# THE BARK TREE

RAYMOND QUENEAU, born February 2, 1903. Novelist, poet, mathematician, philosopher, encyclopedist, pataphysician, ex-surrealist, translator, academician (Goncourt), etc.

*Novels*

LE CHIENDENT
LES DERNIERS JOURS
ODILE
LES ENFANTS DU LIMON
UN RUDE HIVER
PIERROT MON AMI
LOIN DE RUEIL
SAINT GLINGLIN
LE DIMANCHE DE LA VIE
ZAZIE DANS LE MÉTRO
OEUVRES COMPLÈTES DE SALLY MARA
LES FLEURS BLEUES

*Novel in Verse*

CHÊNE ET CHIEN

*Poetry*

LES ZIAUX
BUCOLIQUES
L'INSTANT FATAL
PETITE COSMOGONIE PORTATIVE
SI TU T'IMAGINES
CENT MILLE MILLIARDS DE POÈMES
LE CHIEN À LA MANDOLINE
COURIR LES RUES
BATTRE LA CAMPAGNE

*Other Books*

EXERCISES DE STYLE
BÂTONS, CHIFFRES ET LETTRES *(essays)*
ENTRETIENS AVEC GEORGES CHARBONNIER
BORDS ("Mathematicians, Percursors, Encyclopedists")
UNE HISTOIRE MODÈLE ("A Mathematical Meditation on History")

*English Translations*

THE SKIN OF DREAMS (1948) (LOIN DE RUEIL)
A HARD WINTER (1948) (UN RUDE HIVER)
PIERROT (1950)
THE TROJAN HORSE *(short stories)* 1954
EXERCISES IN STYLE (1958)
ZAZIE (1960)
BETWEEN BLUE AND BLUE (1967) (LES FLEURS BLEUES)
A BLUE FUNK *(short stories)* (1968)
THE BARK TREE (1968) (LE CHIENDENT)

*Books on Queneau*

RAYMOND QUENEAU, by Jean Queval (Seghers, 1960)
QUENEAU, by Jacques Bens (Gallimard 1962)
QUENEAU DÉCHIFFRÉ, by Claude Simonnet (Julliard, 1962)
QUENEAU, by Paul Gayot (Editions Universitaires, 1967)

# THE BARK TREE

## *(Le Chiendent)*

*a novel by*

RAYMOND QUENEAU

*Translated from the French by*

BARBARA WRIGHT



A NEW DIRECTIONS BOOK

Library of Congress Catalog Card Number: 75-145934



Manufactured in the United States of America

Originally published as *Le Chiendent* by Librairie Gallimard, 1933
First published clothbound and as New Directions Paperbook 314 in 1971

New Directions Books are published for James Laughlin
by New Directions Publishing Corporation,
333 Sixth Avenue, New York 10014

To Janine

# INTRODUCTION

*Le Chiendent*,[1] Queneau's first book, is a book with a history. When it was first published, in 1933, it was so different from anything that had gone before that it was appreciated only by a minute minority. Now, though, it is not only regarded as a classic but also as a vitally contemporary book. Robbe-Grillet recently called it: "the new novel, twenty years ahead of its time."

*Le Chiendent* contains in embryo many of Queneau's later books, and perhaps even poems. Queneau started to write it while on a journey to Greece in 1932. Here he became acutely aware of the difference between classical, written Greek and modern, spoken Greek, and this acted as a catalyst to the ideas he had long been forming about the French language. Written French had become fossilized, spoken French was a totally different language; since he wanted to write in what he considered his maternal language, he could not possibly use "the conventions of style, spelling and vocabulary that date from the grammarians of the sixteenth century and the poets of the seventeenth."[2] He wanted to write in a living language, the language of the ordinary man. He wasn't merely aiming at a transcription of the "language of the ordinary man," though, but at a transformation of it, something which would become a third language, a new, viable literary language.

[1] The title, *Le Chiendent*, has many meanings. *Chiendent* is the weed, couch grass. *Voilà le chiendent* is Hamlet's: *Ay, there's the rub*. The word is made up of *chien* (dog) and *dent* (tooth). Dogs have always had great significance in Queneau's private mythology . . . And so on.

[2] *Bâtons, chiffres et lettres*, (Gallimard, 1950).

Queneau considered that the first statement in this new, third language "should be made not by describing some popular event in a novel (because there people might misunderstand one's intentions), but, in the same way as the men of the sixteenth century used the modern languages instead of Latin when writing on theology or philosophy, by putting some philosophical treatise into spoken French."[3] He has described how, on his voyage to Greece: "I had taken Descartes' *Discourse on Method* with me, so I decided to translate it into spoken French. With this idea in mind I began to write something which later became a novel called *Le Chiendent.* You will find a good deal of popular language in it, but also a few efforts in the philosophical sense, I seem to remember."[4]

Descartes and demotic French, though, were not the only elements in the genesis of *Le Chiendent.* Another factor was Queneau's equally early and equally lifelong conviction that there was no essential difference between the novel, as he wanted to write it, and poetry. Classical poetry has rigid rules, and Queneau, in *Le Chiendent* (and to a lesser extent in many of his later novels) invented for himself a rigid structure to which he strictly adhered.

"A novel is a little like a sonnet, though is is much more complicated. I believe in things being highly constructed. I don't expect everyone to do as I do, but that's the way it is with me. I like my characters' entrances and exits to be very precise. If there are repetitions, they are intentional. That's how I work. I hope it isn't obvious. It would be terrible if it were obvious. Though I all but count the lines that separate the entrances of each character. Certain words, certain phrases, must be repeated during the course of the book—for my personal pleasure."[5]

He cannot bear the idea of leaving the number of chapters to chance. In *Le Chiendent,* for instance, their number and form were decided on for "egocentric" (and also for complicated mathematical) reasons. The seven chapters are each

[3] id.
[4] id.
[5] Conversation with Marguerite Duras (March 1959), reproduced by Jacques Bens in his *Queneau.*

divided into thirteen sections; the last section of the last chapter is simply headed: XCI. Each section observes the three unities "as in a tragedy," and the last section of each chapter is quite separate; it is "in another direction, or dimension." *Le Chiendent* is a cycle; it ends as it began: "like a man who has been walking for a long time and who finally comes back to his point of departure."[6]

"I hope it isn't obvious"—Queneau said about his framework for *Le Chiendent*. It wasn't obvious in 1933, and it isn't obvious now; no one might ever have realized it was there if Queneau hadn't later referred to it in an article on the technique of the novel. I doubt if anyone could have known, either, that the germ of the idea for the book was that it should be a transcription of Descartes; Queneau very soon realized that the original idea had got extended, and that he was in fact writing a novel. The connection with the *Discourse on Method* remains, though: Etienne is the embodiment of "cogito, ergo sum"—he doesn't begin to exist as a person until he (accidentally) begins to think. Pierre, a character who is both *in* the story and *outside* it, is necessary to the book as the gratuitous observer who is the only person to be aware of what is happening to Etienne. Already in this first book there is much that in retrospect can be seen as typical Queneau; the accident which is to transform Etienne's life is not something noble, magnificent, transcendental: it is merely the ridiculous sight of two little rubber ducks swimming in a shop window—in a hat. To prove that the hat is waterproof. This, and particularly the fact that he discovers that the little ducks have been there for two years without his noticing them, is enough to start Etienne off on a metaphysical journey and a new life—in which outwardly, however, nothing is changed.

The effects of the little ducks is reinforced by something equally banal, but which this time has consequences not so much in the domain of mind as in that of matter. From his commuter's train, Etienne notices in the desolate suburbs north of Paris a hut which has CHIPS (*i.e.*, French fries) written

[6] *Bâtons, chiffres et lettres.*

up on it in large letters. When he decides to visit this forlorn place, *for no reason,* he there meets several people who are to have a vital importance in his life. The other objects that Queneau chooses to set Etienne off on his meditations on appearance and reality, and on the further train of reflections in which he becomes so passionately involved, are also no more world-shattering than an ordinary potato peeler and a hard-boiled egg cutter. But these ducks, these chips, and these kitchen utensils, are on a par with Queneau's preferred characters. No marchionesses leaving their elegant houses at 5 o'clock for him. There is a key passage where the obnoxious Madame Pic reflects bitterly on this. She "appears to accept her comedown in the social scale with resignation, but . . . her heart bleeds . . . when she remembers the people they used to know—Lieutenant de la Boustrofe, a titled gentleman, and M. Béquille, the lawyer, and M. Dife, who wrote poetry that actually got printed—and compares them with the people she is with at the moment: a junk dealer, a café proprietor, a concierge, an N.C.O., a magician, a midwife and a waitress . . ."

These are the stuff of Queneau's novels, these are the ordinary human beings (even if they have their fantastic sides) through whom Queneau chooses to express himself. There are some of his characters, he has admitted, whom he comes near to detesting, and obviously beastly old Cloche in this book is one of them, and beastly young Théo another. To say nothing of that incarnation of evil, Bébé Toutout. Nevertheless, Queneau is always fair enough, human enough, to give his readers every reason to understand why these people had to become the way they did.

Claude Simonnet, whose short, discreet and enlightening book on Queneau[7] no one interested in *Le Chiendent* can afford to ignore, says that "like all Queneau's novels, *Le Chiendent* both has no meaning and at the same time conceals a profusion of meanings." Talking about the book as a "supreme example of the novel-poem," he describes it as therefore "a supreme example of the novel whose story cannot be told." Jacques Bens, who has also written an excellent

[7] *Queneau déchiffré (Notes sur "Le Chiendent").*

study of Queneau,[8] was required by his publishers to give a brief résumé of the plot of each of Queneau's novels. Ingeniously, he got over this difficulty—this impossibility—by quoting the books' blurbs—written by Queneau himself.

What is *Le Chiendent* about? Well, it is not *about* anything, it *is* something. And that "something" includes a vast amount of what goes to make up human life. There is the terrible, and terribly sympathetic, and all the more realistic for sometimes being fantastic, description of the ordinary man (and woman) caught in the ordinary meshes of trying, unarmed, to make a living, to live a life. There are many of the eternal philosophical themes, humanized as the eternal problems of ordinary suffering humanity—Etienne's anguished cry: Who am I?—the Greek chorus of the wedding party waiting for Ernestine's tragic and beautiful death: Ernestine—who is she? There is the terrible prophecy (six or seven years before the event) of the phoney war of 1939–40, and the *reductio ad absurdum* of all wars, when the French army is finally reduced to eight men, holding out against the superior force of thirty Etruscans. There are the comic passages of irrepressible verbosity (the fight between Yves le Toltec and Hippolyte), a presage of many such later exercises in style. There is great pity for humanity. There are the passages that lead to mental speculation: "The moment you look at things disinterestedly, everything changes." There are the elliptical descriptions: "Suzy is a blonde, and goes to the cinema three times a week." There is (in 1933!) the preoccupation with communication: "Even though I'm trying to tell you something, I see that I have to admit that I find it impossible to be precise about its nature." There are reflections on education—Théo struggling with his list of battles, and his isolated, useless German words.

How it is—that is what Queneau, in his own way, is always describing. How life is. His own way is not anyone else's—hence something of his quality, and hence, also, the difficulty people do sometimes have in knowing how to read him. In the blurb he wrote for his second novel, Queneau said: "After

[8] op. cit. Another enlightening study of Queneau is Jean Queval's *Queneau*.

all, why shouldn't we demand a certain effort from the reader? We always explain everything to him. In the end, he gets fed up with being treated with such contempt." Queneau has no verbalized message. That is perhaps why it may be necessary to reread him (or to read other books by him) in order to understand him. He has nothing to sell—but when the reader finishes a Queneau book, *he* has become enriched.

BARBARA WRIGHT

# I

The silhouette of a man appeared in profile; so, simultaneously, did thousands. There really were thousands. He had just opened his eyes, and the teeming streets were seething; seething, too, were the men who worked all day. This particular silhouette emerged from the wall of an enormous, unbearable building, an edifice which looked as if it were designed for suffocation, and which was a bank. The silhouette, detached from the wall now, oscillated, jostled by other shapes, not visibly behaving as an individual, pushed and pulled in various directions, less by its own anxieties than by the sum of the anxieties of the thousands of people surrounding it. But this oscillation was only apparent; in reality, it was the shortest distance between toil and sleep, between affliction and boredom, between suffering and death.

The other man shut his eyes for a few moments, and opened them again just as the silhouette was being pocketed by the metro, and disappearing. There was a wave of silence, and then the *Intransigeant* and its fellow evening papers started yelling on the boulevard again.

For years now, this same instant had been exactly repeated, every day, with the exception of Saturdays, Sundays and public holidays. *He* had nothing to do with all this. He didn't work, but he had got into the habit of coming here between five and eight, and not budging. Sometimes he would stretch out a hand and pick something up; that day, it was a silhouette.

The silhouette, meanwhile, was arriving at Obonne. Its wife had got the supper ready; she too worked in an office.

The assistant manager was always maneuvering her into a dark corner, and so was the manager. No sooner had she got away from their hands than she became exposed to those of the metro. And no sooner had she finished work there than she began all over again here. The child was dozing under the lamp, waiting for supper. The silhouette was waiting for supper too, feeling its feet swelling, with one arm hanging between its legs, its hand gripping the crossbar of its chair, for fear the chair might run away. He was reading the *Journal.* Or rather, he wasn't reading it. He was staring at the letter *n* in the word Ministry. He went on staring at it until the soup was served. And after a bit of cheese with a lot of bread, he hypnotized the letter *i.* The boy didn't wait for the cheese to make his escape, and went off in a complete daze to live through numerous pollutions in his childish bed. The wife did the dishes and various household chores. And by 10 o'clock, the trio was fast asleep.

---

The next day, there was a woman in his place, his usual place. He had observed this habit and thought: they're all the same. The first day he had come to this café, he had been escaping from the rain and had had no hesitation in choosing a place; the only free one, as it so happened. And ever since, he had always gone to the same place. He mused for a moment about French café life, but didn't linger over these ethnographical considerations and sat down at random, which meant that he happened on a table he wasn't familiar with, studied its marble veins, and drank his Pernod. When it was time for people to stop work, once again the silhouette emerged from the wall, the wall of the enormous money market that was called the Audit Bank.

"Have you got your passport?" said a young man in a very low voice.

The woman, she was extremely young, winked. She was happy, she was going to travel. She smiled, with one hand on the very respectable young man's knee; with the other, she was scratching the crocodile of an old-fashioned handbag, and She went on smiling. She was looking into his eyes; he was quite simply drinking mineral water.

He noticed, not on purpose, though, that his shoes were down-at-the-heels; so were those of the next man next to him, and of the next man, too. He suddenly had a vision of a civilization of down-at-the-heel shoes, a culture of worn-away soles, a symphony of suede and box calf, in the process of being reduced to the remarkably minimal thickness of the paper tablecloths in restaurants for the hard up. The silhouette's movements followed the same rhythm as the previous day; with the same skill, it sought the shortest distance between the monumental door of the Audit Bank and the squeaking gate of its suburban house.

The silhouette owned a house; it had had it built, or rather it had started to have it built, for the money had run out, and the first floor was still unfinished. The house had something of the look of a devastated area, which was now somewhat out of fashion. The child—he has arrived at the age of puberty —his elbows on the table, was learning by heart a list of battles; the wife, who had got home before him, was starting her household chores. Habit.

His eyes moved on from the down-at-the-heel shoe to the silhouette; the daily drinker realized, with some satisfaction, that he had recognized it. At last, out of these thousands of totally undifferentiated people, one had registered on him. Why this particular one? Because of the greater speed with which it made for the metro? Because of its jacket, more threadbare than most? Because of the kind of bun its badly cut hair fell into? Not because of its worn-down heels, not that. What, then? Would he discover why, the next day? The silhouette had already been swallowed up by the shadows, and disappeared.

And, naturally enough, it reappeared at the squeaking little gate of the half-built house. You couldn't say it was a materialization; it was strictly two-dimensional, and didn't deserve such a grand word. But, just like that, all of a sudden, it emerged from the mud in the winter, and from the dust in the summer, just in front of the lock, by a sort of multiple hazard. The cat was purring, and scraping its back along the badly painted iron gate, where the red lead was showing through here and there. The cat was pleased to see its master again, and rubbed itself against the red lead. Pretty puss. The gate was carefully shut again. The child shut his book of battles. And they ate.

After dinner, the wife sat down for a while. The child made himself scarce, taking with him, in anguish and jubilation, a copy of *Le Sourire* which a school friend had lent him. The silhouette watched the cat, which was dreaming. The wife finished her work and, on the stroke of 10, the youngest of the three was still not asleep.

---

At midday, you have to go and have lunch; not too far away, because you have to hurry back to work, and it mustn't be too expensive either, of course. A net, cast no one could say quite how, hauled a thousand human being into these premises and here, in exchange for cash, they were fed. The silhouette is one of them, it's been caught. It eats: a magnificent rancid sardine, a very thin piece of flesh garnished with bits of wood and, when a delectable moment comes for it to sample the banana with jam, its fastidious neighbor is eating cod. The silhouette was used to it, it was the same every day. One anonymous individual, who had been caught in the first cast of the net, rapidly absorbed the muck bestowed upon him and was quickly replaced by the fastidious fish-lover, which latter started to raise hell when, having himself arrived at the yogurt or dried fruit stage, a latecomer started stuffing himself with tripe, and this by means of a fork which the day before had served to shatter the mirror of two already ancient eggs, as witness the golden yellow of its prongs. Around 2 o'clock, in the deserted, but still stinking, restaurant, a few fat waitresses were mopping their armpits.

At about 3 o'clock, the silhouette blew its nose; at about 4, it spat; at about 5, it bowed; at about 5:50 it was already hearing the squeak of the little gate of its headless house.

At 6, the other man was there, on the dot, at his café table. This particular day, the man on his right couldn't stop choking, and was drinking a yellowish potion straight out of a little bottle; the meussieu on his left was absent-mindedly scratching his genitals while reading the racing results. To the southwest, a couple was coupling in front of a St. Raphaël-and-lemon. To the south-southwest, there was a lady on her own; to the south-southeast, there was another lady on her own. To the southeast, most unusually, a vacant table. At the zenith, a cloud; at the nadir, a cigarette butt.

At 6 o'clock, the silhouette emerged. This amused him enormously. He really did recognize this particular one. One day he'd amuse himself by following it. At this moment, he observed which great concern that the silhouette, instead of going straight to the metro, had made a detour and stopped at the window of a hat shop, where he was watching two little ducks floating in a waterproof hat that had been filled with water in order to demonstrate its primary quality. This distraction had an immediate effect on the silhouette which was not lost on the observer; it acquired a certain density and became a flat entity. This modification of its structure was, moreover, perceived by the people who were in the habit of traveling in the same train as he, in the same carriage, in the same compartment. The atmosphere became oppressive when, at the liberating sound of the whistle, the door opned and, at the last moment, the place next to the right-hand corner seat, facing the engine, was occupied. Something had changed.

A game of *manille* got going in the left-hand square. The ex-officer, now a wine salesman, made a lot of noise opening his paper; the young lady opposite went on with her crochet, which she'd begun at Easter. The man opposite the flat entity was dozing, but his sleep was agitated; he was dribbling, and every so often he would retrieve his saliva, thus exhibiting a violet tongue which made you think that its possessor must either suck his pen or have some atrocious disease, such as the bashi-bazouk, or the violetteria. Looking as if he were permanently hanging by the neck, the man opposite went unnoticed. On his right, the retired officer was nibbling at the horsehair on his upper lip and muttering politics; his eyes were fuming; a war in view, no doubt. He too was frightening. Violet-tongue emerged from his somnolence and opened a paper, the *Cross*. One after the other, two serious events occurred: the young lady pinched her finger in the fastening of her handbag and hurt herself badly and, in the other corner, the *manille* players started bawling. "Ace of spades, king of hearts, diamonds, must be a half-wit to play like that." Speak for yourself, Meussieu, people that play cards need to watch what they're doing, if they don't know how to play then they don't play, no one can play with anyone like that."

Play, play, play, play. And the young lady gurgling and sucking her finger. The failed general, lifting his nostrils from his patriotic literature, wanted to join in. The man reading the *Cross* was watching a fly with wide-open eyes, his paper firmly popped up on his thighs. Look out! a sweeping movement with his tongue. And the others were still at it. "That's twenty-five centimes you've made me lose, playing so stupidly. If you'd only realized . . . Meussieu, Meussieu, Meussieu—"

These meussieus, as emphatic as if they were titles, replaced the slaps on the face that they didn't dare to distribute, for fear of getting them back. And it went on, and on. It would go on like that until the next station. Twenty minutes. The flat entity felt like crying. He felt vaguely responsible for this lamentable departure from the compartment's habits. It was the fault of the little ducks and the waterproof hat.

Two the *manille* players get out at the first station, muttering terribly, with the horrible eyes of angry tame rabbits. The young lady, sucking at her finger, got out too. The soldier in civvies spread himself out and picked his teeth with the nail of his index finger, and the Christian started avidly reading an article on the salvation of Chinese children. Things were looking up on this side of the compartment, but the *manille* players went on arguing, and their passionate voices grated on the eardrums of the flat entity, who had just that moment realized that he knew one of them. They had stayed in the same pension in Pornic. This coincidence completely changed the tenor of his thoughts, which were diverted into a little reverie about sea-bathing, it wasn't long till vacation, in three weeks' time he'd have four weeks off, when the wine salesman, deciding that it was getting stuffy, lowered one of the windows. The *manille* player from Pornic couldn't stand drafts. He complained. The salesman refused to close it. And once again cries of "Meussieu," I tell you, Meussieu," "But Meussieu," went flying from one end of the compartment to the other, a Brennish, polite form of artillery, wretched, pathetic bullets that the man reading the *Cross* gulped down as they went by, like rotten eggs. And things were going from bad to worse, as they say; just like kids who load their snowballs with stones, these Meussieus were packing their "Meussieus" with abysses of perfidy, chasms of sarcasm, precipices of defiance and mixed grills of spite. But they wouldn't come to blows. The flat entity again felt that it was the fault of the little ducks and the waterproof hat; the next stop cut the argument short by the premature exit of all the gabbers, plus the Catholic, the flat entity was left alone and anxiously asked himself: Why? And he went on saying, why, why, to the rhythm of the train. At the next station. He got out.

After the inevitable pushing and shoving on the way out, he made his way to his house, jumping from one mudhole in the road to the next, starting stones rolling with the sightless point of his oxford shoes. After twenty minutes of similarly arduous progress, he arrived at the squeaking gate. The cat wasn't there. He shut the gate and went up the four steps to the house.

Now he's in the dining room. Everything seems as it should be. The child with the rings around his eyes slowly closes a *Vindication of Socrates* in which he has hidden a photo that he prefers to keep for his private contemplation. He raises a pure forehead—pure, though heavy with numerous obscenities. The wife brings the shoup.

She thinks he looks odd.

"You look odd, So and So," she says.

He does in fact feel odd.

"Yes, So and So-ess, I feel odd," he says.

The child absorbs his shoup in haste. His spoon goes click click on the bottom of his plate. The flat entity takes his courage in both hands, those hands which he feels down there at the end of his arms; he takes his courage—in other words, he creates it. After a violent effort, he starts:

"You know, today, I stopped at the hat shop, the one on the left as you come out of the bank. There's something very strange in the window. A waterproof hat."

The child, who is waiting for what's to follow (to eat), is listening carefully.

"They've put some water in it to prove, to show, that is, that it's waterproof; and two ducks, too."

The family meditates for a moment. The wife asks:

"Two ducks?"

The flat entity, embarrassed, answers:

"Yes, you know, two little rubber ducks."

Now he's furious; this stupid story *always* ends badly; the absurd idea of looking in that window. What's more, now the child is speaking, and uttering these words:

"It's been there for at least two years, that thing."

The flat papa doesn't know what to say. The noodles are brought. *Are* brought—by the wife, of course. There's no meat tonight. Then, quite bluntly, she informs him that one of the neighbors has killed the cat. Which one, they don't know.

Where is it?

Old Ma Tyrant brought its corpse back. She's a poor old woman, she wanted its skin. She found it against the wall of Hippolyte's café. It had a bullet in its head.

The flat entity can't accept the idea of anyone killing his cat; he starts getting inflated, like the meussieus in the train. Then he gets deflated. He goes to bed. He feels odd. He'll make love to his wife tonight. As for the child, he will abstain from any sort of pollution, because he's got a mathematics test tomorrow, and whenever he does it the night before, it always brings him bad luck.

---

The observer is hatching something; what it is even he doesn't know yet. But he is preparing himself; either he will continue to study his quarry, as he calls him, or he'll look for some other random event, just as pointless, just as useless. After wavering between various possible occupations, he settles for Pernod and the silhouette. And with his eyes open, seeing the beings he encounters with perfect lucidity, he decides to play a waiting game. On his way, he meets his brother, whom he hasn't seen for a very long time; he makes out he's in a great hurry, and also very busy, and arranges to meet him at midnight. Finally, he attains one of his goals: his place is free;

the man with emphysema is sitting next to him. Further to the south, the young man with the passport is brooding, all by himself. At the nadir, a cigarette butt, at the zenith, a striped awning, for the vigilant proprietor is preparing for his customers to get the perfidious drops secreted by the alleged protector down the back of their necks.

The storm is taking its time; so is the flat entity, because just precisely today he's doing an hour's overtime. Finally one, two, three drops of water fall on to the asphalt. The observer, who has been disappointed by the 6 o'clock exodus, remains at his post. Four, five, six drops of water. Some people, anxious about their straw hats, raise their noses. Description of a storm in Paris. In summer. The timid take to their heels; others raise the collars of their jackets, which gives them an air of bravado. It begins to smell of mud. Many people prudently look for shelter, and when the rain is at its height, all that can be seen are blackish groups clustered around doorways, like mussels around the pile of a pier. The cafés are doing a brisk trade. 7 o'clock. Streetcars, buses and trains will be missed, dinners burned and appointments unkept. A few ostentatious thunder claps try to make people believe this is a real storm. Certain learned people declare that it had been working up to a storm and that it will cool the air, and that it's a good thing, a little rain like that from time to time, and that it won't last long.

The observer allows these vain words which tell nothing but the truth to reach him; he notes with some bitterness that these banalities correspond perfectly to reality. The present reality couldn't ask any more. And the silhouette has still not appeared. Yes it has, though; he sees it on the steps of the Audit Bank, patiently waiting for the rain to stop; in any case, it isn't a silhouette any longer, but a flat entity. The other man catches his breath; the rain stops; the flat entity runs for the metro.

The observer gets up, leaves without paying (he'll be back) and starts to pursue his quarry. Now he's going down into the metro. He's right at the bottom of the steps, he's about to go through the iron gate. Luckily, the other man has some tickets. A train arrives. What an incredible crowd! The flat entity is there in the second second-class coach; so is the observer; the first in front of the right-hand door, the second in front of the door he went in by.

What a remarkable change, thinks the second, but it's pointless to study him like this. I wonder what station he'll get off at. Much shoving; Saint-Denis; he's going to change.

Rearrangements as far as the Gare du Nord. Which train will he catch, the local or the one that is an express more or less? The 7:31 or the 7:40? Come on, dig your elbow into that obstructionist's stomach; step on that charming girl's toes—otherwise you'll miss your more or less express train, and if you look at that woman you'll miss the slow one. The flat entity only misses the faster one; the slow train is still waiting. He's made it. No more habits here, the faces aren't the same, the 7 o'clock commuters are an unknown world to the 6 o'clock commuters, and he is one of the latter. He knows neither the little man with a moustache whose jagged-edged straw hat is threatening to bite a tall man next to him who is dozing with his mouth open, nor those two girls absorbed in a book-based-on-the-movie, nor that mother and brat, the latter watching two flies coupling on his grazed knee, because he took a hell of a spill down the escalator at the Pigalle metro station, what a business that was, nor that blond young man staring fixedly at the landscape as it goes by. He has a feeling he saw the young man in the metro earlier, but he isn't sure. Now he's thinking about his cat, about whose assassination he is in despair. He counts up the proofs of affection the animal used to give him. For instance, it used to wait for him every evening on the little wall, by the gate. A dirty beast has killed it. He thinks of its corpse, its hide, its skin that Ma Tyrant is busy tanning. The flat entity becomes indignant, he rebels. And he tells himself so.

Instead of being cut out like a tin soldier, his contours are starting to soften. He is gently expanding. He is maturing. The observer can clearly perceive this, but can see no outward reason for it. He now has in front of him a being who is endowed with a certain consistency. He notes with interest that the features of this being endowed with a certain reality are slightly convulsed. What can be happening? This silhouette is a prize specimen.

The kid murmurs something to his mother; everyone guesses what it is. The little man with the moustache has gotten into a conversation with his neighbor; he informs him in pensive tones that the weather was oppressive and stormy, but that the storm just now cooled the air. The listener agrees. Then, by association of contiguous ideas, he talks to him about journeys into the stratosphere.

Between two stations, without any explanation, the train slows down, and then stops. Heads abruptly appear at the windows; the ones on the right-hand side have to retire into their shells immediately, under penalty of decapitation, because a train is going by in the other direction, but it's going pretty slowly at that. There must have been an accident. Indefinite delay. This news provokes something of a stir in the compartment. The brat takes advantage of it to get out and piss. The man with a mustache loses his listener, who's gone to sleep for good.

---

Narcense and Potice are following a woman. That, actually, is Potice's main activity; his conquests are multiple. A benevolent conformist, he doesn't despise his fellow men, and thinks about them as little as possible. He detests it when some great event occurs and interferes with his ploys. This particular day seems to him to be just as good, if not better; than yesterday; he doesn't really know, though, he doesn't give it much thought. But he doesn't worry about tomorrow. He collects women.

Whereas Narcense, he's an artist; neither a painter, nor a poet, nor an architect, nor an atcor, nor a sculptor, he plays music, to be more precise, the saxophone; and he does this in night clubs. At the moment, he's out of work anyway, and is looking for a means of earning his daily bread by the exercise of his abilities, but he can't manage it. He's beginning to get worried. Today, at about 4 o'clock, he met his old friend Potice, who persuaded him to join him in pursuit of a woman he had chosen out of all the thousands of others; he'd only seen her from behind; her face was doubtful. Risky. 5 o'clock.

Narcense and Potice are very Parisian. They follow women at 5 o'clock.

The lady in question is walking with resolute, hurried steps. Right, now she's in the streetcar. A number 8. Going to the Gare de l'Est. Narcense and Potice run after the streetcar. Some cars run after Narcense and Potice. In the streetcar, the lady sits down, looking lost. Lost in her thoughts, she doesn't look at anything or anyone, isn't interested in anything, or anyone. She just sits there, with some packages on her knees. Not pretty, but beautiful: Narcense and Potice admire her.

At the terminus, still resolutely, she goes toward the Gare du Nord. Does a little shopping on her way. Potice tries to get into conversation with her, but fails.

At the Gare du Nord, they're lagging behind, somewhat. A volley of automobiles has come between them. The lady is going to disappear. They swear. Is this the right moment? They press on, they leap between the delivery wagons and the buses, they avoid the one, and the other. Narcense has time to see the lady on platform 31. He runs and finds out where the train is going, and takes an appropriate ticket (Potice isn't following him); all down the platform he looks into the compartments. This one's full, this one, this one. She's in there. There's still a bit of room in the corner. He climbs in, slightly out of breath. The lady is staring straight ahead, and doesn't seem to see anything. She looks exhausted. Narcense wonders what has happened to Potice. He looks out of the window, but doesn't see anyone. The train starts. At Obonne, the lady gets out. So does Narcense. Lots of people in the street. Narcense doesn't dare to risk it. He nearly does, but then he chickens. So that he finally finds himself all by himself at the gate of a little house. He hangs around a bit, and looks at the house, which is either half built or being demolished. He thinks it's magnificent. He understands that such a woman, such a beautiful woman, should live in such a strange place. Meanwhile, the beautiful woman is peeling onions, quite exhausted.

Narcense is still prowling around, extremely perplexed. Doesn't know what to do. Very fortunately, a definite external event makes up his mind for him. It starts raining hard. And he rushes off to the nearest shelter. A bistro.

I look like a rabbit, today, he thinks. Running all day long. A rabbit playing a little drum. What a beautiful woman! What a presence! He undresses her as he absentmindedly orders a mandarin–curaçao, and he's biting her breast, not the one on the left, the one on the right, when at a nearby table he hears a voice reminiscing.

"Shanghai, that's where the biggest bar in the world is . . . I know all the brothels in Valparaiso . . . I once sailed on a steamer that was transporting Chinese corpses . . . On my first trip, I was sixteen, I went to Australia. In Sydney, I nearly got myself killed by a great big Swede, who . . . I got three years' hard labor. I got over it . . . I'm off to the Pacific in a month. I got a nice little chick in Valparaiso . . ."

Narcense comes out of his dream and looks; a very nondescript individual, but with a seaman's jersey and a leather-peaked cap. Three local youths surround him, listening. It's still raining outside. The proprietor blows his nose loudly, wipes the counter and would like to say something. The other tables are empty, except the one at the far end which is occupied by a truculent mongrel. The sailor goes on jabbering. Then he decides to start up the player piano.

Narcense absently leaves some money on the table and goes out.

---

The child was hypocritical and solitary. Sometimes at the top of his class, he didn't hesitate to win his way to the bottom, if his inner anguish pushed him that way. He had never had a daddy; killed in the war, they told him; but he knew perfectly well that he was illegitimate. His mother, who had some idea of sin, went out to work to bring him up. Then she married a very young man and went on working. The child knew all this; no one had told him, but slowly, skillfully, he had pieced the whole story together. And in any case, this story didn't interest him.

Apart from the solitary pleasures, which took up a considerable portion of his leisure hours, he didn't like anything very much, didn't collect anything and read little.

This evening, he was sitting studying as usual, waiting for his stepfather to come home, but just this evening the stepfather was keeping them waiting. Extraordinary. The mother kept coming and going, from the dining room to the kitchen, and elsewhere. "What could've happened?—your father's not back yet. Something must have gone wrong. I haven't heard a train for the last hour." The question didn't worry him hardly at all. He was trying to remember whether the abscissa was the vertical, and the ordinate the horizontal. He couldn't manage to keep it in his head. Constant is annoyed with him because he hasn't given him back the photo of Marlene Dietrich. To go and see *The Blue Angel* all by himself. This idea excites him considerably. He knows that it starts in a school and that the pupils are showing each other this photo; and this woman sings and she's always undressed, he's been told, and the way she's undressed, you just can't imagine how.

"Definitely, something must have happened. Why don't you go to the station and see? Maybe there's been an accident."

He doesn't wait to be asked twice. In a little garden, he takes one single deep breath. It's warm, it's moist. The ground's wet. It's shining a bit. The moon is three-quarters full. He looks at it and remembers the severed giant's head he used to think he saw when he was younger. This memory embarrasses him a little. He takes a couple of steps in the darkness. It's silly, but he's a bit scared. Suddenly he catches sight of a man standing in front of the iron gate. In the darkness, he stands still; gradually, he begins to make things out. Yes, a man; his head, it looks as if it's trapped between the bars of the gate; it can't be, he's going to wrench them apart with his forehead; his eyes are shining terribly, his mouth is half open. Something seems to be shaking him, though he doesn't move from the spot. The hidden child can see him very well, and with what interest! Pushed by the weight of this desperately isolated body, the little gate squeaks and squeaks. The man lets out a deep sigh, then, in a low voice, moans frantically: "Ah, ah, ah, ah," indefinitely, like a litany. The child suddenly feels like counting how many times he repeats the sound: Ah, but this idea comes to him too late, like at night when you're trying to count the number of times he repeats the sound: Ah, but this idea comes to him too started soon enough. "Ah, ah, ah." He's almost talking out loud now, he seems delirious, he's shaking the bars of the gate with one hand, he's banging his body against it rhythmically. All of a sudden, very quietly, but with his mouth wide open, he intones "Aaaaaaaah" and his head drops. He stays there for a few moments without moving, with his head against the bars of the gate, and his forehead dislodges a bit of the paint, which peels off. Then, abruptly, he goes away.

The child doesn't know what to think. He runs over to the gate, and sees the fellow disappearing into the darkness. Opens the gate. He'd guessed right. The gate has marks on it. From the gate, yes, that's it, you can see into the kitchen, his mother is sitting there, seeing that it doesn't burn. They can't afford that. The child thinks his mother is very beautiful. Then he remembers what he was supposed to be doing. He runs toward the station. At that moment, a train arrives. Three hours late. His father is bound to be in it. All of a sudden, he laughs. "Zdad going to see the gate?"

---

After he'd telephoned his brother to tell him that he was going to spend a few days in the country and therefore not to expect him tonight at midnight, the observer, dying of hunger, sat down at a marble table ingrained with filth, on which had negligently been laid a spoon, a fork, a glass, a knife, a salt shaker, let me just think whether I haven't forgotten something, a knife, a salt shaker, a spoon, a fork, a glass, oh yes!—and an unchipped plate. In spite of the lateness of the hour, a similar set of equipment had been placed on a nearby table, and its occupant was making full use of it. When he had carefully wiped his plate clean, he raised his nose from it and stared at the customer, grumbling: "A hell of a delay today, what a company!" The customer was absent-mindedly looking at the photo of a transatlantic liner on the front page of a newspaper.

"Well, there's a catastrophe for you," exclaimed the voracious customer, not addressing his remarks to anyone in particular. "It reminds me of when the *Clytemnestra* went down off Singapore. It was bedlam! All the passengers mowing all the others down, trying to get into the boats. The captain, he had his revolver in his hand, and bang! he picked off the men trying to get into the lifeboats before the women. Yes M'sieu, he shot them, bang!"

"What a brute," murmured the observer to himself.

The sailor, put off stride for a moment, pulled himself together: "Hm, talk about brutes, he was one all right. One day, for no reason at all, the bugger, begging your pardon, shoved his bloody great fist right in my mug. And Le Touchec, oh my, he was always kicking him up the arsehole, begging your pardon." And after five minutes: "Shanghai, that's the biggest bar in the world is . . . I know all the brothels in Valparaiso . . ." He doesn't manage to get around to his nice little chick in Chile because at this moment a man came in and asked for dinner. Such an event filled the little dive with silence. The newcomer looked odd. From his shoes, which were covered with mud, you could tell that he must have been wandering about the housing development for quite some time. There was a little patch of rust on his forehead, which was traversed by an old scar. He collapsed onto a chair. The proprietor placed the necessary equipment for eating in front of him, and the newcomer started scratching the table with the end of his knife. It made a rasping sound.

"If you don't mind, Meussieu," said the sailor, "that sets my teeth on edge."

The newcomer didn't answer, and stopped. The proprietor looked at the sailor and gave a knowing wink. Which surprised the observer, who asked discreetly:

"Do you know that meussieu?"

"No, but I have a kind of feeling that he wouldn't like to be asked what he does. He came here this afternoon. He went off for an hour. And now here he is again, looking as peculiar as ever. Hm, I'd know how to describe him to the police if I had to."

Another one who wants to have his picture in the paper for free. The proprietor was still exchanging signs of mutual understanding with the sailor, who was meditatively picking his teeth with his own pocketknife. The observer was overcome by infinite disgust. The other man saw nothing of this maneuver.

A man got up and, standing in front of the table of another one, said:

"Pierre Le Grand."

"Oh yes."

"May I?"

"Oh yes. Do. Narcense."

"Delighted."

Handshake.

"I," began the one, "know of no more lamentable spectacle than that of drunken sailors sobering up in sordid cafés on housing developments; nor do I know of any more ignoble than that of the owner of a sordid café who has no other aim in life than spying, spying day and night, until some criminal or other finally happens to come within his reach and he can finally serve society by denouncing him to the police. They are both there: the degenerate from the latitudes and the informer; their encounter makes you feel as if someone has shoved a sponge full of ink down your gullet."

"You know," said Narcense, "I'm not some criminal or other. I haven't committed any crime, in spite of the mud on my shoes. At the very most, an outrage against public decency."

A silence.

"You're very sensitive, Meussieu Le Grand. I don't see it the way you do. That sailor is very amusing, even though his stories are a bit antiquated. He repeats himself, but don't you repeat yourself? Who doesn't repeat himself? He doesn't do it as well as other people, that's all. I like sailors; they please me, their life, something in their eyes. Personally, I hardly even move out of Paris, as you see. But these people who've seen so many different countries, when they come back to their home town, they bring . . ."

"That's a load of bull."

"Thanks," said Narcense. "The fellow behind the bar, though, I can't say I like him much. Look how he's trying to hear what I'm saying. But isn't this little suburban bistro amazing? What's the time? 10:30. Look, when you come down to it, though, it's true for the sailor. Why the hell did he go so far? *I* find this bistro great and tragic. The half moon in the window. The owner pretending to be dozing behind his bar, but really all ears. The sailor's going. Bell. The lousy dog, very odd, that dog, raises its head, and lets it fall again. A railroad worker comes in and drinks a boiling hot black coffee, laced; then goes back to work, after exchanging a few brief words about the accident with the boss. The phonograph was going, earlier. It was touching. I'm sorry, but I just can't be skeptical. What's more, I'm not a philosopher. No, really not. But it just happens, every so often, that something very ordinary seems beautiful to me and I'd like it to be eternal. I'd like this bistro, and that dusty light bulb, and that dog dreaming on the marble, and even this night—to be eternal. And their essential quality is precisely that they aren't.' "

"Really—don't you ever suffer?"

"There were women in my life, before. Now, there's one. One I despair of."

"You were talking just now about an outrage against public decency?"

"What of it? Don't things like that ever happen to you? Do you think there's still a train for Paris?"

"Innkeeper!" (Um er, um er, the last-named insinuates.) "What time's the next train for Paris?"

"Um er, um er, 10:47."

"Excuse me, I'm going back to Paris. What about you, do you live here?"

"No, in Paris. But I'm going to spend a few days here. I'm observing a man."

"Well, well. Novelist?"

"No. Character."

"Good-by, Le Grand."
"Good-by, Narcense."

---

On the platform, a black mass of human beings waiting. You might have thought it was flypaper. The day, a bit dazed, hadn't yet properly dawned. The air, perfectly purified by the night, was again beginning to stink slightly. The number of waiters was increasing all the time. Some were barely opening their sleep-worn eyes, others seemed more exhausted than ever. Many were bright and cheerful. And almost all had a newspaper in their hands. This abundance of paper didn't mean a thing.

Outside the signal room, a being of curious shape was also waiting: he had as you might say only the minimum possible density for a bimane, even though anyone who had seen him only a few days previously would have been amazed at his rapid tridimensional development. This character was also reading a paper, the *Journal*. Friday. He skims through the politics, skims through the news; takes his time over the sports, which slightly intrigues a young man who is assiduously observing him. After which he carefully studies the week's programs. A glance at the classified advertisements, 5 minutes 12 seconds! he's finished his paper.

Singing its usual little song, toot-toot, the train comes into the station with much gusto. The papers are folded and their owners courageously dart into an appalling melee, each is trying to conquer his usual seat. When everyone is accommodated, the receptacle is closed. And once again, the merry train sets off for the big city (taking good care not to walk on the track. Strictly forbidden).

The being of minimal reality looks out of the window. He calculates the number of times he's probably seen that particular factory and is surprised that he's never noticed that weatherboarding hut CHIPS a bit further on. Like the little ducks, he thinks. He suddenly conceives a really extraordinary project: one day he'll go and have some French fries (chips) in that hut. Has a moment's anxiety wondering whether CHIPS isn't someone's name: Mr. Chips. (Good-by.) But he doesn't think it's very likely, and smiles.

A meussieu in the corner notices the smile. But what's caused it? Last night, wasn't the face convulsed? From another seat, a great sack of potatoes also observes the smile. "Another nut," he decides. "Soon have to be put away." He discreetly presses his foot on that of the man opposite him, who raises his snout from a rag which is the simultaneous defender of public decency and the metallurgical industry, and directs his attention, with an artful movement of his neck, to the nut. They smile at each other. They know the being of minimal reality, and the being of minimal reality knows them. They've exchanged: goodmorningmeussieuhowareyouthismorningnotso-badandhowareyouthere'sabitofanipintheairbutit'sgoingtobehot-laterons. The one facing the engine is a bearded and short-sighted hatter who made a fortune during the war manufacturing very French caps; since he has a lot of children, he thinks its his duty to travel third class, on account of their future (the children's). He has a car too, but its' only for Sundays: it's used for carting the brats about. As he's shortsighted, the local people don't think his brats' chances of survival are very high. Only yesterday, the silly dope ran into the barrier at the Outer Circle level crossing.

"Just as well I'm a good driver; otherwise, my friend, there'd have been a catastrophe, a ca-tass-trophy. If I hadn't had all my wits about me, we'd all have been dead, a terrible accident —terr-rrible; but I kept my wits about me (slap on the thigh of the meussieu with his back to the engine) hahahahahahaha-ha."

The meussieu with his back to the engine, who has some regard for the hatter, smiles admiringly. The observer looks at them both ferociously. The minimal reality has stopped smiling, he's still cherishing his project: he'll go and have some French fries. Which day? He can hardly do so other than on a Saturday afternoon. What will his wife think of this curious venture? She'll think it very odd. He'll never be able to explain to her. Either he won't do it or he won't tell her about it, he'll tell her he was working late. He doesn't at all like lying. Right, now he's really in a quandary. He frowns, and purses his lips.

"When I was seven years old, I was working ten hours a day for my father, who was a china merchant. And he didn't spare the blows when I broke something, believe me. That's how I was brought up, and I've no complaints. Ah, it's not like that these days!"

It's the back-to-the-engine perorating. The observer is amazed: then there *are* people who talk like that, and then he smiles (inwardly, because he aims at impassivity) at his naïveté. Now he's appreciating it. The back-to-the-engine carries on imperturbably; *he* is a banker. At least that's what he claims; he's suspected of being at the very most an exchange-broker. But in any case, he's a very respectable meussieu. He contributed fifty francs to the prize-giving and twenty-five francs to the firemen (or something else). The mothers are a bit suspicious of his white hair; they're afraid he might be a satyr; they keep their little girls shut up when he's about. He's very respectable meussieu, but he mustn't get giddy. So he exaggerates his pomposity in order to avoid this.

"I can go and have some French fries tomorrow. When she asks me, 'Well, you're late, aren't you?' I'll say: 'Yes, I went to have some French fries at Blagny.' If she looks at me in amazement I'll say: 'Yes, I just suddenly felt like it.' It's idiotic, this business. I shall go home tomorrow just as I always do. Hm, that young man was in the same compartment as I was last night."

They are nearing Paris. The hatter and the banker are discussing an important question: how much is the pension of the holders of the military medal? The train throws its load out onto the platform. The mass moves quickly towards an aperture, and there disintegrates. Some take the B train, others the V, others the CD, and others the metro. Others walk. Others take a time to gulp down a coffee with a croissant. The observer yawns, and goes home to bed.

---

Ever since she'd seen a man run over, at about 5 in the afternoon, outside the Gare du Nord, Mme. Cloche had been in ecstasy. Naturally, she said she'd never seen anything more horrible; and that must have been so, because poor Potice had been carefully laminated by a bus. By a series of carefully prepared chances, she happened to be sitting, at about the same time, opposite the same place, on the terrace of a café that a blessed coincidence had placed precisely there. She ordered camomile tea, and patiently waited for the same thing to happen again. That was it, so far as she was concerned; she'd be there every day. Waiting for an accident. Absurdly, the ideal line from pavement to pavement that Potice hadn't been able to traverse to its extremity, absurdly, this line now seemed to her to be necessarily linked to fate, destiny or fatality. Something shocking had happened there: yellow brains on the asphault; so there, indefinitely and inexplicably, horrible accidents were bound to recur, and Mme. Cloche adored the shocking and the horrible. The camomile tea was tepid and the sugar inadequate; the waiter was informed of this extremely bluntly. She took off her fur wrapper, for it was very hot, and scrubbed her face with a gray-checked handkerchief; the customers avoided looking at her. As for her, she was waiting.

There were two taxis whose fenders had come into collision, and another which had fallen foul of the law for some trifling reason. But that was all. For an hour, thousands of cars and thousands of pedestrians followed their respective paths without any serious disturbance. Waves of bipeds and a few rare quadrupeds flowed into the station; waves of bi-, tri-, and quadricycles went by. But nothing happened.

The camomile tea had been drunk for a long time, and Ma Cloche was still frustrated; then she had an idea: to stop thinking of the accident, and that way, perhaps, another would occur. She started thinking about professional matters (she was a midwife) and abortional and gynecological difficulties went running through the old bag's head, while the waiter was looking at her contemptuously, making her feel that she should either quit her observatory, or reorder. The insolence of this character became such that Ma Cloche finally realized that she would have to remove her undesirable self from these premises. So she put her fur wrapper back on, looked at the time on an enormous old turnip which she took out of a carpetbag, paid for her camomile tea, leaving a most ungratifying gratuity for the waiter, and left, in despair. She'd hardly gone three paces when she heard a loud scream behind her, a *fairly* excruciating scream, then a terrific hullabaloo, whistles, people calling out, cars hooting. Her heart stopped beating for a moment, then, with unparalleled velocity, she turned on her heel and ran to the scene of the accident.

But this time, alas, nothing serious had happened: a person had been slightly grazed by a car, but he seemed to be all right, though a bit shaken; he was dusting himself off and explaining how it had happened. He was stammering a bit as he explained. It was nothing. No, really, he felt perfectly all right, he was surrounded by people. Some took the driver's side, others his, even though he didn't have one, himself. He expressed the wish to forget about it, because he was going to miss his train. The taxi fare apologized to him; in a way it was his fault, he'd told the driver to hurry, he too was afraid of missing his train. He was going to Obonne; so was the other. So they went to the station. The crowd gradually dispersed. Mme. Cloche shuffled off, furious at *not even having seen* the taxi butting the idiot in the back. All the fault of that waiter. But she'd never go back and sit on that café terrace, no, she'd never go back there, she swore she wouldn't, their camomile tea was too rotten, they didn't even give you any sugar, and, even though the next day, when she went to see her brother at Blagny, she had to take a train from *that* station, well, she wouldn't stop and have a drink in *that* café. No, that she wouldn't.

---

The two men got into the same compartment. The being of lesser consistency had skillfully managed to get his usual seat. The *manille*-playing quartet had disintegrated. The young lady must have found a better place. The wine salesman was sitting in a corner looking important, waving a newspaper like a flag; opposite him, the reader of the *Cross* was trying his hand at doing an addition problem on the back of an envelope; every so often, he scratched his head with his pencil. Two female railroad employees occupied the other two corners: they were sewing (or embroidering, or lace-making. Pierre didn't make up his mind which of these occupations it was). Next to them, face to face, silent and hostile, an old man and an old woman of the silver wedding type.

At the moment when the little trumpets of the people authorized to play them were making their pretty symphony heard, a young man, out of breath, penetrated into the compartment which was already as full as an egg; he remained standing, and his head was lost in the luggage racks. Opposite his jacket pockets, to the right and left, Pierre and his victim were sitting.

Up to Blagny, nothing happened (nor after, so far as anyone could tell). The train was nonstop as far as that station; everyone was occupying himself according to his particular tastes; two women were sewing, two men were reading, two old people were dozing; the latecomer was yawning, and from time to time lowering his eyes to the seated humanity. As this individual's father was not a glass-maker, Pierre couldn't see the modifications in the consistency of the employee of the Audit Bank, the one who had registered on him among thousands of others.

This second journey to the suburbs, in such conditions, he found only moderately enchanting; he remembered with horror the night he had spent at Hippolyte's; the sheets so filthy that he had preferred to sleep fully dressed, the smell of mildew that came from a bedside table of a most uncomomn style; the layer of thick dust floating on the water intended for his washstand; the sickly, yellowish light that had pretensions to illuminating the whole, and, above all, the feeling of abandonment he had experienced when the innkeeper, having taken him up to his room, had closed the door behind him. Even the first day when, in a barracks in the east of France, he had found himself dressed in the uniform of a French soldier, and realized that the next eighteen months he would have to salute innumerable N.C.O.'s and make his bed in the approved fashion, even that day, he hadn't felt as lost, as hopeless. He didn't sleep that night; from time to time he went to the window and contemplated the building sites of Magnificent Vista and then, full of horror, went and lay down again on the shrieking bed.

And the hours struck at the Obonne church, the Blagny church and the Courteville church. Around 4 o'clock, the dawn began. He sat on a chair for something like an hour, and then went downstairs. Men were already going to work. Hippolyte, all smiles, was serving black coffee and calvados to this one and that.

He wasn't going to repeat that lamentable experience today; he'd go back to Paris by the fastest train. At Blagny, half the compartment got out, treading on the toes of the other half.

Pierre said:

"It's the next station, isn't it?"

"That's right," replied the other.

People looked at them.

"And have you been living in Obonne long?" asked Pierre.

"Nearly three years, now. I'd started having a little house built on one of the Magnificent Vista sites, but I haven't got any further than the ground floor."

"How come?"

"Oh! it's a long story. There's a lot of funny business with these sites. I thought I'd have enough money, I was left a little, to have a house built, and then I came up against various circumstances that made me realize my mistake. I had to give up all hope of having a second floor built. So I live in an unfinished house."

This narrative interests the other passengers considerably; the others, that's the two old people and the latecomer, who has finally got a seat.

"And you, meussieu, do you live on Obonne?"

"No, no," replies Pierre, who is horrified by such a possibility. "I'm going to see some friends, Meussieu and Madame Ploute. Do you know them?"

"No, I don't know them."

"A gentleman with a long black beard and gold pince-nez, and a very tall, very slim lady."

"No, I can't place them. Oh, you know, I hardly know anyone here."

The two old people ruminate over this, and try and remember whether they know the Ploutes. But they don't remember having seen a genleman with a black beard and gold pince-nez at Obonne, and yet they know a lot of people. What it is to have a failing memory.

Here's Obonne. The being of minimal reality says good-by and I hope to see you again to the observer, who apologizes once more for the taxi accident. "But really, it was nothing to do with you." Pierre doesn't try to see the Ploutes, and waits for the next train back to Paris.

---

The next day, Saturday, was a great day. After working a couple of extra hours he took the local train to Blagny. He didn't know that suburb. He had to ask his way because, to get from the station to the factory, you had to make a long detour. He finally arrives at the weatherboarding hut: CHIPS. There's no one in the road. Perhaps it's shut? He walks past it casually and stops a bit farther on, turns back, and bravely pushes open the door. And goes in. There's nothing alarming about the place. Some tables and benches. At the back, the kitchen (?), another table where two women and a man are playing cards and sipping some marc. No one else.

He sits down and raps on the table. Someone grunts in the back room; then a fairly immense woman comes up.

"I'd like some French fries." (He takes the offensive.)

"French fries, at this hour?"

She looks at him curiously. Who can he be, this bourgeois?

"Aren't any French fries ready, but we'll make some. And what'll you have to drink?"

"Some white wine."

The being of minimal reality doesn't know what to think of himself. He looks at the other woman and the man in the back room. The French fries start browning. All this seems prodigiously absurd to him.

Now he has the French fries and the glass of white wine in front of him. The French fries are delicious, the wine is excellent. He does himself proud. Goodness, another customer. It's a workman. He calls out. This time it's the other woman who gets up, an old woman who shuffles. As she passes him, he observes that she stinks. She goes and takes the order; the workman, an Italian, also wants some French fries and white wine.

When she's back in the kitchen, the old woman starts talking volubly to the two others, who look into the room. The being of minimal reality suspects that something odd must be going on. He turns around and looks at the workman, who's quite calmly reading a paper. Could it be he himself, then, who is causing this emotion? It seems so, because all three of them are studying him with interest. He begins to feel uneasy. All this is idiotic. What a stupid idea! He calls out, wanting to pay. All three come rushing up. For his part, it's all he can do not to take to his heels. Courageously, he stays on his bench.

"How much is that?"

"Well, I don't know," exclaims the oldest of them, "if that isn't the most peculiar thing. It was you, wasn't it, who nearly got run over last night outside the Gare du Nord?"

He hadn't been expecting that. It was indeed. He couldn't really believe that that could confer such celebrity on him.

"Just think, meussieu, I was there; I saw it all, when the taxi came up."

And she relates the whole accident. Her brother and sister-in-law (Meussieu and Mme. Belhôtel) listen to the tale with interest for the seventh time. The Italian is pretty well forced to listen, too.

"It must have given you quite a shock," opines the gigantic Mme. Belhôtel.

"Oh yes," he sighs, and feels weaker and weaker, and more and more unhappy, and thinner and thinner.

And the old Cloche explains to him once again that he was in the right, and that he could claim compensation, and that he could get the careless taxi driver's license taken away. Meissieu Belhôtel suggests they have a drink together. They go and open an old bottle of white wine. The customer doesn't dare refuse. They all sit down around him.

"Hm, I don't know, it's peculiar to meet again like this."

For old Ma Cloche now considers herself an old friend of

the near-victim, whose smile is turning into a terrible grimace. Belhôtel uncorks his bottle in masterly fashion; they drink each other's healths. Emotion is at its height; the proprietor smacks his lips.

"This is good."

"Oh yes," says the patient, "it's terribly good."

He takes out a packet of cigarettes and offers him one. Belhôtel throws himself on it; it's not possible, he's going to eat them. Mme. Cloche accepts one, simpers, and goes on with her story.

"And the day before, Meussieu, you can't imagine how horrible it was. Well, that one; he didn't have your luck, that he didn't. A bus ran right ovaries body, the paw meussieu. Oh! there wasn't much left of it. It was all flattened out and all over blood, and there was brains even on people on the pavement's shoes. Then a pliceman put his cape over it and everyone was looking and the cars were hooting, on account of they couldn't get by. Well, no, huh, zno doubt about it, he didn't have your luck, did he, eh Meussieu? Meussieu?"

"Meussieu Marcel."

"Are you a hairdresser?"

"Oh no, my name's Etienne Marcel."

A silence. The innkeepers look at each other. "But in that case," says Meussieu Belhôtel, "you've already got a street named after you in Paris."

They laugh like mad. Etienne, to whom people have been making this joke for something like twenty years, laughs too. He finds everything more and more grotesque. He'd very much like to wake up, but he knows he can't. A little sentence starts running through his head: "Such is life, such is life, such is life." The little sentence turns into the vast thuds of a tolling bell. Boom that's life, boom that's life, boom that's life. He drinks another glassful. Belhôtel tells how the day before there'd been a brawl between some Arabs and some Italians here. One dead. Boom that's life, boom that's life, boom that's life.

Etienne suddenly gets up.

They look at him in stupefaction.

"You're not going to leave us like that?"

But he looks so determined that they don't insist on his staying.

"It's on me," the owner declares. "Nothing doing, about paying."

They shake hands effusively. They make him promise to come again. Mme. Cloche calls out: "See you again soon!" A real idyll . . .

Etienne makes his way to the station. The sun beats down on the grey grass of the embankment. A smell of sour candy comes from the linoleum factory on the other side of the track. Refuse and wastepaper complete the landscape of wasteland and weatherboarding. The Warsaw express goes by, making the yellowing old newspapers fly. Then silence reigns again, a Saturday afternoon silence. Etienne trudges on to the station, repeating from time to time: Such is life.

---

Everything seems to be flowing from a dense cloud that remains motionless above the rabbit hutches. Neither beginning nor end; to the right and left, the beaten track; beyond the horizon, those little rabbit hutches, the Magnificent Vista housing development. The milkman, the baker, the butcher, they only venture along the wider paths; and so, along the little tracks riddled with potholes, the housewives come hurrying, in bedroom slippers and curlers. They exchange a few words, and then quickly go back into their holes. Over there, the husband is stubbornly gardening; cleaning out the hens or rabbits; if he isn't gardening, he's watching the grass grow. The younger generation is playing games.

Théo goes up to the unfinished first floor of the paternal house; this is his favorite place; he observes how the bricks are crumbling, how the walls are disintegrating, the effects of the wind and rain, the construction of a ruin. He takes with him the second volume of *Les Misérables*. When it bores him, he looks round at the other houses.

In general, there's nothing interesting to see. Backs bent over lawns, men tomatoeing or onioning. From time to time, the woman suddenly comes out and throws a big bucket of water, splosh! over the gravel, and goes in again. Over there, a little girl is running round in circles. Over there, the druggist's son is fixing his bike; over there, Mme. Pigeonnier, draped in her kimono, is taking the air and sucking candies. Mme. Pigeonnier is forty-five, but it's known that she has a past. Théo suspects a good many things about Mme. Pigeonnier. But Mme. Pigeonnier goes in, proudly draped. Théo once again immerses himself in *Les Misérables*.

The father, down below, is pretending to be interested in string beans, but it's not convincing. He straightens himself up and yawns, then moves on a bit; really, he isn't doing a thing, the father. The mother comes in with the shopping. Confusion (and how!) in the kitchen. The father grinds the coffee. It's nearing twelve. They're going to have lunch in the garden. His father is just about to call him to take the table out. How right he was.

"Théoooooooo;" Théo comes down from his roost. They put the table under the Lime Tree. Ts very hot. The water has to be cooled. Today, it's cucumber salad; meat and vegetables; cheese, fruit. It's Sunday. The two males attack the salad. The wife sits down quickly, eats a few slices and hurries off to see to the meat. With the meat, there's a bit of peace. Théo, his nose dug into his plate, guzzles; that's because he's growing. Fifteen years old, I think. Next year, Théo is going to take his baccalaureate. They're quite optimistic; they slave enough for him.

With the coffee, Etienne opens the *Journal,* and Théo the *Sunday Excelsior;* the wife clears the table. When she's finished, she reads the short story; Etienne has finished the paper a long time ago, and is dozing. Théo does the crossword puzzle.

The sun easily pierces the consumptive leaves with which the Lime Tree is trying to resist it. The Sunday calm is steeped in the lukewarm air. They can hear Mme. Pigeonnier's maid singing a sentimental song. The druggist's son goes off on his bicycle; he's going to watch the E.C.F. team play the A.S.T.V. In the distance, the trains whistle. The flies apathetically drag themselves through the tired air; here and there they hold conferences around various sorts of refuse. Etienne comes out of his doze and goes and fetches his Sunday meerschaum; he fills it, he lights it, he puts it in his mouth, he pulls at it (not the way people pull in a tug of war), and the smoke spreads out around his head, but hasn't enough energy to climb even up to the lowest branches of the Lime Tree.

At about 2 o'clock, they decide to go for a walk in the woods around the old castle, in Obonne. Dressing operations. Théo thinks up various methods of escape; next year, he'll start playing games; that'll save his Sundays for him. He incidentally touches his genitals, but doesn't insist. He's the first to be dressed in his Sunday best. Etienne next; he's put on his beautiful straw hat with the serrated edges, and is whistling. He's certainly not there.

At last, the mother's ready; very elegant, the mother. Théo and Etienne don't say anything, but they don't conceal their pride. She works well and, when they take her out, what a beauty! She's still fussing around quite a bit because everything isn't just as it should be; at last it's all right, and they start. The gate squeaks, once, twice, and the three beings make their way to the woods.

The woods, naturally, are teeming. People have been picnicking, and there are bits of greasy paper all over the place. People are sleeping here and there, couples are tickling each other and women are laughing very loudly. Théo takes a sly look at a girl lying on the ground somewhat immodestly. This gets him into a terrible state; his day hasn't been wasted. Etienne, on his arm, feels his wife hanging. He takes his family along their habitual route. They'll go as far as the old castle, rest there, and then go down to the river again; a lemonade at the little café, and then back home.

The walk takes three hours and is accomplished without a hitch. In any case, it's a famous walk. The river is charming, at the bottom of the hill and the castle; people come all the way from Paris to see it. They drink the tepid lemonade under the cool arbor. Etienne tells them about the intrigues of the assistant manager in his office. At the next table, a man on his own is drinking the tepid lemonade and listening closely to their conversation; every so often, he casts an admiring eye at

Etienne's wife, but she doesn't catch it, seeing that she's got her back turned to him.

Théo, whose father bores him, has spotted what's going on, of course; suddenly, he begins to wonder whether that fellow isn't by any chance? He immediately forgets the woman's thigh he got a glimpse of just now and becomes passionately interested in this adventure. He's jubilant, he's got a secret; now he knows; no more doubt about it, it's the fellow of the other evening, the day when the train was late. The fellow sees that the brat it watching him and is a bit embarrassed. His embarrassment increases. He blushes. He goes away. Théo is now very annoyed; he shouldn't have stared at him so obviously. Maybe something would have happened.

But it's time to go home. The crowd is starting to make its way to the station. 6:30. They'll wait half an hour for dinner, then a pipe, then a last walk around the garden, night, sleep. Tomorrow, work begins again.

---

*Here, the body is curled up like a fetus, turned in on itself, its fists clenched, it's met a childhood friend. The friend is dressed as an ambassador. "What are you doing these days?" He doesn't make excuses for himself. Here's another childhood friend, a dentist; he tried to combine this position with that of inspector of weights and measures, so he went broke. They are all three naked, now. Etienne takes them to the art students' ball. His right leg is relaxing a bit.*

*Here, on his back, his mouth opens wide. He's trying to buy an amusing children's paper. He doesn't dare, with any of the paper sellers he goes to, because there are customers. He goes to a lot of paper sellers like that. In the end, he finds himself at a butcher's, he's sharpening some long knives, he turns around, it's his father. He starts. Agony. Théo gets a bit restless; sleep wins; he subsides.*

*Here, a naked body is lying peacefully outstretched, windows wide open. He sees himself at his grandmother's in the country; they're going to kill an old cock; his mother, he can hardly make her out, is against this execution. The word exe-*

*cution somehow weaves the woof of a canvas on which before long an old cock is painted, a cock of the species that has a featherless red neck. He walks a bit crookedly, in a very particular way that Pierre recognizes. He's the one who's going to kill the cock, he's aware of that. He wakes up very gradually, smiling. He feels marvelous; he looks at the time. Through the darkness, he makes out 4:20. He turns over and, on his other side, goes back to sleep.*

*Here, a globulous, greasy mass is wrapped around dirty sheets; only a few grey hairs emerge from the conglomeration. The conglomeration is reviewing a regiment, a regiment of grenadiers. She's their general. The grenadiers are singing as if they were in an operetta. Aren't they handsome! Suddenly, she's a little embarrassed; the trousers of one of them are open. She'll have him shot. Her embarrassment increases and increases until an enormous white louse comes out of her mouth and flies away. The grenadiers cheer the unspeakable animal. Ma Cloche is dreaming.*

*Here, a man is tossing and turning; he's in a sweat; he's stifling; what a hot night, what a warm night. He looks at the time, 4:20. He gets up, goes and drinks a glass of water. Walks around a bit, rubbing his forehead. He falls back onto the bed, which groans. He wrings his hands, in a way that he himself finds grotesque. Narcense isn't going to get any more sleep tonight.*

*The office is finished; she goes to the grocery store at the corner of La Fayette Street, to buy several things. Just as she's crossing the street she realizes she's forgotten the strawberries. She goes back to buy them. As she is coming out of the grocery store someone bumps into her and the bag of strawberries gets squashed against her white dress. That's what she was dreaming.*

*Meussieu and Mme. Belhôtel aren't dreaming. They are carrying down to the river a little parcel that contains nothing other than the corpse of a dead child, that of the waitress and Meussieu Belhôtel. The waitress is called Ernestine; she has a snub nose and greasy hair. Whereas Meussieu Belhôtel, he, from time to time, makes himself useful to the local copshop.*

## Second Chapter

"HUH, here comes your sister," says Mme. Belhôtel. "I'm off up to the fif floor."

"Or right, or right, you do that. If she annoys you, well, let her be."

"Sjust what I'm going to do, don't you worry!"

When Mme. Cloche arrives, she finds her brother Saturnin huddled up at the back of his lodge, like a spider; he's examining the mail, which, today, is confined to one post card.

"Your wife all right?"

"Oh yes, she's busy."

"Znever there when I arrive."

"Just the way it happens, you know. How's our brother?"

"Things aren't too bad. Isn't too much unemployment out that way. Sa good position, where he is. And then, with two bistros, he can get by."

"And the waitress?"

"I fixed that."

She smiles.

Saturnin gets up and puts the post card back in a pigeon hole. He spits skillfully into a receptacle for that purpose, and stretches his arms. He takes a few shambling steps.

"Want summing to drink?"

"If you ask me."

"Some marc."

Slowly, he gets the bottle, and brings it over. All his actions seem ponderous: all his looks, heavy with thought.

"Still not ezactly overworked?"

"Still no one. Just one tenant for an eight-floor apartment house with all mod. convs.; and what's more, he doesn't even pay, the one and only tenant. It's an uncle who arranges for him to be here."

"You've already told me that. The one who was a musician."

"Mm; at the moment, hasn't got any work. No idea what he does. He looks very weird, at the moment."

"Zthat a card for him?"

"Mm; comes from the suburbs. Says: 'Alberte doesn't read your epistles; if you don't mind too much, send them straight to me, then I won't have to stick the bits together. Best wishes, Théo.' It's postmarked Obonne, 3:45 yesterday."

"Tsit mean?"

"Way I work it out, Théo, he must be Alberte's husband, and a friend of Narcense's. He's writing to tell him to stop importuning his wife with his assiduities. Tsas plain as the nose on your face."

"What's he going to look like when he reads that, eh, your tenant?"

She laughs.

"Yaren't half lucky to be able to take it easy all day."

"Oh, I don't take it easy all the time. I've got work to do."

"Your thing you're writing."

"Yes, my thing I'm writing. Makes a lot of work for me. But it's getting on."

"You're a bit nuts, you know. For a concierge, working as a penman, snot right."

"Tcha, can do what I like, can't I? If you don't understand, just too bad."

"What if I started to write?"

"Write then, write then, my beauty. Well—seen anything nice recently?"

"Oh yes! I saw a horrible accident outside the Gare du Nord. And another the next day."

"Nice—accidents?"

"The first wasn't bad. There was brains all over the shoes of the people standing round. A guy squashed by a B bus. The other—wasn't anything to it; but the following Saturday, it was the Thursday it happened, the guy who nearly got run over, I saw him at Dominique's. He came to have some French fries. Scalled Etienne Marcel."

"Like the street?"

"Mm, Dominique even passed the same remark."

"And what sort of guy?"

"Looks like a meussieu. Probably works in an office. But it was funny meeting him like that. And then, I just wonder what he was doing at 4 in the afternoon, at Dominique's; and a Saturday, at that! Eh, what do you think?"

"Maybe he lives thereabouts."

"Aren't any houses for that sort of people round there. Zonly the factory, and a few huts for people who come and dig in their garden patches. After that it's the railroad sidings, and then old Taupe's shack. It certainly couldn't have been old Taupe he wanted to see."

"Maybe's a cop. On account of your whatsit."

"Oh, go on. Dominique's not worried, he's too useful to them. Me neither, I look after one of the local superintendent's wives; I'm not worried."

"Never know."

"What I thought: maybe it's on account of Ernestine. Za pretty girl, Ernestine. Maybe she's scored.

They laugh.

"Your marc's better than Dominique's."

"So he's doing all right, Dominique?"

"Oh yes; course there's the depression, but even so he reckons he'll be able to buy a brothel soon. In which case his kid, he'll be able to go to the lycée. Dominique'd like Clovis to be an engineer."

"I'sa good trade."

"And how."

"But if his father keeps a brothel, that'll count against him later on."

Mme. Cloche considers that Saturnin is no fool; yes but it's a pity he's a little nuts; what an idea, taking it into his head to be a writer; it's not for the likes of him. Ah, if he'd only wanted to, he could really have done something! But it's time for her to go. Her work is calling her.

Her brother says into her ear:

"Tell Dominique to watch it, though; snitching on people, that can make trouble for you; you never know what you're letting yourself in for; tell him that."

Just his imagination. Still, if it'll please him, she'll tell him. Right. So long.

No sooner has Mme. Cloche disappeared around the corner than Mme. Belhôtel number two reappears.

"The old bitch gone?"

"Mm hm, she's gone."

"What did she have to tell you this time?"

Saturnin gives an accurate report, which is interrupted by the arrival of a telegraph messenger; it's a telegram for Narcense. This is a rare and important occurrence. Will they have time to steam it open and discover some secret? . . .

Saturnin seals the telegram up again; nothing of any interest; "Grandmother dead." *That's* not a secret. They'd have known about it anyway.

---

The night light revealed three to four shapes, deflated by slumber, trying in vain to find a comfortable position to sleep in. The head of one of them, who was merely sitting, was oscillating; the feet of another adjoined a cavernous face, its eyes bunged up with fatigue and embellished with an incipient rheumy discharge. Narcense, sitting motionless in a corner, with staring eyes, didn't see the badly dressed bodies but, beyond the brown boards of the third-class coach, caught sight of a house that hadn't had the strength to reach its second floor and remained acephalous. Now and then his grandmother went by with her retinue of foraging hens and her prehistoric old woman's idiosyncrasies and her three aggressive teeth and her never-ending need to piss. She'd been a decent old woman. In the kitchen, getting the dinner, that very beautiful woman. One of the slumberers went out into the corridor, which made the man next to him move restlessly and automatically take up more room. The other came back a few minutes later and insinuated himself into the reduced space.

A multiplicity of little lights announced the approach of a big town. A bridge was suspended over a suburban street. Narcense caught sight of a mangy dog zigzagging about in search of garbage. Then, in the station, the train, gradually, stopped. Some passengers got out, with swollen eyes and flabby hands. Narcense leaned out of the window, watching the people walking up and down and fussing, and the buffet on wheels, and the man hiring out pillows and blankets. Five minutes later, the train started off again, asthmaticizing. Narcense sat down again. A newcomer was occupying one of the corner seats left vacant by the departure of the first slumberers. This was a person of extremely singular aspect; not on account of the fact that he possessed two arms, two legs and a head, but because these arms, these legs and this head were of such exiguous dimensions that it would have been possible, without much fear of being mistaken, to call the man a dwarf. What was more, a pointed white beard adorned his face, in which scintillated two beady eyes; the beard reached as far as the penultimate button of his waistcoat, starting from the top.

He asked if it was all right to leave the light on. It didn't worry Narcense. Wasn't sleepy. The dwarf began to read a number of *Gay Paris* with great attention. When he'd finished, he crumpled it up, threw it under the seat and started muttering into his beard: "What a life, what a life, what a life," which made Narcense laugh; he had been scrutinizing this odd bird for the past forty-five minutes.

"Anything wrong?" he asked him, nicely.

"Shit," replied the dwarf, and, taking a tiny comb out of the top right-hand pocket of his waistcoat, he started to comb out his tangled, whitish beard.

Narcense didn't insist. When he'd finished combing his beard the little creature picked his nose with an index finger, contemplated at length the product of his explorations, and then rolled it up into a ball.

"It's awful, it's awful," he started grumumbling again. "What a job!"

"What job?"

"That any of your business?"

Narcense was really beginning to be amused by so much misery and bad temper reduced to such minute proportions. By this impotent, squashable ringworm.

"I bet," said Narcense, "I can guess what your profession is."

"Let's bet! Ten francs you don't guess!"

"Ten francs I do guess!"

"'Cross my heart and hope to die,' as my very dear friend, the Countess of Rut's farmer, used to say. What *is* my profession?"

"Well, adventurer."

"Let's say you've won five francs," said the dwarf, and took them out of a greasy wallet.

Narcense was enjoying himself.

"I'm glad I met you," he said, pocketing the five francs. "You're taking my mind off things."

"Is that what you needed?"

"That any of your business?"

The cow-pat deigned to smile.

"And to what do I owe these five francs?" Narcense went on.

"Oh yes. Well" (he lowered his voice) "I'm a parasite."

"Ha ha."

Parasite, just look at it, that mite, that micron, that molecule, that neutron—a parasite!

"And I operate—through fear."

Fear, just look at it, that crumb, that shaving, that scraping, he operates through fear!

"Yes, I frighten old women and children. Sometimes adults, even. I live on other people's cowardice. Stupid, isn't it, eh, to be afraid? Just imagine what sort of a shithouse the person's soul must be. Don't you think, Meussieu? Meussieu?"

"Narcense."

"Nice name, and you're . . . ?"

"A musician."

"Delighful."

"Jobless and penniless."

"Like me. Just think, I was on to a gold mine, and then . . . But it'd take too long to tell you all that. Here's the K. tunnel. I get out at the next station."

"I'm going as far as Torny," said Narcense.

"Tell me. You don't happen to know of a house where they'd put me up, do you? It's for in a few months."

"No."

"Never mind."

Suddenly, just like that, it occurs to Narcense:

"Just a minute. I know a house. Rue Moche. In Obonne. Half built. There's a child. A father. And a . . . Yes, that's it. A horrible brat."

The tiny tot wrote the address down in a notebook.

"Do you always succeed in frightening people?"

"Yes. When I want to. Even you, I can make you . . ."

"You don't say?" laughed Narcense.

The train braked. The dwarf was already in the corridor, suitcase in hand.

"One day I'll do the dirty on you, you'll see, I'll play such a dirty trick on you, it'll knock the bottom out of your life."

He disappeared.

Narcense smiled. Poor, miserable, blighted creature, unjustly reduced by nature to the proportions of a louse. And he's going to knock the bottom out of your life. As if he had any need of that. Poor sap.

---

Marcheville, some thirty miles from Torny, the industrial center, is more like a large village than a small town; a peasant population, a few bourgeois, among whom are the lawyer and his dog. The lawyer's dog is a white poodle, answering to the name of Jupiter. Jupiter is highly intelligent; if his master had had the time, he would have taught him arithmetic, perhaps even the elements of formal logic, fallacies and all. But his various pursuits have obliged him to neglect Jupiter's schooling, and he only knows how to say woof woof from time to time and sit on his behind to get a lump of sugar. However, though there may be some doubt as to the extent of his learning, there can be nothing but admiration for the care he takes of his person. Shorn like a lion, he swaggers about within a radius of fifteen yards of the notarial house. At any greater distance, enormous beasts, jealous of his elegance, menace him with their vulgar, ill-bred fangs.

On this particular morning, Jupiter's habits are upset; so are those of the lawyer and his family. Everyone is restless, and dressed in black. Forsaken, Jupiter goes to sleep in the hall. A person with a small suitcase in his hand comes in; woof

woof, says the poodle intelligently; the lawyer, who has lost his collar stud, comes down in his shirt-sleeves. Good morning, good morning, he seems to be saying; Jupiter shows his approval with his tail and gets a smack on the thigh for his pains. Then another meussieu arrives, a very tall, very fat one. The greetings start all over again; Jupiter wants to take part in the palaver, but the tall-and-fat person treads on his toe nails. Owch, owch, says Jupiter, and goes and hides under a chair. The meussieus talk with restraint and compunction, like the day of the little boy's first communion. Eulalie brings some coffee. Maybe there's a chance of a lump of sugar. Jupiter sits up and begs, but he realizes from the uninterested looks of the meussieus that he's put his foot in it. This isn't the moment for playing the fool. He goes over to the door to get some air; so far and no farther, because Caesar, the Butcher's dog, is watching for him out of the corner of his eye.

The meussieus start walking. He follows at their soles. Caesar is close behind. They get to a house that Jupiter knows well; it belongs to an old lady who's generous with her sugar. The old lady isn't there; there's a meussieu dressed up as a widow, it's true, but that's not the same thing. The meussieu in petticoats starts singing, accompanied by two little boys dressed up as girls whom Jupiter recognizes only too well as being the bullies who, last Sunday, tied a corned beef tin onto his stump of a tail. Then they take a great big packing case out into the street; he goes and has a sniff to see what it is; it smells of the old lady. A kick in the ribs teaches him to respect the dead.

With the big packing case being towed in front, and the crowd following behind, the ensemble makes it way toward a garden surrounded by walls and planted with huge great stones sticking up at right angles. Jupiter runs up and down and is amazed that his master, who's usually in such a hurry, doesn't try and get in front of the big box; he's walking slowly, leading the way, with the young man with the suitcase and the tall, fat meussieu.

At the entrance to the garden, Jupiter's heart misses a beat; he's just noticed Caesar waiting for him, with an ominous look. So it's advisable not to stray too far from the blackened bipeds.

Everyone has come to a standstill around a hole. In the middle of the gathering, the man-woman mutters a menacing song; the bullies wave steaming teapots. Two professional drunks lower the box into the bottom of the hole. Then the guests toss in drops of water. Jupiter is losing interest, and he wanders off and goes scrounging from grave to grave; but, just behind that of Madame Pain, that most worthy lady who kept her idiot daughter in seclusion for fifteen years, he finds himself muzzle-to-ass with Caesar. This encounter gives him wings; he gallops, he flees, he decamps; he jumps onto a mound of loose soil, near his master; the soil is loose, as we said, it crumbles, and Jupiter tumbles, in a cloud of humus and compost, onto the grandmother's coffin. Some people burst out laughing; other exclaim: How shocking! and a few murmur: Putrefaction! The lawyer let out a kind of strident shout, his personal roar of laughter, and then recovered his dignity. But he wasn't going to forgive Jupiter.

That evening, the young man said to the poodle, as he handed him a lump of sugar:

"Will they put a chin strap on *you* when they bury you?"

"Woof woof," says the other, who hasn't understood a word.

The next day Jupiter is hanging at the end of a rope, because he has assailed the dignity of the dead and of the living.

---

1. I am only now answering the very extraordinary post card you sent me three days ago, as I have only just gotten back from my grandmother's funeral. So far as I can gather, you claim to be the son of a certain person to whom I had the presumption to write. This person, it would appear, has torn up my letters, and you, it would appear, have stuck them together again? If I am not mistaken, you must be the schoolboy of perverse appearance and with decayed teeth whom I saw, some ten days ago in the little café by the river, near Obonne castle. I realized, from your narrow forehead, that you were of limited intelligence, and, from the rings around your eyes, that you were addicted to self-abuse. I now see

that you combine with these deficiencies the efficiency of the informer and the pretension of the spy.

I herewith send you, young Théo, the kick in the ass that your filthy initiative deserves, and I remain, of your mother, the respectful admirer.

Narcense.

2. Monsieur,

You polluted the gate of my stepfather's house. I therefore demand satisfaction.

Théo.

P.S. I hope your *filthy* grandmother's funeral was amusing.

Th.

3. I see it's not possible to conceal anything from you, not even the hygienic practices of my deceased grandmother. I might add that your hope was fulfilled; a grotesque incident marred the orderly procedure of this ceremony; a dog belonging to one of my uncles went up to the grave, slipped, and fell on to the coffin, yelping pathetically. Several people laughed; my uncle was of their number. I might add that the latter, considering that on the one hand his dog had fulfilled all his obligations on this earth, and on the other that it was *human* to spare him a rheumaticky old age, hanged him from the cord on which the clothes are put to dry. For a quarter of an hour, Jupiter, the faithful white poodle, swung between a pair of pants and a napkin.

I'm wondering whether it wouldn't also be *human* to apply a similar treatment to you; you would thus be spared a furunculous and degraded youth. Think it over. I would put the rope around your neck with loving care—a rope of tested strength; I wouldn't need to have two shots at it. You would find it an easy death, and I would have the satisfaction of having rid Obonne of a perfect little swine.

I suppose you are on vacation at the moment and don't really know what to do with your time. I won't give you any advice on this subject, as I prefer not to waste mine in writing at any greater length to the most sour-faced, cross-eyed chicken it has ever been my hard luck to encounter.

Be so good as to give your esteemed mother my most humble respects.

Narcense.

4. Monsieur,

On this day of national rejoicing my mother has been crying for hours because I told her you wanted to murder me. It's shameful to make my poor mother suffer so, Monsieur.

Her son,

Théo.

*P.S.* Bet you anything you get cold feet.
*P.P.S.* Not especially funny, your dog.
*P.P.P.S.* See how tactful I am, this time my envelope is sealed (like my mother's panties).

Th.

5. I am convinced that your removal from the number of the living becomes daily more essential. The dog Jupiter's fate seems to me to be the one best suited to you. You can be quite sure that I won't "get cold feet."

I take your jokes about your mother as they should be taken. Tell her that because of my great love for her I forgive her for having begotten such a splenetic bit of vermin as you.

Narcense.

6. Got cold feet yet?

Théo.

P.S. In one of your idiotic letters, you said I was addicted to self-abuse. What about you.

7. Monsieur,

On any day and at any time you choose, I'll be in Obonne forest, in the place they call Les Mygales.

I'll bring the rope.

Narcense.

The stalls put up for the Fourteenth of July modified Etienne's oscillations to some extent. He couldn't avoid the one where the man was peeling potatoes; every day, he stopped and listened for three seconds, without being able to see, on account of the crowd, and then made his escape. Farther on, he had to escape the snares of stylography and the pitfalls of perfumery; finally, avoiding these various temptations, he was able to throw himself into the gloomy stairway that led him to a cruel and automatic gate that had no hesitation in mercilessly crushing whosoever transgressed the severe commandments applicable to the subterranean traveler. The stairway had forty-seven steps; that of Obonne station had the same number. Etienne had just made this discovery and, comparing it with that of the little ducks and that of the place where they sold French fries, he concluded that the world is big and fearsome, full of mysteries and even, as you might say, enigmas. It seemed unfair that so simple an established fact as that of the equivalence of the number of steps in these two stairways should have been hidden from him for so long. Then he stopped blaming the universe for it.

It's not its fault, but mine. All I had to do was turn my head to the right instead of turning it to the left, to take one more step, and I discovered things I passed every day and didn't see. I used not to turn my head; I did turn it. But why did I turn it? It started with the little ducks, those little ducks which even Théo had seen. The same day, if I remember rightly, the cat was killed. Then I saw the place where they sell French fries, then I nearly got run over. Yes, that's how it started. All of a sudden, things changed, from one day to the next.

The potato peeler wasn't doing very well, for a change. The crowd was thinner than usual, so that Etienne, coming out of his bank, was finally able to see the gadget and how it was supposed to be used. And in any case, it wasn't the only marvel they sold at that stall; the avidity of those of a practical turn of mind was also tempted by a mayonnaise whisk with a little funnel which let the oil through drop by drop; an instrument for cutting hard-boiled eggs in thin slices; another for making shelled-shaped butter pats; and finally, a horribly complicated sort of brace and bit whose application the demonstrator didn't deign to explain and which was no doubt nothing but an improved-model corkscrew, At least, that was what Etienne thought.

Having followed the demonstration with some attention, he made the acquisition of a potato peeler; just as he was walking away, he found he couldn't resist the charms of the cutter-of-hard-boiled-eggs-in-thin-slices, and bought it. Then, when he had gone three paces, parcel in hand, he began to get a bit worried about this new new departure; for he suddenly realized that the last thing these objects were destined for was the improvement of his household facilities; anything but—because he'd somehow got the idea that he ought to give the potato peeler to the fellow who sold the French fries, whereas the cutter-of-hard-boiled-eggs-in-thin-slices he intended to keep for himself.

This revelation disconcerted him.

And thus he arrived at his habitual eatery; it was semi-deserted, because it was Saturday. It was horribly hot inside. Etienne sat down and ordered, and while he was waiting for the rancid gudgeon fished out of the bottom of a carburetor, a gudgeon which affected the name of sardine, he undid his parcel and contemplated his acquisitions. Yes, there was no doubt about it, the one had to go to Blagny, and the other had to remain in the bottom of a drawer. The waitress brought the oily gudgeon, reputed to have been fished off the coast of Brittany. Etienne did his parcel up again and fearlessly absorbed the oleaginous chow which he was being sold as hors d'oeuvres—at a reasonable price, though, it was true. Then, with a piece of livid putty, he wiped his plate; he ate the putty; he raised his head and saw, sitting opposite him, a fair-haired young man who was watching him closely. He had a feeling he knew the fellow; the feeling became a certainty; he did know this fair-haired, crooked-mouthed, prematurely balding young man. Where on earth had he met him? The name of Ploute occurred to him; yes, that was it, Meussieu and Madame Ploute . . . The young man interrupted this research:

"I have a feeling, Meussieu, that I've met you somewhere."

"That's just what I was saying to myself."

"Watcha going to have next?" asked the waitress.

"I'll have tripe," said Etienne, "*—gras-double.*"

"How ghastly," thought Pierre, and he ordered: "Steak and French fries." And, turning to Etienne:

"*Now* I remember. My taxi nearly ran you over, about two weeks ago, outside the Gare du Nord, and after that we went to Obonne together."

"Ah yes, ah yes," exclaimed Etienne, happy to meet an involuntary actor in his transformation. Why actor? He doesn't know; and he is equally ignorant of the fact that Pierre has also been watching him closely and vigilantly and, this very day, has seen him attain tridimensional reality. Naturally, Pierre keeps this to himself. He introduces himself:

"Pierre Le Grand."

And thinks he's going to suffocate when the waitress insinuates a plateful of *gras-double* under Etienne's nose, because he only knows the little bistros where you have *foie gras*. He is served the most terrifying bit of leather that ever haunted the nightmares of a hypochondriac cobbler; it has a few charcoal nails with it. It takes him some moments to realize that this ensemble is entitled steak and French fries, especially as it smells of pigs' intestines. He asks:

"Do you come here often?"

"Yes, every day."

"Do you think it's a good place?"

"It isn't too bad; the thing is, it's my sort of price."

Ah yes, he hadn't thought of that. Even so, what muck!

"And Meussieu and Madame Ploute—how are they?" asked Etienne.

"Fine, thank you," replies Pierre, who has no recollection of his creation.

"Do you still go to Obonne from time to time?"

"My goodness—not since last time."

"Ha, ha," says Etienne.

Pierre, who has given up his attack on the charcoal, orders a yogurt; Etienne orders a banana and jam.

"They're very ingenious, these gadgets, aren't they," says Pierre, innocently.

"Oh yes. Very ingenious. They're very useful," replies Etienne, his voice full of restraint.

"They're very amusing, these little inventions. There are always some very interesting ones at the annual Lépine exhibition."

"I've never been to it."

There's this, and that, and then this, Pierre tells him. Etienne listens in amazement. Here's someone else who can see things; *he* would never pass some little ducks for three years without noticing them. This very restaurant, he's been coming to it for three years now, and perhaps he hasn't seen what he ought to see in it. And he, Le Grand, perhaps *has* seen it—he's *sure* to have seen it.

"At the last exhibition," continues Pierre, getting quite worked up, "there were some blotting-paper gloves for accountants and men of letters . . ."

"Have you noticed anything here?" interrupts Etienne.

"Have I noticed . . .?"

"Yes, have you noticed anything here, in this restaurant?" And he leans over and stares at him. He's waiting.

Pierre looks around him. He doesn't notice a thing. Nothing. He feels he *ought* to notice something, that *everything* depends on what he notices. A long half minute goes by.

"You don't notice anything, then?" Etienne asks again, anxiously.

Pierre stiffens, goes tense. Those eyes staring at him. He must look petrified himself. If I don't notice anything . . . at least ten silent seconds have passed.

"Then you don't see anything?" questions Etienne, whose distress is becoming despair. He clutches at the tablecloth and looks as if he's going to scream.

One more second, and Pierre leans over to Etienne's ear.

---

Ernestine, her hair falling over her nose, applies a lethargic dishcloth to the tables, this way and that. Bread crumbs and bits of fried potato fall on to the floor; wine stains radiate. The table thus cleaned, Ernestine goes on to the next. Now and then she stops, blows at her hair and wipes her forehead. It's horribly hot, in spite of the draft. The corrugated-iron hut gently cooks all its contents. Bluebottles buzz; a few advance on Ernestine, who scatters them with her elbow. Only one table is occupied, by a small group of workers from the chemicals factory. At the other end, M. Belhôtel is taking a cork out of a bottle with a slipknot; when he's finished, he sits down by himself at a table and pricks up his ears. Of the five sitting there, he knows two by name and two only by sight; with a vague and absent-minded air, he carefully examines the fifth.

Near the French fries pan, Mme. Belhôtel and Mme. Cloche are playing *belote,* but their hearts aren't in it. While they're waiting, they doze. They are slowly emptying a bottle of cointreau. The cards are getting sticky. A fly, stuck to the bottom of a glass, ties to free itself from the viscous substance that is Mme. Cloche's stomachal joy; it's just about to succeed when it's squashed by a finger in mourning; it's Mme. Belhôtel, killing time.

A little breeze has risen and, periodically, wrapped in the odor of sour candy, a cloud of dust enters the hut and goes and sprinkles itself over the tables as far as the fifth row. There are fifteen, with gangway down the middle. Ernestine ignores the dust and goes and starts to string the beans. Old Taupe comes in, staggering, and orders a liter of white wine, just for himself; When Ernestine brings it, old Taupe indulges in some bold and unambiguous pawing which makes him jump for joy and chortle. He used to live modestly on an income derived from some Russian investments; he now lives in a sort of shack behind the chemicals factory. Poverty and filth seem to have made him immutable. For this living, he picks rags and sells junk. The five workmen get up and go. Old Taupe, who has got through half his bottle, has fallen asleep and is snoring. An express train goes by and makes the badly fixed corrugated-iron sheets rattle. One of the women claims ten points, without much conviction. Dominique Belhôtel yawns. A cloud of dust reaches the seventh row; behind it, Etienne comes in.

It takes them some moments to realize the situation; when it is realized, the attack is launched. Etienne is surrounded.

"We are very glad to see you," declares Belhôtel solemnly; the two women nod assent. "Ernestine! just run over to High Street and buy a bottle of that sparkling wine at 6.85."

Ernestine disappears, gone with the wind.

Then they all three start talking at once, very fast, and avidly:

"Your name *is* Marcel, huh? You *have* a son called Théo? You *do* live in Obonne?" Etienne doesn't know how to answer so many indiscreet questions.

"It's very serious, it's very serious," declares Mme. Cloche, who's managed to get the cross-examination into her hands. "If it's true that you're called Marcel, and that you've got a son called Théo, and that you live in Obonne, well, I've got summing very serious to tell you."

"Tell me, then. My name *is* Etienne Marcel, I *have* got a son called Théo; or rather, he's my wife's son, his real name is Nautilus, but he's always called Marcel. And I *do* live in Obonne.

"Do you know a Meussieu Narcense? A musician, zaround thirty, dark-haired and fattish, not very tall . . ."

Etienne thinks; no, he doesn't know him.

"You really sure?" insists Ma Coche. "A dark-haired guy, with a scar in the middle of his forehead."

Oh no, really that's incredible! That's the fellow who was behind him, earlier on, in the restaurant; the one Le Grand was referring to when he said: "You'll know him one day—soon perhaps;" and he, Etienne, had thought he was pulling his leg.

"Well"—long silence; Mme. Cloche looks all around her,—"that man, tonight, he's going to hang your son."

Etienne bursts into long laughter. The Belhôtels and old Cloche, shocked, cry:

"It's the honest truth, it's very serious, it's horrible, it's abominable."

Etienne, who's beginning to get worried, calms down; Mme. Cloche tells all.

"It's like this, Meussieu, this is how I heard about it. I've got a brother who's a concierge, in the Boulevard of the Unknown Officer. It's a big apartment house, but there's only one tenant."

"Goodness me."

"Oh, that's another story. This tenant, sname's Meussieu Narcense. Thother day, must be a week ago, praps longer, I goan to see my brother, sname's Saturnin; we're chatting of this and that and he happens to say: 'Yknow, there's this person called Théo, he's writing to my tenant to tell him to stop writing to this person called Alberte, that'll be Théo's wife'—sfarz I remember, that's what he said. After he saw he'd gotten it wrong. And that Alberte, she was Théo's mom. On account of after, some more letters came from Théo, see what I mean? The first one next, he told Meussieu Narcense that he'd polluted the gate of his stepfather's house, must say it seemed a strange sort of story to us, and after that he insulted Meussieu Narcense's deceased grandmother, when he'd only just come back from her funeral— the grandmother's, that is. The second one he wrote, that was when it dawned on us that he was the son of this Madame Alberte; he said that the other guy wanted to murder him. After that, he wrote to Meussieu Narcense that he'd got cold feet. And smorning, I'm at my brother Saturnin's; there was a letter from Théo where he was telling him: 'Bring the rope to hang me tonight at midnight in the place they call Les Mygales, in Obonne wood.' And it was signed Théo Marcel. So it just happened to occur to me 'at that was your name and that it wasn't often that people's last names were called Marcel and that you must live on this rail line. So I thought I'd warn you. If you hadn't come here, I'd of gone and seen you and told you. And even without all that to-do; my brother'd of gone and stopped it; seeing as we know them like the back of your hand anyway, Les Mygales and Obonne and the woods and places round. Me and my late husband, we often used to go for walks there, a whole gang with Saturnin and Dominique, that's this one."

This tale completely staggers Etienne. At first, he considers asking Mme. Cloche how it happens that her brother reads *his* tenant's letters; then he decides it's pointless to start the discussion at that point. Apart from that, what does it all mean? The things that emerge most clearly are that Théo wants to get himself hung by the guy with the scar and that this guy has written to Alberte. Etienne finds it difficult to understand what could have been going on. The trio watch him cogitating.

He asks Mme. Cloche to repeat her story; she doesn't wait to be asked twice and starts all over again. So Théo has been writing to Narcense, since that is the name of the man with the scar, to tell him to stop writing to Alberte, that Alberte tore up his letters, and that it would be preferable for him to write directly to him. Even that isn't very clear. Next, he writes that he has polluted the gate of the house. Etienne has never noticed that. And he insults Narcense's *deceased* grandmother. None of it makes any sense at all. Next, he claims that the other man wants to murder him and that he's got cold feet. And finally, he makes a date for him to hang him. But it's absolutely idiotic.

Mme. Cloche has come to the end of her second narration; she's quite prepared to start all over again. But old Taupe's just woken up. "Nestine! Nestine!" he bleats; seeing that no one answers, he finishes his bottle. "Deevning, Meussieu," he says to Etienne. He sings:

"But the best of all dreams is the sweet dream of love,
That you dream by the sea,
As the stars appear above."

Ernestine comes back with the sparkling wine; as soon as she's within reach, old Taupe is patting her buttocks. He warbles:

"Then a magical voice
Is heard from the waves as they part . . ."

It's become impossible to carry on a serious conversation.

". . . 'Tis the voice of the heart."

Etienne stands up.

"What about the sparkling." exclaims Belhôtel, "surely you're going to have some sparkling?"

"No time," says Etienne. "And keep all this to yourselves. Do you promise me?"

"We promise," swears the trio.

"I'll deal with it myself."

"You'll let us know what happens?"

Etienne promises to come back. Ah! he was forgetting something.

"Here, Meussieu Belhôtel, I've got a little present for you."

And he hands him the potato peeler; he wonders for a moment whether he won't give Mme. Cloche the cutter-of-boiled-eggs-in-thin-slices; no, the first contraption has exhausted his generosity.

"Adieu!" he calls.

As he goes out, a cloud of dust half chokes him. He hears the frail voice of the old man singing: "*On the Shores of the Riviera* . . ." A freight train goes by, infinitely long.

The thought of seeing Pierre again makes Etienne feel lighthearted.

In the hut, the trio contemplates with dismay the potato peeler that Meussieu Marcel has just given it. Unembarrassed, Ernestine pulls her stocking up over her thigh; she is wearing pink garters which have a little black lock and a glass key to add spice to them. They make old Taupe's eyes all red.

The dust accumulates; the flies multiply; two Arabs have come in silently and are sitting near the door. They are dreaming. The number of beans decreases. The spud peeler is lying on a table, riveted, by uncomprehending looks, to the zinc.

---

When they left the eatery, Pierre took Narcense in his car for a little drive in the Chevreuse valley. Paris was pouring thousands of cars into the country. The roads were impassable. At Jouy, they let the week-end wave pass them by, Narcense had said he was free until about 10 o'clock; ever since lunch, he hadn't let go of a small suitcase, whose contents singularly intrigued his companion.

"Well, Le Grand, that man you were observing—what became of him?"

"He became someone."

"And before that?"

"Before that, he was a flat entity."

"Really?" said Narcense gently.

Pierre was silent for a moment, then went on:

"He was with me in the restaurant just now," said Pierre. "He thought there was something of note to notice—if I may say so—in that unspeakable place. I didn't notice anything, but I saw you. I told him that the two of you were soon going to make each other's acquaintance."

"Prophet?"

"Agitator—that is, mixer; all I'd have to do would be to introduce you."

"If I'm willing," said Narcense gently.

Pierre was silent for a moment, and then went on:

"He wasn't satisfied with my remark. He left abruptly, disappointed. Yes, I'd disappointed him. He wanted a *simple* marvel, and I'd given him a complicated one."

"Thanks," said Narcense gently.

"When he's met you, he'll realize that I'd noticed the only thing of note: your meeting. I forgot to tell you, he has a historical name, like me; he's called Etienne Marcel. He lives in Obonne, he's married, a father, and works in the Audit Bank."

Narcense: "How far can I trust you?"

Pierre laughs: "As far as my cynicism goes."

Narcense: "Very obscure. Are you capable of abstinence?"

Pierre: "Very obscure."

Narcense: "Of not interfering—if I ask you not to?"

Then Pierre: "Yes."

Then Narcense: "Your ex-flat man, I'm going to kill his son tonight; or rather, I'm going to cause him to commit suicide."

"I beg your pardon?"

"It's quite clear, I think: I'm going to cause young Théo Marcel to commit suicide."

"You're going to make his son commit suicide?"

"Do you want to stop me?"

"Not at all, not at all. But why this suicide?"
"Why? He insulted my grandmother."
If Pierre has wasted his time with Etienne today, Narcense is more than recompensing him. A hundred times, a thousand times. Even so, he still can't believe it:
"You're joking!"
"Joking! Joking!"
Narcense starts swearing under his breath; he has an abundant repertory; he swears for a good five minutes, and then goes on:
"I've lived in such an abundance of dead people in the last week or so. If you only knew. First of all, there was my friend Potice, who got run over outside the Gare du Nord. By a bus, it would seem. You must have seen it in the papers. His brains were spattered all over the road, so they said. Potice's brains. Can you imagine it? And my grandmother, they hadn't yet shut her up when I got there. She was in her bed, with that absurd chin strap. She was eighty-seven. She looked as if she was made of wood; a Breton nutcracker, like they sell in Saint-Malo. It was very simple. During the funeral, a grotesque event occurred: my uncle's dog fell into the hole that had been dug for the coffin. My uncle burst out laughing, but, the next day, when I went out into the yard, I saw the dog hanging with the washing. He was ridiculous and pathetic—and dead, of course."
"Hanging a dog!"
"Yes, isn't that odd? I might tell you that my uncle is rich, extremely ferocious, and very thick in the head. They're all like that in my family; another uncle, no less rich, ferocious and thick, gives me a luxury apartment rent-free, but apart from that lets me rot."
"Don't you think," said Pierre, "that it would be preferable to hang him, rather than Marcel's son?"
"That remains to be seen," replied Narcense. "You understand, I need two stones to kill two birds."
"But the kid—do you stick to your story that he's committing suicide because he insulted your grandmother?"
"Ah, shurrup!" said Narcense rudely.
And he started, swearing under his breath again.

"At 11 o'clock," he went on, "I get off at Blagny. I walk as far as the place they call Les Mygales, in Obonne wood. The kid will be there at midnight."

"Are you sure he'll be there?" asks Pierre.

"Yes, absolutely sure. At five, or ten, or a quarter past twelve, either the kid will have hanged himself or I'll have hanged him. With that rope."

He indicates, with his chin, the suitcase he has left in the car.

Pierre looks at him with skepticism and admiration. He's quite prepared to play this game with Narcense; he doesn't for a moment believe in the reality of the project.

"I can drive you to somewhere near the place you mentioned, if you like, I'll wait for you. That'll make things much easier for you."

This suggestion pleases Narcense, who adores going for drives in cars.

"That's nice of you, Le Grand," he says gently. "Thank you."

"That's all right, that's all right."

They fall silent. It's nearly 7 o'clock. In the calm little square, a few rare natives go from time to time. The car sleeps peacefully near the sidewalk. They can hear the road living, in the distance.

"To come back to the conversation we had the other day," says Pierre, "I can imagine you prefer special cases to general cases, the particular to the universal. An affective preference, not a reasoned statement, I think."

"Yes, that's right. I prefer what exists to what doesn't exist."

"I'll introduce you to my brother, he'll interest you."

"Really—and why?"

"He's a Cantorian," replied Pierre.

---

Saturnin picks up a big hunting knife which had come to him from his grandfather, puts it in his pocket and says: "I'm ready now." He kisses his wife, who says: "Your false beard's tickling me." He says: "Don't worry. If the father's there, I shall leave it to him; if he isn't, I'll deal with the whole thing." She says:

"Whatever you do, don't catch cold, the nights are quite chilly." Saturnin is dressed accordingly. He adjusts his false beard. Let's go. He arrives just in time to catch the 9:31. Not many people at this late hour. He is the only passenger in his third-class compartment. He looks through the tiny window at the neighboring compartments; no one. The train stops at every station and is desperately slow; Saturnin cleans his nails with his hunting knife. Then he takes a bit of pencil out of his pocket and, in a little notebook jots down: "Cut out the fifth part." He draws a line; underneath it: "Put this as an epigraph: Descartes, why is it that, in cafés, cardplayers so often call the waiter by this name?"* He sucks his pencil for a moment, crosses out what he's just written and underneath it: "Why is it that, in cafés, cardplayers so often call the waiter Descartes?" He replaces *so often* by *always*, and closes his notebook.

The train is passing through various badly lit suburbs. Saturnin tries to make out the landscapes by the light of the street lamps which are as feeble as they are rare. The number of lights increases; the train stops. Blagny. That's where my swine of a brother lives, thinks Saturnin; but he has hardly thought this when he sees on the platform Mme. Cloche, his sister. Forgetting his false beard, he pulls his head back in again so as not to be seen, and flies into a rage. That old bitch Sidonie, what's it got to do with her? She doesn't really mean to go to Les Mygales, does she?

Saturnin tries to guess what his sister's going to do—to stop her doing it, if need be. The stations go by. He can't think of anything. Blangy. The next station is Obonne. Saturnin idly looks out of the window. The train starts off again. At this moment, Saturnin catches sight of an old woman making for the exit. This time he's disarmed. Why is she getting off here? Has she got off at the wrong station? He doesn't know what to think. Did she intend to walk from Blangy to Les Mygales?? Most unlikely. And yet . . . Mme. Cloche has got her brother worried.

The train finally arrives at Obonne. A few passengers get out. Narcense isn't there. He wasn't at Blangy, either. Saturnin is sure of that. Hell. Could it really be a joke, as his wife be-

* Asterisks in the text refer to the notes on p. 281.

lives? 11 o'clock; he reckons he has time to indulge in a pick-me-up, as he calls it to himself. But all the cafés are already closed. Too bad; he starts walking down the road leading to the forest, a road he knows well, because he's been there several times to picnic with the family. He advances into the night with a sure step. He is fairly soon brought to a halt by a light that's trying to penetrate a dirty window. No doubt about it, it's a bistro, and it's still open. Saturnin presses on the handle, pushes, and, giving rise to a carillon, enters. Two sleeping men wake up with a start; a bald, four-footed bastard barks in such a high key that he goes out of tune. One of the two men orders him to shut up; the other character, who seems to have emerged from a deep sleep of alcoholic origin, starts making various vehement asseverations: "Tsonly in Brittany ch'ou'll find real sailors! Yep, tsonly in Brittany ch'ou'll find real sailors!"

"Shurrup!" says the boss. "Well, beardie, watcha want?"

"A rum please, boss," says Saturnin.

"M'names Yves le Toltec," shouts the sailor.

"Tsmore than mine is," replies Saturnin politely.

"Ha, ha! that's a good one!" chortles the boss, "I shall copy it."

"Hey, that's some beard you've got," retorts the sailor, who has no idea how lucid he is.

Saturnin is embarrassed, and swigs down his rum.

"Another one," he orders, "and the round's on me."

"Oak, eh! replies the boss (He learned this expression from the sailor.)

Yves le Toltec is drinking hard liquor; he tosses off his glass with decision, wipes his mouf, and starts holding forf:

"Four times I've been shipwrecked, yes M'sieu, four times. Best of the lot was the *Clytemnestra* one, off Singapore. It was bedlam! All the passengers mowing all the others down, trying to get into the boats. The captain, he had his revolver in his hand, and bang! he picked off the men trying to get into the lifeboats before the women. Yes, M'sieu, he shot them, bang!"

Saturnin listens. The boss yawns.

"Here, I'm closing. It's 20 to 12, and I close at a quarter to."

"Twenty to! Oh! shit!" says Saturnin; he leaves a five franc note on the counter and hurries off as fast as his legs will carry him.

"Hm, that's odd, too," says the sailor.

"Yes, there's some odd customers hanging around these parts at the moment. Looks fishy to me. Tslike the guy came here a month ago. Summing's going on."

The sailor hiccupped his agreement.

"Tslike the kid from the ruined house: that's twice I've seen him sneaking into old Pigeonnier's place."

"What a shame! Debauching a brat that was still in short trousers last year! Someone oughter tell his parents."

"Pyah! His father's too much of a dope. Nanyway, snone of my business. Come on, Yves, move it. I'm going to bed."

The sailor stands up rather waveringly, hangs about at the door for a moment or so, and then dissolves into the night.

---

Théo swears he won't try and go to Les Mygales, kisses his mother and goes to bed. Etienne takes his hat: 11:30.

"I'll just get there on time."

Alberte wipes her eyes; she's been crying all evening. Seeing Etienne about to leave, she's frightened.

"You can't come with me, though. Listen you've got nothing to be afraid of here. And I won't be in any danger. No, you've got nothing to be afraid of."

Alberte sighs.

"I'll be late," he says.

"Go on then," she says.

He locks all the doors, even the garden gate, although he knows perfectly well that anyone can easily climb over it. He's going to be late. He starts walking more quickly. He takes the short cut, a little path covered with refuse. He walks over broken bits of plates, and stumbles over empty cans, which go rolling off with a clank.

The moon passionlessly illuminates a landscape of hen-houses and leeks. Finally, Etienne comes to the edge of the forest.

The village church struck 12.

For Les Mygales, it's the path on the left. I'm going to be ten minutes late." Luckily, the path is quite easy to follow. A variety of insects accompanies the halo of his flashlight. More precisely, some mosquitoes are singing in Etienne's ears. He arrives at the intersection with the path to Pourvy. A little farther on, the place they call Les Mygales; there's a big oak in the middle, with a circular bench. From the end of the path, Etienne can see the thick, short grass of the clearing, lit by the moon. When he gets there, he looks for Narcense. He goes up to the bench—no one; walks around it—no one. Then, raising his head, he sees a man showing him the soles of his shoes; Etienne, horrified, is rooted to the spot. The man is still swinging.

At this moment, someone comes galloping up; a strange individual appears, a hefty, bearded man, but his beard seems to grow in a most peculiar fashion—exclusively on his left cheek, and perpendicular to the same.

He gets to the ancient oak and stops, braking on one foot. He pants. He sizes Etienne up:

"Narcense?"

Etienne raises his chin.

"Oh, oh," says the peculiar person with the horizontal beard.

Etienne is amazed at the strange way in which the hairs of this beard are implanted.

"Give me a boost."

Etienne perches on the bench, the bearded man climbs into his hand; he manages to reach the lowest branch of the oak tree; he hauls himself up onto it; he crawls along it; he reaches the rope, he brings out a knife, his grandfather's hunting knife; he cuts the rope, and Narcense falls to the ground in a most undignified way; if he's still alive, he must have hurt himself badly. Etienne, who has now got his wits about him again, rushes over and undoes the slipknot; the bearded man, who has rapidly gotten down again, grabs hold of Narcense, massages his larynx and moves his arms rhythmically up and down. Etienne follows all this with interest. The scar hypnotizes him; this man is indeed the one Pierre had pointed out to him in the restaurant. Narcense breathes; he's going to be all right.

"He's going to be all right," says the bearded man.

Narcense opens his eyes.

"Where am I?" he says, trying to start the conversation along well-known lines; suddenly changing his mind, though, he faints.

"What are we going to do with him?" says the bearded man.

Then Etienne says:

"We'll take him to my house."

"Are you the one that's called Etienne Marcel?"

"That's right. How do you know?"

"My name's Saturnin Belhôtel."

"Aha!" says Etienne. "Pleased to meet you. Your sister has told me about you, and . . ."

"My sister is a sour-faced bitch," interrupts Saturnin. "Well, are we going to move him?"

"Yes, yes," says Etienne. "That's what we'll do, we'll take him to my house."

One takes his head, the other takes his feet.

"I'll go first," says Etienne. "I know the way."

After a few moments:

"Tell me, do you read your tenants' letters?"

"Oh, I've only got one; otherwise it'd take too long."

They rest for a moment; Narcense is sleeping peacefully.

"Who is this person?" Etienne asks.

"Narcense, my tenant."

"His age?"

"Thirty-four."

"Profession?"

"Musician."

"Nationality?"

"French."

"Father?"

"Dead."

"Mother?"

"Deceased."

"Education?"

"B.A."

"Height?"
"Five foot six."
"Weight?"
"One-sixty-five."
"Chest measurement?"
"34¼."
"Ha ha," says Etienne. "Address?"
"8 Boulevard of the Unknown Officer."
"Earns his living . . ."
"Playing the saxophone in night clubs; at the moment unemployed."
"Important events in his life?"
"Childhood: mumps, measles, scarlatina. First communion. Typhoid fever."
"Adolescence?"
"Adolescence: appendicitis, eczema, boils. First part of the baccalaureate. Journey to Marchville, to his grandmother's. Whitlow. Second part of the baccalaureate. Conservatory. Fall on head. Scar."
"And then?"
"Then: military service; musician in the 167th Infantry Regiment. Gonorrhea. Gonorrhea again. Adultery (wife of the drum major). Released from military service. Writes music. Doesn't eat. Hunger, famine, starvation. Plays the saxophone in night clubs. Honeymoons, females, skirts. Depression; unemployment. No more saxophone."
"Shall we take him to my place?"
The two men start off again. Frequent pauses, because Etienne is not very strong and soon gets tired. Narcense sleeps.
After two long hours of walking, they arrive at the little gate. The moon, going down, illuminates the silhouette of the unfinished house. While Etienne is making the gate squeak, Saturnin holds Narcense up against the wall.
"You know what, it's true, what you say about people that've been hanged."
"What's that?"
"*In re* virility."
"Well, that's odd," says Etienne.
Now the front door to be opened.

Alberte rushes up. She's been crying the whole time. She now looks at Narcense with some interest.

"Where are we going to put him?"

In Théo's bed: the only solution. Théo can sleep in the dining room. What about Saturnin? Saturnin too.

"Ah. I was forgetting to introduce Meussieu Saturnin Belhôtel."

"Meussieu—thank you," said Alberte.

"Not at all, not at all."

Narcense, who has been put in an armchair, goes on sleeping doggedly. Well, that's what they'll do, they'll put him in Théo's bed. Etienne opens the door of Théo's bedroom. He calls gently: "Théo"; no one answers; through the darkness, he sees that the bed is empty. Then, that the window is open.

"We'll still put him to bed here," says Etienne.

---

After a fruitless week of standing guard opposite the Gare du Nord, the widow Cloche (Mme. Sidonie, née Belhôtel) renounced her vision of further accidents. But she immediately sank into an incoercible and crushing state of ennui, from which even chartreuse and the hazards of her profession couldn't manage to extract her.

She didn't, in any case, want to miss the great tragic scene which was going to take place at Les Mygales. It had certainly occurred to her that if she hadn't warned Meussieu Marcel, she could have been present at a hanging, a real one (she didn't doubt the reality of Narcense's threat for a moment); but she'd promised Saturnin she'd tell Meussieu Marcel everything, and in any case, Saturnin would probably be there. Saturnin's presence she found rather a nuisance. So she took it into her head to get out at Blangy instead of Obonne. She knew the district, because on two separate occasions she had had as a patient someone who lived in Obonne, Mme. Pigeonnier, and she had many times gone there for picnics with her late husband and her brother. Coming back to Saturnin, she told herself that she didn't give a damn; and as for the promise she'd made to Etienne, she'd already forgotten it.

At Blangy she got her bearings surely and swiftly; she must take the road that went past the town hall; then she'd come to a crossroad; there, she remembered very well, was a signpost that showed the way to Les Mygales.

All went well until she got to the edge of the forest, but when she saw its black mass rising up in front of her, she suddenly felt afraid. She hadn't thought that once she was in the wood it would be *dark;* the road suddenly turned into a sort of underground passage which was completely obscure.

So Mme. Cloche sat down on a bank, quite determined to turn back. But the path behind her wound its way through the fields so ruthlessly, so drearily, that it terrified her. She imagined what might happen to her: a tramp might rape her, a highwayman might kill her, a dog might bite her, a bull might charge her; two tramps might rape her, three highwaymen might kill her, four dogs might bite her, five bulls might charge her; seven tramps might bite her, eight highwaymen might charge her, nine dogs might kill her, ten bulls might rape her. A great big caterpillar might fall down her neck; a bat might go ooh! ooh! in her ear; a night bird might pierce her eyes and dig them out of their sockets. A corpse in the middle of the path; a ghost taking her by the hand; a skeleton eating a piece of bread.

This last idea made her shudder a little, but its absurdity reassured her. "It's all amphigories and dillydallying," she told herself, "rigmarole and bibble-babble, balderdash and buffoonery, piffie and fiddle-faddle, gibberish and galimatias."

The village clock struck midnight. When she'd counted the twelve strokes, the widow Cloche suddenly became furious with herself; fool that she was, she'd missed it all. What a boob she'd turned out to be. Her considerations had brought her to this point when a human silhouette was outlined on the path; someone was coming. She got to her feet, with all the agility of which she was capable, and plunged into the forest.

There, it was almost total darkness. It was not long before Mme. Cloche was stumbling over roots, colliding with trees and getting scratched by brambles. Her hat got caught in a branch, and she couldn't find it again. She tottered on and on, scratching her hands, bumping her forehead, getting her hair torn out. It seemed to her that this went on for a very long time. Finally, she perceived a patch of light. She straightened herself up; the path was vaguely illuminated. She was coming to the place where the paths crossed.

Luckily for her, the signpost pointing the way to Les Mygales was lit by a moonbeam; she congratulated herself, and once again disappeared down an obscure path, and once again tottered on, colliding with trees, getting scratched by brambles and cut by branches. And once again, it was a very long time, it seemed to her, that this went on. And once again, she perceived a patch of light.

Her hair tousled, her hands bleeding, her clothes torn, her forehead bruised, one eye red, her cheek scratched, having lost her hat and her umbrella, but still firmly clasping her carpetbag, Sidonie emerged from the path and stopped in the middle of the clearing.

Nothing was happening. No one was there. The silence was absolute. She walked around the oak, looking up into the air; no one hanging there, any more than in the hollow of her hand. She sat down on the circular bench, completely exhausted, and was just going off to sleep when she noticed, there, in front of her, on the grass, a rope, a slipknot. She threw herself onto it, and fell on her knees. She grabbed the rope. Yes, a rope to hang someone with. But who had been hung? On her knees, on the grass, she held the noose in both hands, and looked at it, and trembled, quite upset.

For a long time, she looked at that rope. The moon disappeared behind the trees. The darkness became total. Mme. Cloche, exhausted, lay down and went to sleep, her head on her carpetbag. The night was soft and clear, and multifarious constellations feebly illuminated the clearing.

---

"And if you go home to your parents, what'll you say to them?"

"I'll tell them I was walking for a long time, all night; and that after that, I came home."

"You won't tell them anything about me?"

"Oh! no, I won't say anything about you."

"That's right"—and Mme. Pigeonnier kissed Théo on the forehead.

"What about your father—what'll he say?"

"Nothing. Ztoo stupid."

"Oh! aren't you ashamed, talking about your father like that?"

"In the first place, znot my father. I've never had a papa."

"Poor boy," sighs Mme. Pigeonnier, kissing Théo on the cheek.

Théo is sitting stiffly on a chair; but he is not unaware of how this conversation will end. He looks straight ahead of him; only his sense of smell reveals Mme. Pigeonnier's presence to him, or her chaste kisses.

"And your mother?"

"She'll cry."

"Doesn't that make you sad?"

"Oh, yes!" says Théo, grinning on the other side of his face, the one Mme. Pigeonnier can't see. "She'll be so happy when she sees me again."

"Doesn't take much to console you."

A short silence. Théo sniffs. It smells damn good. But the preliminary moralizing bores him.

"Your parents work hard enough to bring you up. Just think, they aren't rich, but next year you'll have taken your baccalaureate, thanks to the sacrifices they make for you."

"That's all a lot of boloney: primo, did I ever ask them if I could take my bac.? segondo, the sacrifices, I have to put up with them just as much as they do, the daily grind, I do it just like Dad and Mom; and tertio, if I get my bac., it's because I'm intelligent and work hard."

Mme. Pigeonnier finds these remarks pleasantly titillating, and laughs.

"Naughty thing," she chuckles, and kisses him.

Théo preserves his immobility. He looks at the time. Midnight. What, actually, could have happened? If Narcense started beating up his stepfather, what a joke that would be! This idea makes him join in Mme. Pigeonnier's laughter.

"You know, there's a meussieu that's in love with my mother."
"How d'you know that?"
"He's written to her. Mom, she tore up the letters, but I stuck them together again."
"Aren't you ashamed of being such a snoop?"
"Oh sure." A short silence. "This meussieu, I know him."
"How d'you know him?"
"Wurl, I saw him one day, one evening, by our gate."
"Really?"
"He wz looking at Mom through the gate."
"You got a good look at him?"
"Yep. And then, he wz doing something funny."
"But what?" questions Mme. Pigeonnier, who doesn't understand.
"Well, he wz behaving zif he was all by himself."
Mme. Pigeonnier, who has finally understood, looks at Théo, highly shocked. Théo remains imperturbable.
"Wossmore, he mucked up the gate."
"My stepfather's gate," he adds.
He turns his head to see what Mme. Pigeonnier thinks about it. Well, she's highly shocked, is Mme. Pigeonnier. He reassumes his hieratic position and changes the subject.
"I'm hungry," he observes, authoritatively.
"What would you like to eat?"
"Summing nice," he retorts.
"D'you want me to get the maid up?"
"You do that. I want summing hot, and then some dessert."
Mme. Pigeonnier waves a bell. Catherine comes running, draped in a Chinese dressing gown. She pushes her hair back over her forehead:
"Yes, Madam?"
She ogles Théo and yawns; this time, he blushes.
"Catherine, get us some supper," says Mme. Pigeonnier.
Catherine whistles in admiration.
"Coming up," she says, and goes out.
"You know, she's impertinent, your maid," says Théo hypocritically.
Mme. Pigeonnier is lighting a cigarette, and doesn't answer.
"She isn't like that in the daytime," he persists.

He takes the lighted cigarette he is offered.

"Thanks. They won't let me smoke at home. It's idiotic."

"Come on, don't criticize your parents all the time."

"You know, my stepfather, he isn't funny. There's nothing in his head."

"How d'you mean?"

"Never says a word. Talks about his office; that's all. Looks at the papers with half an eye, but he never reads them."

"How d'you know?"

"I watch him. He's asleep on his feet."

"But he's nice to you?"

"Yes, course he is; he's too much of a dope to bother me much. Never knows how to pass the time. And Mom, who's at it all day long. All my pals, they live in Paris. And I'm stuck in that half-demolished house. My God, it isn't funny. I get so pissed off."

"What?"

"Yes, I'm labefying my crumpet with all these nigmenogs," replies Théo volubly.

Catherine comes in, bringing the cold supper. She hasn't forgotten herself; she lays the three places and sits down with Théo and Mme. Pigeonnier. As she cuts up a piece of cold chicken, she tells them:

"Something must have been going on next door, earlier on. I heard footsteps in the garden, and some men's voices. There must have been several of them. I recognized Meussieu Marcel's voice."

As she speaks, she pretends to be unaware of Théo's presence.

"I looked out of the window; I saw two men in the garden, they were carrying a third one, who looked as if he was dead, or 'd fainted. Someone opened the door. It was Meussieu Marcel. Him and the fellow with him, they got the one who was dead or who'd fainted into the house. The door shut again. That's all I saw. In any case, I'm not particularly interested in what goes on in that house. Would you care for some white wine, Madam?"

"Thank you, Catherine, just a drop."

"Me too, I want some," says Théo, "and a whole glass."

"As I was saying," continues Catherine, "I'm not particularly interested in what goes on in that house; all the more so as nothing ever does go on there. It's absolutely typical of the sort of house where quiet, mediocre people live, and get old, without anything ever happening. Aren't I right, Madam?"

"As you see very well, Catherine, something *was* going on there tonight."

"It's probably because it was never finished."

Catherine pours herself out a large glass of wine.

"What do you think of this wine, Madam?"

"It's very good."

"It isn't bad, but you ought to buy some champagne, Madam, a small crate of a dozen bottles for special occasions. You could allow yourself that, Madam."

"All right, Catherine, order a small crate, then."

"Certainly, Madam. When Meussieu Théo passes his baccalaureate we'll open one."

"I hope we won't have to wait as long as that," says Théo.

Mme. Pigeonnier laughs. Then Catherine starts talking to her about dresses and all that. Théo, while this is going on, devours everything within reach of his fork. When they finish their supper, Catherine clears the table; it's getting late.

"Ah, I'll leave you," says she.

"Good night, Catherine," sighs Mme. Pigeonnier.

Théo says nothing. They hear Catherine going downstairs, and then coming up again to her room.

"I'm going to bed," says Théo, yawning.

---

His mother had put on a false beard to serve the boiled eggs; this unpleasant vision was followed by an access of very profound, but very short-lived, anxiety; the next moment Etienne opened his eyes. The night was barely over. He felt that Alberte, at his side, was awake; he himself hadn't slept more than two hours.

How could he find Le Grand? There was no reason why he should meet him again, no chance. Was it entirely his fault? He had been asking for some actual revelation, some light to be thrown on the environment in which he had lived an hour a day for the last three years, and Le Grand had given him a prophecy. Yes a prophecy. Wasn't there something phony about his pointing out Narcense like that? You'll know him, soon. That brown scar. And after all, Narcense, what a curious name! Is it a last name or a first name? He's a musician. He loves his wife. He's written to her. He loves his wife. He loves Alberte. He loves her. So Alberte exists for other men. The folly of wanting to hang Théo; a joke, that threat, a joke in bad taste; a joke, that absurd story about the dog Théo had told them; yes, Narcense's uncle hanged Théo, no, the dog. He hanged his dog because he fell onto the coffin, onto Narcense's coffin, his grandmother's, and Théo has disappeared, has run away. Alberte is in despair. Narcense loves her, other men see her, follow her, yes, in the metro, touch her, often. That happens to me, I don't do it on purpose, my hand just happens to be touching a woman's body; when I was carrying the gadgets, for instance, uh-oh, I must have left the hard-boiled-egg-cutter on the table; why did I buy it? I didn't tell Le Grand about it perhaps he could tell me why I've changed a lot in the last few weeks I'm aware of it now yes the world isn't what it appears to be, at least when you live the same thing every day when you don't see anything any more and yet there are people who live in the same way every day but I—I really didn't exist, it all began with the little ducks before I didn't think I didn't exist you might say at least I don't remember any more other people were living near me things were there there or somewhere else and I didn't see anything and yet I must still look the same and other people if they're like I was before perhaps other people don't think they don't exist they go from one place to another like I used to go from one place to another but it doesn't mean a thing you might say even so it would be odd perhaps it's the other way around and I was the one who was the exception I was the only one who didn't exist and when I looked at the world I started to exist perhaps all this is in the philosophy books perhaps they explain it what sort of book would tell me Le Grand's the one who'd know *he* is alive he's always existed he sees everything he knows what you have to do to think I didn't read when I was little I must have existed for instance when I was five I cried when the cat died so I did exist then and my cat that they killed it was the day of the little ducks everything happened on the same day it's all confused yes what activity all of a sudden all these things happening there's something else today as well Narcense hangs himself and gets cut down fundamentally that's all part of everyday life whereas the hard-boiled-egg-cutter no that's the difference one can be explained the other can't be explained for Narcense perhaps it can't be explained for him he is going beyond his own everyday life but he doesn't make me go beyond mine now Le Grand he could make me go beyond it just like that you can go beyond it without appearing to that's the odd part I live just like I used to before all I have to do is just give a sideways look as you might say and there I am out of it now Narcense he gives himself a lot of trouble a rope at night it's very tragic with me it's much odder I'm getting very good at it it's very amusing to be in charge of your thoughts like this to talk to yourself in the old days when I woke up during the night I used to look at the fifth acanthus leaf on the wallpaper now I know how to tell myself extraordinary things I wonder if all this has been written down in books you can't know that beforehand Le Grand will be able to tell me but how am I going to find him again how could he guess I'd meet Narcense perhaps he's a friend of his he doesn't seem to be or else he arranged things so that it's very odd it's funny he must be very clever if it wasn't a prophecy then it was a conjuring trick in either case he's very good at it perhaps one day I'll be able to do conjuring tricks too the little ducks conjured themselves up for me by themselves that's the odd thing but for Théo it was the opposite they were there they'd been there right away from the word go Théo was the one who'd seen who is he that kid he was here he's disappeared I don't know who he was I know the color of his eyes now I don't know what his nose is like or his mouth I can't manage to see his face isn't it funny I've seen him every day and I find it impossible to remember his face what about Alberte can I remember her face her eyes her mouth.

Etienne, much distressed, leans over and looks at those eyes, that mouth; had he forgotten them? He heard, in the next room, a metallic sound; an object had just fallen off something. The hard-boiled-egg-cutter. A cock wailed; others, stupidly, answered it. In the distance, a train whistled. A door opened; two voices whispered for a few moments.

---

*Ffteen hundred feet high, the cliff damned the sea and the cliff looked as smooth as a mirror and perfectly vertical and the sea came and pulverized itself against it. Along the whole length of the cliff, the sea was turning white. It was the cliff that marks the limit of the Ocean, against which every wave is shattered. It rose up like a phallus, and stretched out like an arm.*

*Parallel to it, a man was swimming: himself. He wanted to go ashore, but no hand was held out to him. He also had to avoid being crushed against the rock. While swimming parallel to the cliff, he wondered how long he would be able to go on holding out against fatigue and cold; then he realized that night would not fall, because the sun was motionless. As he was swimming, his head in the water, he saw, very far beneath him, a stretch of fine, luminescent sand, unsullied by seaweed or sponges; he saw neither fish nor shell nor octopus nor crustacean. No living being reached that depth and, when he took a breath, he felt that even the smallest bacteria would not survive in that crystal air.*

*He swam, then, for a very long time; more precisely, the visual perception of the cliff was immediately followed by that of the flight of steps that made it possible, so it seemed, to climb up to its summit. These steps were composed of metal rods, driven into the rock horizontally; a distance of about six feet separated each rod from the next.*

*He went ashore without trouble and, grasping the lowest rod, he started the climb, that is, he had to balance himself, upright, on each rung, grasp the rung above and then pull himself up onto that rung on which he would again have to balance, and so on about two hundred and fifty times. Even though he had never done any gymnastics, he managed the climb without difficulty.*

*When he had reached the hundredth rung, he looked down and saw that the seething foam of the sea had been reduced to a fine, whitish border. The sea was perfectly clear and lay on a bed of sand that was everywhere the same; no shadow was projected onto it. He looked up, and saw nothing but the rungs. He looked into the distance, over the Ocean; it seemed to him that he could make out the Eiffel Tower, but this was a mistake. The horizon, that universal castrator, allowed nothing to emerge.*

*At the hundred and fiftieth rung, it seemed to him that the number of rungs above him had hardly decreased. At the two hundredth rung, this semblance became a certainty; he could go on climbing like this for a very long time. To such a situation there was only one possible solution; he continued, knowing the procedure, and reached the two hundred and fiftieth and last rung. Unfortunately, that still wasn't the summit of the cliff, for it was crowned by a thick layer of ice. To tell the truth, what at first looked like ice, was rock crystal, as smooth as the cliff; the layer was some thirty feet high.*

*He looked down; the sea had disappeared, and the rungs, and everything. There was nothing but this crystal. He touched it, and it was only with difficulty that he could release his hand; what he had taken for ice, and then for crystal, was solid and perfectly transparent glue. Climbing was now no more than a game. Stuck to the wall, he went from the bottom to the top, foot after hand, hand after foot, and reached the summit.*

*When he had got there, he saw three things: the fringe of glue, which seemed to be for the cliff what the whitish border of the seething foam of the shattered waves was for the sea; an expanse of something that seemed to him to be a lake; and the rest, which he described as a meadow. He was by the lake. On all fours, he got to the edge; it really did seem to be a lake, but the water wasn't genuine. He had immediate confirmation of this, for a clockwork horse came to drink at it; the animal leaned over the surface of the alleged water; before he'd touched it, he suddenly raised his head again, turned around, and went off on his little wheels.*

*Marble tombstones were drifting across the lake, very peacefully, very calmly. And then Narcense felt a pain on both sides of his neck. The sun was still motionless. The pain spread around to the back of his neck, and around to his larynx. The sky, Narcense only realized at this moment, wasn't blue, but white. The pain became circular; that white sky could only be* made *of very special air, of air which was not* made *for man to breathe; for me to breathe, thought Narcense. He started panting or choking; the tombstones went on floating on the atrocious liquid where toys go to drink; the sun was still motionless. Narcense died.*

*The morning twilight filtered through the shutters. Narcense sat up in the bed and swallowed a mouthful of air; then he fell back again. The dawn spread through the room, a very sad, very grey dawn, the dawn that surrounds railroad stations. In the small, narrow room, there was only one chair and one table; on the chair, Narcense saw his clothes, on the table, a little parcel.*

*He sat up in bed again, and drew a breath. He could breathe. He got up. He could walk. The sea and the cliff and the flight of steps and the lake and the wooden horse suddenly reappeared, all together. He tries to rearrange these elements. I started with a shipwreck—he took a few steps—a shipwreck in a forest. He leaned against the table. He grabbed the half-open parcel and looked at the strange object it contained. In the half-light, it looked like a little musical instrument, but he couldn't grasp how it could be played. The clockwork horse reappeared; Narcense felt something like a wave of nausea and dropped the cutter-of-hard-boiled-eggs-in-thin-slices onto the floor.*

*A few seconds later the door, gently, opened; a head appeared. Narcense recognized his concierge. A cock crew; others answered it. In the distance a train whistled. Narcense thought he could make out the Eiffel Tower, but this was a mistake; the horizon, that universal castrator, allowed nothing to emerge.*

## Third Chapter

As the train started, Pierre waved, and then turned his back, deciding that any other byplay was unnecessary. Skillfully avoiding the multiple threats of porters' baggage carts and ferocious and overloaded latecomers, he reached the exit, hailed one of those tiny taxis which are the beauty of Paris and had himself driven to the Audit Bank. He would arrive just before the bank closed. That Narcense had not hung Théo, he knew from the silence of the papers; but he knew no more. When, the day before, he had woken up at dawn, lying near his car, he had indeed thought for a moment of going to see Etienne at his home; on second thought, though, he had preferred not to.

He got to the Audit Bank at ten to. While he was waiting, he contemplated the building and calculated the degree of stupidity and abjection of the architect who had elaborated that arabesque. Even so, he had to admit that the bas- or haut-relief representing the Five Continents laying their "products" at the feet of a heavy-jowled goddess of Commerce was not without some charm for him. The cluster of bananas, pineapples and elephants' tusks, which a Negress with beautiful breasts was offering with an inexplicable smile, seemed to him particularly pleasant.

At the stroke of six, he abandoned these superficial observations and brought his gaze down to human level. Etienne caught sight of him and raised his arms, giving him to understand that he was expecting, or better still, hoping to see him.

"Oh, I am so pleased to see you again! How nice of you to come and meet me. I didn't know how to find you again. I wasn't very polite to you the day before yesterday, I was a bit rude, even . . ."

"Oh no, oh no."

Etienne was speaking very rapidly.

"Yes I was. I was rude to you, and I'm sorry. I thought you were making fun of me, that you were playing the prophet. But in fact, what you foresaw did happen. That same night. How did you know? Do you mind if I tell you what happened, first? The man with the scar is called Narcense. I discovered that the same afternoon . . ."

Pierre takes Etienne off to a quiet little café and listens to him as he recounts the whole story. So Narcense tried to hang himself, and Théo disappeared.

"The next morning, Narcense and his concierge left very early, without any explanation. I heard them talking; but I went back to sleep, like a fool. During that time, they cleared out. By midday, Théo still wasn't back; my wife was in despair; I went and reported it to the police. What a day! At six o'clock, he came home. He said he'd been afraid, and that he'd been wandering all night and all day—he seemed very tired. I think he was lying, but I really don't care. As for Narcense. I don't know any more about him than what I've told you."

None of this was particularly fascinating; only two points interested Pierre: Etienne's visit to Blagny, and Narcense's address.

"But how on earth did you come to know of that bistro in Blagny?"

Etienne gave him a strange look.

"That was a discovery."

Then:

"You still haven't told me . . ."

Pierre could guess well enough what he wanted to know; but what could he tell him? If Etienne were to see Narcense again, he would hear of his part in the Les Mygales adventure; and perhaps Narcense would even repeat everything he, Pierre, had been rash enough to say. He'd lose ground. Until it actually happened, the best thing was to keep quiet.

Etienne is staring at him. What insistance! What passion! What gravity! What innocence! Pierre, suddenly, feels ill at ease. For a moment, he lowers his eyes, but then quickly pulls himself together, and goes on:

"That French fries place at Blagny, I'd very much like you to take me there. What an odd place it must be!"

"Would you like to go there now? Although—no, not today, if you don't mind; I'd be too late; as it is, I must leave you right away. Tomorrow, if that suits you."

"Tomorrow—that's fine. Here?"

"Yes, that's right."

For a moment, Etienne doesn't quite seem to know where to look.

"There are so many things I'd like to ask you." (He holds out his hand.) "About existence."

He leaves.

Pierre has remembered an address: 8 Boulevard of the Unknown Officer. That's worth knowing; but, watching Etienne disappear, he suddenly has the disagreeable impression that things have gone beyond him.

---

Sitting astride a chair, Saturnin was meditating. He was picking his teeth; more precisely, one. A well-dressed gentleman said to him.

"I would like to speak to Meussieu Narcense."

Saturnin raised his head and answered:

"Not in."

The well-dressed gentleman persisted:

"Out or away?"

Saturnin explains:

"Znot in, I tell you," and resumed his meditations. The gentleman retreated a few steps, about twenty, and turned around; he saw Narcense, who was going out, and was coming straight toward him without seeing him. When he reached him, Hello, he said, and Narcense looked at him. He started by using exclamatorily the adverb the corresponding adjective of which would be good, then uttered the syllables that composed the name of the person he had recognized. Not at all surprised, at that; questioning, rather.

"I haven't seen you since the other evening," said Pierre. "I waited for you until morning. Yesterday, Etienne Marcel told me what happened; and what's more, your address. I came to see you."

"Thank you. I do actually owe you an apology."

"Not at all, not at all."

"What do you think happened?"

"How do you mean?"

"Well, between the time you left me and the time Marcel found me?"

"I'm waiting for you to tell me."

Narcense was silent. Changing the subject:

"Actually, how on earth did you get into my life?"

Saturnin was watching them talking with feigned indifference.

"You can talk to a woman in the street, not to a man. Unless you're a homosexual. Are you a homosexual? No, you aren't a homosexual. I remember you spoke to me in Obonne, at that bistro that I found tragic, then at the restaurant, the other day. It's very simple. What do you claim to be?"

"Nothing," said Pierre.

"At least, you're rich. My pursuits don't allow me to be that."

"I'd like to help you."

"Lend me money? No thanks. He's a strange guy, my concierge, you know. He reads all my letters, he opens them and seals them up again. I don't resent it. Not because he saved my life; no. Nor Théo's life. But, as he says himself, he's an oddball. I can't resent his incursion into my private life."

And, after a silence:

"I'm in a terrible predicament."

"I can help you," Pierre repeated. "I know Shibboleth . . ."

"I know him, too."

"He'll give you a job in one of those night clubs he promotes during the summer in fashionable resorts. He'll do that for me."

"Thank you. I'm in a terrible predicament."

They started walking.

"The world is fascinating," said Narcense, "and death is part of the world. When I found myself climbing up into that tree with the slipknot around my neck, I laughed like anything, I assure you. I laughed for at least fifteen seconds. It was no ordinary situation, and the clearing was so incredibly beautiful . . . I looked to see whether Théo was finally coming. I heard footsteps. A bird sang in a tree. All this happened very quickly.

I raised my head and lost my balance. Saturnin can't explain why I didn't break my back; I think I was holding the rope in one hand and the knot didn't tighten till a few seconds later. In any case, the consequences were very unpleasant. I'd rather not talk about them."

"Which means that no one knows whether you tried to commit suicide or not," Pierre insinuated.

"I didn't mean to present you with a psychological problem," said Narcense.

Pierre had not the slightest desire to solve any problems of that kind; Narcense's impressions of being hung left him completely cold. He should get this saxophone player sent to some seaside resort. He suddenly wondered why he was talking to this person; really, there was no reason. What did he have to do with him? He was amazed to find himself in such company. Nothing Narcense said was of any interest to him. He started to hate him. For a moment. Leaving him without ceremony, he hailed a taxi, promising himself that he certainly wouldn't ask Shibboleth to do anything for him. As for Narcense, he went on his way, which led him straight to uncle. "He was annoyed because I mentioned psychology to him." he thought, "but even so, he's a decent fellow."

---

Old Taupe had his own idea of happiness; he had acquired it in poverty; he had elaborated it in penury. Happiness, for him, consisted in excessive security. Since he had been ruined, he no longer feared ruin. Having reached the minimum of existence, he was afraid of going beyond it. Supported by a heap of junk and scrap iron, he thought himself happy; he thought himself wise; he was, moreover, alcoholic and lecherous.

Junk and scrap iron, he was afraid of dealing in more valuable objects; he only allowed himself dog-eared novels, dilapidated furniture and battered household utensils.

The whole week he entrenched himself in a distant shack, hidden in a sort of cul-de-sac behind the chemicals factory, a dusty, stinking desert, where no human creature ever ventured. On Sundays, he went and exhibited his rubbish in the market in Blagny; that was taking great risks. He always trembled when he came out of his shell; confronting the world terrified him; but this market had become a habit; he wasn't afraid of it any more, he liked it.

After five years of this life, he persuaded himself that his wisdom had reached its apex, and he started drinking methodically. Then he became libidinous, and his desires were centered on the Belhôtel's maid, Ernestine. This affected his serenity to a certain extent, but he didn't notice it. He still thought he was happy. He dreamed of Ernestine, and doubled his dose of alcohol. He even went as far as buying a door.

"The less you own, the less you suffer," he informed Belhôtel, "*You* want to make money, but you'll lose it one of these days. You don't know what it's like to be rich. Yes, the less you have, the happier you are. Here, give me another liter of white."

At the far end, Ernestine was laughing as she served a group of workmen. Several tables were occupied when the chlorine and sulfur knocked off, and the men were drinking aperitifs.

Old Taupe went on:

"The more you want, the more you find yourself in the shit."

He sometimes affected a vulgar mode of speech.

"The only way to be happy is to keep yourself to yourself."

"You and your moralizing," someone shouted at him, "you're a damn bore. Go and preach all that in church."

"That's the sort of stuff the priests try and sell us," added another.

"Not at all!"

Old Taupe faced them.

"The priests want a lot of things; they want paradise. That's all! to be happy for all eternity! No, but really, any fool can see what you have to go through for that!"

A few workmen laughed, but one returned to the charge:

"All the same, if we believe your crap about the rich being so miserable and the poor being so happy, we'd let ourselves be exploited without every saying a word."

This was a point of view that old Taupe refused to envisage. He emptied his glass and was getting ready to start perorating again when a couple of middle-class types appeared at the door. The customers looked at them in silence, which silence was broken by Belhôtel's voice recognizing the presence of Meussieu Marcel. He started by using exclamatorily the adverb the corresponding adjective of which would be good, then uttered the syllables that composed the name of the person he had recognized.

Etienne came in, followed by Pierre; Belhôtel held out his hand to him and wished him a good day. He would have liked to ask him some precise questions, but in front of so many people, he didn't dare. Etienne and Pierre sat down. Dominique hadn't seen Mme. Cloche since the previous Saturday. He still didn't know the sequel to the strange business of the hanging. Meussieu Marcel didn't seem much inclined to talk about it.

The conversations at the other tables started up again. Old Taupe, happy to have a high-class audience, addressed his remarks to the two newcomers, telling them that in the old days he used to have a little money, which he had had the good fortune (that was how he put it) to lose, and that he'd never been so happy as he was now. They were young, young and rich; what troubles were in store for them they'd see later on. *He* didn't want anything; nothing could touch him. Etienne laughed at having wealth ascribed to him. As for Pierre, he listened without sympathy to old Taupe's moralizing. However, when he heard, from Belhôtel, that the moralist was a junk dealer, he immediately foresaw some discovery, because junk excavation was one of his hobbies, and wanted to go looting then and there. The old boy cackled: wouldn't be anything that'd interest him, but Pierre insisted so much that he agreed to take him to his shack. Etienne wasn't interested, but went with them.

They walked along the factory wall parallel to the railroad line, and then at right angles to it. The path they took was a blind alley; the Northern Company repair shops, built on a mound like a bogus plateau, cut it short. They turned left; between the factory and the workshops there with a triangular stretch of wasteland that a series of planks forming a fence made into a trapezoid. Old Taupe lived behind these planks.

Two rows of barbed wire capped the fence; a triple lock secured the gate. They entered the lair. With his first glance, Pierre realized that there was in fact nothing to discover among the rusty old nails, the solitary mattress springs, the dirty, stinking rags and the broken chairs. There was junk strewn everywhere outside Taupe's house, in his house, it was piled up. Pierre was terrified, and didn't dare go in; so much filth appalled him.

---

And what if they'd only been there since the day before or even for an hour or only a few minutes? But I was sure of the opposite at once I was right but I hadn't imagined that I might be wrong and that the hut might only have been built for several days or several hours for the first I've got Théo's evidence and for the other it's obvious. What's Le Grand going to discover? Is he thinking about discoveries? What a smell. Now I'm stuck with this place with that hut with that factory and now perhaps with this old man trotting along in front of us he's half drunk of course and he says he's happy what does that mean? he's happy because he isn't anything because he doesn't want anything because he doesn't desire anything. Why doesn't he die? If he killed himself he would want something yes that's true this is a cul-de-sac ah yes the workshops of the Northern Company railroad you see them from the train and those old German trucks Narcense wanted to kill himself he's unhappy why yes that's true he must be desperate a bit mad he didn't stay he wants to die because he's unhappy in fact if happiness consists in not being anything but that old man he must be afraid of dying what can Le Grand be thinking of at this moment? What is he seeing? It's a fortified castle this junk shop three locks yes there are three locks and there's barbed wire along the fence what can the old man be afraid of he protects his happiness with barbed wire if he shut himself up in a safe it would be better when I was a child and the whole world was turning against me I built myself a place where nothing could get at me you could only get into it through mysterious tunnels it was defended on all sides and I could live there indefinitely all by myself this old man's the same but he makes a sermon out of it so his padlocks and bolts and barbed wire don't go with all the rest if nothing could get at him he wouldn't need all that Le Grand looks very disappointed with all this old muck am I happy was I happy I didn't exist so I couldn't have been when you come down to it how stupid and yet when I think back to my childhood how very unhappy I was and later it was habit I think of far more interesting things it's this old man who's got the wrong idea doesn't it stink in there Le Grand looks highly embarrassed he must think it stinks he's not wrong what did he think he was going to find here what curiosity! and the old boy giggling in there sitting on his bed that's the sort of thing that must be called a pallet-bed sitting on his pallet-bed I think he's pulling our legs why is that door there it can't lead anywhere he hasn't dug a cellar in the embankment it looks odd that blue-painted door it wasn't there originally it must be for sale that door Le Grand is asking him whether its for sale no it isn't for sale that's interesting Le Grand is interested why doesn't he want to sell his door now he's getting angry don't let's press the point obviously he hasn't dug a cellar in the embankment a sort of lair a real hole for his happiness this old man's ideal is a fetus that door has some sort of value in his eyes perhaps it's connected with some incident in his life perhaps it revealed happiness to him Le Grand is catching my eye yes of course let's go that door behind it there is only boarding so long good-by yes it isn't happiness I'm concerned with but existence.

"What value can that door ever have for him?" asks Etienne.

"I doubt whether it has any value," replies Pierre. "Maybe the old dotard has hidden some money behind it. Classic type of old miser."

"There's something very odd about that door. Even so," says Etienne.

Ideal, a fetus, totally uninteresting. CHIPS.

"Hey, Hippolyte! come navva look," exclaimed the sailor.
Hippolyte came running.
"Stavva look at that"—and the sailor pointed at a stylish sports car that was carefully negotiating a fearsome gully.
"That's the guy from that half-finished dump," observed Yves le Toltec.
"He's not worried," observed Hippolyte Azur.
"Must cost a mint, a car like that," observed the sailor.
"He's stopped at his house," observed the innkeeper.
"Zgetting out bime self."
"Yuther one doesn't want to get out."
"They're being polite to each other."
"Must be asking him to come to dinner."
"How come an ordinary bank clerk like him can know a guy that's so loaded?"
"Could be a relative."
"They don't look much alike."
"What can they be cooking up between them?"
"Here, now he's turning around."
"His wife must've called him."
"Here, now she's rushing out."
"Oh, look, seems like she's crying."
"Aha, aha, summing xtraordinary must be up."
"Zgiving him a piece of paper."
"Ztaking it."
"Zcrying."
"Zreading it."
"Zrereading it."
"She's leaning against the gate."
"Za good-looking piece, eh?"
"Maybe the loaded one wants to taker away from him."
"Ha ha ha ha!"
"Ztalking to his wife."
"Zpointing to the rich one."
"The rich one's saying hello to her."
"Ja see how gracefully he lifted his ass off the seat?"
"Ha ha ha!"
"That's a laugh, he's showing him the letter."
"Other one's reading it."

"Must be pals."
"What is it, that car?"
"It's a Bugatti."
"Oh go on, not with a hood like that."
"I suppose you know more about it an I do?"
"And how! You'd hardly've learned much about cars on your laundry boat."
"Tabout you? Not on your bicycle."
"I certainly know more about them than a Swiss admiral."
"You mean me, I'm a Swiss admiral?"
"Yaren't even an admiral."
"Just say that again, that I'm a Swiss admiral."
"I'll say it again if I want to."
"Just see that you don't want to."
"Oh, but they're going to fight," exclaimed Alberte.
"Not a chance," said Pierre, "words are enough for them."
"Go in, Alberte," said Etienne.
"They're grabbing hold of each other," said Pierre.
"They are actually starting to fight."
"They must be evenly matched."
"They both look formidable."
"They're on the ground."
"They're banging each other's head."
"They're twisting each other's arms."
"They're biting each other's eyes."
"They're loosening each other's teeth."
"They're warming each other's ears."
"They're crushing each other's toes."
"They're making each other's nose bleed."
"They're butting each other's tibias."
"They're blacking each other's eyelids."
"They're hitting each other's stomach."
"They're pulling each other's hair out."
"They're breaking each other's back."
"They're tearing at each other's cheeks."
"They're putting out each other's joints."
"They're squeezing each other's larynx."
"They're shattering each other's shoulder blades."
"They're crowning each other's knees."

"They're flattening each other's genitals."
"They're dislocating each other's articulations."
"They're straining each other's muscles."
"They're epilating each other's eyebrows."
"They're pulverizing each other's chin."
"They're luxating each other's testicles."
"They're unscrewing each other's penis."
"They're malaxating each other's ribs."
"They're gnawing each other's intestines."
"They're pounding each other's liver."
"They're bloodying each other's face."
"They're flaying each other."
"They're mutilating each other."
"They're triturating each other."
"Frightful combat!"
"Horrible conjuncture!"
"The timid postman does not dare separate them."
"Meussieu Cocotier's dog is barking at them."
"Mme. Sélénium, at her door, is trembling with fear."
"The trees are shivering."
"The birds have stopped singing."
"The sky is becoming overcast."
"The sun is becoming obscured."
"Nature refuses to contemplate this atrocious haggis any longer."
"Let us go in," said Etienne, "to our half-house, and discuss the fate of Théo, once more a fugitive. Alberte advises me to find Narcense, and Le Grand argues against it. What shall I do?"
"It was bound to end like that, in a fight," said the postman.
"I have always thought that sailor a most undesirable individual," said Meussieu Cocotier.
"Personally, exhibitions of that sort quite take my appetite away," said Mme. Sélénium.
"Well, is it a Bugatti?" asked Hippolyte.
"He says that, and he's quietly strangling his opponent," observed the postman.
"No, it isn't a Bugatti," admitted Yves le Toltec, "but you owe me at least a quarter of a liter to celebrate your victory."

"Cock-a-doodle-doo, cock-a-doodle-doo," bawled Meussieu and Madame Exossé's cock.

In its youth, this animal had fallen on its head; ever since, it had crowed at sundown, even when there was the extra hour for summertime; it was roasted, the following year, and its flesh delighted the omnivorous palate of its stupid owners.

---

The Belhôtel's son, whose first name was Clovis, like his deceased grandfather, the one that had died of apoplexy on hearing of the declaration of war in 1914, the Belhôtel's son, as he was saying, had, for nearly twenty-four hours, been keeping a secret. He had spoken of it neither to his father, nor to his mother, nor to Ernestine, nor to his pals, nor even to his little girl friend Ivoine, who was twelve years old and blonde. Serious and thoughtful, Clovis considered that his secret deserved better than to be shouted from the rooftops; one person, and one only, was, in his estimation, worthy of sharing it with him, and while he was waiting for that person on the road he was throwing stones at a condensed milk can.

Hector (Totor) and Dagobert (Bébert) came by:

"Hey, Cloclo, coming up to the repair yard with us? We're going to throw stones at the switches."

"No, I'm waiting for my aunt," replies Clovis.

"Oh well, if you're going to be with your family, then so long," says Totor.

"You know, that Saponaire, the one who snitched on us the other day, we tied his cat's tail up to his bell, the other night. Dick thought that one up."

"And then," added Totor, "Dick, he slopped a great big pail of water all over Polyte's mother's feet."

"That'll teach the old bitch," Clovis commented.

"Well, so long."

A few paces farther on, Dagobert turned around:

"You know Tatave, he's making eyes at your chick."

"Let him try. I'll bust his goddam nose."

Hector and Dagobert ran off, laughing.

With renewed conviction, Clovis started stoning his condensed milk can again.

At about 6 o'clock, an old woman appeared around a bend in the road; Clovis rushed up to her.

"Hello, Aunt Sidonie."

"Hello, Clovis," replied Mme. Cloche.

She was anxious to see her brother, and didnt' take much notice of her nephew.

"You know, Aunt Cloche, I've got something serious to tell you."

"What? What?"

"I've got a secret for you."

Oho, if it's secrets, she's ready.

"You're the only one I'm telling it to. It's a real secret."

"Tell me, then."

"Promise you won't tell it to everyone else?"

"Yes, Clovis, my nephew, I promise."

Clovis gives a little cough, and looks all around to see whether anyone can hear him. Then, in a low voice:

"Ole Taupe, he's a millionaire."

Mme. Cloche receives the blow without flinching.

"Howdger know?"

"Th'yuther day, I was walking along the embankment by the Company's workshops; I saw two well-dressed men coming out of ole Taupe's. They passed very close to me, they dint see me, and one of them said: 'Zno doubt about it, he hides his money behind the door,' and th'yuther, he said: 'He's an old miser, he must be very rich,' and the first one, he said: 'It's quite certain he hides his money behind the door.'"

"Then they never said he was a millionaire."

"*I* say that."

"And wattad they look like, those two men?"

"Wz a tall fair-haired one, and th'yuther, I think he's been and had a drink at Dad's before."

Mme. Cloche cannot contain her joy. She holds the key to the mystery. Etienne Marcel wants to get hold of old Taupe's hoard! That's why he came to have some French fries at Dominique's! There's no other explanation. And he has an accomplice, and maybe that Meussieu Narcense is an accomplice too. The business of Théo's hanging, that was a settling of accounts. Among international gangsters. And old Taupe's hoard must be pretty sizable for gangsters of that kind to bother about.

Hah! But the tall fair-haired one, he was the one whose taxi nearly ran into Meussieu Marcel. Etienne Marcel! outside the Gare du Nord! Yes, a tall fair-haired guy, that's him all right! That accident, naturally it was all show, it was on purpose.

Clovis contemplates the warty nose of his aunt twitching with the strain of meditation.

Well, old Taupe! Always shouting from the rooftops about how you mustn't own anything. It's plain as the nose on your face, that's just a cover! You old miser, you! you won't keep your hoard much longer! I'm certny not going to stay here like a half-wit and let other people get their hands on it. Oh no, that snot the way it's going to be. Those gangsters, they may know a thing or two, but I'll find a way to get summing out of this business, I will.

"Listen, Clovis, that wz very nice of you to tell me that. We'll talk about it later on. And don't tell a soul, eh? whatever you do."

"No, Aunt Cloche, I promise."

The old girl trots off to the French fries place; watch out, though, mustn't mess around. First thing is to keep your trap shut. Dominique doesn't need to know about it for the moment, nor his wife; and let's hope the brat can hold his tongue.

Dominique's place is crowded. The factory's finished for the day. Old Taupe is sitting at a table, knocking down his liter of white; he's holding forth to a couple of workmen:

"Yes," he's saying, "when you want something you can't have, you're unhappy, and if you've got a lot of money and piles of things, you're afraid of losing them, so you're unhappy."

"Old hypocrite," thinks Mme. Cloche, as she goes by.

Dominique is very busy; his wife receives her.

"You know Meussieu Marcel, he came back."

"And what did he say?"

"Nothing."

"Nothing?"

"Yes, he was with a fair-haired young man 'at wanted to go and have a look at old Taupe's, maybe he'd find summing interesting. They both went off to his place. Don't think they found anything. They came back past here again; they said hello, but they didn't stop. What about you—seen Saturnin?"

"Yes. He told me all about Saddy night. Well, nuh'ing happened. Kid didn't turn up. Nor did Meussieu Marcel. Saturnin found Meussieu Narcense, all by himself, with the rope in his hand. He spoke to him, he persuaded him to go away, they went back to Paris together."

"Nuh'ing happened, then?"

"No, nuh'ing."

"Nuh'ing ever does happen," sighs Mme. Belhôtel, disillusioned.

Mme. Cloche smiles. Nuh'ing happens to slobs like her sister-in-law. But to her . . . Mme. Cloche looks at old Taupe; he's going on; mustn't have anything, he's saying, if you want to not have any trouble. And women, they're trouble all right. He makes jokes on the subject. His eyes, observes Mme. Cloche, never leave Ernestine; he follows her all the time. She happens to pass near him: if you don't want to have any worries, mustn't desire anything, proclaims old Taupe, and he pinches Ernestine's bottom.

Mme. Cloche has an idea.

---

Even though it was absurd, and Le Grand was against it, Etienne, the next morning, went to see Narcense. He got the morning off and, at about 9 o'clock, turned up at 8 Boulevard of the Unknown Officer. Saturnin was sweeping up outside the door. Etienne recognized him and asked him whether his health was good. The other replied that it was not at all bad; and the fact is that he was extremely well. Then he too inquired after the health of the visitor and learned without surprise that the latter had nothing to grumble about in that respect. These preliminaries lasted only a few seconds, for their apparent complexity concealed a profound simplicity.

Saturnin taught Etienne how to work the elevator, and the two latter immediately took flight toward the upper floors of the uninhabited apartment house. At the seventh, the elevator came to a halt and its contents having arrived, *mirabile dictu*, at the required landing, rang the bell at Narcense's door, which Narcense almost immediately came and opened.

Etienne apologized for the trouble he was causing, Narcense requested him to think nothing of it and, at the same time, to come in. When they were seated, for Narcense offered Etienne a chair, the latter, while inviting his interlocutor not to believe that his visit implied any suspicion of him, the latter, I say, informed Narcense that his son, Théo, had once again disappeared from the family residence; he added that, even though it seemed to him to be highly improbable, Narcense might perhaps be in possession of some information on this matter. Narcense appeared to be just as amazed as he was in reality, and stated that it was a grave mistake to believe that he might spend his whole life thinking about Théo; that it must not be imagined that this child was his sole preoccupation and his sole anxiety; that, on the contrary, he was extremely little concerned with his acts and deeds and would even prefer not to hear anything about him. Etienne rejoined that he had not thought his question would have irritated him to such an extent; to which Narcense replied that he was in no way irritated, but that he had not the slightest wish to have Théo dogging his footsteps all his life.

Etienne agreed with him, which did not fail to astonish Narcense, who added that, furthermore, he had no news of the fugitive adolescent. He inquired as to the possible causes of this departure; Etienne knew of none; he feared an accident, and alluded to his wife's despair.

After a few moments' silence, Narcense asked Etienne whether he was not a bank clerk and, on receiving a reply in the affirmative, added that he, Narcense, played the saxophone; that it so happened that at the moment he was out of work, but that their mutual friend was going to get him some. Etienne was amazed, for he knew of no one who was also Narcense's friend, but when the latter had mentioned the name of Pierre Le Grand, Etienne realized his mistake—and many other things as well. For the prophecy in the restaurant was immediately transformed into a remarkably successful conjuring trick; and Etienne was still unaware of the fact that Pierre had driven Narcense to Les Mygales in his car. This discovery of Pierre's duplicity fascinated Etienne more than it disconcerted him. The conjuring trick seemed to him to be skillful, and he admitted being quite incapable of accomplishing anything of the sort. He asked the musician whether he knew anything of what their friend did or how he lived; Narcense knew nothing; they both knew only one thing about him: that he had a car. Each inquired of the other how he had got to know him; one of them had seen him for the first time in Obonne, in a little restaurant. Etienne preferred not to ask *which,* because that reminded him of the reasons why Narcense had gone to Obonne; he himself had made Pierre's acquaintance as a consequence of a slight accident outside the Gade du Nord—and Narcense then remembered his best friend being run over in the same circumstances, and, once again, he thought of death. Once again, because that same morning, when he was only half awake, he had seemed to see a clenched fist outside his window; and while he was describing his friend Potice's death to Etienne, he was seeing before his eyes a succession of pictures which started with his grandmother's chin strap and finished with his own hanging, by way of the absurd incident of the incongruous poodle.

While he was continuing to stem the tide of mental pictures, from the hanging to Théo, and from Théo to Alberte, he revealed to Etienne the fact that before Pierre had got to know him, he had been observing him. And as Etienne asked for details, Narcense told him that Pierre had observed him changing. Etienne admitted this change; but that anyone else could have noticed it seemed to him to be singularly mysterious. He didn't try to go any deeper into the problem, and decided that from now on, Pierre Le Grand would be his friend, even though he had, at least once, played a trick on him. As for Narcense, what he was seeing was not Etienne, but, very far away, behind him, a woman.

The series of revelations concerning Etienne was interrupted by the entrance of Saturnin bringing a post card addressed to Narcense; on the back, these words were to be read: "Best regards, Théo"; it came from a seaside resort on the Atlantic coast.

---

After they had covered with humus and compost the rectangular parallelepiped in which the fermentation had already begun of the mortified mortal remains of the sordid old man called Bousigue by custom and Thomas by his father, his pointed-nosed daughter returned to the dead man's house at the very end of the village.

For years and years, he had been moldering in a rabbit hutch near the old tile works; during that time, his daughter was selling split peas and vegetable butter a long way away from him, in one of the suburbs of a big town. People used to give the old man alms; she never went to see him, for business does not forgive absenteeism. For the demise, however, she did put herself out, and pushed open the door. A straw mattress was recumbent on the floor; a chair adorned a corner; some packing cases; everything was covered in filth. It would all have to be burned. She got hold of the mattress, rolled it up, and threw it into a corner; something fell out of it.

Soon, the news spread that Bousigue's daughter had found two hundred thousand francs, in bank notes and defense bonds, hidden in the mattress of that old bum, her father. The whole village soon heard of it, and to think that we used to give him alms, said they, the villagers of the village. The news reached the neighboring town, and there the druggist, who was a correspondent of the *Petit Tourangeau*, wrote about it for his paper; and in Tours it was thought of sufficient interest to be sent to Paris.

There, this news item was held over for three days, until the end of the Tour de France. And then, when its last echoes had died away, they found a little corner on the fifth page to place:

A MISER, etc.

Chinon, etc.

This was printed during the night, then, with the first light, the paper left, and some people bought it. A lot of people, because a lot read the papers, even some who don't read anything else, so they say. Belhôtel Dominique was one of these. He read his paper in the morning, while he drank his coffee; then his wife read it; then the customers read it.

The paper hung around on the table all day. Toward the evening, covered with blobs of wine and grease marks, and slightly torn, it was rescued by Ernestine, who opened it carefully and smoothed out its crumples with her hand. Her head between her hands, she read the serial, then various crimes, and finally:

A MISER, etc.

Chinon, etc.

Bousigue, two hundred thousand francs, Bousigue two hundred thousand francs. Behind her, someone whispered in her ear:

"Two hundred thousand, huh, my girl."

"Yes, two hundred thousand," murmured Ernestine, shattered.

"Some luck for the heirs!" Mme. Cloche went on.

"Whew, talk about luck, that's luck all right."

"And he used to beg, too," added Sidonie.

"Mm, he used to beg."

"Pooh," said the old woman, "zbags of 'em like that, old men people give money to, and in a corner of their wardrobe, or in their mattress, they've got a fortune tucked away. Misers, huh, there's hundreds of 'em, you just don't realize, honey. They look poor, yet they could live in the swankiest places. There's tons of 'em like that."

"Yes, of course," replies Ernestine, overwhelmed.

Ernestine wasn't counting on spending her whole life serving white wine and half pints. That she wasn't. She'd find a way to put some money to one side. Belhôtel had promised her that she'd be assistant madame in the brothel he was going to buy. But even so, to make your fortune overnight like that, it was enough to give you an apoplectic fit. When she was a kid, she'd once read in *Belles Images* the veracious account of the treasure of the Incas. And this news item and the odious life she led reminded her of that wonderful tale. But she suddenly thought that really, she wasn't the sort of person who had the luck to become the heroine of an adventure like that. Not like the daughter of that Bousigue, whose name kept running through her head now, pulling its little trailer of bank notes and defense bonds behind it.

"There's things you go a long way to get, and very often they're right under your nose," murmured Mme. Cloche pensively.

"Could well be, but snot me things like that'd happen to."

Ernestine added:

"I've never had any luck."

"One day, your luck will change."

Could be so, could be. And Mme. Cloche pressed the point:

"There's things you go a long way to get, and very often they're right under your nose."

"Now that's *very* true," said Etienne, who had just come in.

Mme. Cloche remained speechless for a few moments. She stood up convulsively.

"Ah! hello, Meussieu Marcel."

"Hello, Madame," rejoined Etienne, with infinite presence of mind. "It's getting late. I've got an appointment with a friend who will be here in a few minutes. Ernestine, a white wine!"

At this late hour, there wasn't a single customer. The Belhôtels were at their bistro in town.

"And how is that old junk dealer?"

"Oho, oho," said Mme. Cloche.

"Does my question surprise you?"

"No, no, no, Meussieu Marcel. Oh no! Old Taupe, well, he still lives in these parts."

They heard a car stopping. Pierre came in.

"You might tell him that this gentleman would still like to buy his door."

"Ah, you're talking about the old fellow we saw the other day," said Pierre. "Why don't we go and wake him up?"

Mme. Cloche paled:

"He'd welcome you with a shotgun."

"Goodness me! I'll have a white wine, too."

The two men drank; Ernestine fell asleep; Mme. Cloche—secretly—was exultant. It really was so. And what if they went now . . . No, though, they wouldn't dare. They didn't dare, because they were in a hurry. So they said, at least. And the car disappeared into the night.

---

"Ernestine, why d'you think those two meussieus come here?"

"How should I know?"

"You don't think it odd?"

"Why should I?"

"Meussieu Marcel lives in Obonne, and the other one lives in Paris. Why do they come here?"

"They stop to have a drink."

"Snot on their way."

"Oh no, it sure isn't."

"Do you think it's natural, for rich people, to come n drink here, where it stinks of the chemicals factory and where there's nothing but white wine and beer to drink? D'you think that's natural?"

"Hm, that's true, Madame Cloche. Dnever thought of all that."

"And coming here at this hour. Isn't that odd?"

"Well, yes!"

"And what'd they come to do?"

"Mjust wondering."

"Don't you member any more, honey?"

"Did they say why?"

"Course they did—try and remember."

"Can't."

"Being lucky comes down to remembering what matters. Get that into your head, Ernestine."

"Yes, M'dame."

"They said they were going to wake old Taupe up."

"So-o they did! an that they wanted to buy his door! that really is a laugh, to buy a door!"

"Yes, but, Ernestine, isn't it peculiar, wanting to go and wake a poor devil up at this hour?"

"You even told them he'd be after them with his shotgun. which he certainly would've been."

"You ever been to old Taupe's?"

"Mm, with the boss, to buy a lock."

"Zanything interesting there?"

"Ja mean?"

"Well, nice things?"

"Yiy-yi-yi, just a norrible lot of old junk. Nothing but a lot of rotten old broken things."

"You think there'd be anything there that might interest a moneybags like the blond guy?"

"Course not."

"Isn't it peculiar, then, that he should come here at this hour to buy summing from him and want to wake him up to do it?"

"And to buy a door."

"To buy a door, there's a peculiar idea."

"Well, yes it *is* a peculiar idea."

"And those, two meussieus, what d'you spose they might want to do with it?"

"Mjust wondering."

"What do they do for their living?"

"No idea."

"One of them's a bank clerk, so he says."

"Don't you believe him?"

"And the yuther one doesn't do anything."

"Ah!"

"Well then, Ernestine, what d'you think of it all?"

"It's a screwy idea, wanting to buy a door."

"And then what?"

"Well—swot it is. It's a screwy idea."

"So you think they're screwy?"
"Howshd I know."
"Couldn't be summing else?"
"Ida know."
"And old Taupe, who's he?"
"An old satyr! Every time he gets a chance he pinches my rear, and tries to touch my thing."
"He's got a thing on you."
"Ha, ha, ha."
"And?"
"Dirty old bastard! at his age!"
"Yeah, sure—and apart from that, what does he do?"
"You know as well I do. Why're you asking me all this?"
"I wanted to know what you think of old Taupe."
"Well, he's an old satyr."
"And then what?"
"He gets boozed."
"And then what?"
"He's a junk dealer."
"And then what?"
"He's at the end of his rope."
"Ernestine, you're a fool."
"That's what you say, Madame."
"Ernestine, you're touched."
"That's what you say."
"Ernestine, you could make your fortune, and you're letting it pass you by!"
"Eh?"
"Ernestine, if you listen to me, you can live on the Côte d'Azur and have a car and go to the movies every evening and go dancing every night. Ernestine, happy days are here. No more French fries and white wine! No more chemicals and suburban trains! No more of my brother's attentions and my sister-in-law's insults! No more work! No more being broke! It's gigolos for us, and bottles of kümmel! We're going to have a good time! It'll all be coming out of our ears! Everything—cakes, and *foie gras,* and caviar. And this, and that, and whoopee!"
"Madame Cloche! Madame Cloche! don't get so excited!"

"Yes, Ernestine, I'm getting you out of the slums, out of the gutter, out of the shit! I'm getting you out of poverty, penury, indigence! I'll get you covered in jewels, I will I will! Every day, Ernestine, you'll be able to eat raw artichokes with vinaigrette sauce, your favorite dish! Every day, Ernestine, you'll be able to go to the Trianon-Lyrique and hear your favorite operettas!"

"But whatsa matter with her? But whatsa matter with her?"

"Ernestine, if you listen to me, you'll be rich."

"But how come?"

"First of all, though—we'll go fifty-fifty."

"How come?"

"I tell you watch gotta do, and you give me half you get."

"Half. That's a lot."

"What a bitch! Won't tell you, then!"

"Ten per cent, that's plenty, I would think."

"What a cow you are, Ernestine. Half, or I won't say a word."

"A third, Madame Cloche."

"Half, Ernestine."

"If I give you half, then I won't be as rich as all that."

"You'll still have more'n you need . . ."

"Huh! And what if I didn't give you anything?"

"Then you wouldn't know anything."

"And what if I knew without you telling me anything?"

"Knew what?"

"Madame Cloche, I'm not such a silly cunt as I look. I know very well what you're getting at."

"Which is what?"

"Well, you're trying to get me to believe that old Taupe, he's a millionaire."

"Ernestine, do you really think so?"

"Whereza proof?"

"Precisely. Half—and I'll prove it."

"Or right, or right, Madame Cloche. Half."

"You mean it?"

"I mean it."

"And whatever you do—not a word to a soul."

"I promise, Madame Cloche."

"Well, then, Ernestine, it's like this: the yuther day, Cloclo, he was playing near old Taupe's hut when the two men came out. He heard them saying: his money, it's hidden behind his door, 'swhy he wont' sell his door. And the tall blond one, he was saying: Sobvious that he's more than a millionaire. That's how it is, my girl: Meussieu Marcel and his buddy, they want to get their hands on old Taupe's cash. They're a lot of thieving robbers. But we'll get there before them. Couldn't be simpler: you marry old Taupe, and the cash is ours."

"And what if ole Taupe doesn't want to marry me?"

"*He*'ll marry you, don't worry. He goes nuts when he sees you."

"And the yuthers, what if they have it in for me?"

"Course not, course not! You've got nothing to be afraid of."

"Not so sure."

"What d'you spose they'd do?"

"Seems risky to me."

"What, Ernestine, would you allow this magnificent opportunity to pass you by?"

"I see it all. I risk my skin, and I get myself saddled with ole Taupe so's I can give you half the proceeds. Don't think much of that."

"You're just making difficulties, Ernestine. I can think of dozens of girls would take that risk."

"Swot *you* say. Way I look at it, the others, the moment they saw the cash slipping out of their hands, they'd get rid of me. Any fool could see that."

"You're dreaming, Ernestine."

"No, Madame Cloche, I'm not dreaming. I won't play."

"Oh come, Ernestine."

"I won't play! I won't play! I won't play!"

"But you're a fool! An absolute fool! There's millions at stake."

"Maybe, but I'll do without them . . . No, M'dame Cloche. Count me out. Thank you. Nenni case, you've got to go. I'm closing, sten o'clock."

"Well, that's really too much. Look, Ernestine, a fortune, and you're letting it slip through your fingers. You really must be touched, then."

"It's all very fine, but I'd rather be a waitress here than a millionaire in the cemetery. Nenni case, zno proof he's a millionaire."

"Look, Ernestine, watch want, and you really think those two guys keep coming here just for the hell of it? isn't it proof, what Clovis heard? What more ja want? and you think it's natural to go on going on about how the way to be happy is not to own anything, and a lot of boloney like that? If he was really poor, ole Taupe, well, he wouldn't go on about it so much. It's as plain as day. Yes, I mean it, it's as plain as day."

"That's all very fine, Madame Cloche, but it doesn't interest me. And nenni case, it's 10 o'clock, I'm closing."

"Right, I'm going. But you'll see, you'll change your mind! You'll change your mind!"

---

It was goddamn stinking hot. Old Taupe was sitting on a rickety chair, his tongue hanging out and his left eye oozing. With the other eye he was idly observing the movements of a big green fly in search of sustenance among the odds and ends withering in the sun. Few flies frequented this place, being disgusted by the smell of chemicals. On the other hand, you sometimes met a few rats. Old Taupe ignored this kind of livestock, even though one of them had, one night, bitten one of his toes. For the moment, it was goddamn stinking hot, the factory chimneys were smoking abundantly; from the sidings came the sound of a train being put together and the jolts that reverberated from car to car as they were coupled. Trucks were going by on the road to Blagny. Old Taupe was vaguely trying to recall the dates of the hottest summers he had known; this tiring effort of thought was accompanied by an abundant secretion of saliva. He came up with the summer of 1895, that of 1904, that of 1911, then he filled a clay pipe whose bowl he had carefully tied on with a bit of string, and started smoking: the pipe gurgled, the man spat; a little corner of paradise in the middle of the hell of the Paris suburbs.

Old Taupe went to a lot of trouble over his happiness; to the pleasure of his pipe he added that of scratching his head with his index finger and watching its nail gradually blackening. A feeblish, tepid wind brought a little more dust into the enclosure; a tattered umbrella gently flapped its wings; an old newspaper shifted a little; a slack spring tried to take a few steps but couldn't make it. The sun, without discrimination, beat down on nails and color prints, on locks and cauldrons, on water jugs and candelabras; the nail had become quite black, and the gurgle intensive. Perfect bliss reigned in this corner of paradise which had struck root inner miggle uvver Parris suburbs.

Old Taupe heard an ancient pair of shoes slopping along the path, and, next thing, summon knocked on the gate. And a voice sang: M'sieu Taupe, M'sieu Taupe; it was a woman's voice. It nearly made the old man swallow his pipe. What a thing to happen! M'sieu Taupe, said the woman's voice. Who a nurth could it be? He trotted over to the drawbridge and asked: "Who is it?" and the answer was: "Nestine." He opened the gate.

Ernestine wanted to buy a vase to put flowers in. That was the only excuse she'd managed to think up. The junk dealer was amazed.

"Who's giving you flowers, then, you hussy," said he, in the most licentious tone of voice he could produce.

Ernestine made a few jokes. The old man tried to pinch her; she made him take his hands off, but how the hell was she going to get him to ask her to marry him? Not the very first time, obviously. She went into the hovel and saw the door. Obviously it was there, the door. A door for no reason at all, and blue, furthermore; behind it, it was the railroad embankment. Maybe the old man had dug a cellar there. Ma Cloche didn't know the details. Ernestine was making superhuman efforts to rise to the occasion.

Old Taupe had fetched a vase which made a beautifully decorative impression; a pink shepherd and a mauve shepherdess were negligently leaning against its flanks. A blackish mud hid the rest of its ornamentation. He muttered:

"Like it, m'girl?" in a choking voice.

She looked at him; was he really a millionaire? He thought he detected untold depths of perversity in her eyes; putting the vase down on a toothless chest of drawers, he started dancing up and down on the spot and clucking like a guinea fowl.

"Well, Pop, how much y'going to charge me for your vase?"

And this acrobat, who had one foot in the grave and the other in the cradle, this acrobat whispered:

"A kiss."

Ernestine saw only the comic side of these goings-on, and turned around, to stifle her laughter. The sound of breaking china made her turn back again; the old man didn't like people making fun of him, he'd just broken the rosy shepherd and the mauvish shepherdess.

"Oh! my vase," said Ernestine, suiting the appropriate mimicry to these words.

Old Taupe regretted his gesture.

"It's not right to make fun of me, my dear," said he.

And she understood at once what he was referring to.

The good fellow then heard some surprising words; the girl wasn't rejecting his advances any more, but she seemed to attach a condition to them whose meaning he couldn't quite grasp yet. He went and fetched her another vase, adorned with a Neapolitan moon, which he sold her for three francs fifty; she left, smiling pleasantly. She had said some things to him which, if she really meant what she said, well, there was no getting over them.

---

Sidonie sat down on the terrace of her favorite café, opposite the Gare du Nord. It was there, three weeks before, that she'd seen a bus run over a young man in a hurry; it was there that she'd first seen the two accomplices, Etienne Marcell and X . . .

They had then acted, before her very eyes, a mysterious scenario whose exact meaning she hadn't succeeded in understanding, any more than she had understood the exact meaning of the conversation she'd just had with Narcense.

At first, her brother Saturnin had made a terrible fuss: out of the question for her to go and see Meussieu Narcense.

What did she want with him? What business was it of hers? Ek cetra, ek cetra. Summing streamly important, she'd replied, and then, sit got to do with you? Her brother, he'd had to shut his trap. No but . . . an anyway, he was the youngest. Another good thing was that the meussieu in question was in. He'd looked surprised to see her, course he had, and he'd asked her nice and politely to sit down. Wasn't anything ticularly interesting to look at in his apartment. Wz a piano, and then a jazz-band whatsit, and then some photos, and then he was in the middle of writing some music. All for show, of course. It was the first time she'd seen him. He had a scar on his forehead, and he looked a tough customer. Wasn't wearing a tie, and he was in his shirtsleeves. So he asked her: Watch want me to do for you? Just like that, abruptly. So she'd answered: I've come to suggest doing a deal, and he'd said: Well, well! Whereupon there'd been a silence. Then she'd gone on: You do know M'sieu Marcel, Etienne Marcel? "Yes," he'd answered. "And his pal, oh beg yours, his friend, the fair-haired meussieu that's got a car," and he'd said: Pierre Le Grand. So that was what that one's name was. Certainly not a real name; it's like Narcense, odd sort of name that is. Ah well, duh matter.

N then she said: You had some matters to settle, the two of you, and she gave him a wink. The fellow, he said he din understand. "What about Théo," says she. "Don't know 'im," says the fellow, looking furious. "Oh, beg yours," says she. She hadn't been going about it the right way.

There wz another silence; Narcense was the first to break it, and he said: I haven't the vaguest what you want from me, Madame. Natch it was difficult to explain it to him. "The other two, they're hatching summing up," she finally made up her mind to say. "Watch mean, the other two?" "Well, Marcel and Le Grand."

Then he'd said: "What the hell d'you think I care?" Then she'd said: "You and me together, we can stop them." Then he'd laughed like anything and said: Why should we stop them? And there wasn't any answer to that. "Oh, it's a big deal," says she, and Meussieu Narcense had said: You don't say, and he gave her a peculiar look.

Then he asked her: Do you know them well, those messieus? "Do I know them? Course I do," she'd replied. "They're always coming to have a drink at my brother's, not the one that's the concierge here, but the yuther one that's got a bistro at Blagny, you know, on the Obonne line." "Then Saturnin, he's your brother," says he. "Yes, M'sieu," she'd replied. "And those two messieus are always going to have a drink at Blagny?" "Oh yess, M'sieu," she'd again replied. "Well, that takes the cake," says he. "And is that all they do at Blagny?" he asks.

She winked: No, that isn't all, it's just precisely there that they're getting ready to do the deal. "A big deal?" says he. "At least a million," she answered. "Well, well," says he, and she added that if he liked, the two of them could stop them. "Yess, M'sieu Narcense, I can see what they're after, but then I know all about it. Me, I'm only a weak woman, I can't risk it all by myself; sa question of at least a miyun, think of that, eh, so it'd be better for it to be me and you rather than them, doncha think? That's what she'd said to him. Then he'd answered: Who d'you think I am? And she'd told him what she thought: that his music, it was all for show, wasn't it? Slike Marcel, that makes out he's a bank clerk. Believe me, M'sieu Narcense, I know very well who you are. I'm not from the police, believe me. It's on the up and up, the deal I'm offering you, and there's no big risk. It's a profitable deal, believe me, and it's in the bag if you'll only do something about it."

She'd said all that to him, and all that time he'd been walking up and down. "How d'you know that Marcel and Le Grand are cooking something up?" says he. "Ah, now that I can't tell you." Natch, she couldn't tell him that just like that. And then he'd said: Msorry, Madame, but I can't do anything about your business, at the moment I'm busy smuggling cream cheese in North Africa; you understand, that takes a lot of my time, and then, at the same time, I've got a lawyer to liquidate not far from Castelsarrazin, a little business which ought to bring me something like two million, not counting the extras, so, you understand, I'm extremely busy; naturally, this is just between you and me.

Yuh, tswot he'd said, and after that he'd said: Good-by, mso sorry, Madame.

But what did he mean, not counting the extras? And then, smuggling cream cheese, do people do that? It was certainly international gangsters' slang. Like the correspondence with Théo in code, it meant something different from what was written. A guy like that who goes about hanging little children and smuggling cream cheese, better watch out. Maybe Ernestine isn't so wrong not to get mixed up with all that. Guys like that are danjrous, they do in the people that get in their way, and they, well they never get caught. Two mijun not counting the extras, Lord, that's something. Old Taupe certainly hasn't got that much. You never know, though, if the yuthers are mixed up in it, then it must be a deal that's worth something like that.

"Yes, Madame?"

"A cointreau," replied Mme. Cloche, "and make sure you fill the glass up full, I don't want any of your half measures."

"Well, there's a vulgar one for you," said the waiter to himself, wiping his nose with his napkin.

---

"Here, Saturnin—is that your sister, the old girl who just left?"

"Yes, M'sieu Narcense. What on earth did she have to say to you?"

"Didn't she tell you?"

"Not a word. As she left, she said: If the meussieu wants to see me, give him my address."

"Hm! And she didn't tell you anything about me?"

"Not a word."

"Is she drunk or mad or drugged?"

"Nothing like that, M'sieu Narcense. She's in her right mind, my sister is. And she didn't touch a drop today, my sister didn't."

"Saturnin, do you know who I am?' '

"M'sieu Nar . . ."

"Not at all. I'm a crook, a thief, a dangerous gangster. Your sister just told me so."

"Dnever've thought it."

"Nor would I."

"If she said that, it's because she had a reason for saying it."

"Obviously, Saturnin. Etienne Marcel is a crook, too."

"The guy from Obonne?"

"That's the way it is. He's cooking up a scheme involving a million."

"Jesus," said Saturnin.

"I fear you may be carried away by fraternal love, Saturnin, when you say that your sister is in her right mind. Watch her closely. Examine her attentively. Ask her, for instance, if she knows anything about the traffic in cream cheese. You'll see what she'll answer. In any case, come what may, I don't ever want that individual of doubtful cleanliness and repugnant aspect to set foot on my premises again."

"Right, M'sieu Narcense."

"And you can also tell her not to count the etxras when she adds things up."

"Right, M'sieu Narcense, If I get a chance, I'll tell her."

Narcense hasn't heard from Shibboleth yet; too soon; Le Grand couldn't have had time to get around to it; it can't be long now, though. Once again, he thinks about the old madwoman and wonders how she managed to come to such conclusions; and the frequent visits to the bistro, as she said, at Blagny. Was that true or false? What on earth could Marcel and Le Grand do there? That must be just as imaginary as all the rest. Blagny, on the Obonne line. Obonne—Narcense hadn't been there since the Mygales business. That was five days ago —only five days.

In the train, he looked out of the window at a landscape which he found atrociously hopeless. He liked the engines, but those hovels, those shanties. Now a row of conventional houses. This goes on for some time; there are a few trees here and there; then some waste ground, some workmen's tenements, some more allotments studded with sheds, a factory here and there, we're coming to Blagny. No animation in the square at this time of day. The train starts off again. More allotments studded with rabbit hutches, more wasteland and there, just before the chemicals factory, he can read CHIPS in enormous letters, and underneath, modestly, *D. Belhôtel.* That's the famous bistro, then, and *D. Belhôtel* is certainly Saturnin's brother. At least that much was true in the old girl's tale. Suddenly, he catches sight of the very same old girl. In person. On the path that runs along the factory wall, just by the railroad line, she's shuffling along with decision. She certainly knows where she's going. Narcense can't resist it. He puts his head out of the window and shouts: Belhôtel! Belhôtel! and waves a handkerchief. The old girl finally sees him; she stops dead, petrified, salted, desiccated. So long as the train remains in sight, she doesn't budge. He sits down again, highly pleased.

Obonne, houses, houses and more houses. There's only one touching one, it's only half finished and the paint on the gate is flaking off. He prowls around. From a neighboring "Mon Désir" come the yells of a toothless baby; at "Dun Romin" a miserable dog is howling in a destitute voice; at "Mon Repos" a duck is screaming because it just broke its foot on the flying trapeze (it's not true); at "Mon Rêve" you can hear Rome, unless it's Madrid or Toulouse (in any case it's Latin, they're playing Tortoni's serenade, oh, to hell with it!).

In the half-house, nothing stirs. The shutters over all the windows are closed. Meussieu Exossé watches Narcense out of the corner of his eye from his doorway. Abandoned houses provoke the immoral desires of burglars, thinks Meussieu Exossé.

Narcense looks at the house for a long time. Then he finds he's near the little café; will he go in? He hesitates; the door half opens, he hears: "the last time I went to Singapore," and goes back to Paris.

---

*Saturnin was trying to write; but it wouldn't come. He wasn't in form. His pen in the air, he was staring with a baleful eye at the pigeonholes with not a letter in them. Then, lowering his pen, he committed this sentence to paper:*

*the bird flue a way,*

*and replaced the instrument on the inkstand. Very ill at ease, Saturnin, very ill at ease. Lurking at the back of his lodge, the shutters tight shut on account of the heat, he has opened a little exercise book, a third of which has already been written in, uncorked a little bottle of ink and picked up a slightly nibbled pen. He intended to write something. But it isn't so easy as all that to write something when you haven't anything to say. All the more so as Saturnin doesn't write any old prose or romantic stuff. No no; what he writes has been thought out; so when he doesn't write, it becomes painful. Your stomach gets hollow, like when you're hungry; this is especially odd. Your eyes blink and your temples get hollow like your stomach; a slight pain moves down from the fontanel to the cerebellum, and vanishes.*

*Saturnin picks up his pen again and crosses out*

*the bird flue away*

*He hadn't had the slightest intention of writing that; all the more uninteresting. He continues his stroke, and finishes it in a most effective doodle. He puts down his pen.*

*There are some days when his head is full of things, when he makes judicious, original, profound observations, there are some days when he sees clearly that this is that, and then that, and other days when he understands this and that, and then that, and others days when he feels a little spasm at his heart because he perceives that this is not this, but that, and still other things. He often gets ideas, or if he doesn't get ideas, there are things that can be written; then it seems so funny. Where does it come from? You really don't know. He often gets the impression that what he has to say is very important; sometimes, even, that it's the most important thing in the world what he's just written or what he's going to write, what's in his head, huh. Yes, sometimes, the most important thing in the world is there—staring him in the face; yes, that's how he sometimes thinks, Saturnin the concierge, whether he's sitting on a chair, or lying in his bed, whether he's in his lodge or at the door of the apartment building he has been entrusted to look after, whether it's day or whether it's night, whether he's alone or whether he's in the company of his wife, who detests sewer rats and prawns that are still alive; yes, Saturnin, sometimes, that's how he thinks.*

*But at other times, Saturnin the concierge, he isn't at all like that. As we were saying just now, his head is empty and his eye baleful, he doodles on his paper and he nibbles at his pen. But he doesn't have anything to say; it isn't that that's what's painful, but that he'd thought the contrary. For, as we mustn't forget to say, there are some times when he wouldn't be capable of writing anything, but when that wouldn't make him in the slightest uneasy, because he doesn't in the least feel like it. That's the difference, there's the tra-la-lacuna. Spose he wz to take his feather duster and move the anonymous dust in the elevator from one place to another, then he wouldn't suffer. Spose he wz to get some polish and a brush and make himself look so handsome in a parquet floor, then he wouldn't suffer. Spose he had a lot to do, spose he had a lot to keep him busy, then he wouldn't suffer. But he wants to write, and so he suffers, because there's someone, behind him, who's thinking. That, at least, is what he believes. He had been scratching his shoulder for some minutes and thinking vaguely of various incidents in his past, when he gradually realized that, behind him, someone was thinking. Then, immediately after, that there was really no one there, thinking.*

*The various images that were interfering with his will to write began to fade away; the faces of his little friends who used to spit in each other's mouths at school, for fun, then the silhouette of the teacher who'd fallen downstairs—these faded away, then the last echo of the laughter provoked by this incident faded away, then some vague obscene pictures faded away, the image of a warship, that of a naked, tattooed arm, more slowly, that of a bottom, and once again a few vague obscene pictures. Then a bouquet of roses he'd seen going by that morning, carried by a uniformed delivery boy.*

*He drew a vertical line,*

*and nothing was left but coenesthetic impressions: his stomach hollowing, his temples hollowing, his fontanel hollowing, and then turning into a sort of well, of well, of well without bottom or rim, into which stones fall indefinitely, without ever coming into contact with the surface of the black water entirely and forever bereft of light and movement, the surface of this perfectly carbonic, arachnoid water, the skin of a brain. His chest became constricted and his heart started beating wildly; his breath became jerky. Saturnin fell into his own well belonging to his own brain, where there was now nothing; no more well, no more brain, no more Saturnin, no more concierge, no more camels, no more sunshades, no more laundry boats.*

*Saturnin, with his mouth open.*

*After—after—what? he picked up his pen again and, carefully tearing up the crossed-out, scribbled-over page, he wrote on the opposite page:*

*There isn't anything.*

*And reshut the little exercise book, recorked the little bottle, and put down the little pen. Then he got on with his work, while there was still time.*

## Fourth Chapter

THEY arrived at noon; aperitifs were in full swing. Pierre's sports car received the warm approval of the public. Alberte shut herself up in her room. Etienne started searching for Théo. This vacation was starting in an original fashion. One night in the car had advantageously replaced the ten or fifteen usual hours in the sardine can, and Pierre's company was becoming a necessity to Etienne. Forgetting the little ducks and the hard-boiled-egg-cutter, he saw in this meeting the cause of the change whose reality he perceived daily. He didn't even think of reproaching Pierre for the conjuring trick he had been responsible for in relation to Narcense. And in any case, he considered it preferable not to let him know of his acquaintance with the facts of this matter. At least for the moment. As he was very thirsty, he went into a local American bar and asked for a lemonade. The bartender was amazed that anyone should ask for such a strange beverage, and replaced it on his own initiative with a djinn-phiz. Etienne drank, and thought it not bad. He paid, without looking startled at the price, and left, delighted with his new experience. He loitered outside the bookstore-cum-newsstand; he felt like buying a book, not a novel, a serious book, but the display offered nothing he wanted; he contented himself with a few post cards. A little farther on, he asked the price of a souvenir; just so as to know. Then he made a detour in order to look at a few old houses, very local color, built the year before by the tourist bureau. He retraced his steps, again examined the books and papers, bought some cigarettes, and found himself back at the hotel. Pierre was waiting for him, drinking an aperitif, like everyone else. Then Etienne remembered Théo, turned around again and went to look for him.

He asked in the hotels whether they didn't know a young man of about fifteen, with greasy, badly cut black hair, his face covered with spots, his eyes ever so slightly rheumy, and with permanently dirty hands; but no one had seen a young man answering this description. Then he wandered through the little town, and came to the beach. Of the few bottoms still roasting there, none belonged to his stepson, the future holder of the baccalaureate.

At 1:30 he went back to the hotel, very tired. Pierre was still waiting for him. He sat down, discouraged.

"It's not funny—no Théo. Alberte waiting for him in her room . . . What's in a djinn-phiz?"

"It's a squeezed lemon with gin," replied Pierre.

Etienne rubs his forehead. Where on earth can he be? The moment you look at things disinterestedly, everything changes. That's quite obvious, and that is what makes it difficult to accept the obviousness of what you see at first. Not to take the destination of an object into account, what a strange activity! You start by not seeing anything because you're living in a whirl, then you look because you want to do something different, and after that you contemplate because you're tired of working.

"And what do you intend to do?" asked Pierre.

"Damned if I know. If I went to the police—what a business! What a bore! What a bore!

"What sort of boy is he, your stepson?"

"He's a young man of fifteen; he goes to the lycée, he has brown eyes, his nose—how should I know? I don't think he likes me very much, I even think he detests me. It often happens, doesn't it, that a child detests his stepfather? I think he takes me for an imbecile, I didn't go to a lycée, and until recently I didn't know much about the world. About existence. Whereas he's one of the first in his class; he'll get his baccalaureate. So, you understand, he thinks he's someone. I'm not cut out to be a father . . . Not Théo's father, at any rate."

"You ought to go and tell Mme. Marcel."

Etienne stood up. That was when he saw Théo. The latter, his hands in his pockets and his hat on the back of his head, had just sat down in the next café. He looked contemptuous and bored; he opened a book and started pretending to read. A few seconds later, Etienne was sitting down in front of him.

"So this is where you are," he said.

Théo, prodigiously astonished:

"Yes, this is where I am."

"What got into you?"

"How did you know I was here?"

"What are you doing here?"

"Is my mother here?"

"Why did you go away?"

"I wonder how you managed to find me."

The conversation continued on this note for some time. Théo took advantage of it to make up a tale, for his parents' benefit, about his new escapade.

Pierre, who was beginning to get bored, went and joined them.

"Are you coming to lunch?"

"Le Grand, this is my son Théo. Monsieur Le Grand."

"Pleaseder meecher, M'sieu," said Théo, who had some notion of Politeness.

"I'll go and tell Alberte right away," exclaimed Etienne.

Pierre and Théo were left tête-à-tête. They didn't exchange any interesting remarks.

---

If I ignore the practical side of a manufactured article," said Etienne.

"Then you're involved in aesthetics," interrupted Pierre. "Or magic."

"But I don't want to have anything to do with aesthetics, or magic," Etienne protested. "Men think they're making one thing, and then they make another. They think they're making a pair of scissors, but what they actually make is something else. Of course, it *is* a pair of scissors, it's made to cut and it does cut, but it's something quite different as well."

"Why scissors?"

"Or any other manufactured article, any manufactured article. Even a table. A house. It's a house, because people live in it, but it's something else as well. That isn't aesthetics, because it isn't a question of beautiful or ugly. And as for magic, I don't understand it."

"What *would* be interesting, would be to say what that 'something else' is."

"No doubt. But it's not possible. It all depends on the circumstances, or else you can't put it into words. Words are manufactured articles, too. You can think of them independently of their meaning."

Etienne had just discovered that, as he was saying it. He repeated it to himself, and was pleased with himself. Now *that* was an idea.

"Apart from their meaning, they can say something quite different. For example, the word 'teapot' indicates *that article,* but I can consider it apart from that meaning, in the same way as the teapot itself, I can consider it apart from its practical sense, which is—to be used for making tea, or even as a simple receptacle."

"Have you been thinking about these questions for long?" asked Pierre.

"Oh no," replied Etienne, "I'm inventing them as I go along. I talk, and it means something. For me, at least; I suppose so, at least. Does what I say mean anything to you?"

Pierre nodded his head several times; he meant by this: yes.

"And things that are natural, and consequently don't have any meaning, would you attribute one to them?"

"I haven't thought about that yet. But why *consequently?*"

"No doubt. Do you think that birds and stones and stars and shellfish and clouds have a meaning? That they were manufactured for some purpose?"

"I don't think so," replied Etienne, "though I haven't studied the question in any detail. In any case, natural things can acquire a meaning; when men give them one."

During the ensuing silence, both men moved a few steps forward, for they were walking.

"That's what so odd," murmured Etienne: "you think you're doing this, and then you do that. You think you're seeing this, and you see that. Someone says something to you, you hear something different, and it's a third thing you should have understood, All the time, everwhere, it's like that."

"For me, too," said Pierre, "things, the world doesn't have the meaning it attributes to itself, it isn't what it claims to be; but I don't think it has a different meaning. It has no meaning."

"Is that what you think?" asked Etienne, "What *I* was saying was: you think you're seeing one thing, and you're seeing another."

"And what *I* say is—you think you're seeing something, but you aren't seeing anything. And you know," added Pierre, "I don't so very much like what I've just been saying. I don't often express myself in metaphysical terms."

"What metaphysical terms? I don't know any," Etienne objected.

"Maybe, but that's what it is."

"What?"

"Metaphysics."

"Really? Well, it's about time," replied Etienne.

Pierre, disconcerted, kicked at some stones. They passed (the two men, not the stones; the stones didn't pass, they *were* passed) by a group of young gentlemen and young ladies, very young gentlemanlike and young ladylike, who were singing the latest hit.

"That stupid tune again," sighed Pierre. "What idiots."

"*They* don't think they're what they are, either," remarked Etienne, "for," he added, "you think you're this, and you are something else, not counting what you appear to be."

"Who do you think you are?"

"A man who thinks," replied Etienne. "That's what's odd, because I'm certainly *something else*. As for what I appear to be, you ought to know that better than I do. Weren't you observing me? Don't deny it. Narcense told me. What am I like? What was I like?"

"At first," Pierre began, "you were only a silhouette."

"Is that all?"

"At first, you were only a silhouette; you went from the bank to the metro and from the metro to the bank; that was when I noticed you. One day, you made a detour, and you became a flat entity. But perhaps you yourself have never seen such individuals; my description is probably becoming obscure."

"Please go on," said Etienne, politely.

"This transformation, needless to tell you, increased the interest I already had in you. One day, I was sitting opposite you, in a train; I saw you slightly swelling. You'd just acquired a certain consistency; but personally, I was unaware of the cause. When my taxi bumped into you, you were still in the same state. But when I saw you again, in the restaurant, as you no doubt remember, you looked as you still look; like a man, and one who thinks."

"So that's what you saw."

Etienne pensively examined a piece of orange peel, then, raising his eyes, saw—not without amazement, at that—someone he knew.

"Excuse me," he said, speaking to his companion.

And, taking a few steps:

"I am surprised and pleased" (that was the formula he used) "to meet you here."

Mme. Pigeonnier nearly fainted; Catherine, who was with her, supported her with her arm and encouraged her by pinching her energetically.

"Meussieu Marcel," sighed the lady, "how nice to see you!"

And the polite remarks were let loose, while Etienne couldn't manage to understand the remarkable emotion the sight of him had provoked in his neighbor from Obonne. Who, in any case, gradually recovered her composure, and it was with the greatest *sang-froid* that she asked for news of "your big son." They arranged to meet again.

---

A few steps farther on, Pierre asked what Théo had said about his escapade.

"He claims he doesn't remember what he did," said Etienne. "I don't believe a word of it; it's a facile excuse, but I don't understand what made him come here."

"Didn't he say anything else?"

"No. He says he woke up here. I asked him whether he remembered writing a post card; he said he didn't. Then I mentioned the one Narcense received. He looked very astonished. I think he's a great hypocrite. But Alberte—that's my wife—is so happy to see him again. She's coming back to life. He simply doesn't care, I'm afraid. Shall we call each other *tu*? Though really, I hardly know you. All I know is your name. Nothing else. What do you do? Where do you live? I've no idea. You don't seem to belong anywhere, or to anyone. Have you parents? friends? mistresses? a wife? children? Are you a poet or a financier? a journalist, an engineer?

Etienne stopped talking; but Pierre didn't answer him.

"Look, the fishermen are going to spend the night at sea. All the boats are leaving the harbor."

"I simply wanted to say: who are you?"

Pierre stopped for a moment, silently watching the fishing fleet putting out to sea.

"I apologize for my curiosity," said Etienne.

"Not at all, not at all," said Pierre. "You probably think I don't answer your questions very frankly. That's not so. But where shall I begin? Have I any children? no; a wife? no; any mistresses? not at the moment. A father? no. A mother? yes, with whom I live. And I have a brother, too. Look, they've all gone. They won't be back until morning . . ."

They were near the harbor, now; phonographs and radios were bawling; people were enjoying themselves like anything, because not a minute of liberty must be spoiled. Behind one wasted moment there were eleven months of worries, anxieties or servitude. This resort was almost entirely frequented by clerks or petty officials; everyone felt at home; many met there every year. A few shopkeepers from the nearby big town came there to spend the week end with their women, they shocked the population and drank American drinks; they were having a good time, eh. Apart from them, almost everyone was extremely respectable, and the extramarital affairs could be counted on the fingers of one hand. The swimming instructor had hairy legs; you were forbidden to urinate against the wall of the school; in the evening, after 10 o'clock, you were requested to respect your neighbor's sleep; you had to ring once for a waiter and twice for the chambermaid, and it was always the other one who came, which in any case wasn't the slightest importance. Et cetera. Et cetera.

"That's enough small talk," said Etienne. "What about your brother?"

"I'm going to see him tomorrow. I shall stay with him for a few days. It's not far from here."

"I had a brother," said Etienne, "two years older than me. He taught me to make cages for flies, and to draw tankers. I don't know why, but he didn't like those boats; I don't think he'd ever seen one; in shape, they looked like any other boat, but my brother decreed that they were tankers. He died of Spanish flu, in 1919."

"Mine is a professor of mathematics."

"Ah," said Etienne. "Younger?"

"Two years older," replied Pierre.

"It's odd," Etienne went on, "that lady we saw just now, she lives near me, in Obonne."

"The girl with her was charming," Pierre observed.

"Yes, she is. I know her, anyway. Isn't it funny. Just think, she's the maid, Catherine."

"They look more like two friends."

"Odd."

"And Théo, does he know Catherine?" Pierre insinuated, malevolently.

Etienne pretended to be deaf. The remark displeased him, but he admitted to himself that it was idiotic not to have thought of it sooner. And how had Théo got the necessary money for the journey? He hadn't thought to ask him, and, after all, what importance could it possibly have? He was beginning to find these paternal worries singularly disagreeable. And any minute now, meeting of Théo, Alberte and Mme. Pigeonnier; and perhaps even Catherine. Feeling aggressive, he preferred to turn on Pierre.

"And Narcense, do you know him well?"

"A little; a charming young man."

"Oho, a charming young man; that's too much. I do find him a little odd, though."

"Oh yes, I was forgetting. Has he said anything to you about me?"

"Yes," said Etienne simply, "we talked about you a lot."

They had come to the harbor. Alberte and Théo were waiting for them.

That young man was drinking a lemon squash in silence; his nose in his glass, he was sucking at his straws, the second volume of *Les Misérables* was lying in some sugar and soda water. The two men finally found some chairs and sat down. A few superficial remarks were exchanged; these ready-made utterances killed time for a few minutes.

There was much animation around the Marcel family's table. The café tables had invaded the harbor; the Paris papers had just arrived, alcohol filled the glasses, and ash the saucers. Phonographs and radios were screeching. Taking advantage of a lull, Etienne told them whom he had met, and watched Théo; but Théo was sucking at his straws, and didn't blench.

---

A huge car stopped; its occupants got out; they weren't the usual sort of visitors to X. . . . They ought instead to be going to Y . . . , the fashionable resort thirty miles farther on.

Pierre, who had recognized Shibboleth, hurried over to him.

Shibboleth was driving four women to Y . . . to enhance the luster of his night club; two of them were going to do a dancing act, the only merit of the others was to sleep with him. He was fond of haremizing. The gang sat down with a good deal of commotion; the harbor kids came up to study the great big bus; Shibboleth, who was sporting a pink sweater and riding breeches with small checks, did a few exercises to restore the circulation in his legs. In short, it was a sensational entrance.

"Le Grand. It caaaaaaaan't be. What are you doing here, my dear fellow? Having a real vacation? No, you live here? Ah, I must introduce my women; Oréa and Koukla, Oriental dancers; Camille, who used to be the mistress of a poet, and little Oque. Ah! sit down and have a drink. What'll you have? Hey waiter, we've been waiting five minutes. D'you think we've got time to waste? You don't move very fast. Send us a couple of picon-cassis and four red ports. And no garbage, eh.

Yiy-yi! what a hole, what a hole. Just look at the mugs of those wage slaves. You can smell the bureaucrat a mile off. A family resort. Yiy-yi-yi, and what families! And these pure young ladies, oh mother, no doubt they sneak up to the top of the cliffs in the evenings and get tickled by future tax collectors. So you're vegetating here, eh? What a trip, though. Have you seen my new car? I'm very pleased with it, you know. I left Paris this morning, and I'll be in my dump by 8. It goes like a treat, a car like that. What about you, do you still have the same one, the eight-cylinder one with a supercharger? Of course, it isn't bad. What's your gas consumption like? I don't get more than nine or ten out of mine, but I do up to ninety-five on the straight. Hey, Koukla, stop making eyes at that choirboy in his Sunday best. Waiter, oh waiter, do you really think that anyone can drink picon without ice? Think again. Nothing more necessary, and transparent ice, eh? This is a moron's paradise, my poor Le Grand. And they're Parisians, too. No really, just look at that fellow with a face like a tadpole, sucking his lemonade! and their clothes are all two years out of date, at that. It'd make me sick if I had to stay in a dump like this. By the way, did you know that Ted and Léon are cruising with the de la Sentines on their yacht; the last time they got smashed, it was at my place a week ago. Claude Poupou is in Norway and Odéric Sauleil in the Tyrol. In short, there's absolutely no one who's anyone left in Paris. How's your brother, all right? Still the great highbrow? They can't even manage to serve a picon-cassis. Well, Oque, is their port good? After all, there's nothing you can do about it, you have to put up with what you get when you're traveling. Did you read Paul Tontaine's last book? He didn't put himself out all that much. My champagne doesn't seem to inspire him. Did you see that little thing over there, the one in green, she isn't bad, but just look at her getup. By the way, you haven't told me what you're doing here. Then you really are spending your vacation in this cheap little hole? Are you trying to start a new fashion? But you'll ruin me, my friend. You'll ruin me. Well, children, feeling better? Another round? What about you, are you going to have another? Waiter! Waiter! He's always miles away, this waiter. Ah, there you are, well, the same again.

What, you've forgotten already? Four ports and two picon-cassis! Yi-yiy-yiy, what a barbarian. Oréa and Koukla are going to do an Oriental dance number. You must come and see it. Very original. A great novelty. Beats the Negro dancers to a frazzle. Hm. Apart from them, I've got a new jazz band, it's terrific. You must come and hear it. Not like this foul music, listen to it! No but really, listen to it! and these people drinking in these ancient old tunes. Yiy-yi-yi, poor France. Look at the way those brats are ogling my women; they're vicious, these kids; and they're only babies, pinch their noses and milk would come out. And you know, at Y . . . I've got my regular customers, the Prince of Wales, the Aga Khan, the Trouvadja of Bizère and the Duke of Sentinel. People above all these depressions, my boy. And who guarantee me a rich and respectable old age. For you, the first bottle of champagne will be on the house. You see, permanently openhanded, that's me. What's the time? Oh hell, a quarter to. I must go, I must fly. Come on waiter, get moving. How much for all the swill? Six saucers at six and four at three. You're just giving it away, not like at my place. And keep the tip. Come on, girls, get going. Well, my friend, don't vegetate too much here. It'd be bad for your health. No but really, just look at that car. What a line, eh, what a line! A classic beauty, and does she go! Yiy-yi-yi! how she goes! And your first bottle of champagne on the house, eh! Come on, kids, don't squabble, it's Camille's turn to be in front. And my regards to your brother. There's another one who won't make my fortune. By the way, young Lanlalaire, he just killed himself. A bad business. Well, girls, fairtish? Oak, eh. 'Bye, my friend, enjoy yourself, but don't stay here too long, it'd be bad for your health, just a friendly word of warning. Don't forget to come and see me."

The engine started to turn over, in silence.

"By the way, Shibboleth, you wouldn't have a job for a saxophonist at the moment, would you?

"For a saxophonist? But my friend, I'm positively giving them away, saxophonists and drummers, the whole bunch. It's raining saxophonists, positively raining them. Nice to see you. 'Bye! Your first bottle of champagne on the house!"

The car drives off amid general admiration; something of

the Grandiose is left floating in the Atmosphere. Pierre goes and sits down again at the Marcel family's table.

---

"Did your parents believe what you told them?"

"Yes, or else they pretended to. Which comes to the same thing, for me."

"Now that your father's seen me, haven't they changed their minds?"

"How should I know? They haven't said anything to me. If they leave me in peace, that's all I ask. We're here on vacation, aren't we? They've turned up—just too bad!"

"You oughtn't have written to that Meussieu Narcense."

"How could I have known?"

"And the young man that's always with your father, who is he?"

"He's gone off to see his brother at Z . . . , today."

"And who is he?"

"He's in business, so Dad says."

"What sort of business?"

"Howshd I know?"

"It he a friend of your father's?"

"Yes, he juss can't do without him any more, doesn't talk of anything but him, an' what he says. It's getting monotonous."

"But how did they get to know each other?"

"His taxi knocked my father down outside the Gare du Nord. He was inside. That's how they got to know each other. He drove them here in his car. What business is it of his, the snooper!"

Théo was walking up and down in the room, trying to look important, furious and fuming. Secretly, he was pleased that his escape had finished so well. The journey with Mme. Pigeonnier and Catherine had scared him stiff; his flight had filled him with anxieties and fears. Now that everything had turned out for the best, he was sorting out his feelings and keeping only the most high-flown—the taste for risk and adventure, the awareness of responsibility, the virile decision and the scorn for the common opinion. He had thus attained ethical heights of which, up to now, he had not even had the slightest suspicion. He was walking in the clouds, and breathing the pure air of heroism.

Mme. Pigeonnier, on the other hand, had flown from Obonne in a spirit of absolute unconcern; she considered this adventure the best she'd ever had. She was still radiant with joy, she was beginning to get worried now. She multiplied her anxieties. Wouldn't the Marcels discover all, simply by using their reasoning powers? For how could they not see some connection between her presence here and Théo's flight. And should she not also fear that some mischief-maker would reveal all to his parents? Or that Théo would give himself away in the course of conversation? or that she would? Didn't the law punish her act as a crime? She could already imagine herself up before the judges, or even with a public hue and cry after her. And so, lying on her bed, she was tormenting herself in multifarious ways, while Théo, standing at the window, was lighting a cigarette and looking Life in the face.

There's a knock at the door; it was Catherine. She came in apologizing for disturbing them and, sitting down on Mme. Pigeonnier's bed, at her feet, started telling them the various things that had been happening among them that, early that afternoon, a young man had accosted her, and that the said young man was Meussieu Marcel's friend. He had tried, so she said, to "worm" various things out of her, but she'd "played the innocent," and he hadn't found anything out. But he certainly suspects something: he looks very bright, that young man.

"And he's such a gentleman, Madame."

Catherine went into ecstasies over various sartorial details that had struck her and described the elegance of his speech and the distinction of his gestures, then she went on to say that he had paid her a lot of compliments, that he'd told her that he had something to do with the movies, that he'd find her a part in a film, and that she would certainly become a star.

"Must be crazy to believe such whoppers," opined Théo.

The two women didn't answer him.

"He's gone off to visit some property he's got at Z . . .

today," Catherine went on. "He made a date with me for when he comes back."

Théo shrugged his shoulders and began turning over the pages of *The Three Musketeers,* Mme. Pigeonnier's favorite reading. While Catherine was starting to tell them about her flirtation with Alexis Considérable, the son of the Mayor of X . . . , Théo was pondering the subject of a poem; a man loves a woman in silence; she either loves someone else or despises him; he doesn't dare declare his love; he writes a sonnet to describe all this; the woman who has inspired it reads it, but she doesn't understand that it's about her. There. He'd just found the first line: *Mon âme a son mystère, ma vie a son secret,* but, counting on his fingers, he discovered that his alexandrine was walking on thirteen feet; he tried to think of a synonym for *mystère, Enigme,* no, *Cacher,* all right; but the corresponding noun? *Se taire,* not bad. *Mon âme se tait,* no. It didn't work. Once again, he counted on his fingers the number of feet in: *Mon âme a son mystère, ma vie a son secret.* There really were thirteen.* Mme. Pigeonnier asked him:

"What are you counting like that?"

"How many days we've got left in this moldy hole," he growled.

---

Then Etienne experienced the power of boredom.

After two days. Pierre had gone; he had to go, he said, and see his brother, not far from there; some friends were expecting him in Y . . . , too; in short, mundane and family obligations caused him to disappear. So they gave themselves up, without reserve, to the pleasures of X. . . .

Going for a dip, walking on the cliffs, meals, fishing(?) made up the daily routine. They got to know the lady from Obonne better; she taught them to play (here the name of a game in fashion three years previously). They renewed their other acquaintanceships; Théo was allowed to go out with Sensitif junior and young Nécessaire, but not with that girl Catherine, who lost no time in getting herself talked about in the neighborhood because she was carrying on a flirtation, so they said, with Alexis Considérable. In the evenings, there was an open-air jazz band, and they danced by lantern light. Sensitif junior asked Alberte to dance; but he didn't dare show her the poems he'd written for her. Young Nécessaire was absorbed in the contemplation of Mlle. Considérable, the mayor's daughter, and a distant star. Théo didn't have any success with the first line of his sonnet, worked wonders of imagination and diplomacy to meet Mme. Pigeonnier, and read *The Three Musketeers* in secret. All this totally escaped Etienne, who only seemed interested in ridiculous details, and went down more and more in the estimation of his son by marriage.

Alberte took the pleasure in this vacation which there was to be taken by a person who throughout the year worked, either bureaucratically or domestically, ten to fifteen hours a day. She was touched by Sensitif junior's homage, and charmed by Mme. Pigeonnier's friendship. The fine weather continued uninterrupted.

After a week, Etienne suddenly realized that he was terribly, totally and irremediably bored. He discovered this while he was lacing up his shoelaces. These shoes were white and beige, and most impressive. He was putting them on to go and meet the ladies and the young things down at the harbor. He had just been shrimping with two young employees of the C.N.A. who were highly skilled at it, and he was now changing. For when he went shrimping, he obviously didn't wear his beautiful white-and-beige shoes any more than he wore his trousers with the vertical crease. He was dressing for dinner, then (even though he wasn't wearing a dinner jacket), and lacing his shoelaces.

The sea was beautiful, the sun was lovely, the earth was beautiful, the sky was lovely, the beach was beautiful, the harbor was lovely, the town was beautiful, the country was lovely, the atmosphere was beautiful and the air was lovely.

The room was on the second floor; the window of this room opened onto the roofs; if you leaned out to the right, you could see the vasty deep (the briny element, you might call it).

In the dining room, they were starting to set the tables. The doctor had not notified them of any contagious diseases in the area belonging to the commune; the hens wouldn't have to fear the staggers, the pigs swine fever, the turkeys the pip, the cows mammitis, the dogs rabies or the horses glanders.

The barber's wife had just auspiciously given birth to a viable teratological phenomenon capable of being shown in public and bringing in some cash.

Youths and girls, adults and old people, children and the maids of the same, fishermen and lighthouse keepers, swimming instructors and waiters, big and little short and long, aphonic and stentorian, Catholic and Orthodox, trepanned and legless, country people and peasants, vacationers and summer visitors, they all, all, breathed in the perfume of quietude with the lungs of happiness.

The hour—sweet.

While lacing his shoelaces, he realized this; not that the hour—sweet; not that the ones and the others were breathing in the perfume of happiness with the lungs of quietude; not that the mewing monster represented a fortune for the poor barber; not that animals and men had nothing to fear from the microbial tribe (!); not that the forks and knives were being artistically arranged on quasi-clean tablecloths, not that if he leaned out of the window he could see, over on the right, a fragment of green enamel which he would know was the sea. No, no and no again.

He realized that he was bored; terribly, totally and irremediably. He had finished lacing his right shoe; he sat there, shoehorn in hand, dreary-eyed, and the laces of his left shoe lay on the floor like snakes run over by a truck. He had said nothing against the world, for the world existed only in so diminished a form that it could scarcely be said to exist. A grey mist lay over everything. Who could want anything, then? Who could love, then? Who could suffer, then? Shoehorn in hand, Etienne contemplated, with a dreary eye, the laces lying on the ground like bits of macaroni under the table of a transalpine glutton.

Existence was losing all its value; things, all their meaning—and it wasn't only this existence that was present here and now that was losing all its value; it wasn't only these things here and now that were shedding all their meaning, but also the existence that was behind and above and over there, and everything that was elsewhere and beyond and everywhere. The universe was squeezed like a lemon, and no longer seemed to him to be anything other than a despicable, unattractive piece of peel, like an infinitely thin skin to which he couldn't (didn't want to, or didn't know how to) adhere.

At the same time as the world, he himself lost all value and meaning. He was dissolving, becoming obliterated, being annulled. He could no longer distinguish himself from the uniform fog that was absorbing everything. He threw the shoehorn on the bed and finished lacing up his shoes. Then, with his elbows on his knees, his head in his hands, he yawned. Perhaps he was hungry.

He got up slowly and, when he was on his feet, stood still. His arms reached a jacket; before he put it on, he took a few steps up and down. He noticed some dust on the mantlepiece; with his finger, he traced a few ornamental patterns in it. In the distance, he could hear the phonographs and radios in the harbor. He looked at what he had just drawn, but he felt no interest in it; the tip of his finger was now black with filth, he ran some water on it and wiped it. He put on his jacket. Then he yawned at the copper balls on the bed. He made as if to hold his hand out toward one of these balls, but immediately checked the movement. He had very vaguely felt like unscrewing it. He sat down again, without good reason, and counted how much money he had to last out the vacation. He looked at the time, and immediately forgot it.

He formulated his state in vulgar terms: "I'm so goddamn bored today," he murmured. Then he made up his mind, and cast a last glance at the designs traced in the dust. As he shut the door behind him, he yawned. Perhaps he was hungry.

In the hall, he passed various faces he more or less knew. He admitted their existence, but not their interest; they appeared to him as abstraction of no value, and not as living people near him. At the door, the proprietress greeted him, using his name; he replied in symmetrical fashion. In the street, people were nonchalantly walking up and down; the shopkeepers were emerging from their obscure lairs; a newsman was hawking the Paris papers. Everyone was agreed in acknowledging that the weather was superb.

---

Bang, bang, bang, bang, bang, bang! Six revolver shots.

Who has fired these revolver shots? We don't know yet. What's going on, then? Quick! Let's go and see. We run. We're going to see.

Horrors! There lies on the ground the corpse of a young man, almost a child.

Isn't he hideous, though. But that doesn't matter much, for he is dead. Hats off! The corpse is weltering in blood, in a lot of blood, in barrels of blood.

Could it be suicide? Some despairing young man? A disappointed love? A question of honor? Ah, but no! It is not suicide, it is murder!

Terror! Atrocity! Who, then, with cruel and bloody hand, could have . . . et cetera, this young man? almost a child?

Who then? There he is! there she is, rather. For it is a female felon.

People are throwing themselves on her, they are disarming her, they are shouting and yelling! Oh! Oh! that such a quiet little seaside town for Paris tourists should be agitated, upset, congested by such a petrifactive crime. The customers will fly away and flee this apprehensive place, like little birdies abandoning our so-called temperate regions at the approach of the rigors of the cold winter. But tell me, if you please, who are the two protagonists of this seaside drama? This young man is named and is called Théo Marcel! That woman sells toys—and in particular that toy which is named the cup-and-ball!

Oho! here's something out of the ordinary. But how could this honorable tradeswoman commit such a heinous crime?

Well! lend me your ears, and I will pour into them the bitter essence of this long and distressing story.

Not long after the death of Julius Caesar, the Gallic chieftain Péponas emigrated with his whole family to a more hospitable land, for in Arvernia, that year, the chestnut harvest was extremely poor.

While telling himself the tale of this comforting murder, Narcense is slowly absorbing the ham sandwich which will comprise his one and only meal of the day. His situation is daily becoming more critical; he has nothing left to pawn; he neither dares, nor wishes to touch Saturnin for any more; he despairs of hearing from Pierre and Shibboleth. He has thought of subletting the apartment his uncle gives him, but he can't find any takers; and his uncle, whose stupidity and ferocity increase with age, has merely offered him a ten-franc note which he has preferred to refuse with a disdainful air. And here he is, this August Sunday, sitting in front of a small glass of beer and a ham sandwich. After which, he will still have two francs left. And what of tomorrow? So he goes on telling himself stories.

Well then, the Gallic chieftain Péponas, deeply grieved by the poor harvest, emigrated with his family to a more hospitable region; after having wandered aimlessly for some time, he came to the shores of Lake Aral and settled there. He dealt in pawns, a trade that was not at all tiring and fairly lucrative. Unfortunately, an invasion of lancinating spinning-tops obliged him to move on, and he, and all his family, fled by bicycle to a more hospitable region. N.B.: He had just invented the bicycle when the invasion occurred, and this invention had been forced on him by the necessity of cutting four-wheeled carts longitudinally in two when he wanted to go down certain narrow paths. In any case, the chieftain Péponas was a highly educated young man; he spoke the Gallic tongue to perfection and could count up to two thirds; when they got to Trebizond, he and his family had a breathing spell; it was then that the cup-and-ball was invented. The cup-and-ball immediately enjoyed an unparalleled vogue both in the Mediterranean world and in the Extreme Orient, an incomprehensible vogue, at that, for Péponas had omitted to give directions for the use of this singular object. In general, it was recognized as a weapon of economic cast, since it returned its projectile to its sender; in short, a perfected version of the boomerang; it was through replacing this archaic weapon by the new invention that Alexander the Great made the Macedonian phalanx the invincible instrument of his great and well-known ambition. Péponas junior—for the father, full of years and honors, had departed this life—was decorated, pensioned, beatified, statufied and embalmed.

From generation to generation, the Péponases continued the manufacture of the cup-and-ball, to such effect that, throughout the Middle Ages, there was a proverbial saying (Ah! the good old days): there are no cups-and-balls like those from Trebizond.

In 1453, the genius of Christopher Columbus discovered a way of considerably improving the cup-and-ball; abandoning the projectile to its flight, he abolished the string; the weapons became more costly (since its entailed a new projectile each time), but certainly more efficient. Then, taking his inspiration from the ordinary hen's egg, he replaced the wooden ball by a very fragile sphere filled with an evil-smelling liquid; this modification necessitated another: removing the hole from the ball and putting it in the stick, thus turning the latter into a tube; the whole was mounted on two wheels and equipped with a spring with a knob to pull to provoke the expulsion. So Péponas's son, who had acquired the patent, started manufacturing cannons, and prodigiously multiplied their fortune. They were ruined and suppressed at the time of the Armenian massacres in 1912, and the sole survivor of this illustrious industrial family established herself at X . . . , a little port on the Atlantic coast; but she only made the old-fashioned type of cup-and-ball, having lost the secret of the type called "Columbus's egg." Twenty years later, a young man comes into her shop and says: "Madame, the obscene trade in which you are engaged is an insult to Christian youth." "Oh, Meussieu," says she, blushing. The young man goes away. He is Théo Marcel, a little cretin who goes bathing in the sea and indulges in practical jokes in bad taste. The next day, he comes back and says to the lady: "Madame, the obscene trade in which you are engaged is an insult to Christian youth." "Oh Meussieu," says she. The young man goes out.

Narcense, who has decided not to finish his story until he gets home, and who is still only halfway there, makes the adventure last for twenty-seven days.

On the twenty-seventh day, a young man comes in and says to the lady: "Madame, the obscene trade in which you are engaged is an insult to Christian youth." Mme. Péponas doesn't answer, but the moment she sees Théo going out of the door, she pulls out a revolver which she had hidden in her blouse and mercilessly slaughters the insolent clown. Justice is done, she cries, ha, ha, ha, ha! no longer will little humorists insult the senile industry created on the shores of the Black Sea by the Arvenian chieftain, Péponas, whose geneaology was even then lost in the night of time; so just imagine what it must be now. As for Théo, he is voiding his blood on the pavement.

"Hallo, Saturnin. Haven't you gone to the country this beautiful Sunday?"

"Oh, Meussieu Narcense, I muss tell you the latest about my sister. She's still got the idea that that young man from Obonne and his friend are gangsters she's got to be leery of; she found out, no idea how" (here Saturnin is just slightly embarrassed; very slightly) "that they've gone to X . . . for their holidays. And do you know what she's done? She's persuaded my brother to send his son there, to stay with a lady she knows, a midwife, to spy on 'em."

"Now that's very nasty," says Narcense.

"Don't you think she's becoming very alarming, my sister?"

"Mm, hm, Ida know, Ida know."

"Meussieu Narcense, you don't look very well."

"Too true; but what d'you suggest I should do?"

"If you'd let me, I might maybe help you a little."

"No thank you, Saturnin, no thank you."

"Bet you haven't had anything to eat today."

"What an idea, what an idea. By the way, am I still a gangster too?"

"Of course! There's no shaking her on that one."

"I hope, Saturnin, that you aren't spying on me on her behalf."

"Don't worry, I don't tell her anything. Zit true you've had summing to eat today? You look so pale."

"Saturnin, you're getting to be a damn bore. Good night."

Narcense is invited to Théo's funeral, he gets a big letter with a black border; your presence is requested, etc. He borrows some money from his concierge and goes off to X. . . . Etienne and Alberte are crying: he offers them his condolences. He can see the little room where the scene takes place. As for Mme. Péponas (mustn't forget her), she's been hung.

He opens the door and goes into his apartment.

Théo's funeral is going to be magnificent; the general has sent a squadron of hussars; a battleship is going to fire thirty-six cannon shots; the bishop *in partibus* of Pharmacopolis is going to come especially for the occasion; he's going to follow the cortege on horseback and the coffin-bearers will be soldiers. The children will be given lollipops, and every adult will be entitled to a lottery ticket.

Narcense undresses; he's going to bed; 8 o'clock, that's a good time when your stomach is cracking.

On the appointed day, everything goes smoothly; bishop on horseback, hussars, lollipops, etc. . . . Théo's tombstone has been temporarily made out of gasoline cans. In short, everyone expresses satisfaction. After the ceremony, a great banquet with the bishop, the hussars, the general, etc. On the menu: sheep's brains and pig's feet.

Narcense shivers; he changes the subject.

He is at the banquet, too, as are Etienne and Alberte; at a certain moment the latter gets up and disappears; without anyone noticing, he does the same; he looks for her. He finds her: she's stopped halfway up the stairs and is doing up her garter. The most beautiful leg. The most beautiful thigh. Narcense's mind starts wandering.

---

After two weeks, Pierre came back to X. . . . He was only passing through, because, he said, he had to go to Paris on important business. The Marcel family, to which were agglomerated Mme. Pigeonnnier, Sensitif junior and young Nécessaire, gave him a warm welcome; he amazed this little group with marvelous tales about the other resort, Y . . . , which was frequented by the Prince of Wales, the Aga Khan, the Trouvadja of Bizère and the Duke of Sentinel; where you could count yachts by the dozen, Rolls Royces by the hundred, and thousand-franc notes by the thousand. He also told them about his brother, the mathematician; he lived, so he said, in a little castle on the banks of a river which were overgrown by reeds; near it was a farm where, every morning, they drank fresh milk; then they rode through the fields and forests; the fruit was ripening, they were bringing in the harvest, and they would soon be picking the grapes. His brother was putting the finishing touches on a big article for *Acta Mathematicas,* in which he proved that the cardinality of the continuum is aleph one. An admiring silence followed this revelation. Young Nécessaire timidly alluded to Pythagoras and Henri Poincaré; Sensitif junior, much impressed, there and then conceived a poem about the square of the hypotenuse which is equal, if he is not mistaken, etc.;* Mme. Pigeonnier started to say something about Inaudi,* but Théo shut her up with an insolence that surprised the assembled company. Etienne wanted to know what the cardinality of the continuum was. But Pierre admitted that he had no idea. Later, the two of them went for a walk along the path leading to the cliffs.

"When you're back in Obonne, will you sometimes go to Blagny?" asked Pierre.

"Probably. I don't know why, but there's something in me that is attached to that horrible place, now. Because it is horrible, isn't it, that bistro?"

"Yes, it's a sinister place."

"And those people! the owner, Belhôtel, he seems to be a brute and a boor. And his sister, Mme. Cloche, seems to be a terrible virago."

"She doesn't only seem to be one," Le Grand corrected him, "she undoubtedly is one."

"It isn't because those people got mixed up in that strange incident at Les Mygales that I feel attached to that shanty. That's got nothing to do with it. To tell you the truth, it isn't

I who have become attached to the place, but the place that has become attached to me. It extends me, mysteriously."

"Do you remember," said Pierre, "that blue door the local junk dealer didn't want to sell us?"

"It's odd, eh," said Etienne, "I sometimes think of it. That door intrigues me terribly."

"And me too! I dream about it! I suspect it of being of uncommon value, I imagine it to be inestimable—and in particular, I'd like to see—the other side."

"That's it; that door ought to be opened."

"We'll go back there together," suggested Pierre, and Etienne agreed.

Pierre went on:

"What about Narcense, you don't know what's become of him?"

"Not at all. How would I? I'm not on any sort of terms with him. I know him far less than you do."

"How's that?"

"Listen, Le Grand, I'd like to speak frankly to you, and I'd like you to do the same. When, in the Langlumet restaurant, you pointed Narcense out to me as someone who was going to play a part in my life, you already knew him, didn't you? He told me so himself."

"And did he also tell you that it was I who drove him to Obonne wood, that evening?"

"He didn't tell me that," replied Etienne, profoundly astonished.

No, that he didn't know; he couldn't even have suspected it. This revelation upset him. He thought he knew, and he didn't know. He thought he understood, and he didn't understand. The world, like a game of hide-and-seek—again he had this vision. Was life a continual surprise, then? He had a coherent, definite memory of the night at Les Mygales, a global representation of which he had thought he could say: that's how it was—and yet there had been something missing in it, a vital intervention had remained hidden. Then Etienne began to doubt everything he thought he knew, everything he thought he understood, everything he thought he saw and heard. *Naturally,* Etienne doubted the world. The world was playing with him. There was a secret behind this fishing port, there was a mystery behind this cliff, behind that milestone, behind that cigarette butt.

"Yes," he said, "even a cigarette butt hides its own truth."

"What did you say?" said Pierre, who had just seen, on the road, coming toward them, Catherine, on the arm of Alexis Considérable.

"I was saying that even a cigarette butt, you don't know what it is. I don't know what it is! I don't know! I DON'T KNOW!" he shouted.

Catherine and Alexis turned around, surprised.

"Ah yes, that's the one who, you think, might have had something to do with Théo running away?"

"Oh, I have no theories," Pierre rejoined.

"It's possible, isn't it? Everything is possible. Do I know anything about Théo's flight? No, I don't know anything. There again, I don't know anything. Even Théo, perhaps you think I know who he is? Well, I don't. Théo? Who is he? It's very simple: I don't know anything about him. Even if I were to ask him, that wouldn't get me any further; obviously. Even if I were to think about him all my life, I wouldn't know in the end. And what about me, eh, who am I? I've already told you, I don't know who I am. And in any case, has that question any meaning? Does it mean anything, to demand like that: who am I? has it the slightest meaning? Who am I? But I'm Etienne Marcel, born in Besançon on the 23rd of May, 1905, clerk at the Audit Bank, living in Obonne, in an unfinished house, et cetera, et cetera. I have such and such a character, I have such and such feelings, I live in such and such a way. The psychologists ought to be able to analyze me, oughn't they? And after all that, I'm still asking who I am! But that's what I am! and in spite of everything, I can still persist in asking this sempiternal question. It torments me; that's stupid, isn't it? And that's not the whole of it. This question—has it, in itself, any meaning? has the verb *to be* any meaning?"

"You've made great progress in metaphysics," said Pierre.

They had got to the top of the cliff; that was the end of their walk; they went down to the town again.

---

*Saturday*

Dear Aunt Sidonie,

I'm very grateful to you for having had me sent on vacation to the seaside, and I like the sea very much. If you hadn't told Dad, I'm sure I wouldn't have come to the sea this year, because Dad makes out that business is bad, but you know as well as I do that that's because he doesn't want to part with his cash. So there it is, dear Aunt Sidonie, I've settled down with Mme. Corcoran, she's very nice to me, my room is a little attic where it's very hot during the daytime, but that doesn't bother me because I'm never there then. I go out with my pals, we go shrimping and then we go bathing and then we go and climb the cliffs, in short, we enjoy ourselves. What I don't like, it's because we have fish every day, I don't like that because of the bones, but Mme. Corcoran, she says that teaches you to be patient, so she makes me eat it, but I don't like it.

It didn't take me a minute to recognize the Monsieur that you say is called Marcel. He's staying in a hotel with his wife and son who looks about the same age as him; no one says anything against them except about the son, people say things about him, but I'm too young to understand them. They spend all their time with a lady that they call Mme. Pigeonnier and a couple of gigolos who look a bit dopey and who call themselves students. In short, they all seem to be respectable sort of people and they do the same as everyone else; they go bathing, they play tennis and all that, and there's nothing you can say about them.

That's why, dear Aunt Sidonie, I haven't written to you, because I didn't have anything to say. But yesterday there was something new: the fair-haired young man with the sports car, the one that's called Le Grand, he arrived and started telling heaps and heaps of stories. And after that, the two of them went for a walk on the cliffs; I followed them, and I heard everything they said. Le Grand asked Marcel whether he remembered the door? And then the other one replied that there was a fortune behind it and that he wouldn't forget it so easily as all that. Then Le Grand said that they had to get hold of the fortune, and for that the door would have to be opened. Marcel replied that they'd get hold of the fortune that's behind old Taupe's door and that nobody would stop them. Then Le Grand said that old Ma Cloche, that's what he said, if she started interfering, she'd have him to deal with, and the other man added: She'd better look out. After that they said that they'd go to America and have a good time there on old Taupe's money, they'd buy a big house with tons of servants, and cars, and a swimming pool, like in the movies, and they'd invite all the gangster friends they know there.

There, dear Aunt Sidonie, that's what I heard that day, that's to say yesterday. So you see how careful you've got to be with these people that's such terrible gangsters. I'd like to know whether the date of Ernestine's marriage is fixed, becaues I'd certainly like to be there; there's sure to be some fun. I like it very much here where I am, but I wouldn't like to miss Ernestine's wedding. So, if you know about it, see that I come back so's I can be there.

Very soon, dear Aunt Sidonie, you'll be able to stand me the trip around the world you promised me. Aren't I just pleased, to say the least.

With love,
your nephew,
Clovis Belhôtel.

*Sunday evening*

Dear Aunt Sidonie,

I'm writing in haste to tell you that a lot of things have happened here since the last time. Yesterday evening, Saturday, an extraordinary sort of man arrived and started by doing lots of peculiar things. In the café, he drank five or six aperitifs: when Marcel and Le Grand arrived he went and said hello to them, and they looked very surprised. Then he sat down with them and drank another aperitif; he was completely boozed. Then he wanted to fight the one that's called Le Grand, but they calmed him down, only when the Marcel kid turned up he started yelling and breaking glasses and saying a lot of things you couldn't make head nor tail of. It was a terrific scandal. People were scared; in the end they shut him up in a room where he wrecked everything. Naturally, you can imagine the commotion it caused around here. Everyone was talking about it. People were asking who the man was, but no one knows anything about him, not even his name. This morning, at about 7 in the morning, Le Grand came to fetch him in his car and took him away, I don't know where. We haven't seen them since. In any case, the Marcels seem very fed up on account of the scandal, because every one looks at them now. It's attracted attention to them, so they aren't pleased.

If I find anything else out I'll write to you; in any case, don't forget me for Ernestine's wedding. I'm always thinking, dear Aunt Sidonie, about the beautiful trip your promised me.

With love from,
Your nephew,
Clovis Belhôtel.

Pose crypt: the nut's called Narcense; he was accusing Le Grand of having let him down, of promising and not keeping his word, etc. I got this from the page boy. So you can see that he's another member of their gang, and he's fed up, no one knows why, exactly.

Clovis.

*Tuesday*

MAXENCE SCAR FOREHEAD URGENT CLOCHE

*Tuesday*

YES SCAR CLOVIS

*Tuesday*

My poor child,

What you've just told me is terrible. This Narcense that you saw knows that I know that the others are getting ready to strike and he'll tell them and I'm only a weak woman, so's Ernestine, and you're only a child. Whan can we do against these three dangerous evildoers? Ernestine's wedding is on the 25th of August, your father will see that you're back for that day, don't worry unless in between time, you never know what may happen; in any case keep your trap shut in all directions and burn my letters. Be sure and write me everything you see, it's all very serious, but if I pull it off, think of the beautiful trip you'll go on.

Your affectionate aunt,
Sidonie Belhôtel
Widow Cloche

P.S. The two of them are certainly coming back to Paris.

*Thursday.*

Dear Aunt Sidonie,

Here's what's happened since last time. It's been raining a lot, which means that people haven't been out much, me neither. I've been playing backgammon with a pal. The tourists are fed up because it's raining.

There, my dear Aunt Sidonie, that's what been happening since last time. I'm looking forward to having a whale of a time at Ernestine's wedding.

Your affectionate nephew,
Clovis.

---

Sensitif junior was the first to arrive at the rendezvous; young Nécessaire was close on his heels, but they had to wait for Théo.

"Théo's always late," grumbles young Nécessaire, whose first name begins with the letter P.

Sensitif junior, awkward and virginal, nods his agreement, at the same time turning over the pages of a dilapidated little book covered with brown paper.

"What are you reading?" sighs P. Nécessaire.

Sensitif waits a couple of minutes and then answers:

*"The Song of Roland."*

Intimidated, the former dares to ask:

"Is it good?"

And Sensitif junior snaps his fingers admiringly. They say no more, and wait for Théo Marcel, who finally arrives. They can see by the way he looks that he knows more than he's going to tell them and that he's going to tell them more than he knows.

They rush up to him. To start with, they had despised him a little because he hadn't got his baccalaureate, but since he had discovered that they weren't students, but simply future members of the top class at school, they could no longer cash in on their title:

"Well? Well?"

Théo sits down, makes himself comfortable and, smiling:

"Huh, what a business!"

"Oh, tell us what happened?" implore ess and enn.

"I don't know whether I ought to tell you everything."

"Oh yes! Oh yes!"

"Well then, slike this."

"Ah! Ah!"

"That," Théo begins, then, "guy who came yesterday is called Narcense; he's the one I told you about that hung himself in the wood . . ."

"The one that had a thing on your mother?" asked P. Nécessaire.

"Yes."

Sensitif choked back his saliva with a nervous movement of his larynx.

"Well, that's the guy that arrived yesterday evening by the 6:20 train. He went straight to the *Café des Fleurs* and there, it seems, he drank five aperitifs. And then my father arrived with Le Grand. He got up and went over to say hello to them. They all three knew each other; they sat down together and Narcense ordered another drink. That time, it didn't do him any good. He started cursing Le Grand. Because, if you can imagine such a thing, he'd promised to find him a job, because he hasn't got one at the moment and he's at his rope's end, and then he hadn't done anything about it; so he was fed up."

"I don't understand very well," sighs Nécessaire.

"It's not complicated. Narcense is looking for a job and Le Grand was supposed to get him one; but he didn't find him one and Narcense thought he'd let him down . . . *Inde irae.*"

"Ah yes. And what does he do, Narcense?' '

"He plays jazz. Thought I'd already told you. So then he starts cursing Le Grand: "Yerra fraud! You take people ferra ride! You look down on people from the heights of your idleness, you promise and you don't keep your word! and what happens to me, while all this is going on? I just starve to death!' That's what he said, and Le Grand replied: 'But Shibboleth can't do anything for you.' Because Shibboleth, he's the guy who came through here bout two weeks ago with a huge car with terrific broads in it. He owns some bars and night clubs; he was the one Le Grand was supposed to talk to about Narcense so's he would strike it lucky. After five minutes, they were coming to blows. My father stopped them. And people were already starting to look at them, in the café. And just then, I turned up. Oh, when he saw me he jumped up and shouted: 'You filthy little swine.' But I went up to him, I didn't turn a hair, I said to him: 'Are you addressing your remarks to me, Meussieu?' "

"Go on, is that what you said?"

"Just like I told you."

"But why did he say you were a swine?"

"All that, that's because of the first business, the letters he wrote to my mother. Squite true that I was a little nasty to him, but that's no reason to try and kill me, like he already has once."

"He was boozed, eh?"

"Hang on. So then I said to him: 'Do you wishter speak to me, M'sieu?' And then he banged on the table, the glasses flew all over the place: 'I'm fed up,' he shouted, 'I'm fed up with all these swine that don't have any guts.' Yes, that's what he said, but it was Le Grand he meant when he said that. 'I'm fed up with all these swine that don't have any guts, and this kid that plays with me like a cat playing with a mouse. A kid. All these creatures who look on and never do a goddamn thing.' Yes, a kid, he dared call me."

"What's it all mean, what he was saying?" young Nécessaire interrupted again.

"Well, the guy's sick," explained Sensitif, emphatically.

"And then," added Théo, "you need to understand who Le Grand is. I finally found out. He's a rich guy who doesn't have anything to do and amuses himself watching other people live. Which means that Narcense, who's starving to death, he says so himself, and hasn't got a bean, he's had enough of this guy who's taking it easy acting the voyeur."

"Oh, a voyeur!" exclaimed young Nécessaire, inexplicably.

"How d'you know that about Le Grand?" questioned Edgard, the son of M. Sensitif senior.

"I realized it from what my father said. Because my father, from what I guessed, Pierre Le Grand was watching him too, doing all this and that; and he used to follow him in the street."

"No!" exclaims, incomprehensively, Paul N.

"Yes, that's how it was."

"I dont' know," insinuates Sensitif, "that's odd, a man that follows men, like that."

Théo laughs *(sic)*.

"You're getting ideas into your head. Pierre Le Grand, well, he just kidnapped a woman."

Nécessaire shuts his eyes and his ears tingle. Sensitif leans over:

"Who is she?" he vibrates.

"Oh but," Théo goes on, "I haven't finished yesterday's story yet. Everything in its proper place, eh? Well, I'd got to the point where Narcense was starting to break the glasses. People were afraid. The manager came up, you know, the bald one with the little beard. 'What d'you want with me?' shouts Narcense and he flings a glass in his face. Then the waiters jumped on him; Le Grand said to take him to a room upstairs. And there, it was as if he was delirious, a very thin man; he wrecked everything; his nose was bleeding and he was puking . . . It lasted a good half hour. After that, he looked as if he was dead. Then my father and Le Grand took him to the hotel. There he went to sleep. But that's not all. This morning, at 7 o'clock, Le Grand came and fetched him in his car and took him away, I don't know where. And what's more, in the car, there was a woman with him. Guess who?"

The others remain silent.

"Catherine."

"No?"

"No?"

"Yes, Catherine's his girl now."

"Well, that's a funny one."

Sensitif, giving a little cough, asks:

"What about your mother, what does she say about all this?"

"If anyone asks you, you must say you don't know anything about it," replies Théo, who likes historic words.

---

"Natch," went on Sidonie, "everyone's going to wonder why you're marrying ole Taupe that hasn't got a bean."

"Yes, that's a difficult one to essplain," Ernestine agreed.

"Gotta get our brain boxes working," declared Mme. Cloche. "It's ticularly for Dominique and his wife that we've got to find a likely essplanation."

"Strue," Ernestine once more agreed. "M'sieu Belhôtel, he's going to think it's peculiar. What'll we tell him?"

The two women fell silent. The sweat radiating over their skin, which was sprinkled with dust. The CHIPS shack was melting in the August sun. This was the time of day when they were manipulating the chloride and sulfuric acid in the factory with the blue windows. The two women were alone.

"And who's going to pay for the wedding breakfast?" questioned Mme. Cloche.

Ernestine didn't answer, but then hazarded:

"Old Taupe."

"No, he won't give anything away so long as we haven't taken anything."

"Well then?"

"Haven't you got any money saved up, Ernestine?"

Ernestine blushed.

"Yes, Madame Cloche, I've got a savings bank book."

"Well then, you'll pay for it. We'll have the wedding breakfast at Dominique's. We can pay him back later."

"That's right, Madame Cloche."

Two truck drivers came and interrupted this important confabulation. While Ernestine was serving the two dust-covered men a liter of white wine, which she embellished with a few piquant pleasantries destined to reawaken their eroticism, which might have been deadened by their exhausting work, Mme. Cloche, with one fist on her hip and the other supporting her chin, was putting her brain box to work. Her nephew's letters were not calculated to reassure her; Narcense's arrival at X . . . , the brawl that had followed it, his departure with Le Grand, all this boded no good. For it was quite clear that he'd come to demand his share of the loot, in exchange for giving them some information. And that information could only be about her own visit! What an absurd thing to do! And the very same day! when he'd shouted something at her from the train! that she hadn't understood! Ah, if only that idiot of an Ernestine had agreed right away! None of this would've happened. Stead of which, she'd had to try and play it *her* way; she'd wanted to bring it off on her own. But Ma Cloche was there. What an old fox, huh! she thought, referring to herself, and young Ernestine had after all had to agree to give her half Taupe's treasure. As for that one, he was obviously an old rogue; he agreed to everything; talmost looked zif he was letting himself be married on purpose. And not a sausage to be got out of him! Yes but, after the wedding, they'd soon see about getting his small change out of him. Funny thing was, he wasn't as old as all that after all: only sixty. He looks much much older. Natch, not a word to Ernestine about the new conspiracy that had got under way at X. . . . Mustn't scare the little thing. As it was, she wasn't feeling too happy about it. The most awkward thing was to get Dominique to accept her marriage to Taupe. After all, she was what you call his concubine, and he'd promised her all this and that when he'd got his brothel. So he wouldn't be very pleased. That was a nuisance. What were they going to tell him?

The two men had gone; Ernestine came and sat down with Mme. Cloche again.

"And who'll we invite to my wedding?" she asked.

"I've already thought about that," replied Sidonie. "There'll be me, natch; and then Dominique, Eulalie and Clovis; and then Saturnin and his missus. With the two of you, that makes eight. And then there'll be your relations. Who're they?"

"Vonly got two brothers; there's Themistocles, that's an N.C.O. in the Zouaves, and it just so happens he's on leave at the moment; and then Pierre, that's married. He's a magician, plays the music halls; he calls himself Peter Tom the Anchorite. I've got some cousins in the provinces, too, but they won't come."

"Then that makes three more, that makes eleven."

"And then my girl friend Suzy."

"That makes twelve."

"And ole Taupe, he's sure to invite the Pics."

So they'd be at least fifteen; apart from that, they couldn't find a valid reason to explain why Ernestine, young and almost pretty, and an ordinary waitress in a bistro, should marry a self-styled beggar.

"If we leave it like that, everyone'll say that it's because Dominique's got you pregnant," says old Cloche, "and the child's got to have a father."

Flies were fluttering around their brains.

"What the hell does it matter if they say that," exclaimed Ernestine, confidently.

"Yes, that's true, we don't care. Here, give me a cointreau, Ernestine."

Impelled by the effort of thought, Sidonie was scratching the table with the nail of her index finger, a familiar gesture.

Could they also say that Ernestine had developed a liking for the junk business? That old Taupe had won her heart? If the idiot didn't always claim to be so badly off, none of this would present any difficulty. But he was really lousy. And yet, after all, he *was* someone; everyone knew he'd been a gent and that he'd lost all his money in the Russian

Revolution. The most difficult is Dominique. How to get him to swallow it? This was going to cause more trouble, this business. She'd tell him 'at Ernestine had fallen for Taupe. That swot she'd tell him, her brother. She was perfectly entitled to get married to anyone she wanted to, wasn't she? And then, after all, Dominique, he'd be very pleased that it'd worked out like that for Ernestine. And Mme. Cloche was very pleased, too, that it should work out like that in her mind, because all this was making her feel tired. Whereupon, in came old Taupe.

"Hello, Madame Cloche, Hello, my little Titine," and he pinched her waist.

"Hands off, I tell you. Y'not to touch me till we're married."

"Isn't she naughty," said the sexagenarian. "I've just been to the town hall; it's all fixed. We're going to get married on the 25th of August."

"It's the 25th, then?"

He sat down, and didn't look as if he was thinking about anything much.

"I'll have a white wine," he declared automatically, moving his hand about in his pants pocket.

---

The beach was strewn with bodies without number, which were turning it from golden yellow to fly-black; there were some very little ones who cried without respite, and some very big ones who slept all the time. There were some who had breasts, and there were some who hadn't; there were some in bathing suits, and some with more clothes on; some were deformed, and some were formed; some were bulky, and some were transparent. The ensemble was not impressive. Sitting on a broad, flat stone, that he had chosen with care, Etienne was following with listless eye the reduced activity of his balneal colleagues. Some suddenly got up and went to have a dip, and then came back to snooze until it was time for the well-filled aperitif. Sometimes the women going by caught his eye: Etienne was thinking of Narcense, of that man who, tormented by love and poverty, behaved in such a strangely agitated fashion. He saw him again, hanging in the forest, and the sole of his shoe with a leaf stuck to it; he saw him again, struggling, being taken away by the waiters. And the correspondence with Théo, and the meeting in the Langlumet restaurant. He noticed Alberte with Mme. Pigeonnier; then young Sensitif waved to him with great elegance. The water was lovely today, the people around him were saying. Pierre and Narcense, who had been gone for two days, hadn't given any sign of life. Nor had Mme. Pigeonnier's maid, and this worried Mme. Pigeonnier. It didn't seem to affect Théo particularly. Odd, if what Pierre had insinuated was true? Then he wondered. "Why am I not Narcense?" and felt uneasy about the meaning of such a question.

He had been on his flat stone for about an hour, when a hand touched his shoulder. He followed it. It was Pierre, whose eyes were shining with excitement.

"Come somewhere quiet, I've so many things to tell you."

And in spite of his habitual calm, he was practically trembling. They went to the end of the little jetty and sat down. Pierre spoke:

"First piece of news: you and I are dangerous crooks; at the moment we're preparing a coup which ought to bring us a million: Mme. Cloche is also concerned with the same business and Narcense, another gangster, has refused to work with her. As she is suspicious of us, she has got her nephew to spy on us."

"I don't quite follow," said Etienne.

Then Pierre described in detail the Cloche-Narcense interview just as Narcense himself had recounted it to him.

"The strangest thing of all," he commented, "is that the old woman isn't mad, and that it really does seem that a million could be behind our machinations. But how we can *look as if* we are preparing the said swindle, that's something that seems very odd to me."

Etienne didn't say a word: the fact that, after having looked like a silhouette in Pierre's eyes, he should have become a gangster in those of Mme. Cloche, started him off on meditative paths such as his grey matter had never yet set its neurons on.

"It's obvious," continued Pierre, "that all her conjectures are based on your visits to Blagny. How could you expect that anybody as artful as Mme. Cloche seems to be could conceive of someone going to have a drink at her brother's just for the pleasure of it?"

"One day," said Etienne, "I gave Belhôtel a potato peeler; that must have seemed funny to them, too."

"And that business at Les Mygales, they know about that, don't they? With all these data, Mme. Cloche's effervescent brain has had something to work on, and so we've become dangerous gangsters. The transformation isn't particularly unpleasant, so long as that romantic midwife doesn't set the cops on our heels. Though it's true that, you and I, we're irreproachable from all points of view? isn't it?"

"Do we know?"

"Marcel, you're becoming skeptical; a dangerous obstacle to your meditation."

"It isn't being skeptical, to destroy error, and what graver error is there than to think you know what you don't know? Now, do I really know whether you aren't a thief and a murderer?"

Pierre didn't answer; even though he didn't find either of these hypotheses particularly unpleasant, as he said to himself in these words. Taking advantage of Etienne's silence, he went on:

"There's one way of finding out, and that is to find the little spy, Mme. Cloche's nephew."

"What for?" Etienne asked politely, just to look as if he were interested.

"It won't be difficult; he's staying with a midwife; there cant' be many, here. We'll easily find him."

"All right, let's try."

They discovered where Mme. Corcoran lived, without trouble; but that day the midwife was out visiting, and young Clovis must have been amusing himself somewhere, either down at the sea or in the country. The description they were given of him was too vague to rely on; he was due back about 7. While they were waiting, they walked up and down, talking of this and that. Etienne referred to Catherine's disappearance;

Pierre didn't hide from him the fact that she had become his mistress and that she was waiting for him at Z . . . , at his brother's, as was Narcense himself. It was then that Pierre realized sadly that he couldn't parade all Catherine's revelations; he was always forgetting that this young man had to keep up the appearance of being a paterfamilias. Another thing he wouldn't have been able to do.

At about 7 o'clock, a few steps away from Mme. Corcoran's house, they saw a child of thirteen or fourteen who looked like Clovis to them. He was carrying a basket full of shrimps, or stones, or rubbish, or which may well have been empty, and he didn't see them. Pierre called: "Clovis!" Clovis raised his head, and saw them. They didn't look so terrible, but, as this unexpected meeting, the child lost all his self-control. He dropped the basket and scrammed. Pierre Le Grand caught up with him and held him by one arm. The brat started yelling for help. A passing fisherman said to Pierre:

"What d'you want with that kid?"

A lady exclaimed:

"What a brute!"

Pierre let go of Clovis, who fled. The two mens' attitude elicited some stern comments.

The latter made themselves scarce, leaving the ill-informed crowd engulfed in its error.

A few steps farther on, Pierre burst out laughing:

"I don't think we acted very cleverly there."

"I'm afraid not," agreed Etienne. "For international gangsters, it isn't very impressive."

Pierre didn't answer.

---

*It is with as much surprise as indignation that we have heard about M. Système being bitten. We would like to inform the canine race that such deviationist behavior will not be tolerated within the area under the jurisdiction of the commune. Dogs were made to bite the dust, and not good citizens.*

*

*Little Octave Tandem, five years old, found a rusty knife in the street. He lost no time in taking it to the police station. The voice of conscience had spoken to this child.*

*

*Mme. Tendre Soucoupe, while clearing her dining room table, dropped a glass made of Czechoslovakian crystal. The purely material damage will be reimbursed by the France Assurance and Co., 11 rue des Moutons-Pressés, in the cantonal county town of the canton.*

*

*Some practical jokers having inserted a bullet in the head of M. Oréor Serventi, and this by means of a rifle disposed to this effect, the consequence has been a passage from life to extinction of the person incriminated. The wags were immediately taken to the recruiting office and appointed corporals first class.*

*

*A wine party was held last night in honor of Rude Agricole, postman in Blanc-Yeux, to celebrate his forty years of service. The mayor gave a little impromptu speech which impressed with its charming good nature. The most charming cordiality reigned throughout in this charming assembly. A dance brought this charming evening to a close. Next day, Rude Agricole resumed his duties, saying: On the fiftieth now. This charming utterance earned him the applause of the whole village who had hastened to the charming spot.*

*

*You can't think of everything. Caromel Blanc, thirty-seven, a tailor at Cinq-Epis, suffering from a violent migraine, took twenty aspirins last night; but having omitted to take them out of their tube, the treatment had no effect. A subscription list has been opened.*

*

*Count Adhémar du Rut has returned to his castle for a few days, to rest from the fatigue of taking the waters. He will be exercising his* jus primae noctis *on Tuesday, Thursday and Saturday of the coming week. Young men will be admitted.*

*

*Market Prices for August 11th.*

| | |
|---|---|
| *Bread* | *1 franc per quantity* |
| *Beef* | *7 francs per piece* |
| *Potatoes* | *3 francs per heap* |
| *Radishes* | *1 franc 30 per fragment* |
| *String* | *0 francs 10 per bit* |

*

Pause for laughter.

*Q. What's the difference between an asthmatic pork-butcher and a party given by intellectuals?*

*A. One's all chine and wheeze, and the other's all wine and cheese.*

*Q. Why is a gambler like a man whose wife is called Elizabeth?*

*A. They both like to lay their bet (Bet).*

*

*Isaac Poum will visit you at your home every day from 5 to 7. He omits nothing, and remains expressive. Results guaranteed.*

*

*Colonel and Mme. Pot have pleasure in announcing to those who were kind enough to be their guests last night that Private Louis Gamahuche has been sentenced to thirty days' imprisonment for having replaced the Sauternes 1919 with a well-known brand of bleach. This regrettable error having been thus rectified, Colonel and Mme. Pot request their yesterday's guests to be kind enough to come back this evening to finish the turkey, of which there still remain several good portions.*

*

*Théodore Marcel, 15, now on vacation at X . . . , has just finished reading the third volume of* Les Misérables. *All our congratulations to this young representative of the French intelligentsia.*

*

*M. Curieux Fontaine, lawyer, of Pinceau, informs the tradesmen of here and elsewhere that he will no longer be responsible for the debts of his wife, who is gadding about like a whore, with alcoholic bravado. Such behavior, alas!, seems to be on the increase in our land; nor does the scourge now spare the cradle of our ancestors now reposing in the tomb. Ways must be found of reacting against the profligacy of the new layers of society and the insubordinate and lascivious ventures of noncommissioned officers on bicycles.*

*(Official Announcement)*

*

*Codicille Plusdun, Freemason, was observed last Thursday answering the call of Nature against the wall of the Enfoui cemetery. This new proof of the disrespect of Judaic and pro-Bochian masonry toward the best and most healthy of our institutions could not be suffered in silence.*

*

Does this apply to you?

*Working late into the night on my archaelogical studies I had gotten into the habit of drinking very strong black coffee. I gradually felt my heart beating tumultously, and this made the exercise of my ministry very painful.*

*The doctor in the county town prescribed pure water without caffeine, my trouble has disappeared, and it seems I have recovered my youth, I feel so fit.*

*M. le curé de V. . . . (Ardeche)*

*Do you, like this ecclesiastic, suffer from an inexplicable feeling of indisposition? Cure it by taking pure water without caffeine. On sale at all good druggists': 5 fr. 95 a liter.*

*

*The coffee that you purchase*
*From Jean-Baptiste Averse*
*Is good, but it is better*
*At the Café du Commerce.*

*(Advertiser's Announcement)*

*

*Why neglect your beauty after death? Look after your bones.*

Just think that in five hundred years, or a thousand years, or more, your remains may be exhibited in a museum. Don't you want to appear there at your most advantageous?

*Thanks to the potion of the Eternals, you can prepare to have skeleton of pleasing aspect, and guaranteed unbreakable.*

IT WILL BE THE ADMIRATION OF THE FUTURE GENERATIONS.

Twelve-liter flask: *Price by arrangement.*

*Apply to Dr. Effaré, 15 rue des Mages, Paris.*

*

After carefully reading this fragment of the *Little X . . . Echo,* Narcense made use of it and threw it down the hole. Then he went up to bed.

## Fifth Chapter

SEVEN o'clock, they're not back yet. The fire's boiling under the pots, the table's laid, the wines are waiting. Camélia, the new one, is drying up glasses and sniffing: it's a habit. Plenty of regular customers. Mme. Belhôtel is sitting at the cash register proud of her culinary efforts. It won't be long now before the wedding party comes back from the country where it must have spent a happy afternoon.

Good old Taupe! Getting married at his age! Out of the entire neighborhood, there was only one person who said: It's obvious he doesn't mind if his wife deceives him, and the same person had added: She's got a screw loose, Ernestine, marrying an old boy that hasn't got a bean—and had then also added: It's Dominique that wants his child to have a father. Mme. Belhôtel repeats these words to herself, and *adds nothing of her own invention.* The new one was snub-nosed; Dominique didn't like that; they'd replace her later on. Had she put enough salt in the soup? Huh, there goes Jojo, the haberdasher's son. All the same, really *can't* mind if his wife deceives him.

In the billiard room, all that can be heard is the toc-toc of the balls in the midst of a great silence; the local champion has had a run of twelve caroms, among the general admiration. There are many onlookers; people are standing up to have a look. Mme. Belhôtel is beginning to get impatient, something will get burnt. A customer comes in, lugging an enormous beige canvas suitcase; a young woman follows in his footsteps. He is wearing knickerbockers, a thick sweater and a stableboy's cap; he is smoking a pipe with one of those enigmatic airs that it takes years to learn. Who is he, this citizen? He asks for a green menthe; so does his wife. No one takes much notice of him, for everyone's attention is directed to the billiard room where the toc-toc is continuing; in the midst of the general emotion, the champion has just pulled off his fourteenth carom. Mme. Belhôtel gets up to see to her cooking; Camélia serves the green menthes, sniffing with a disgusted air; it isn't that the menthe nauseates her, but it's a habit. The customer calmly draws her attention to the fact that she's given him a picon; she can't get over it; she distinctly remembers picking up the bottle of peppermint; how extraordinary. She goes back to change the drinks. Mme. Belhôtel returns to her cash register and starts working out the cost price of Ernestine's wedding breakfast.

In the billiard room, people have stopped breathing. With a dry throat, the champion is preparing his twenty-fourth carom; he screws the balls to the cloth with a confident look, lines up his cue; no doubt about it, till his dying day he'll be able to describe and redescribe this twenty-five point break. His ball is off, exactly following the path he has mapped out for it; it hits the red according to the anticipated angle and continues on its course; but a bit farther on it stops, flabbergasted, not encountering the object of its trajectory, for the third ball is no longer there. The champion, overcome with astonishment drops his cue on his toes, without feeling any pain, and yet he's got corns; the onlookers lean their foreheads over the deserted green cloth; no doubt about it, one ball is missing. Who has dared steal it? The champion goes red with fury and green with despair; there is chaos and confusion. The onlookers search, go through each other's pockets, suspect each other. Mme. Belhôtel is worried about all this havoc. Camélia stops drying up glasses to find out what's going on. The players are yelling with fury; one asserts that if he knew who was responsible for this idiotic joke he'd give him something to remember, wouldn't he now! The other, from the depths of his envious heart, is laughing derisively at the misfortune of his opponent. Which opponent declares that he'll never set foot in such a lousy dump again. And then they discover that the three balls are once again on the table, just as they were at the twenty-fourth carom. Everyone exclaims, everyone is amazed; you could knock them down with a feather, they can't believe their eyes. It's overwhelming. Camélia starts drying up her glasses and sniffing again, the customer and his wife calmly drink their menthes.

"In six months at the most," thinks Belhôtel, "we'll have our little house, our little whorehouse. I'd like it in a nice quiet safe neighborhood; regular, bourgeois customers, seven or eight girls, no more; but well chosen. It'll be all gold and red velvet, and we'll live in peace and plenty and Clovis will become an engineer and he'll marry the daughter of a rich industrialist and the little children will have an English governess with big teeth and blue ribbons hanging down over her bony bottom. Later on, we'll buy a little house in the country where Dominique comes from; maybe he'll be elected mayor and Clovis will come and see us in his car with his little children." A tear begins to well up in the flabby eye of the proprietress of the Café des Habitants. She gathers it up with her finger and smears it on her blotting paper and gets on with her accounts. That's a funny one, she says to herself, looking at the man with the big suitcase.

All of a sudden she thinks: "But it's Ernestine's brother! The one who was coming from Brussels!"

It was, it was Peter Tom the Anchorite, real name Pierre Troc, and the timid person with him was none other than his wife, the girl who, during his act, presented to the public the doves that came out of the top hat, curtsying like a convent schoolgirl. Peter Tom knocked his pipe out against the heel of his left shoe and opened his mouth twice, the first time to spit and the second to speak.

"Well, Ernestine? eh! marriage! Who to? A man, of course. An old man. Eh? What am I supposed to think about it? What do you? Doesn't matter much, eh? Taupe, he's called, eh?"

"Yes, that's right, zcalled Taupe," volubilized Mme. Belhôtel, who had been afraid she wasn't going to be able to get a word in edgewise. "And he's a junk dealer."

"A junk dealer? Not rich then, eh? What's she thinking of, then? Good old Ernestine. Little girl—already a half-wit. Now —no change. So she used to work for you?"

"She did an all; she's a good girl, not fraid of a biv hard work."

"Can believe it, can believe it. No idea how to make life

easy for herself. She'll never find out. By the way, what about my brother, the military gent?"

"He arrived this morning. The whole wedding party has been spending the afternoon in the country. Be back soon."

"So Totocle is here! Good old Totocle! Haven't seen him for three years! must have a lot of hardware on, eh? And Titine, haven't seen her for two years, either. Time passes, eh, Madame Bitôtel."

"Belhôtel, Belhôtel."

"Belhôtel. One day in Carcassonne, th'next in Angers, after that in Swisserland and Spain and Italy. Certainly see some countries in our perfession, Madame Belhôtel. Even as far as Brittany, I've been. Now there's a nice bit of country for you. Vjust now been in Brussels, and after that I've got an engagement in Lyons."

"You're a . . . ?"

"Magician. Even better: professor of white magic. I can make ten-franc pieces come out of the noses of babes in their cradles, and even babes not in their cradles. And plenty of other things besides. My act, well, it's one of the best of its kind, Madame Belhôtel. I invented the dancing scissors trick and the one with the little bit of string made of thin steel. I did them to a gathering of more than fifty colleagues and not a single one discovered how they worked. Eh, Madame Belhôtel."

"Oh yes."

Peter Tom the Anchorite is making a great impression on Mme. Belhôtel; the woman with him starts murmuring:

"Oh, Pierre, he's very intelligent, but he never has any luck; he can't seem to make a name for himself; he always has to go on one of the first."

"Stupid creature," mutters Peter Tom.

Mme. Belhôtel nearly falls off her chair in surprise.

"Me; never had any luck? Me? No luck? Here, you'll see!"

He goes over to an automatic machine, stakes on the red, and it's the green that comes up.

"See that, eh, Madame Belhôtel? No luck!"

And, with a casual gesture, he takes a guinea pig out of this honorable tradeswoman's blouse.

This feat focuses everyone's attention on him, amid many exclamations; Mme Belhôtel shivers, and rubs her breast in stupefaction; the cavy is charming. Peter Tom the Anchorite picks up a *Paris-Midi* that happens to be on a table, screws it into a cone, puts the animal into it, puts the ensemble down on the counter, takes a pistol out of his pocket, fires at the paper, and unfolds it: the guinea pig has disappeared, and *Paris-Midi* has turned into *Paris-Soir,* fourth (sports) edition. Applause crepitates, the magician bows, and the wedding party has still not arrived.

---

It won't be much longer now; the car transporting it cleaves the air; its bodywork is trembling with impatience; like unto a high-spirited steed bearing on its back the chief of police who is afraid of arriving at night school when the poetry class is over, so the powerful quadricycle carries the joyous wedding party toward its destiny, eating up the kilometers and shitting dust, roaring like a lion and snoring like a sleeper with a cold. It tells, one by one, the beads of the intermediary villages, it jumps the ditches, the gutters and gullies; bicyclists cannot make it flinch, hens are flattened by its unpuncturable tires, fascinated corners allow themselves to be cut; it ravages the countryside and subjugates the towns, the intelligent and the imbecile admire it alike. As it goes by, people cordially cry: Long live the bride! Long live cuckolds! The car, scorning these facile, yet benevolent, witticisms, continues on its way with the speed of running champion and the obstination of a six-day-man. Its goal has been fixed, this goal it will attain; it is the Café des Habitants where, in the kitchen, the cauliflower au gratin is simmering; but it must make haste, if it doesn't want its occupants to find the roast burned. And therefore does its bodywork tremble with impatience, therefore does it flit over pothole and quagmire with more facility than a skater over a frozen lake. Now it is moving over the territory of the commune of Blagny; it leaves on its left the building development hight The Desert, where the roads are ravines, where neither water, nor gas, nor electricity are known, thanks to the artful skill of some honorable traders in square meters; it leaves on its right the papier-mâché factory where they manufacture indiscriminately cheap bricks or army bread; it rushes through the district called Venice the Beautiful, thus named because it is flooded every winter; it jumps over the main road and plunges into the Rue Pasteur, which leads it straight to the Place Victor Hugo. Snorting, it stops outside its terminus; carried away by its store of speed, was it not about to pass it?

People run up from all sides, they form a circle and line the path; Mme. Belhôtel comes out of her tavern, followed by Peter Tom the Anchorite, by Mme. Troc, his spouse, by Camélia, the new waitress, and by all the delighted customers. The car door is opened and the wedding party trickles, drop by drop, down onto the pavement.

In the first place comes Dominique Belhôtel, larger than life, twice as handsome and freshly hatted; he is wearing spats and has stuck an artificial pearl in his tie; when he moves, his muscles burst the seams of his jacket. His nose has taken on the fiery color of campari and his eyes are sparkling like lemonade. Powerful and Olympian, he holds out his arms to the bride and deposits her on the ground with the elegance of a Hercules who thinks he is lifting a couple of pounds of lead but who is in fact shifting a couple of pounds of feathers, which thus flutter from the car onto terra firma.

Ernestine astonishes the crowd by her grace and elegance; her elegance is costing her dear, it is true, and her savings have evaporated; but is she not rich now? The café habitués rush up to congratulate her, some claim a kiss. They're having a good time today, all right!

Then follow the pageboy and the bridesmaid: to wit, Clovis Belhôtel, who is christening—lucky coincidence—a new suit, and Florette Pic, who is thirteen, and depraved. Ivoine is certain to be jealous; Clovis will have to put up with her tantrums the next day. For the moment, he allows himself to be tickled without demur, and exchanges looks for full of pride and mystery, and some slight anxiety, with his aunt.

Then Themistocles Troc gets down onto the pavement;

Ernestine's brother is sporting a superb Zouave uniform, studded with four decorations, its sleeve adorned with silver ribbon, a token of his rank. His appearance provokes various kinds of appreciation among the spectators, some of the women admiring his colonial splendor, but most of the men mistrusting his stripes. Imitating Dominique's gallant example, he tries to get out with Suzy, Ernestine's friend, on his arm; but he goes about it in such an awkward fashion that she twists her foot.

"Blessed idiot," says she, massaging her ankle.

Suzy is a blonde, and she goes to the movies three times a week.

Next appears Meussieu Gérard Taupe; an astonished murmur accompanies his descent. How could anyone recognize old Taupe in this elegant, closely shaved old gentleman, his grey hair plastered down on his skull, wearing a morning coat, a bit greenish, it's true, and a pair of trousers whose impeccable crease seems to have been cast in reinforced concrete? Patent leather shoes and white spats complete his getup. Taupe looks twenty years younger, such is the common opinion. To raise to its apogee the stupefaction of the population, he covers his hoary head with a genuine top hat, from which the grease has been carefully removed.

After which, it's a real free-for-all. Mme. Saturnin Belhôtel, Meussieu Saturnin Belhôtel, Meussieu Jérôme Pic, Mme. Jérôme Pic, appear one by one, without anyone paying much attention to them. Finally, the car expels its last occupant, Mme. Sidonie Cloche. Her hat, embellished with parrot feathers, her billiard-green dress, her tartan cape, her gigantic carpetbag, subject her to the mocking homage of the youth of Blagny. But what does she care about her appearance? She has plenty of other things to worry about. She is accomplishing her purpose; Ernestine's marriage brings fortune in its wake, and it won't be long now; in a few days she'll know exactly how much the treasure, as she calls it, is worth, and in a month, two months at the most, she'll start cashing her bundles of bank notes. It's perfect; but there are the *Others,* and the *Others* worry her all the more in that for the last two weeks she hasn't known what has happened to them.

As a consequence of his abortive abduction, Clovis took fright, and wanted to come back to Blagny at once; according to Saturnin, his tenant's absence continues, and, five days before, in the course of an excursion to Obonne, she was able to ascertain that the Marcel house was still unoccupied. What are They going to do? The easiest thing for Them would be to burgle the shack. To guard against this eventuality, Mme. Cloche has not hesitated to grease the palms of the security men at the Company's workshops, to get them to keep a close eye on the old man's fortified castle. But she considers this precaution superfluous; for she calculates that the *Others*, knowing her to be aware of their dishonest projects, have abandoned all hope of appropriating the Taupic treasure to to themselves. Perhaps they'll want to take their revenge? They wouldn't dare, she consoles herself; and thus repeating these historic words, she holds her head high and defies destiny, while the whole wedding party is getting ready for the ultimate aperitifs.

---

Ernestine, escaping from the compliments of those whom, for more than a year, she had served, perceives her brother, the professor of white magic, and her sister-in-law. Goodness, isn't she pleased! Isn't it nice of them to have come! These remarks inaugurate a series of embraces and handshakes, the former full of affection, the latter of cordiality. When Peter meets his brother, Themistocles, he says to him:

"Well, Totocle, still a mercenary?"

And his brother replies:

"And you–still a juggler?"

And they look very friendly. Suzy, who now feels full of contempt for the Zouave on account of his clumsiness, is attracted by Peter's Anglo-Saxon elegance; the latter completes his conquest of her by extracting a bouquet of tricolored flowers from a bell push.

They'd had a good time in the country, all right. The new arrivals still seem all red and out of breath. They had danced to a player piano, they had drunk white wine and lemonade, they had picked little flowers in the fields, they had been boating, they had played games of *tonneau,* they had sung in chorus old ditties and new couplets. Mme. Cloche had nearly made one of the boats capsize, and Florette had nearly been bitten by a dog. Meussieu Pic had imitated a cow mooing, and Themistocles had imitated a belly dance. And when, as the sun was sinking, their stomachs had started to feel empty, they had climbed back into the car, satiated with pleasure. It had been a gorgeous day, all right!

And now a little aperitif before the great feast Mme. Belhôtel has prepared. Dominique makes the ordinary clientele evacuate the Café des Habitants; clear decks for the wedding party. Camélia serves the bitter picon and the germicidal Pernod, and sniffs more than ever; she has eyes only for Ernestine. Camélia, who is no cynic, is amazed that people should make such a fuss over the wedding of a waitress and a pauper; because old Taupe, she knows him very well, she's seen him often enough on Sundays, in the market, displaying his old iron and junk. What amazes her most is Ernestine: Ernestine is radiant. Ernestine is resplendent. Ernestine is scintillating. Is it marriage, or the day in the country? Camélia, who isn't in the know, thinks it's peculiar, Ernestine's transformation, but if she did know more about it, she would no doubt attribute it to incorrect reasons. Because Ernestine, for the moment, has completely forgotten the Taupic millions and the sumptuous life of which Sidonie Cloche has sketched so brilliant a picture; her joy has other causes: one afternoon in the country after four hundred and eighteen consecutive days of washing glasses and scrubbing floors. If she is smiling, it is not because she is thinking of her future wardrobe, but because she's still gliding downstream; if she is smiling, it isn't because she's thinking of her visits to the beauty parlor, but because she can still see herself drinking lemonade under a big old green tree; if she is smiling, it isn't because she already thinks she's driving in her own car, but because she can still see, through the heavy atmosphere of the café, a cow majestically dunging while grazing the crimson clover. Ernestine feels, growing in her heart, an enormous little blue flower, which she waters with a Pernod whose 60 percent content of alcohol is slightly quenched by the addition of a few cubic centimeters of pure, but not distilled, water.

As one man, all the guests have raised their glasses: fifteen glasses have been raised. What does their content matter—nothing counts but the feelings that animate this symbolic gesture. Fifteen glasses, fifteen feelings: that's fourteen too many; there should only be one: the joy of seeing the foundation of a new family, a new hearth and home. But very few are capable of rising to these civic heights; one is thinking, with hatred, of his brother, and that one's Themistocles; another is suffering horribly because his clodhoppers are too tight, and that one's Meussieu Pic. But zygomatic muscles are sufficiently stretched, and gullets sufficiently sonorous, for us to be able to state that sympathy and cordiality reign. Fifteen glasses have been raised, we have said: a few seconds later, they clink; everyone striking his glass fourteen times, that makes a hundred and five encounters. A hundred and five times, then, the glasses tinkle, a hundred and four times, more precisely, for Themistocles and Peter, by common consent, have not drunk to each other. Once more they shout: Long live the bride! Long live Taupe! and they drink. Meussieu Pic, putting down on the cracked table a glass snowing with anisette, says:

"Not so good as when you used to serve it, Ernestine."

This piece of gallantry gives rise to an admiring hubbub from the men, and delighted exclamations from the ladies. The latter have a weakness for Meussieu Pic, a dealer in dried and salted goods, whose civility has become proverbial throughout Blagny. Meussieu Pic is Meussieu Taupe's friend. Meussieu Pic, too, had known better days, reverses of fortune; both had had a secondary education, and learned Latin. Even while Taupe was leading his misanthropic existence, he used to meet Pic every week and measure his strength with him at dominoes. The one would say: *tibi*, and the other, scorning the vocative: your turn, *civis romanus*, and both considered that they were soaring over the heads of the *belote* players. Meussieu Pic, though, was already married, and a father. His wife, the daughter of a druggist, if you please, appears to accept her comedown in the social scale with resignation; but when she thinks of the little Louis XV drawing room she used to have, her heart bleeds; it's even worse when she remembers the people they used to know—Lieutenant de la Boustrofe, a titled gentleman, and M. Béquille, the lawyer, and M. Dife, who wrote poetry that actually got printed—and compares them with the people she is with at the moment: a junk dealer, a café proprietor, a concierge, an N.C.O., a magician, a midwife, and a waitress. She, the daughter of a druggist, a guest at the wedding of a waitress! and her heart bleeds, while her lips, maintaining an affected and contorted smile, dip into the contents of a glass of grenadine, around the rim of which Camélia's fingerprints are profoundly engraved. And her heart bleeds once again when she sees her daughter, Florette, focusing her dark-rimmed eyes on the flies of all the men. The child of old parents, Florette shows a remarkable predisposition toward what Mme. Pic calls vice, and Meussieu Pic calls trifling.

Meanwhile, the general attention, concentrated for a moment on the interesting personality of the latter, chooses a new pole, determined by the bouquet of tricolor flowers extirpated from the bell push by Peter. A magician. Mme. Belhôtel tells about the guinea pig and insinuates about the billiard ball; there is noisy admiration. Peter refuses to give any sort of explanation, but promises them a session after the dessert. They certainly are going to enjoy themselves. The children jump for joy, but Themistocles frowns; for Suzy has insulted him by choosing Peter as her cavalier (if I may make so bold). He envelopes the serpents of contempt in the handkerchief of jealousy, and throws the lot into the depths of his ulcerated heart; then he thrusts out his chest, and finishes his aperitif.

Everyone meditates for a moment before the final apotheosis, which is announced by a raucous yell emitted by Mme. Belhôtel; this savage cry was answered by the joyful exclamation of the guests; couples were formed, but owing to the fact that the reduction into prime factors of the number fifteen does not cause to appear among those factors the number that comes after one—and it is thus that the most abstract theorems of the theory of numbers have occasionally in everyday life some direct application—owing, as I was saying, to the nondivisibility of the number fifteen by the number two—and you may observe that if French wedding parties walked in triplets instead of walking in couples, such considerations would become superfluous, since Ernestine's wedding party would then appear as forming five triplets, and one can even envisage ethnographical circumstances such that, wedding parties walking in lines of five people, Belhôtel's guests would have been able to conduct their maneuvers as a combination of three quintuplets—in short, owing to the fact that fifteen is an odd number, only seven couples could be formed, one person remaining solitary. This person is a woman; a simple piece of reasoning suffices to demonstrate this, since, out of fifteen guests, there are seven men and eight women, and since two individuals of the same sex could certainly not have been coupled together, such habits being restricted to homosexuals and, thank God, we have nothing to do with people of *that* sort. But who, then, is the woman who is thus forsaken? Two methods are available to the mind: reason and intuition. Owing to its rapidity, it is preferable to employ the second, even though by means of the first it is equally possible to arrive at the desired conclusion.

---

The couples form, they make their way into the private room. The table is resplendent with its fifteen places laid on a strictly white tablecloth; the knives gleam, the plates blaze, the forks sparkle, the glasses glisten, the spoons shine, a real feast for the eyes. They sit down, they unfold their napkins, which have become stiff with waiting, and the soup starts flowing over the shoulders of the guests. For things have been done properly; two waiters, lent by the Restaurant des Alliés, create a luxurious atmosphere. Mme. Pic, privately, approves of this ostentatious display. Dominique is collapsing with pride, and his spouse has really earned the right to be pleased with herself. Ernestine, still under a spell, swoops down on her plate, because country air, it gives you an appetite; as for old Taupe, he confines himself to a smiling silence, of which it would be impossible to say whether it is aping dignity or expressing degradation. At the same time as he gulps down his shoup, Totocle runs through his repertoire of jokes. Separated from him by Mme. Saturnin Belhôtel, Pic is doing the same; both are getting ready to shine. Suzy is all the time waiting for the saltcellar to turn into an elephant or the oil and vinegar into a bootblack's box. But Peter, for the time being, refrains from demonstrating his talents. Florette, in spite of her youth, shares Suzy's hopes, and keeps thinking she's just about to see a flight of doves. As for Clovis, he keeps thinking that he's going to see the *Others* suddenly appear, armed with revolvers. On his left, Mme. Cloche, forgetting her fears, abandons herself to the delights of the scalding soup; ever since her tenderest youth she has adored shoup, and that's why she has grown to such great strength, audacity and coriacity. Mme. Peter Tom, who leaves half hers in the bottom of her soup plate, remains, on the contrary, slender, small and slight.

A certain time elapses, marked only by silence. Parallel to the soup, the duration elapses; parallel, and so close that it seems to be it the guests are drinking rather than the nutritious, steaming liquid that is being transported by the electroplated spoons. The plates are emptied, and the soup moves into the past. The varied sounds accompanying this movement deserve careful description, for great events are presaged in this concert of glug-glugs and gargles. If someone sucks in his broth with the very edge of his lips, someone else swallows his with ferocity. To cool it, some blow, and others make waterfalls out of it. Some lap, and some splash. With this one it's a hiss, with that one a dissonance. From this music, little by little an elementary harmony is born; soon, from mouth to ears, words will fly and, passing from the animal to the social and from gluttony to chitchat, each of the fifteen persons enumerated above begins once again to be aware of the presence of the other fourteen. For, when the dinner pail is empty, the head will rise.

To eat the shoup, elbows are raised, and mouths are opened;

after which the gesture becomes a habit, and, apart from the purely gastronomical satisfaction, a pleasure in itself.

The only one of the guests to be fully aware of this is Saturnin: "When they've finished, they're going to feel terribly frustrated," he says to himself. And even he, faced with his empty plate, is horribly bored. "The wisdom of nations," he thinks, "teaches that it is easy to acquire a habit but hard to get rid of it." That's just what's happening here. They've got into the habit of eating their shoup, and now they are all of a sudden obliged to abandon this so easily acquired habit. And so, they are sad. And so, there is a taste of ashes in their mouths. And so, they are in despair. They didn't suspect that a full plate conceals an empty plate, as being conceals nothingness, and, without having any suspicion of the terrible consequences their inconsequentiality was about to make them suffer, from sheer wantonness—they had got into the habit of eating shoup. Ah! if only the plates were infinitely deep. Ah! If the liquid, instead of stagnating, were to renew itself and flow from an inexhaustible fountain. Then, from this eternal two-way traffic of spoons alternatively full and empty, from this eternal repetition of elbows being raised and mouths being opened, from this infinitely permissible habit, would spring something that resembles happiness, the happiness of a peaceful people . . . But that's just fantasy! Plates have a bottom, and in this bottom, the shoup is shtagnating.

But the two waiters lent by the Restaurant des Alliés know this difficult moment and the way to relieve it: they whisk away the empty plate. It's true that another empty plate replaces it; but this one is an expectation, whereas the other was no longer anything but a disappointment; the one is a preliminary, the other a memory. This concealing of a vacuum by another vacuum is not enough; the two waiters lent by the Restaurant des Alliés complete the operation by concealing the vacuum by a plenum; they fill the glasses with wine, which glasses take on the joyous appearance of druggists' display bottles.

That's how you escape from anguish, Saturnin concludes. And then you understand what is meant by the word well-being. Someone smiles, someone else sighs with satisfaction. Someone licks his lips, someone else wipes his mouth with enthusiasm. It's only now that their tongues, which had been tied by hunger, will become loosened; it's only now that their mouths will open for anything other than absorption, it's only now that their quietened stomachs will allow their brains a little exercise; it's only now that the guests, accomplishing a revolution analogous to that of Copernicus' in astronomy, pass from egocentricity to polycentricity; it's only now that, ceasing to be interested solely in themselves, the someones and the someone elses admit of the existence of the someone elses and the someones; it's only now that, having become sociable individuals, the members of the wedding party are going to emerge from their isolation and again become what they were earlier on: the members of the wedding party. In order to make it quite clear that they once again feel they belong to this temporary community of which Ernestine and Taupe are the poles, and Mme. Cloche the indirect and hidden cause, they all stand up and, holding up their glasses, utter identical words in chorus: an exclamatory phrase, the framework of which is composed of the words health, bride and bridegroom.

Then they sit down again.

Then they talk.

"Florette, take your elbows off the table," Mme. Pic starts.

---

When there is nothing left of the fish but its skeleton. Meussieu Pic thinks it's time to get in some of the jokes from his repertoire; Themistocles, too, has the same thought. Both of them, with quivering nostrils, start watching for the keyword from which the anecdote will blossom. But at the moment, the conversation is desultory, which makes their hunting difficult.

"Will you do some tricks for us, then?" Ernestine asks Peter.

Aand Dominique asks Saturnin:

"Still only one tenant?"

Mme. Dominique answers Themistocles:

"No thank you."

And Suzy answers Meussieu Pic:

"Not yet."

Mme. Cloche, over the heads of the two children, harpoons the magician and asks him:

"Why're you called an Anklewright?"

"Anchorite," replies Peter. "It's a Greek word that means: that you hardly ever eat or drink; a fakir, as you might say."

"Seems to me that you eat and drink or right though," Dominique objects.

"Ah yes. Here. But on the stage, I hardly eat or drink at all."

"Ah!" say most of the bewildered listeners.

"Has anyone ever seen people eating and drinking on the stage?" remarks Meussieu Pic.

"Well, really!" protests Peter, "what about sword-swallowers?" (They laugh.)

"Oh go on, that's idiotic, what you're saying," Themistocles says to him. "It's like the guy from Marseilles who . . ."

"It isn't idiotic. I do hardly eat or drink at all on the stage."

"Even so," retorts Meussieu Pic, who's sticking to his idea, "it's very rare for a magician to eat and drink on the stage."

"That's just what makes me different," says Peter, with a knowing air.

They're afraid they haven't understood; Themistocles, who is never afraid of not understanding, formulates the general uneasiness.

"You're pulling our legs. If you're like the others, that can't make you different."

"But I'm not like the others; They don't eat *anything* on the stage. Ever seen a magician eat on the stage? No, eh. Well, me, I eat just a little. Get it, *just a little,* that's what makes me different. To be quite precise, I eat an apple, and then I take it out of one of the audience's pockets. That, Madame? . . ."

"Cloche."

"Is why I call myself the Anchorite."

"Well, strue, that's clever," Dominique admits.

"Oh, Pierre, he's very intelligent," Mme. Peter suddenly murmurs, "he's very intelligent, but he never has any luck, he can't seem to make a name for himself."

"What a bitch!" exclaims the magician, causing general consternation (Florette is the only one who thinks it's very funny). "What a bitch! she will insist on saying that I'm not lucky. She keeps on saying it in every way she can think of. Obviously, that brings me bad luck."

"You're imagining things," Ernestine tells him.

"And then, it's stupid to shout it from the rooftops, that I haven't made a name for myself. What does that make me look like now, eh? A half-wit." (They laugh.)

The leg of mutton makes its appearance.

"Here, to show you that I'm someone after all, would you like me to make the leg of mutton disappear? The whole leg, or just the pope's-eye?"

Everyone laughs and protests. Clearly, he's getting it all his own way. Themistocles smiles; Meussieu Pic wonders whether, apropos of the leg of mutton, he couldn't slip in the story about the Jew, the lamppost and the camel seller. But he hesitates too long; the conversation gets off on another track. A remark of Dominique's about the dog that nearly bit Florette is its source. The subject of dangerous dogs, even though less prolific than that of swimming fatalities, nevertheless produces possibilities of sufficient abundance for them not to be exhausted before the guests have reached the bone of the leg of mutton. Mme. Saturnin, who is now opening her mouth for the first time, tells how her parents went six months without hearing from their son, because their dog couldn't bear postmen. In Themistocles' regiment, so he says, they have done away with bugle calls because they got on the nerves of the colonel's greyhound. They thus pass from dangerous dogs to dogs that are merely cantankerous, and from these to quadrupeds in general. Pic waits patiently until they gradually get down to the gasteropods to bring out his story about the Jew, the bishop and the snails. Alas! his expectations are once again thwarted; the arrival of the cauliflower au gratin causes the animal kingdom to be abandoned for the vegetable kingdom and, by an abrupt twist, for which Dominique once again seems to be entirely responsible, they come back to the lovely day they've just had, the charm of country life and the cultivation of the crimson clover.

While Ernestine is giving Mme. Dominique an account of their boating expedition, during the course of which Mme. Cloche nearly came into contact with the river water, Suzy steps up her flirtation with Peter, Mme. Pic reminds her daughter that elbows are not to be put on tables, and Totocle is plunged into profound inner jubilation, for he has just discovered an excellent pun; all he has to do now is to find the right place for it; the moment Meussieu Pic distinguishes himself to any extent, he'll say: "You're a wit, old Pic." And they'll laugh like anything.

"Hey, Uncle Sat," says Clovis to the Concierge, "you promised to give me a nice book to read on my vacation and you never gave me one."

Unclesat pretends he hasn't heard; it's true that he's completely forgotten about his promise.

"Hey, Saturnin," intervenes Mme. Cloche, whose deep voice makes the teaspoons vibrate, "carnch hear wo' Cloclo's saying cha?"

"Ah yes, a nice book; well, I'll buy you one when you go back to school."

"Huh, yes, you'll buy me a textbook."

"You don't seem to have much confidence in your uncle, Clovis. That's not very polite," says Mme. Dominique indulgently.

"How old is the old boy?" the sergeant major asks her in a very blue-blooded manner (though he's never seen blue blood on the battlefield).

"Thirteen."

"He's big for his age, isn't he?" Peter observes to his brother.

The latter, who hadn't prepared any more remarks, takes refuge in interjections.

"Hm! Hm!" he grunts, like a gourmet discovering a nice ripe Camembert.

"Has he passed his grade school exams?" asks Mme. Peter.

Mme. Dominique swallows her saliva before she utters the incendiary phrase:

"He's starting at the lycée this year."

And Dominique, in a casual tone of voice, adds:

"Yes, we're sending him to the lycée."

People look at Clovis; he blushes proudly.

"He's going to be an engineer," says his father. "We shall make the necessary sacrifices."

"You're absolutely right, Meussieu Belhôtel," says Mme. Pic approvingly, "to sacrifice yourselves for your child, and to want to make someone of him."

"It's better for children to be ashamed of their parents than for parents to be ashamed of their children," sententiates Meussieu Pic.

Immediately after which, he has a vague idea that that's not very flattering to Dominique. Whereupon Themistocles decides to put his oar in, he turns toward Meussieu Pic and says point-blank:

"You're a wit, old Pic."

"*Me,* a wittol!" (he suffocates). But Meussieu I won't allow you to insult me like that! To say nothing of my wife! *I* respect the French army, Meussieu; and *you,* you ought to respect the sanctity of the French family. Me, a wittol, ho! At my age, to be insulted by a, by a . . . Ho!"

He gets up and starts waving his arms about wildly. The ladies calm him down. Madame Pic looks puzzled; fortunately, she doesn't know what a wittol is. Themistocles, alarmed at the effect he has produced, tries to justify himself.

"But it was a pun!"

"Pun or no pun, Meussieu, you have insulted me! And my wife! And . . ."

"I was only saying that you were a wit, Meussieu Pic! A wit!"

"Of course," says Dominique, laughing, "a wit, old Pic!"

"Haha, *civis romanus,* you're a wit, old Pic! Ha ha!"

Taupe has just spoken for the first time since the napkins were unfolded. And yet he's talkative by nature; this evening, though, he hasn't said a word or a phrase, and no one can know what he's thinking about. The pun at the expense his old friend the dealer in dried and salted goods, however, brings him out of his shell, as we have just seen.

"Come on, Jérôme, you don't want to lose your temper on a day like this! for a mere trifle!"

"Ah yes, ah yes, a pun! Oh, very good, very good! I wouldn't want to lose my temper for a mere nothing! Oh, very good! But tell me Sergeant Major Troc, you must see a lot of rivers in your profession, don't you?"

"Rivers? No!" replies the astonished sergeant major. "Why should I?"

"Oh, I'm always hearing people being told: 'They soldier down the river.' "

And he sits down again, satisfied with his revenge. The other guests are a little limp.

---

When this incident has blown over, and as no one wants any more cauliflower, the two waiters lent by the Restaurant les Alliés transport onto the table an impressive quantity of assorted cheeses. Meussieu Pic, who is reputed to be a connoisseur, usually loves to hold forth about the various qualities of Brie and the precautions to be taken in handling Pont l'Evêque, but he is still too much affected by his brush with the sergeant major to be able to take the floor with the necessary authority.

"Oo, good, Roquefort," exclaims Ernestine, delighted.

Taupe smiles, but this hardly changes him, for he seems to have decided to confine himself to this uncompromising type of dumb show. In the meantime, the attention of the company in general, having described a somewhat rugged circle, comes back to its favorite subject, to wit, the magician.

"Mussed oo loh trang?" asked Mme. Cloche, with her mouth full.

"What?"

"You must do a lot of traveling, I said."

"Hah! don't talked me about traveling! A week here, two weeks there. France today, Belgium tomorrow. I even been as far as Syria and Constantinople.

"I've even been," Clovis corrects him.

"Where's that you've been, young 'un?" asks Peter, who seems to be impervious to this linguistic nicety.

"I said I've been and not I been," replies the future pupil of the lycée.

"Ah," says Peter, who doesn't bother about such trifles and, without trying to go any further into the insinuations of the kid, whose mother points out to him that he is speaking without being spoken to, which is extremely bad manners, particularly at a wedding, and even more so coming from a future pupil of the realm of secondary education, continues: "Constantinople! Ah, what a wonderful city! The Golden Horn! The Bosphorus! The Dardanelles!"

"Ha ha, the Dardanelles!" roars Themistocles. "My regiment won the right to wear the red aglet, there."

"Were you there?" asks a lady.

"Oh no, I was too young."

"No one is ever too young to serve their country," observes Peter, sententiously.

"Well said, Meussieu."

Pic, whose emotions have been soothed by a solid chunk of Gruyère, thus makes his reappearance.

"Even so, at thirteen, I couldn't have been in the war in the Dardenelles!" protests the sergeant major.

"It has been known, children of that age joining up," remarks Meussieu Pic, in a distant and faintly scornful voice.

"What about Bara and Viala," cries Clovis.

"Oh, for goodness' sake, be quiet," Mme. Dominique mutters.

"But," says Peter, approvingly, "the boy's right! Bara and Viala, they were children, and yet they were heroes."

"I made up for it," retorts Themistocles, giving his breastplate a great slap, thus causing the four decorations thereon aligned to reverberate.

"Tell the ladies where you picked up all that," his brother advises him.

"Have you finished taking the piss out of me?"

"Come on, Totocle, don't get annoyed," Ernestine intervenes, "You know very well that Peter will have his little joke."

"Me?" protests the latter. "I wasn't joking in the least. It's very interesting to know where you pick up things like that."

"Judging by what you say, Meussieu the Anchorite, it would

seem that you are a pacifist, am I not right? Well, Meussieu the magician, pacifists, I despise them."

"Meussieu Pic!"

"Oh, Meussieu Pic!"

"Oh come on now, we don't want any arguments," Dominique decrees.

"That's right," says Ernestine, in a shrill little voice, "we don't have to talk about war."

"No point in starting any political discussions," says Mme. Dominique B.

"Yes, we're at a wedding, not at an election meeting," says Mme. Saturnin B.

"Daddy's getting cro-oss!" Florette shouts, clapping her hands excitedly.

"Oh, come on, Jérôme, you're not going to start arguing all over again."

"Be quiet, wife! I've said what I had to say. I'm a man who speaks his mind."

"I accept Meussieu's apologies," the magician calmly proclaims.

"But I haven't apologized!" the old man protests.

"It's fine the way it is," Saturnin approves. "Seeing that this meussieu accepts your apology, the matter is now closed."

"Of course, of course, I accept Meussieu Pic's apology! The matter is closed. Let's change the subject."

"Yes, but after all," stammers the dealer in dried and salted goods, "I haven't . . ."

"Come on, Jérôme," his wife says to him, "finish your Gruyère. You're always last."

"Who wants smore cheese?" asks the proprietress.

Calm reigns once more.

"It," says Themistocles artfully to Mme. Cloche, "seems to me that you've missed your vocation. You ought to've been a judge."

"*Me,* a judge?"

"Yes! You'd have been a very wise one, Madame Cloche. You're doing such good justice to the meal."

This is not generally considered very funny.

"He's daft, that fellow," mumbles Sidonie, emptying her glass for the twelfth time.

---

Whereupon the two waiters lent by the Restaurant des Alliés bring in a *gâteau* with cream and butter and vanilla and angelica and crystallized fruits, oh, la la! it makes them tremble! And what a size it is, the *gâteau!* Zenough for everyone. Florette can't get over it and Clovis sits stock still, quivering with emotion.

"Well, Madam' Belhôtel," says Ernestine, "you've certainly done us a treat. Talk about a wedding breakfast—this beats the lot."

"Long live Madame Belhôtel," old Taupe suddenly yells, and then immediately relapses into inaction.

"Long live Madame Belhôtel," they shout in chorus.

It's quite true—talk about a wedding breakfast, this certainly beats the lot. Not everyone is of this opinion, though; Themistocles, for instance, thinks there's a shortage of girls, Mme. Pic considers the company on the vulgar side, and her husband was hoping for a more copious menu. But who could dream of insisting that the wedding breakfast of a waitress in a suburban bistro should be as sumptuous as that of a princess?

The ovations over, everyone throws himself on his portion and wolfs it down, sensually.

"It's terrific," says Dominique.

"Gentlemen don't usually care for sweet things," remarks Mme. Pic, as if it were a reproach.

"Dominique, he likes everything what's good," says his wife.

"Aren't so many good things in this world," adds the tavern-keeper. "No point in letting them pass you by. Have to take advantage of life."

"Of course," agrees the sergeant major, eating a piece of angelica that Clovis, at the other end of the table, had been coveting.

"Even so, there are other things than eating and drinking," says Mme. Pic in an inspired voice.

"Naturally," retorts Peter, "there's walking, hunting, sleeping, doing nothing . . ."

"There is the Ideal, Monsieur," Mme. Pic articulates, "Alas! our civilization is deficient in Ideals," she adds, harvesting with her teaspoon the remains of the whipped cream wandering about on her plate.

"We've had Politics; now it's Morals," murmurs Suzy.

"That's not fair, what you're saying," begins Mme. Dominique Belhôtel, whose brain is beginning to be disturbed by a multiplicity of glasses of wine. "No, it's not fair. Frinstance, Dominique and me, we've got an ideal, and that's that Clovis, he should become an engineer."

"And Themistocles's ideal," adds Peter, "is to become a second lieutenant when he's forty-five."

"And Peter's ideal," murmurs Mme. Peter, "is to have his name up in big letters outside the Empire."

"Silly fool, who wants to know what you think, eh? My ideal is to be free, and for people to damn well leave me in peace."

"To be free, that's terrific," says Ernestine dreamily.

"It's pretty difficult to get people to leave you in peace," Suzy adds.

"Pah, pah, all that's just fine words," says Dominique. "As we were saying: Eating, Drinking, and Sleeping."

"No, *no,*" yaps Mme. Pic, "that's not what *I* call the Ideal. The Ideal is your Family, and your Country, it's Art, Duty, Religion . . ."

"And Property," says Meussieu Pic, finishing her sentence for her.

"Oh la la," mutters Suzy, "things aren't looking up."

"Property, that's the origin of a lot of misery," and old Taupe suddenly starts waffling in a monotonous voice, like an automaton whose secret mechanism has long been sought and which has been accidentally set in motion by pulling on one of its toes. "The secret of happiness is not to possess anything. To live happily, we must live apart, and be poor, because the less we possess, the more we escape our fate. Yes, that's right; the more we escape our fate."

These definitive words worry the assembled company a little; this speech seems to them inopportune, out of place, in bad taste even. Their uneasiness turns into anxious embarrassment when they hear Mme. Pic, in a curt voice, utter these words:

"But Meussieu Taupe, you *possess* a wife, now."

This is just what the others didn't dare say; but they consider it a cruel remark. What can old Taupe reply to that? He replies very simply:

"That's stupid, what you've just said, Madam' Pic, it's stupid, foolish and unkind."

A great silence spreads out in front of each face; Meussieu Pic looks as if he has bitten his spoon so hard that he can't get it out of his mouth, and his spouse, after having imitated the behavior of something sitting on a pincushion, exclaims in a sprightly manner:

"Oh! Meussieu Taupe, you will have your little joke. Look Florette, I've already told you not to put your elbows on the table."

Mme. Cloche does," retorts the child.

"You'll get your face slapped in a minute!" yells her mother.

"I'm setting your child a bad example, Madame Pic, aren't I?"

"Oh! but not in the least, Madame Cloche."

"Ideal . . . ideal . . ." Meussieu Taupe mumbles, absent-mindedly.

"It's true, how can we live without ideals?" Themistocles feels obliged to say. "Without ideals, we live like animals."

Mme. Pic casts him the grateful glance of a bitch being allowed to keep one puppy. But Dominique, on the other hand, makes no concession to her.

"Eating, drinking, sleeping, that's my ideal, and I'm not budging."

"And women," adds Themistocles, abruptly deserting Mme. Pic's camp.

"Materialism is the scourge of our society," groans the latter.

"Sanctimonious old cow," says someone, in a sufficiently low voice for everyone to hear without looking as if they do.

Mme. Pic's eyes become bloodshot; Meussieu Pic's become atrocious.

"Do you know the story about the Englishman and the

sack of flour?" Themistocles suddenly asks, with a presence of mind of which his brother thought him incapable.

"That's right, tell us a story," says Mme. Dominique, backing him up.

"Oh yes, let's have a little laugh," sighs Suzy.

"Ah! the story about the Englishman and the sack of flour," says Meussieu Pic, who has finally disengaged his teeth from his teaspoon, "I have a feeling I know that one. It's not the story of an Englishman who buys a sack of flour from an Armenian, is it?"

"From a Greek," Themistocles corrects him.

"In my story, it's an Armenian who sells a sack of corn."

Themistocles lowers his nose in his plate in disgust, and lets the dealer in dried and salted goods finish the story. He congratulates himself on having done so, however, because it doesn't have the slightest success. It's more a strategic retreat than a defeat, and that wit, old Pic, in the end only wins an emPyrrhic victory.

---

Meanwhile, the two waiters lent by the Restaurant des Alliés are putting the fruit on the table and inquiring as to everyone's wishes with reference to coffee and liqueurs. Mme. Cloche, who has drunk eighteen glasses of wine, scorns the fruit, folds her napkin meticulously, and orders a cointreau. She sighs. The two children have disappeared; nobody takes any notice. Most of the guests look like tomatoes drying in the sun. Suzy and Peter are even closer to each other than they appear to be. Mme. Pic, having a care for her dignity, suppresses some tendentious hiccups. Through the open windows comes a little fresh air, with an aftertaste of coalsmoke.

"You'll let us see your tricks soon, Meussieu Peter, won't you," says a lady.

"As soon as I've drunk my brandy, I'll be at your disposal."

"Why don't we sing something?" suggests Suzy.

Now there's a good idea. Ernestine and Suzy each comes on with a nice sentimental tune. Dominique sings of the baneful effects of the gaming table; Themistocles, more gayly, assures them that he's got a good scheme, and Meussieu Pic makes a big hit with a little song relative to the planting of bananas. Taupe declares he doesn't know anything. Mme. Pic declines. Mme. Cloche, requested to show her talents, bellows out a lugubrious tale about a crippled sailor whose fiancée prefers to marry a young man who is quite a gentleman to start off with but who later becomes an alcoholic and goes mad; the fiancée then tries to find the crippled sailor, but his comrades have eaten him one day when there was a west wind, and all that's left of him is a little bit of his calf preserved in brine. Choking with emotion, Mme. Cloche does away with the contents of her glass of cointreau before she goes on: the fiancée takes the little bit of his calf and eats it, and then throws herself down from the top of a lighthouse into the homicidal Ocean, singing: 'Tis the tale of a sailor boy, a sailor boy of France . . .

This lugubrious adventure makes a considerable impression.

"You might have sung us something a bit more cheerful," says Dominique.

"I yonly know two songs; that one, and then the one about the tragic guillotine. I chose the one that wasn't so sad."

"It's Mme Belhôtel's turn, now," says Suzy.

Ernestine gets up and goes over to the window.

"Smatter?" asks Suzy.

"Don't feel so good."

"You ill?"

Ernestine doesn't answer.

"Well well, certainly are some stars, this evening!" says she, then takes a few unsteady steps.

Peter gets up to help her.

"Go ahead without me. I'll go and lie down for a few minutes. You stay there, Taupe."

Suzy escorts her; they both go out. They wait in silence. Mme. Cloche leans out of the window. Suzy comes back with the two children.

"It's nothing. She's lying down in her room."

"She duh want anything?"

No, she doesn't want anything.

"Snot serious, is it?"

No, it's not serious.

"Where've you been, Florette?" Mme. Pic asks severely.

"I was playing with Clovis."

"Hm! why weren't you playing here?"

"Ida know."

The two children sit down again. They look at each other without laughing. Just no way of being left alone, thinks Florette. She agrees with Peter: the ideal is for people to damn well leave you in peace. That day will come; when she's grown up. And *how* she'll put her elbows on the table. And *how* she'll have fun with the boys in the dark. And *how* she'll go home just when it suits her. They'll see! As for Clovis, he feels slightly embarrassed where Suzy is concerned; the thing is, Suzy, she isn't a little girl, she's a woman, a real one. And furthermore, his uncle, who is giving him an amused look, terrifies him more than his father, who's frowning at him. In short, he is slightly embarrassed.

"What are you looking at over there, Aunt Sidonie?"

"Getting a bit of fresh air, dear."

After a silence:

"It's true, what Ernestine said; certainly are some stars this evening."

One by one, the assembled company leaves the table; some of its members verify Mme. Cloche's statement. Dominique hands around some cigars.

"There's the Great Bear," says Themistocles, pointing to something or other with the tip of his cigar.

"And there's the polestar," adds Meussieu Pic, doing ditto.

"It's funny, all those little lights," says Mme. Cloche pensively.

"Those little lights, Madame, are big suns, only they're so far away from us that they seem no larger than a pinhead," pontificates the dealer in dried and salted goods.

"Well I never!"

"And there's some that's so far away that you can't see them," adds the sergeant major.

"Howd we know they exist, then?" asks Mme. Dominique.

"You can see them through glasses, and the bigger the glasses are, the more you can see. Astronomers count millions and millions of them like that," replies Meussieu Pic, who has been very well informed on this subject by the Abbé Morue.

"Isn't science wonderful!" exclaims Suzy.

"I want to be an astronomer!" exclaims Clovis, fired with sudden enthusiasm.

"Don't spose the gents in that profession get very rich," Dominique thinks aloud.

"In the old days," says Mme. Pic, who'd managed to keep quiet for ten whole minutes, "no one counted all those stars, and they were much happier."

"Sgot nothing to do with it," Peter declares.

"Yes, woss use of astronomy?" questions Mme. Cloche, following this new line.

"It's absolutely no use," Saturnin answers.

"There, you see!" Mme. Pic triumphs.

"It's been useful enough to show that the sun doesn't go around the earth, like they say in the Bible," Peter throws at her, sure of this effect.

Mme. Pic, who has no hope of converting the professor of white magic, registers this blow by abstracting all the remaining *petits-fours* from the table.

"Astronomy is useful in the navy, too," adds Themistocles.

"I remember that my grandfather, who was a master mariner, knew all the stars by name," says Meussieu Pic.

"Have all the stars got a name?" asks Mme. Cloche, thunderstruck.

"Every one."

"Well I never!"

Mme. Cloche, much affected, opens her bag and extracts a large checked handkerchief; she makes immoderate use of it, and then puts it back in its receptacle.

"What are you doing with that dove?" Peter asks her.

"What dove?"

"The one that's in your bag."

"I've got a dove in my bag?"

"Take a look."

She obeys, and a dove escapes from the open bag, flutters

about a bit, and then alights on the frame of a color print. Applause.

"That's just nothing," says Peter. "Child's play! Child's play! The performance is really going to begin, now."

"Why don't we ask Ernestine to come," Suzy suggests.

"That's right! Maybe she's better."

"No, she isn't better," says old Taupe, emerging from the corridor. "She looks ill."

"What's the matter with her?"

"Dunno."

Old Taupe sits down, in a daze.

"Have to get a doctor," he adds.

Then they really get going. Suzy and Mme. Belhôtel go up to Ernestine's room. The men, no point in their going. What could be the matter with her? Indigestion? Migraine?

Mme. Cloche then starts anxiously contemplating the turnip watch she's holding; she's beginning to get worried, to be afraid. Taking advantage of the confusion, Florette tickles Clovis, but the latter is in no mood for fun and games. He shares the avuncular anxiety. Then the heavy tread of Mme. Dominique is heard.

"Dominique! Dominique! have to go and get a doctor!"

---

When the doctor had gone, the members of the wedding party sat in silence around the table, which was soiled with cigar ash and wine stains. Bits of vegetables or meat, which had jumped out of the dishes like absurd acrobats, were scattered all over it, wilting in little pools of gravy. Pips and pieces of peel were mixed up with this debris; a flower petal was transfixed by a huge fishbone, for a bunch of flowers was shedding its petals in the midst of this dilapidation. Upstairs, they could hear Suzy walking up and down in Ernestine's room; old Taupe was there too, and Mme. Dominique. The rest of the wedding party were hanging around in the dining room, their eyes vacant, their stomachs full. The two children were pinching each other with violence, but in silence. Mme. Cloche, very pale, was scratching the tablecloth with the nail of her index-finger, her favorite gesture; but the others didn't budge. Camélia came as far as the door to sniff, looked at the silent assembly, and then went back into the shadows. The two waiters lent by the Restaurant des Alliés had gone. Dominque coughed every so often. Suddenly, he noticed that Mme. Pic wasn't there.

"Huh, where's your missis then?" he said to Pic.

"Ursule? Huh, where is she then? She may be upstairs, I don't know," replied Meussieu Pic, who was falling asleep.

"I think she went out," said Mme. Peter.

But they didn't press the point.

Then, five minutes later, Peter stood up and exclaimed:

"It's rotten, though, just sitting here and not doing anything. Not being able to do anything. Absolutely nothing."

He sat down again, his eyes moist. Dominique coughed.

Saturnin, irritated by his sister's habit, said to her:

"Stop scratching like that. You're not a mouse."

Mme. Cloche stopped; she was getting paler and paler, and seemed to be thinking hard. Her tuberous nose was throbbing, her eyes were passionately animated; with despair, rage, hope and anger.

Florette, who had been pinched a bit too brutally by Clovis, started sniveling. Meussieu Pic took her on his knees, mumbling poor little thing, pore lil thing, pawlthing, pawlthing, pawlthing.

"Ah, sh'urrup," said Dominique, exasperated.

The dealer in dried and salted goods shurrup, and advanced once more toward sleep. A few moments later, Mme. Dominique came down, poured herself out a large glass of wine and gulped it down.

"She's getting worse," she said abruptly, and then went upstairs again.

Themistocles, who had discovered a stray bit of bread on the table, was modeling a little ball into the shape of a phallus.

A bell rang. It was the doctor coming back. He climbed the stairs with speed, like a dead leaf raised by the wind. Then, five minutes later, he came tumbling down to the door and disappeared, his shoulders hunched. Mme. Dominique came down again.

"Well, what did he say this time?" asked Dominique.

"Znothing he can do, he says."

"Znothing he can do," Peter repeated, automatically.

"But what is it she's got?" asked Mme. Cloche.

"He said the name of an illness, but I can't remember it," replied Mme. Belhôtel. "Tsan illness you don't get better from, tswot he said."

The company shivered.

"Isn't there any way of saving her?" asked someone.

"No, the doctor, znothing he can do, tswot he said."

No one spoke; then someone again asked:

"Has she got long?"

"Quarter of an hour, twenty minutes at the most, tswot he said."

No one spoke; then someone again asked:

"She in pain?"

"No. Zjust gently fading away. She's near her end, tswot he said."

"How extraordinary," said someone, pensively.

Mme. Cloche, with a backhander, flattened a fly that was shitting on the tablecloth. Themistocles, with a flick, ejected his bread phallus through the window. Mme. Dominique poured herself out another large glass of wine, and went up again to watch over the deathbed.

"Isn't it a shame," says someone, "dying at that age."

"Alas, we die at every age," says Meussieu Pic.

"She was a good girl, a good girl," says Dominique, deeply moved.

"Isn't it a shame," says someone, "dying at that age."

"And they can't do anything for that illness."

"We don't even know what it is."

"We don't even know what it's called."

"She's forgotten what the doctor said."

"Isn't it a shame to die at any age," says someone else.

"All the same, when you're young, when you haven't had anything out of life."

"All the same, what a shame, all the same, what a shame."

"We don't even know what she's dying of."

"The doctor said a name, but we don't know."

"And us, we can't do a thing, we can only wait till it's over."

"What a shame, all the same, what a shame."

"Ole Taupe now, you could understand him dying, but Ernestine . . ."

"Why'd she marry him? Why youth with an old man? Why?"

"And why is it the young one that's dying, and not the old one? Why Ernestine and not Taupe?"

"How should we know? how should we know?"

"What a shame, all the same, to die at that age," says someone.

Then, once again, no one spoke. They aren't crying; after all, they aren't children. Ernestine—but who is she? She is about to disappear, so they say. She's upstairs in bed, and it will soon be as if nothing has happened. Ernestine—but who is she? "My sister," one will answer. "I've hardly seen her three times in the last ten years. We were the same age, us two brothers, she was just little; we went away to earn our living, more or less well; Ernestine, we didn't really know how she was getting along. We sent New Year's cards, and birthday cards. We were fond of her." But who is she—Ernestine? "A little waitress I made pregnant," Dominique will answer. "She worked well; not a lot, no, but she wasn't afraid of hard work. Day and night, I used to go to her room. Like with Germaine, like with Camille, like with Marguerite, like with the other one too, the one with straw-colored hair. She knew how to keep the customers, an she never complained. The kid, no one ever saw it. The river's looked after it all right. Ernestine—I was very fond of her."

But who is she—Ernestine? "Dominique's waitress," Saturnin and Meussieu Pic answered. But who is she—Ernestine? "My sister-in-law," answers Mme. Peter. But who is she—Ernestine? "The bride," answers Florette. But who is she—Ernestine? "My accomplice," answers Mme. Cloche. But who is she—Ernestine? And they are all thinking: She's something that's upstairs and that's dying. Ernestine—that's not me. Ernestine is someone else, someone else that we don't want to be, that we don't want to see. Some of them might perhaps want to know how it's happening. She isn't in pain, it would appear. But is she talking? Is she delirious? Does she know she's going to die? Because we know *we* aren't going to die. She can't have much more than ten minutes now. That's not much. At least *we* have the whole night, and tomorrow, and the day after tomorrow; well—days. Days and days. And old Taupe, what's he got to say about all this? What could he be thinking? Because really, it's a little peculiar, marrying a young woman and then she goes and dies on her wedding day. No, that's never been known. Old Taupe, what could he have to say? Zno getting away from it, it's all very sad.

The members of the wedding party are becoming a sort of worried and amorphous magma. Their anxiety weakens and dissolves them; it makes putty of them. Because it's a minor anxiety, something very ordinary and a bit degrading. Not an anxiety that'd get you rolling on the floor, not for the moment, at any rate.

For the moment, they're bored. They are waiting—it's almost as if they're waiting for a train. But this particular train, they're not the ones that are going to take it. It's the person that's up above.

If you look a bit closer at it, the magma turns out to be mere semblance. You can discover its molecules. You can perceive the individuals. It is composed of Dominique, who is worried, and Peter, who is sad, and Themistocles, who is sick at heart, and Mme. Cloche, who is seething, and Florette, who is sleeping, and Meussieu Pic, who is dozing, and Mme. Peter, who is doing accounts in her head, and Mme. Saturnin, who is profoundly affected by this lugubrious event, and Mme. Pic, who isn't there.

"Hm, that's true," says Dominique, "Mme. Pic, we don't know where she is."

No one answers, as the family concerned is snoozing, as has been said above.

But the facts soon take it upon themselves to answer the tavernkeeper. Facts—let us rather say: events. For there is a ring at the door, and the sniffing Camélia goes to open it. Four shod feet tap on the treads of the staircase with their discreet heels, for someone in the house is on her death-bed.

Sh! Sh! The four feet reach the first floor, pass the dining-room door, and continue their ascent.

"Good God!" cries Peter. "The old girl has gone and fetched a sky pilot!"

---

Ernestine, with a friendly gesture, invited the crowd into her room, adopted the position of Socrates drinking the hemlock, and uttered these words:

"It was nice of you, Madame Pic, to think of me, but your curé, you know, well, you know what you can do with him, because I know your curé, I've seen him often enough, him and his dirty tricks, to know the sort of stuff he pulls, and snot only this one, it's the ones I knew when I was just a little girl, too, they never deprived themselves of their nasty little pleasures with anything they could get hold of, from their check handkerchiefs to the little boys in the catechism class. Anyway, as you see, Madame Pic, if you thought you were going to inflict your mumbo jumbo on me, you were barking up the wrongest tree you ever could bark up, and your curé, he can stuff his crucifix back in his pants that he hides underneath his soutane. Anyway, even so, it's nice of you to let me know nicely that I'm going to die. Praps I mightn't even have known. You know, Madame Pic, I wasn't so crazy about knowing, but now that you've shown me your gent in black I know what's going to happen. Cept that I don't really know. Anyway, members of the wedding party that are here to listen to me jabbering, I'm going to tell you a little about what's going on. Snot that I want to teach you anything or start preaching at you. They don't have me registered at the town hall for that sort of thing; even so I could do it just as well as that gent in black that's making such horrid faces at what I'm saying. And so, members of the wedding party, open your lug-holes, like we used to say in my village where I was born, and I'm going to make you a little speech; that's as good a way as any to use up the time I've got left to live, doncha think? To start with, I must tell you, then, that the fact that I'm going to disappear amazes me a little. Somehow, I can't quite understand how it's going to happen. I know that everyone can do without me quite all right, and that they'll go on living after me; even so, I can't quite essplain this peculiar adventure to myself. Ten minutes, or an hour, mnot quite sure which, from now . . ."

"Ten minutes at the most," says Mme. Belhôtel.

"Thanks, Madame Belhôtel. I'll see that I finish in time. So as I was saying, in ten minutes from now I'll be disposed of, obliterated, blotted out. That—now that's really peculiar. Snot that I believe in the immortality of the soul, as the abbé would say, or in life after death, like the woman that sells newspapers would say, you know the one I mean, the one that's a spiritualist. I don't believe in all that. I've thought about it. Imagining yourself just like you are, only not having any eyes, or arms, or legs—doesn't make sense. On account of I've realized that what you are, it's not just a little voice that talks in your head, but it's your whole body, too, that you can feel is alive, and everything you can do with it. If you haven't got a body any more, how can you say that it's still me? And so, to come back to what I was saying just now, when I find it surprising that I'm going to disappear, snot that I'm thinking about life after death or my soul in heaven or in hell or any sort of imaginative stuff like that. I'm talking, as you might say, objectively. When something else disappears, that's already odd. But me. *That's* just staggering. A tree catches fire—there's still the smoke and ash left; and yet the tree's gone. It's like me. The decay will be left, but the little voice that talks in your head when you're by yourself, there won't be anything left of that. Mine, when it stops talking, it won't be talking anywhere else. That's what's strange. Tisn't that it worries me much especially. People can do without me. Zno doubt about that. And I can do without myself all right. Snot that I'm trying to make any propaganda for the spiritualists—I might as well use the right words. Even so, there's things you can't stop yourself thinking. On the yuther hand, it's just as crazy to think that there's any reason for you to be on earth, but all the same I can't stop myself thinking: Here

I am, dying, and what the hell will I have done here? I'll have rinsed out some glasses and done some dishwashing—no doubt about that; I'll have slept with some men who were a pretty lousy bunch, in the main—in the moral sense of the word, that is; I'll have had a child that was immediately done away with; I'll have been beaten as a child, after which I'll have somewhat wallowed in the mud. And I'll have married old Taupe, yes, I was forgetting, I'll have married old Taupe. I can't help saying that if that's all I'll have done, I haven't got much to boast about. And after that, what would I have done? Well that's another story. I'll say some more about that in a minute. For the moment, I'm giving you a lecture. Well, coming back to that, I must have plenty of screws loose to ask myself the sort of questions I am asking myself, don't you think? What was I doing among you all? Well, I used to do the dishes. Why try and split hairs, eh? Members of the wedding party, what the hell are you doing here?"

"We're listening to you," they replied in chorus.

"And me, what the hell am I doing?"

"You're talking," they replied once again.

"And what am I saying?"

"You're saying rather vague things," they replied, still in unison.

"I'd really like to give you more details, but you'll understand, I can't. Course, there's something very simple, and everyone knows that: Taupe's wife's going to die, cos sooner or later, that finally happens, and if we live it's because we're going to die. In that right? And then, there's something else, something very simple. Since I'm dying and there's nothing to be done about it and that's just the way it is, well, zno point in making a song and dance about the fate of my little voice that talks in my head when I'm by myself, or in knowing what's been the point of me living twenty-one years on this planet. To sum up, as I was saying, I'm disappearing like so many other people have done before me and like even more will do after. There. But I'd say that's a good five minutes I've been talking."

"A barber's five minutes, even," said Saturnin, politely.
"Then I'll get a move on."
"Just a moment," said Saturnin.
"Yes?" said Ernestine politely.
"If we live, it's because we die, that's what you said, dint you?"
"Yes, I did say that."
"You might just as well have said the opposite," he observed.
"I agree," replied Ernestine.
"Ah, good," said Saturnin. "That's all I wanted to know."
"You see what a good girl I am. Just when I was going to get rich, I'm dying, and I'm d . . ."
"When you were going to get rich!" exclaimed Mme. Pic, amazed.
"She's getting delirious," Mme. Cloche hastened to say.
"When she was going to get rich!" exclaimed Meussieu Pic, flabbergasted.
"Ernestine doesn't know what she's saying any more," declared Mme. Cloche.
"Let her speak," said Peter.
"Yes of course, we must let her speak," Themistocles agreed.
"She's only got five minutes to live and you won't let her speak, it's idiotic," said Mme. Belhôtel.
"Start by keeping quiet yourself, then," said Mme. Pic.
"I'll keep quiet when I want to keep quiet, Madame," replied Mme. Belhôtel.
"Come, come, ladies, you surely aren't going to quarrel *now*," said Dominique.
"Someone's got to start keeping quiet," said Mme. Saturnin.
"*You* start, then," said Mme. Pic.
"And this girl is dying without the sacraments of the Church," exclaimed the curé, who was called the Abbé Leslaines.
"Ah! If that one's going to start, there's more to come!" exclaimed Peter.
"Silence, then!" shouted Themistocles.
"Not so much noise," whispered old Taupe.

"Oh, you know, I'm a good girl," said Ernestine. "If it bothers you to listen to me, I'll keep quiet."

And she kept quiet.

---

Along the river, where antiquated hats and abandoned shoes were rotting, down by the river, where fishermen's lines were vainly trying to tempt the nonexistent gudgeon, by the banks of the river, where a barge occasionally crept past, laden with sand and adorned with a Flemish flowerpot, along the river, it was dark. It was also dark elsewhere, but never mind; by the banks of the river, the darkness was deepening. Through this darkness, two beings were walking. These beings were human; better still, they were brachycephalic; one female and the other male, they belonged the same family, they had had the same mother, and no doubt the same father; and if they did not bear the same name, that is because French law gives the married woman the name of her husband. Now, the sister had married, in lawful wedlock, one Cloche, and the name had remained with her even though she had been the winning party in a widowhood case. The brother had never given up the name of Belhôtel, of which he was in nowise proud. But this brother might well have been another, for two existed, whom a skillful subterfuge made it possible to distinguish, In fact, their father, foreseeing that the same nomenclature might be a source of inconvenience to his two male children, had given them a second appellation: he called the one Dominique and the other Saturnin. In this way people were able to distinguish them. It is with the former that we are here concerned.

Mme. Cloche and Dominique Belhôtel, then, were walking in the dark along the tarry river and, apart from this occupation, were exchanging ideas and interjections. In short, by the side of the mourning-crepe river, Mme. Cloche and Dominique Belhôtel, enveloped in the darkness like truffles in chocolate cream, were having a discussion under cover of the opaque shades of night.

"The little bitch, she nearly let on," the one was saying.

"What a mess," the other was saying, "we'll have to start from the beginning again."

"*They've* had us."

"They've had *her.*"

"They'll get *us.*"

"They *will not* get us."

"What we going to do?"

"Look at this water, it's safe, it's calm, it's water that doesn't talk. When the old boy's at the bottom, he'll never come up again. He'll've committed suicide out of a broken heart."

"How you can go on," murmured the brother.

"And that idiot of a Mme. Pic, she'll go and blurt it out everywhere. There's another one ought to go down to the bottom. Into the mud!"

They walk in silence for a few moments, moving in the darkness along the black, shoe-polish river.

"So you think *They* killed her?" asked the brother.

"Plain as the nose on your face," replied the sister.

The sister added:

"Pore Ernestine! She suspected something of the sort."

"And we've been had."

"Yes, we're the marks, unless the old boy disappears. It's simple."

"Not so simple as all that. And after, have to find his hiding place."

"It's behind the door."

"What if we don't find it?"

"Dominique, I believe you're getting yellow."

"Yellow, seasy to say. You're getting me involved in some lousy goings-on. Personally, I don't need it, the old boy's money. I've got my own. Ten years from now I'll have made my fortune. I'm hard-working, I am, and I know how to look after my cash. When it was just the business of the wedding, that was all right. Just a little favor I did you. But now, to chuck the old boy in the river just for the sake of maybe getting a little sweets, no thanks. An anyway, I'm like Ernestine, I'm wary of the others. They're stronger'n us. We've just seen that, haven't we? Well, no thanks! The cemetery or the guillotine, that's what you're offering me."

"You're talking like a sock merchant or a ham actor," Mme. Cloche told him. "You may not look it, but you've got noodles in your veins stead of blood. You look tough, but your heart's made of macaroni. Won't you just drool at the mouth when you see me go in my Rolls with my gigolos when you're rotting in your whorehouse with three poxy sluts and a Negress. You're like Ernestine. If she'd listened to me right away, she wouldn't be where she is now. You won't play now, and then in a week you'll want to be in on it. Twon't bring you any luck. Snuff chat. Sgo back."

They turned around. The moon was swimming with difficulty in mid-air, and the rare stars were blacked out in the dark mud of the river. Trains whistled now and then, and dogs howled from time to time. A cock even crowed; which didn't cause the dawn to appear. Behind their fragile fences, kitchen gardens were peacefully sleeping, and onions were dozing side by side with lettuces and tomatoes. Over in the direction of Paris, there was a huge glow, because it's a big town with lots of streetlamps and luminous signs. On the other side of the river, a long way away, a factory was still lit up; on the Chemicals and Linoleum side, a few lights spoke of reduced activity. Occasionally, everything subsided into abysses of silence, only to be dragged out of it once again by a train whistling, a dog barking, a cock crowing or a car humming; after which, the houses and the huts and the little gardens and the factories were once more engulfed in an oleaginous silence.

In Blagny itself, one house alone was still alive, and toward this house the brother and sister Belhôtel turned their steps. When they got to the town hall, Sidonie said:

"And whatever you do, you that's in good with the cops, try and see they keep their noses out of this."

"Well, that's one more thing I'll do for you," said the brother.

Then he added:

"What if you informed on the others?"

"Brilliant—and that's all you can think of. When I'm just precisely asking you to see that no one sticks their nose into it. This business is between me and the others. Got it?"

"All right, all right," replied Dominique.

As they were coming to the café, they could see its lights, she said:

"Are you very upset about it?"

"About what?" he said.

And then he remembered the young body that had been murdered, and started to cry, because after all he was very fond of Ernestine. Mme. Cloche turned her head to look at this brother with the heart of macaroni, but the look did not express any precise thought, nor any more blame than approbation.

---

At dawn, the passenger trains started running again, damp and cold, their windows foggy and whitish, like eyes covered in nubeculae. Into one of these climbed the remains of the wedding party, with thick mouths, and brains flabbier than an eider down. Saturnin and his lady were going back to their lodge; an unexpected engagement was enticing Peter and his espoused into a Walloon province; the discipline which is the strength of the armed forces had determined the hour of Themistocles's reimbarracksing, and Mme. Cloche had an appointment for 9 o'clock, something to do with a fetus. The little group, still sprightly after their sleepless night, sat down on the arid seats and allowed themselves to be conveyed into the city with no word either of farewell or protest. Then, when the engine with the powerful whistle had already conveyed them for some minutes along the rails, which were as shiny as a bald head, one of the persons present—it wasn't Mme. Cloche—asked. "Why the devil did she say: 'just when I was going to get rich'?," thus translating the general uneasiness this mystery was causing among the uninitiated. For, at Blagny, the news was already being spread from vocal chords to voice, and being completed by this anxious interrogation, which no one could answer except by imagining romantic adventures or absurd fuliginations. For example, as a result of all its cogitations, Mme. Pic's brain was wrung out like a dishcloth that is being relieved of its moisture; Peter and his wife and brother didn't know what to say about these unexpected riches; but Saturnin, who was more knowledgeable, was beginning to glimpse the somber machinations of his sister, the abortionist. He was reconstituting their framework, not without certain errors. But he didn't answer. Mme. Cloche grunted, and they all became lost in thought, and only resumed contact with the world at the call of a man with a gallooned cap who was demanding in a raucous voice some pieces of cardboard which he wished to perforate.

Then, they separated. Saturnin and his wife were able to utter some words of condolence. The two brothers, moved to tears at the memory of their defunct sister, forgot their differences. They shook each other's hand very heartily, and then immediately turned their backs on each other, and went off toward other atmospheres, both with heavy heart and flowing lachrymal gland. Both disappear, both fade away, we shall see them no more, neither Peter Tom the Anchorite, the subtle magician and his lady, so very slim and slight, nor the trusty sergeant major, the pride of his superiors and the terror of his subordinates. They plunge into their reciprocal destinies, like shrimps into the sand, they withdraw and, as you might say, die.

The brother and sister remain face to face, and the sister-in-law too. The sister-in-law is sick of it all; of the wedding, of defunctitude and of old Ma Cloche. She's had her fill. She's choked. She's fed up. She's pissed off. She's had enough. She gives her spouse's muscular arm a significant pinch, and he puts off until later the explanation he intends to demand from Sidonie. On the street, opposite the Gare du Nord, the final disintegration of the wedding party is accomplished. Meussieu and Mme. Saturnin Belhôtel, concierges by profession, catch a bus. Mme. Cloche stays there, alone and in distress.

People have finally woken up. The traffic is already circulating—that's the right word—and becoming thick. The cars are multiplying. They are emerging from all sides. You couldn't count them, there are so many. It's raining cars and cars. And the pedestrians, that's even worse. They are rushing in all directions and treading on one another's toes. And they really are in a hurry. They're going to work, for goodness' sake, and their bosses won't have any messing around with time. The late bird catches no wages, as the proverb has it. Mme. Cloche, standing squarely on her soles, lets the flow of workers go by to her right and to her left. A memory is monopolizing her thoughts and making them firmer than a rock again which a torrent of insults is breaking. She remembers, yes, it was here, that three months ago—three months, already! —a man got made mincemeat of by a bus, and that the next day the gangster nearly got himself run over by the other gangster. Ah, this café, that's the one where the camomile tea is so bad and the waiter so insolent. She'd forgotten that incredible sequence of events. Taupe's treasure had been entirely dominating her, and she immediately reverts to him, abandoning the field of remembrance.

A bitter taste was grating her tongue. While Dominique was there, she hadn't shown the white feather. Now, in the midst of this bustling crowd, far from the poisoned corpse, she felt beaten. The others had won. The treasure had eluded her. She could see no means of getting it back. This was the end of the long and copious banquets with which she had been promising herself she would stuff her old age; this was the end of the attractive young men who would have taken her dancing in night clubs; this was the end of her travels; car and low-cut evening dresses, itwoz, itwoz itwoz, and chic little dogs that were horribly ugly and expensive, and real genuine jewelry. She'd have to start all over again removing undesirables, and festering in a lousy, rancid flat. It made her sick with disgust. To have discovered a treasure trove, a real one, and then to be done out of it, what a disgusting thing. It made her pale with rage. Looking at her, a meussieu who was two minutes early wondered whether, improbable though it seemed, she weren't feeling seasick.

She remembered something else: two days before, she had shuffled up the whole length of the Rue Saint-Honoré, promising herself both this and that, and then again this, for, in her opinion, nothing could exhaust the resources of that immense miser, the Blagny junk dealer. And nothing could exhaust the desires of a midwife past her prime. She would have taken dancing lessons; she'd have had her rump massaged by some guy with a lot of energy. She'd have learned to swim; to drive a car; to play bridge and bite-me-pussy, which was the latest fashion in games. She would have come into contact with the costly virility of elegant and idle young men. And to come back to the start of the beginning, she'd have stuffed herself to the gills, blowouts would have succeeded banquets, and gorgeographies would have succeeded indigestions.

In the pavement opposite the Gare du Nord, Mme. Cloche remained motionless and solitary, like a rock in the middle of a torrent, contemplating the shards of her ideal, broken by the Others.

A new wave of suburbanites finally uprooted her, and one unit of this wave happened to be Etienne Marcel, on his way to his bank, there to earn his bread by the cramp of his arm. Mme. Cloche didn't see him. She was carried away by the new wave of suburbanites and disappeared with it, into the innermost recesses of the city.

---

*There are ways of laughing, as there are of crying, murmured the green-eyed Romany. What more do you want to know? Which is the gloomiest history? Mine, or that of my ancestors? In the old days, the stakes went up in flames, and my ancestors with them; or their friends. For we have always had friends. But their number diminishes every day. As we ourselves, too, become obliterated. You can easily guess, everything I'm telling you about my ancestors is just supposition, and I myself am acting a part. My eyes are certainly green, and my beard displays a week's growth, but I don't belong to the Romany race; I only look as if I do. I have the Romany Look, and the Romany despair. I am accompanying the outworn races toward their fatal dissolution. The Tasmanians. The Dodos. The Æpyronithidae. The Thises. The Thats. Forgive me if my erudition sometimes fails me. To be frank, it's a real pleasure to appear to advantage in one's own eyes. To be a man who strays through space, suppressing stupendous secrets—mysteries. To be a man who sweats blood at the sight of his own shadow growing grey, growing white. Or the people you sometimes meet in provincial hotels. They have no reason to be there. They are not tradesmen, they are not burglars. They haven't come for a wedding, they haven't come for a funeral. They have no reason to be there, unless it is that they are heavy with the burden of their unhappiness and boredom. Unhappiness is sometimes immeasurable, and boredom continuous. It's a question of secrets that affect the life of peoples and nations; of abortive upheavals that constrict the hearts of these outcasts; of failed endeavors; of anguished memories; of recurrent frustrations. I belong to this race, that is what I was insinuating to you just now. I accompany this race, as it makes its way through the Occidental peoples, telling fortunes. I shall not tell yours, for I prefer to remain silent in this respect in your presence. Yes, as I was saying just now, there are ghosts who bear the burden of heavy silences, and silence strangles them; in their pale way, they come and go as if nothing had happened. Those who have no secrets suspect them, however. Naturally, though, I say that to make a good impression, because, as we all know, everyone has his secret. Thus one man hides the birth of a vice, another the anxiety of a parent, a third a horrible practical joke which was played on him, and which torments him. Naturally, they do not each have the secrets they deserve, because there are such things as idiotic ghosts. Loves can be disappointed, loves can be blighted, loves can be hopeless, loves can be desiccated. Ambitions can be disappointed, efforts of will can be hopeless, pride can be blighted, passions can be desiccated. They still look the same, these men, they remain upright, they walk, but they are sick unto death and their secret is eating them away, eating them to death. Spiders' teeth are not so long as a torment that cannot be avowed. And I too have my secret, my secrets. I have several thousand. One a day. Ever since I was born. I'm exaggerating a little, of course. But still, let's say since I was two, a secret every other day. You can see how obvious this is, and I'm not talking about the everyday secret, the little secret which, if you really had to, you could talk about. The sort of secret that would do for the confessional, when it still existed. A shabby little secret, in short. I'm only talking about big secrets. Naturally, a single one is enough to run you aground. You see, I* am *aground. So I have a big secret. Even though I'm trying to tell you something, I see that I have to admit that I find it impossible to be precise about its nature. Totally impossible. But this has a certain something to do with the downfall of races and the decomposition of nations. I once knew an individual who was in possession of a formidable secret; I met him in a hotel in Avignon, in a very specially lugubrious hotel, in a hotel for people of our sort. I saw at once that something was weighing on him and that he couldn't talk about it. I didn't want to ask him—it would have been a waste of time. He was a very correct-looking person, of pronounced elegance, with an umbrella and bowler hat, and his every action revealed his great distinction. He read little, and went for long walks through the town, looking through the iron bars of the gates. Well, as I was telling you just now, this individual was in possession of a formidable secret, which I finally discovered. He was dead. You can easily see how it was. And this is really one of the most formidable of secrets. I'm afraid that mine is even more appalling. Don't worry, I'm not going to tell it to you. I Am Not Going To Tell It To You. I'm not going to tell it to you. You know quite well that I'm neither an ogre nor a Simple Simon nor a boojum. It's something far simpler. I don't know whether you're aware of it, there are some men who suffer appallingly. And that doesn't stop them getting their toes trodden on in the metro. But you may perhaps not be following the sequence of my sentences very clearly. It doesn't really matter. You can think about it later on, when I've disappeared around the corner with my wives and my sons, my horses and my dogs. The sun is sinking. It's time for me to go. We shall finish the night's march. Farewell, then, and keep your secrets as I keep mine. My sons are calling me and my horses are neighing. Farewell.*

*The clock struck 11 on the mantelpiece, 11 o'clock—all right to go to sleep now. He took off his green-eyed Romany mask and obliterated it between his hands, like a magician making a handkerchief disappear. Then he picked up a face, stuck it over his own, and started speaking.* I *am the dead man.*

*You see how distinguished I look. I'm just as the Romany described me, aren't I? Umbrella and bowler hat, distinguished gestures. I'm exactly like the portrait he painted of me for you. I read little, and I go for long walks through the town. And I look through the iron bars of gates. That's the truth. I admit I am curious; not a very serious failing, eh? Only, the thing is, I have a formidable secret. If you hadn't been told about it, I wouldn't have been able to confess it. I am dead. More precisely: I am a dead man. But naturally, no one suspects it; if they did, innkeepers would refuse to let me a room, and people in the street would say: That fellow stinks, he has a stale, musty smell. Comments, you will agree, which it is very unpleasant to hear. I can't bear people making remarks about me behind my back. It irritates me. And even though I am dead, I am still very sensitive.*

*He snatched off this new mask in disgust, crumpled it up and threw it down the toilet. What an overripe corpse that was! And not a bit interesting. It ought to be planted in the ground and well watered; it might perhaps give birth to a beautiful willow tree or a tomato plant. If not the agreeable, at least the useful. Let's forget about it. Then he yawned, thought for a moment about the appearance of a professor of white magic, and then chose his usual appearance. Pierre yawned again, wound up his watch, blew his nose with circumspection, stretched out between two cloths, and quickly fell asleep.*

## Sixth Chapter

HIS hands in his pockets, Narcense was going home.

"Ah, you're back then!" said Saturnin.

"You see, I've had a vacation."

"I'm glad to see you again, Meussieu Narcense," said Saturnin.

"Any letters?"

"Not a thing," said Saturnin.

"I thought so."

"If you've got time to listen to me," said Saturnin, "I could tell you some most peculiar things."

"Apropos of what?"

"Apropos of my sister," said Saturnin, "and Etienne Marcel and Pierre Le Grand."

"Well, well! I'm all ears."

"Um. Here's the whole story. But let's go in: I don't want this to go any further."

They sat down in the darkness of the lodge.

Then Saturnin described the marriage and death of Ernestine, and her last words: "Just when she was going to get rich."

"So now, Meussieu Narcense," said Saturnin, "you can see that I see it all. My sister Sidonie has discovered, I don't know how, that old Taupe was a rich miser and she made Ernestine marry him so as to get her hands on his fortune. As for M. Marcel and M. Le Grand, she suspects them of trying to swindle him, in one way or another. How did she find all this out? Don't I just wonder! But the facts are there, eh? An zanother thing that's pretty suspicious: that's Ernestine's death. What do you think?—don't you think it's extraordinary? In any case, one thing is true: that's that Taupe's hiding his cash, and another's just as certain, and that is that Sidonie wants to pinch it. As for Marcel and Le Grand, well, don't you think they want to get their hands on it, too? If not, how do you explain their trips to Blagny? Don't have anything to do at Blagny, do they? Well then?"

As Narcense didn't answer, Saturnin went on:

"Do you think Meussieu Marcel is capable of committing a crime?"

Narcense smiled:

"That would amaze me."

Saturnin scratched his hair.

"Well. What do you think about it?"

"Hm. Not a great deal. By the way, do you know where I've been?"

"In X . . . ?" said Saturnin.

"Oh no. I've just spent three weeks with Le Grand's brother, in Z. . . ."

"Ah," said Saturnin.

"I saw Le Grand several times. He's a charming young man, and he's trying to help me. But only when it amuses him."

"Ah," said Saturnin.

"What would you do if you got rich?"

"Oh, oh," said Saturnin, "that needs some thought."

"You must have *some* idea on the subject."

"Of course," said Saturnin, "I think I'd do a bit of traveling."

"Good."

"And after that," said Saturnin, "I'd publish my complete works."

"Good."

"And I'd buy myself a meerscham pipe," said Saturnin.

"Good."

"That's all for the moment," said Saturnin.

"Do you think all that's worth a little trouble?"

"How d'you mean?" said Saturnin.

"Well, are you really itching for them, your mere sham pipe and your trip around the world and your complete works?"

"They do make me feel a little itchy," said Saturnin.

"Would you be prepared to go to a little trouble?"

"Oh oh," said Saturnin. "I see what you're getting at."

"I'm fed up with dying of hunger."

Narcense burst out laughing.

"It'd be more amusing than being a concierge or a saxophonist."

"And I could pay you back the money I owe you."

They both became lost in thought of a singular nature. One would be swindling his sister, and the other a so-called friend.

"Really, it's only a question of a simple theft," said Saturnin.

"We could even go as far as euthanasia."

"What?" said Saturnin.

"I say we could even go as far as murder. Old men's blood, it doesn't stain much."

"Yerss," said Saturnin.

And they both set off once again for that new domain of cogitation as profound as it was joyous, that unexpected, that vast domain, that veritable virgin soil upon which all the suns of hope were shining and tintinnabulating. (Phew.)

"There's Sidonie. There's Marcel and Le Grand. And there's us. Right?" said Saturnin.

"Right."

"Objective: Taupe's treasure. Methods: all."

"That's it, precisely."

"But we don't know which end to start," said Saturnin.

"No, we don't know."

"We dont' even know where the treasure is," said Saturnin.

"No, we don't know."

"We don't know anything at all, eh," said Saturnin.

"No, we don't know anything."

"And consequently, we can't do anything," said Saturnin.

"Too true."

Narcense got up.

"Goodnight then, Saturnin."

"Goodnight, Meussieu Narcense," said Saturnin. "Have you thought about what I was telling you the other day?"

"Yes. Well, I am still attached to plurality, though at the same time I suffer from the becoming."

"Appalling contradiction," murmured the concierge.

"Good night."

And Narcense went up in the elevator, wondering what the future held in store, and then realized, not without some qualms, that he had forgotten to tell Saturnin that the Others had been informed—by himself—of the suspicions Mme. Cloche had conceived about them. But it really wasn't of the slightest importance.

---

Etienne was congratulating himself on the enormous progress he had made in manipulating concepts. Squashed up in his corner seat in the compartment by a fat man suffering from an advanced state of halitosis, he plunged into a series of considerations relative to the necessity of preliminary doubt in all philosophical inquiry.

Everything you come across is disguised. As, for instance, the right shoe of the man in front of me. Naturally, it appears to be covering his foot; it *appears* to be. But it could have some other meaning. In an elementary fashion, it could be a box; there's some cocaine hidden in the heel. Or it could be a musical instrument, it could do a music hall act; or then again it could be edible, he could be a prudent Meussieu who's afraid of running out of money, in which case he'll eat his clodhoppers. And plenty of other things, too, and men, they are even worse than things; and the world, and everything that happens. You think it's this that's happening, and it's that. You think you're doing this, and you're doing that. Every action is deception, every thought implies error. Precisely out of naïveté: we assume that all appearances are genuine, whereas, on the contrary, we ought to doubt them.

Etienne smiled to himself. He looked at the people around him and saw nothing but newspapers; the fat man, who had no doubt not had enough sleep, was the only one snoozing, and was puffing away in fetid fashion. Etienne smiled. He saw, through the window, the minute houses of Coquette-sur-Seine go by, and then the market gardens that meant they were coming to Blagny. Then there were the bits of wasteland, then the chemicals factory, then the CHIPS. Etienne looked away, and stared at the darn in his trousers, near the knee.

"So Mme. Cloche imagines I'm a crook. What an extraordinary thing. I don't look like one, though. Oh, hell."

Etienne paled. His heart had just missed a beat. Two or three newspapers were then folded, and if anyone there had been inquisitive, he would have been able to see the faces of their owners. But Etienne was far from bothering to be inquisitive. For he had just paled.

So Mme. Cloche might be right, then. She doesn't restrict herself to appearances. I make out I'm a bank clerk, honest, scrupulous, married, a stepfather and all the rest of it; in short, like the right shoe of the fellow opposite. But Mme. Cloche isn't taken in by it. She looks further. And she discovers I'm a gangster. Which means that my appearance is that of a gangster. Well, I don't know, it's funny that anyone could take me for a gangster. It's unexpected. It's comic. Pierre drew my attention to it; it must be because of the French fries. The French fries have given me a new appearance—and when I wasn't asking anything from anyone!

Etienne smiled again. The train had just passed the outer circle station and was entering a lacework of rails punctuated by switches. Etienne had smiled.

So you could doubt some appearances, and be wrong, for everything has a multiplicity of appearances, an infinity of appearances. That right shoe possesses an infinity of pretensions. Which are all false. There are pretensions, and there are disguises. This, of course, is all for the Meussieu who looks. The other one, the one opposite me, carefully folding up his *Petit Journal*, that one *uses* his shoe; what does he care about appearances. But what if he hadn't noticed that his shoe was made of a material that was soluble in water, and if one rainy day he found himself paddling in the mud in his socks? That would teach him to take everything for gospel truth. There isn't any gospel, there are only works of fiction.

Etienne tumbled out of his compartment. No doubt about it, he was getting very good at this. And it was so amusing. He hurled himself into the crowd and, carried with it to right and left, allowed himself to be led into a sort of tunnel, illuminated here and there, in which circulated various series of five vehicles linked one to the other and moving with a certain rapidity, a rapidity which naturally didn't equal that of the ourlouri in full flight when it is fleeing before the storm, but which, however, was greater than that of a legless man going up a hill. Compressed by neighbors without number, Etienne pursued his meditations.

I must see that old woman. I'll speak frankly to her. She may tell me what made her suspect me, and also, perhaps, what she's aiming at. And her nephew, the little spy, we certainly frightened him! Two days later, he was gone. That must have confirmed the old girl in her suspicions. Yes, I'll go to Blagny and I'll talk to her, or to her brother. But does her brother know what's going on? And what if I went to see his brother? Narcense's concierge? Perhaps Narcense might be able to tell me something worth knowing. What's become of him? And Pierre? What's he doing? I don't see him any more.

He began to look worried and anxious; a superficial thinker might perhaps have attributed its cause to the force of the compression of a hundred and seventy adult passengers of both sexes. At Saint-Denis, the perpendicularity of the new direction in nowise changed the intensity of this force. Etienne still looked worried and anxious.

That's plenty of things to do: Blagny primo, and secundo the Boulevard of the Unknown Officer. As for Pierre, he's never given me his address. That's odd. Why not? And why does he bother with me? And what if Madame Cloche were right—about him? Why did he drive Narcense to Obonne wood?

Worried and anxious, he started his eight-hour (working) day.

---

Daddy and Mommy are at work; the child is in possession of the house, the garden, the furniture and his liberty. He is doing what he likes. He's promised to work on his German. So, having climbed up to the ruins of the first floor, he is working on his German. He is learning a list of words by heart, but his memory is a bit shaky; he toils away, and finds he has to repeat the same noun a hundred and five times and then some before he can get it encrusted in his memory. And then he's forgotten it by the next day.

Sitting on a little wall, his feet in thick, plastery dust, he rereads and reads his enumeration of various terms relative to agriculture. Axe, hatchet, wedge, billhook, saw, watercan, hod, sieve, plough, ploughshare, harrow, goad, yoke, scythe, sickle, flail, winnowing basket, wine press, that's die Kelter. How's he going to remember that? He repeats winepressdiekelter three and sixty times, then watercan, die Giesskanne also three and sixty times. Good. Now, wine press? How's he ever going to know it- Wine press? Wine press? Wine press?

It's 3 o'clock in the autumn. Calm reigns over the housing development. The neighboring houses can't be heard. Now and then Meussieu Exossé's dog barks; Mme. Caumerse's hens croak; a car goes quack-quack, the postman's bicycle cheep-cheep and the gardener's wheelbarrow squeak-squeak. These diverse and discreet sounds give the greenery of the plane trees a charm that only distinguished minds are able to appreciate. Théo appreciates them.

At this very moment he hears the bicycle cheep-cheeping like a sparrow. The brief-trayger plunges his nose into a big bag full of folded papers, pulls out an envelope and throws it, pulling at a bell. This series of disjointed acts greatly interests the perching philosopher. He repeats kelterwinepress eight and forty times before deciding to go down and see wotitiz.

With his finger in the book to keep his place, he looks carefully at the brief. A fifty centimes French stamp; posted in the rue des Sardines, today at 7:15. Address: M. Etienne Marcel, rue Moche, Obonne. On the other side: Obonne date stamp. Thickness: thin. Transparency: you can't see a thing. Conclusion: wotizit?

If you can say wine press in German, I give myself permission to open it. Wine press in German is die Giesskanne. Very good. You have permission to open this letter. All work should be rewarded.

Théo was still standing behind the gate, his geshprakeshtoff in his left hand and the brief in his right hand. He was just going to turn around and go into the kitchen to boil a saucepanful of water, thanks to the steam of which he would be able to be informed more rapidly than his stepfather as to the contents of the envelope, when he heard a voice; and the voice said:

"Wouldn't have a cigarette to give me, would you?"

Théo looked around. No one was there. He turned pale. He didn't like this sort of joke much. Sure as shootin', there wasn't anyone there; which didn't make it any the less alarming. He took a deep breath, to reequilibrate his coenesthesis, and heard the voice again; the voice said:

"A cigarette, please."

His throat dry, his liver curdling, Théo examined his surroundings. The result of this examination disconcerted him: the garden was empty, and so was the road. He turned from pale to livid. He felt an urgent need to go somewhere. The voice went on:

"You're surprised you can't see me, aren't you? Don't be afraid, little boy. Just open the gate and give me a cigarette."

Théo totters between these two alternatives: either to give vent to his evacuatory project, or to follow the voice's advice and open the gate. Both these acts offering certain advantages, it was difficult for him to make up his mind; but as he had to put an end to this untenable situation, he decided to leave it to chance; to what he called chance, but which, as we shall see in a moment, was just cheatery. In fact, he decided that he'd open the gate if he could remember how to say ladder in German and, if not, to turn on his heel. He remembered the word "floog," and was satisfied with it. So he opened the gate; but how would the fact of opening the gate cause the mysterious beggar to appear? He didn't give it a moment's thought.

"Come come, my child, don't be frightened," the voice encouraged him.

Théo moved forward. He put his book down on the little wall. The gate started to squeak and, the moment it was half open, Théo saw his interlocutor.

"Then you're not frightened any more?"

No, he wasn't frightened any more. He felt more like laughing, stupidly.

"How is it that you live in a house that's being pulled down?" the ex-invisible one went on.

"It's not being pulled down, it's being built. My father hasn't got the money to have it finished."

"Aha. And what does your father do?"

"Huh, you're very inquisitive."

"Don't get angry, my child; this house intrigued me."

"Sjust what I was saying: you're inquisitive."

"And you're rude, my child. Have some respect for my white beard."

"I respect it all right, your beard; but watch want with me?"

"There's nothing to be afraid of, young man. I simply wanted to visit this extraordinary house."

"Whydge ask me for a cigarette?"

"To have one, my boy. Do you have one on you?"

"Don't smoke."

"Never mind; what I particularly wanted was to come in. I would be interested to visit this strange abode."

"Znothing strange about our 'abode.'"

Théo shut the gate again.

"You're very suspicious, young man. What do you have to fear from me?"

"Howshd I know?"

"From a feeble old man?"

"Hm."

Théo frowned anxiously, which gave him a constipated look.

"Come, my child, think a little. What do you have to fear from me? Do I look dangerous? Evil?"

"You give me the shit-squitters."

The dwarf burst out laughing, triumphantly.

"Open the gate, triple idiot."

"What's your name?"

"Bébé Toutout. Open the gate, stupid coward."

"You won't stay long, eh?"

"Of course not."

Théo, very ill at ease, opened the gate a little. The dwarf insinuated himself into the garden, like a cat. He was shabbily dressed, but his white beard made him into a person of some respectability. His big head was covered with a sort of cap, with earflaps of an unusual sort, and in his hand he was carrying a little traveling bag. He couldn't have been more than two-foot-three tall. He crossed the garden rapidly and went into the house without any hesitation.

---

Old Taupe was sitting outside his hovel, smoking. He had the stupid look of a goat that has strayed into a chick-pea plantation. Every so often, he took his pipe out of his mouth and spat a little. Then replanted the object between his lips, and rings of vacuity went floating all around the old man, who was drying up in the sun.

Somewhere around 4 o'clock, there was a knock at the gate. Taupe dragged himself over to it and, in a toneless voice asked:

"Who is it?"

He was answered:

"Vcome from the Abbé Leslaines."

"And you; who're you?"

"The Abbé Rounère," he was answered.

Amazed, Taupe opened the gate, and the Abbé Rounère came in.

"You *are* Meussieu Taupe, I suppose?" says he.

And, confirmation of this identity having been vouchsafed, he walked over toward the hovel, followed by the highly amazed old man.

"What's he want with me?" he was thinking.

The curé, who was very fat, very broad, very red, and who was wearing dark glasses and a cassock that was turning green, sat down on a stack of packing cases and looked around him intently.

"The Abbé Leslaines sent me."

It started like that and it went on like this:

"What's he want from me, the Abbé Leslaines?"

"He dunt want anything from you," replied the curé. "I'm the one what wants something from you."

"What is it?"

"Vcome twask you for some money for a new church to be built."

"Twask me *what?*"

"The new church. Sgoing to be built down by the river, behind the Northern line workshops."

"And you want?"

"In this area, where we have so much trouble saving people's souls, an extra church won't do any harm."

"But what cn I do about it?"

"You could add your mite, M'sieu Taupe. The whole church sgoing to be made of reinforced concrete; inside sgoing to be cubic frescoes and the whyliss so's to listen to the pope. And at the entrance, sgoing to be hot an cold holy water."

"My mite!"

"In the vestry, sgoing to be a telephone, some showers and a fridge. And the bells'll work by electricity. And right next to the church, there'll be toilets with seats; it'll be the finest church in all the suburbs, sgoing to be dedicated to Saint Squit."

"But I can't do anything about it."

"You can give your mite, M'sieu Taupe."

"Is that what you've come to ask me for? But I don't have a sou! Everyone knows that. I can give you twenty sous, that's all I can do for you!"

"Ha ha! twenty sous! one franc! But I'm expecting you to give me at least twenty thousand francs."

"How come?"

"Twenty thousand, I say, thass what I'm specting you to give me."

"Come again?"

"You're getting deaf, old Taupe."

"Just a moment. In the first place, I won't have you calling me old Taupe like that, we never kept pigs together. Eh? Segondo, where'd I get them, your twenty thousand francs?"

"Avarice is a mortal sin, M'sieu Taupe."

"Avarice, avarice! How can you be avaricious when you don't have a bean?"

"And lying, that's a mortal sin, too."

"Oh, go on. M'sieu the curé, you're beginning to annoy me.

When I tell you I don't have a bean, that means I don't have a bean; and I just wonder who could have put that idea into your head."

"So you're saying that you're not a miyonnaire?"

"Me, a millionaire."

"Yes you, a miyonnaire."

"You're loony, with all respect."

The curé had become purple in the face and was walking up and down the room, raising the dust with his steaming clodhoppers. He bellowed:

"It's hell! it's hell that's lying in wait for misers. I'm telling you, that's the way it is, and I know a thing or two about hell. It's hell, for money-grubbers! It's hell, for muckworms! It's hell, for niggards!"

"I don't have a bean, I tell you," yelped Taupe, who was getting desperate.

"It's hell, for tightwads; it's hell, for skinflints!"

"Boohoo, don't have a bean! don't have a bean!"

"You want to go the way your wife did, eh? that went straight to the devil. You want to go and meet her down below, eh? Come on, old Taupe, out with your stuff so's we can make a splendid cathedral with it."

"Boohoohoo." The old man was crying now. "Don't have a bean, not a bean, notabeen, notabene."

Then the Abbé Rounère pointed to the door—not the door that led outside, but the one opposite it, the one that was painted blue.

"And that door—where's it go?"

Old Taupe started, looked at the blackish gentleman in utter amazement, and didn't answer.

"What's behind that door, I asked you," yelled the abbé, banging on it with his fist.

This question seemed to soothe the old man. He almost smiled.

"You're going to break it," he said, in a gentle voice.

The Abbé Rounère stopped banging.

"Well, what's behind it?"

"I'll tell you one thing," replied Taupe "it's none of your business."

The curé's cheeks turned vermilion. His anger was terrible to see. He was drooling with rage, he was incohering.

"I gotta know everything, I do, what's behind the door and even what isn't behind it. It's hell, for pinchfists! You'll go and roast with Ernestine, Taupe. You can take it from me. Out with your cash, you old heathen! Come on, out with it! Or do you want to make it into jam? Behind the door, thass where I want to look! Woss behind the door? Produce your cash, you sordid old hoarder! Ah, aha, aha!"

Old Taupe finally got the jitters, and how! He thought the best thing to do was to get away from this maniac. This decision even seemed extremely prudent, and necessary for the protection of his old bones, when he saw the curé grab hold of the iron bar he used to barricade his door at night. He saw at once the news item it would make, and his photo on the front page with his skull stove in and minus his brains. Terribly afraid for himself. The curé was standing threateningly against the door. Taupe turned green. Oh! What a pain in his stomach he'd got. To die in bed, all right, but to get your skull bashed in by a nut, that's too silly.

At that moment, a car hooted, and someone knocked at the gate. The curé dropped the iron bar and Taupe trotted out to see who it was.

---

With the junk dealer out of the way, the Abbé Rounère rushed over to the mysterious door and tried to open it. But shake it as he would, it was in vain. He looked through the keyhole, and naturally saw nothing. His visit wasn't to have been in vain, though; after careful examination, he was able to make this important observation: there was absolutely no doubt about it— the enigmatic door was hung on the wall like a picture. This made him profoundly uneasy. He didn't understand anything any more. An excruciating doubt pierced his soul. And yet—didn't that make it even more suspicious? At this moment he turned around and saw—and that was really the end—that the visitor to whom Taupe indirectly owed the fact that he was still vegetating, was none other than Pierre

Le Grand, who was accompanied by a rather remarkably beautiful young woman. They had come. so they claimed, to see the curios. There wasn't very much there, volubilized Taupe, who was smiling, happy to be alive. The first time he hadn't found anything, but the second time, you never know, Le Grand was saying, something no one would think of any value might perhaps interest him. He, Taupe, hoped so.

They all three went into the hut. The curé was sitting on a packing case, looking through a dilapidated issue of the Hachette Almanac. He was letting on he was extremely absorbed. Taupe hoped he would go. He didn't. As for Pierre, he was somewhat stupefied by the appearance of this individual, and shocked by his foul smell. Catherine retreated before the fusion of filth and frock; the picturesque left her cold, and she went out and waited in the car.

Pierre pretended to be looking around. With the tip of his gloves, he shifted various rusty screws and crusts of bread. There isn't much, he said. Taupe showed him a teapot with a broken spout, which dated from President Fallières's era (1906-13), and a feather duster from President Loubet's (1899-1906). These didn't interest the customer. Wasn't much. But he had to bring this to an end somehow.

"How much for that door?" asked Pierre.

Panic-stricken, Taupe started stammering, and couldn't manage to compose a rational sentence. The curé raised his head and, throwing the almanac onto a pile of my-movie-mags, opened his mouth and said:

"It's not for sale."

"I beg your pardon," retorted Pierre. "I'm not addressing you, but Meussieu Taupe."

"Meussieu Taupe isn't selling his door," the priest declared.

Taupe continued to look like a slug crossing a main road and terrified by the approach of a fast truck with wide wheels.

"Well, Meussieu Taupe, how much will you sell me this door for?" Pierre again asked him, without deigning to answer God's representative on earth.

"Ah ba ba, ah ba ba," came from Taupe.

"I'll give you two hundred francs for it."

"Meussieu Taupe isn't selling his door," roared the man in

perpetual mourning, bespattering Pierre's right sleeve with saliva.

"I'll tell you one thing very simply: you get on my nerves. I am not dealing with you, but Meussieu Taupe."

"You *are* dealing with me! You won't have that door."

"You're going to stop me, are you?"

"Jesus Christ! I tell you, you won't have it."

"Well, well, so you blaspheme."

"Ah ba ba, ha ba ba," said Taupe, sweating profusely. Pierre was extremely embarrassed.

The man in black looked resolute and violent. A curious person.

"Two hundred francs in cash, and I'll take it with me now," he proposed to Taupe.

"Don't sell it to him," yelled the man in skirts.

"Hehe, hehe," Taupe began, "hetried . . ."

"I beg your pardon?" asked Pierre, leaning over to try and understand what Taupe was stammering.

"Hetried, hetried, hetriedakillme!"

"*He* did?" and Pierre pointed to the sky pilot with his thumb.

"*He* did! with the bar, hetriedakillme!" and the junk dealer collapsed onto his sleeping board.

The curé hadn't turned a hair. Pierre looked at him with interest.

"Are you interested in this door?"

"Zmuch as you are."

"But why?"

"Same reasons as you."

"You have an odd voice."

"Mind your own ass."

"I beg your pardon?"

"Shit. Get lost."

"No."

There would be no point in concealing the fact that the situation was becoming devilish tense. Or divinely so, rather, since a representative of the cloth was present. The trouble was, the dark glasses. A curious person. Pierre turned to the junk dealer again:

"Taupe, what *is* this door?"

Sniveling, Taupe lay down on his bed. This was a subterfuge. Under his pillow was hidden an enormous 2nd Empire pistol; he got hold of it and, pointing it at the two visitors:

"Get lost! get lost!" he screeched, keeping them covered.

"Is it loaded, your pistol?" asked Pierre.

"Take a look," Taupe replied.

Pierre took the fearsome weapon; it was, in fact, loaded. He gave it back to him.

"Idiot, should've kept it," grumbled the holy-water sprinkler.

"I don't stab people in the back," replied Pierre, nobly.

"Isn't poisoning people stabbing them in the back?" Exploded the prayer-stool-pigeon.

"I don't know what you're talking about."

And Taupe was screeching:

"Get lost! Get lost!"

"All right, all right, we're going."

The Abbé Rounère and Le Grand left, and behind them, Meussieu Taupe, so recently widowed, barricaded his gates, and, in a state of great emotion, went and sat down again outside his hovel, smoking his highly seasoned clay pipe, which gurgled merrily in the tranquil, but unhealthy, air.

---

When dinner was over, Bébé Toutout carefully folded his napkin, and, belching freely, declared that he was highly satisfied with his meal. Then asked Etienne for a cigarette, and inquired whether the latter was not in the habit of indulging in some kind of liqueur; but Etienne was not, and this caused the dwarf to look a little glum. In the meantime, the Marcel family was silently watching him. Like a snail who happened to play the trumpet. Like a fly who might perform on the flying trapeze. Like a mustard pot that might be writing its memoirs. Like a policeman who happened to be plucking the petals of a rose. Like a lump of sugar that might have been going for a walk with a stick under its arm.

Imperturbably, the dwarf let them look at him, and smoked in perfect peace.

"What do we have for breakfast? coffee or chocolate?" he calmly asked.

"Coffee," Alberte answered, without thinking.

"I prefer chocolate," retorted the minimus.

The Marcel family didn't say a word; things were beginning to get tragic. There must be no delay in expelling this singular parasite who seemed determined to dig himself in here with them forever; and who wasn't even trying to justify his behavior. Preceding his question with a little cough, Etienne asked him:

"Are you going to stay the night in the hotel?"

"Is there a hotel in Obonne?"

"Yes, not far from here, at Hippolyte's."

"Ah. I prefer to sleep here."

"But there isn't a bed."

"Ah."

Etienne hasn't got much further than he was before.

"It's probably time you left, if . . ."

"I'm perfectly all right here."

Then Théo exploded:

"He's making a fool out of us, this little thing is. So you think you're going to sleep here, eh? My foot. I'm going to take you by the scruff of your neck and chuck you out like a cat that's pissed in the corner."

"Oh, Théo," says Alberte, "How can you be so vulgar!"

"There now!" exclaimed the dwarf, triumphantly, "you see what your mother says!"

Théo gets up, the dwarf is going to get it. But the generous Etienne stops his stepson midway, and advises him to keep calm. The dwarf is enjoying himself tremendously. Théo sits down again and mutters:

"He won't miss anything by waiting."

"We'll see." Then: "Believe it or not, I stayed for more than a year like this with a very respectable old lady, the Baroness du Poil. I had a marvelous life, champagne with every meal, the car whenever I wanted it, and all the rest of it. All I had to do was gnash my teeth like this" (he gnashes), "and she gave me everything I wanted."

"And why didn't you stay any longer?" they ask him.

"She died," he sighs, pretending to wipe away a tear. "She died of purulent hemorrhoids. Poor dear old lady! Poor dear old thing! What a kind heart she had!"

"And after she died, what happened?"

"Her heirs asked me to leave. They were stronger than I was, weren't they? I went. After that I lived with. . . But I'm not going to tell you my life history."

"It seems pretty strange, though," says Etienne.

"Pah," says the dwarf. "Nothing so very extraordinary about it. You do the best you can."

"Then, if I understand you right, you're intending to find the equivalent of the Baroness du Poil here?"

Théo laughs. So does the dwarf.

"Sright."

Alberte smiles. So does Etienne. The conversation is getting very friendly.

"So you think you're going to stay here, and eat and sleep here?"

"Why not?"

"But how are you reckoning on doing that?"

This is becoming very amusing.

"Through fear and cunning."

"Through fear?"

"Well, yes. Meussieu Théo wasn't very much at ease when he was alone with me. Were you, Meussieu Théo?"

Meussieu Théo doesn't answer. Etienne goes on:

"But aren't you afraid of being thrown out by force?"

"That's a risk to be run."

"Do you still hope to spend the night here?"

"Of course."

"You know there isn't a bed."

"You're not going to tell me you sleep on the floor!"

"I mean, we haven't got a guest room."

"An armchair will do for me."

"A saucepan, even," says Théo.

Alberte and Etienne burst out laughing.

"That's right, make fun of me, now! Rude thing! Boor!"

"He's insulting us now."

"I," says Etienne, "think the time has come for you to go."

"You'd even be wise to," snarls Théo.

"Now now, don't get excited," they tell him.

The midget gets down from his chair and goes into Théo's room, to fetch his cap and suitcase, no doubt. But he doesn't come out again; and very calmly shuts the door behind him, and locks it.

"Good night, all," he calls to the Marcel family, who are crying, who are crying with laughter.

"Oh, that's too funny," they say. "Well, what a nerve," they add, in tears, in tears, in tears of laughter.

---

It was decided that Alberte should go and spend the night with Mme. Pigeonnier, their neighbor. Théo insisted on taking his mother there, which meant that Etienne was left alone in the house.

There was still a light on in the dwarf's room. Etienne knocked.

"Tizit?" came from the other side.

"Are you sleepy?"

"Not yet."

"Could you answer a question I'd like to ask you?"

"If it isn't nosy."

"It isn't."

"Go ahead, then."

"I'd like to ask you what you think of Appearances."

"What does that mean?"

"I wanted to ask you if you sometimes think about. . . ."

"Life?"

"For instance."

The dwarf coughed, clearing his throat.

"Wait a moment, will you," Etienne called, "I'm going to get a chair."

Which he did. He sat down, and stuck his ear against the door.

"Well?" he asked.

"When I say life," Bébé Toutout began, "I'm talking about the life lived by men, by myself; not about life in general, including the life of the fish, for instance."

"That's interesting, too," murmured Etienne.

"Oh shit," said the dwarf, "if you're going to start criticizing, there's no point in my going on with my lecture."

"I didn't mean to offend you. I'm listening carefully."

"I won't talk about the lives of all men, either. Now, it's like this. Some lives are full of possibilities, others are full of impossibilities. A man who sees the impossible closing all avenues to him, he's described, so it seems, as despairing. But you also have to know why every road becomes impassable, and why the ship sinks, and why the days are dark. Because if the impossibilities spring from a deficiency in altitude, then it's no longer a question of despair, but of ridicule. You tall people, you must think a despairing dwarf hideous; luckily you mostly only think of him in the category of the grotesque. I might tell you that, for my part, I see all these relationships the other way around. I scarcely care about the laughter of people between whose legs I am forced to pass, or about the giggles of people who at first take me for a child. It's disappointing, of course, but I repeat, I scarcely care. Nor about all the possibilities that my height prevents me from envisaging. I can't be an archbishop, or a general, or an undertaker, or a swimming instructor, or a professor. Among other things, I shall never become a great man. That would be terrible, if I were the right height, but as I midget my way around, it's quite different. I find giraffes comic, and guinea pigs touching. There are only two roads open to me: the circus, or the one I took."

"Which is?"

"Parasitism through terror. I live on old women's cowardice, and I'd live on that of babes in arms if it could be of any use to me. What d'you think of my beard?"

"Very beautiful, but white easily gets dirty, don't you think?"

"It's not so bad as all that. It makes me look like a gnome; one more card up my sleeve."

"Do you ever think of anything other than your tricks?"

"Of course I do. Didn't you hear the result of my reflections on the mass perturbation my dwarfishness causes?"

"Alas!"

"What d'you mean, alas?"

"I don't want to offend you yet again, but I must tell you that I find your reflections on masturbation somewhat irrelevant."

"Oh¡¡" (¡¡—they're indignation marks).

"They don't make sense, your thoughts about the possible, the impossible and the grotesque. Or rather, it's not so much that they don't make sense, as that they're rather confused. They're like trifle."

"You! you have a funny way of philosophizing!"

"There! the dirty word is out! Philosophizing! But, my poor Bébé Toutout, you're the one who philosophizes like a whistle in an old sock."

"I know what it's all about better than you do, though. It's actual experience what I'm telling you."

"No. It's very abstract, on the contrary. I'll tell you what *I* think. In the first place, when I see a dwarf, I'm suspicious."

"Why's that?"

"I'm suspicious because he may well not be a dwarf. It would be too simple if a little fellow with a beard were just quite simply a dwarf. The world is much more complicated than that."

"There *are* dwarfs, though. Me, for example."

"No. All things considered, they don't exist. They're absurd and immoral. And furthermore. I've never seen one."

"Oh! !"

Bébé Toutout jumps down from his bed; the key turns in the lock and the door opens; he appears, dressed in striped pajamas; he's put on his cap with the earflaps to sleep in.

"Well then, not a dwarf? Me?"

At this moment, Etienne flings himself on him, grabs him by the seat of his pants, and carries him off, beard downward, intending to throw him out.

This is a very bad action, and it greatly astonishes Bébé Toutout. He'd never have thought that this young man, who was so gentle, so timid, was so unpleasant. If it had been Théo, he wouldn't have been surprised, but coming from this young metaphysician, it's staggering.

In the meantime, a sports car pulls up outside the half-house. Pierre and Catherine and a third individual in skirts get out of it. Amazed, Etienne lets go of Bébé Toutout, who goes rolling over on the gravel, but immediately picks himself up and runs back to bed, fuming like a thief.

---

Alberte took the train at about 8 o'clock. Etienne had already left. She didn't dare go back home. Théo kept Mme. Pigeonnier company until 10. Then, having had breakfast and suffered the necessary caresses, he decided to go and see what was happening in the house.

He found Bébé Toutout in the kitchen, cleaning his shoes.

"Good morning, Théo," said the dwarf in friendly fashion, without looking up.

To which the young man replied:

"Huh, still there, eh, *you!*"

Bébé Toutout seemed to be in an excellent mood; waves of gaiety were making his freshly brushed beard oscillate; he was zestfully polishing his miniature oxfords.

"Sit down," he ordered Théo, "I'm going to tell you a story." He adds: "A story about your father."

His appetite whetted, Théo sat down.

"Do you know a meussieu called Pierre?"

"Shdthink so; he's a pal of my stepfather's."

"Is he your stepfather, that young man?"

"Shdve thought it was obvious; I look as old as him." (He sits up straight.)

"Yes. And Mme. Cloche, you know her?"

"No. Don't know her."

"And Catherine?"

"Oh, I know *her*. She's Pierre's girl. Wheredger meet them?"

"They came here."

"Last night?"

"Yes. At the very moment when your father, your stepfather, was going to throw me out."

"Go on! How'd he manage?"

"That's another story. He stabbed me in the back."

Théo cackles.

"Finished? Right. Well, at the very moment, a car stopped outside your house. Your stepfather let go of me and I rushed back and locked myself in your room again. Then I heard the people from the car coming in; there were three of them: Pierre, Catherine and Mme. Cloche. They went into the dining room and started a great discussion, it was terribly complicated, about a door."

"A door?"

"Yes. The one called Pierre insisted that there mustn't be any more misunderstanding about it: he didn't know what was behind the door; and your stepfather said the same. Then that Mme. Cloche said that it was all Clovis's fault—you know who Clovis is?"

"No—no idea."

"In the end, she said she'd been mistaken about them; but that now one thing was sure, and that was that the door was hanging on the wall like a mirror or a picture. Which the others thought very strange. Then they started talking very softly, and I couldn't hear anything, except that they were talking about someone called Pôte, and a woman called Ernestine—you know who they are?"

"No—no idea."

"You don't know anything, then, my poor child."

"Obviously, if I was as nosy as you are, I'd find things out too; but personally, you know, I don't give a damn about other people's business."

"In any case, it seems to be a strange business, that door hanging on a wall. They sounded terribly excited when they were talking about it.

"Even Etienne?"

"That's your stepfather?"

"Yes; Etienne."

"Etienne as well. Ah! and they were talking about someone called Maxence, as well."

"You don't say."

"Do you know him?"

"Do I know him! Shink so. He tried to hang me."

"Well, well. So he tried to hang you, did he, my lad? He must have been a vicious one, to want to hang a little lad like you! And how come—why did he want to hang you?"

"I'd insulted him. Oh! that's quite a story. That gigolo, all he did, he made advances to my mother: so I said to him, I said: Hands off my mother, Meussieu. So he said to me, he said: Unless you're a coward, come and meet me tonight at midnight in the forest; we'll have it out. I didn't get cold feet. I went, all alone. He'd told me to meet him in a clearing. In the moonlight. I get there, he was waiting for me. The minute he sees me, he throws himself on me and ties me up. I'm going to hang you, he yells. He'd got a slipknot ready. Huh, what an adventure!"

"Go on, this is interesting."

"Well then, just when he was starting to hoist me up in the air, what happens but a fisherman turns up, and so Narcense runs away."

"He's called Narcense?"

"Yes, Narcense, not Maxence."

"A fisherman in the middle of the night?"

"Yes, he was looking for glowworms."

"Ah."

The dwarf is rubbing away at his shoes; Théo, wanting to look as if he's doing something, absent-mindedly goes through his pockets. He finds the letter for Etienne. Bébé Toutout squints at it out of the corner of his eye.

"Huh, a letter."

"Not for you."

"Who *is* it for?"

"None of your business."

"The letters other people get interest me more than the ones I get. All the more so as I never get any."

"Nor do I."

"Well then. When we've got a chance to read a letter for once. With a bit of steam, it's very simple."

"I know, I know," says Théo, irritated, putting a sore span of water on the gas to heat.

---

If you think I didn't understand all your schemes. And what a laugh they gave me. All your comings and goings and your tricks and your hopes and all. Old Taupe's treasure, what a laugh, eh, oh what a laugh. And you believed in it! I'm talking to you, Ma'ame Cloche, especially to you. And I was always wondering how the idea could have taken root in your nut. How you could possibly have thought it up. I saw at once what it was all about; and I saw, too, that it was ever since those messieus came to see me that I'd begun to look like a miserly millionaire. I'd seen that much, but I couldn't very well make out why. Maybe they were pulling your leg. Madame Cloche, those messieus. My goodness, I really couldn't make it out. But one thing was absolutely certain, and that was that you took me for a millionaire, you and Ernestine. When she came to my place, the first time, I said to myself: Hm, that's odd. What's she want from me? Why should she agree to sleep with me? Then my brain got to work, and it went on working, and I thought, and I watched, and I listened, and in the end I understood: you, Ma Cloche, you'd persuaded her that I'd got a fortune hidden somewhere, and that if she married me she'd be rich. Rich! Rich! Poor Ernestine! Marrying me didn't make her any less broke! She'd have been . . . Eh? Yes, you think it was a lousy thing to do, what I did. Lousy? Because I didn't object. I let myself be married, an old boy like me. Sixty years old. A love match. They don't dare say it's my money they're after. My nonexistent money! Poor Ernestine, she believed in it. She thought she was going to get out of the gutter by becoming my wife. How could you call that lousy? How could you? I loved the girl. And why not? Every time I went to Dominique's, I saw her. What a lovely girl! Whenever she went by me, I could smell her sweat, I got drunk on it; it gave me the shivers, up and down my spine. And her buttocks; like marble, they were, like elastic marble. The bitch, she knew very well what a state she got me in. She never missed—every time I was there she'd hoist up her dress and fix her garter. When she saw I was looking, that's what she'd do every time. And I'd go away, with my liter of white in my stomach, and my head haunted by the sight of her thighs. And then, she was so nice to all the others, to the young men. She'd laugh with them; they'd paw her, and she'd laugh. Not with me, though. Just an old beggar, that's what she thought I was. And I wasn't thinking about anything but her—the whole of her. I could feel her under my hand, when I was alone. What sort of hope did I have? And then, all of a sudden, she offers herself to me, to get her hands on my imaginary money. And you think it was lousy of me to say yes? Afterward, of course, I did ask myself, what's she going to say when she finds out that it was all a lot of nonsense and that she's just as broke as she ever was, and married to me, at that? What would she have done? She'd have gone mad. I was very worried. I'd have had her for a whole night, I said to myself, and then what? What a thing it would have been for her! The despair! To have thought you were going to get rich from one day to the next, and then find yourself in an even rottener position than before. How she'd have suffered. Poor Ernestine! But you know—she didn't know—and I never had her. Never, never. And I can still see her, bringing me my liter of white and the glass she never wiped—I can still see her, with her green eyes and her messy hair and her pointed breasts, then she'd go away and peel the spuds. She wouldn't look at me any more, and I'd just drink my liter of white. And now, nothing. She never got out of the gutter. And to think that I never had her. Never! Never!

And the door? that door, it's always the same story. Yes, the same. The *same* thing always happens to you. Funny, isn't it? When I was twenty, a woman. But I won't bore you with a young man's love affair, eh? Well, a woman who's dead. The door's a souvenir. That's all. Forty years later, I found the door. It had got our names on it. I bought it. That's all. No fortune, no treasure, no mystery. Nothing. And if you don't like it, too bad. Or all the better. Yes, forty years later, I found the door we'd written our names on. And, *because of that door,* Ernestine, that I loved, is dead. That's something out of the ordinary, isn't it? Don't you think it's even tragic? *Fatalitas! Fatalitas!* as they say. It's given me a shock. And what about me? What becomes of me with all this? I'm left—with my head tormenting me and fermenting, with my head haunted by pictures that get more and more obscene. I'm left—slobbering in the sun, becoming more of an imbecile every day. Ernestine, the sweet cheat gone!

---

She couldn't care less, now, whether she saw the door or whether she didn't see it. She caught the train to town and, getting out at the Gare du Nord, sat down on the terrace of her usual café. She was very weary. She ordered a green menthe, which made the waiter smile; of course, though, she was still wearing her curé's habit. Well, she'd gone to a lot of trouble for nothing, and it was well and truly over.

Well and truly over, and no more hope. No more hope—nothing. Old Taupe was really poor, poverty-stricken. There was no more treasure than there was butter up your ass. Well, she was going back to her abortions. That was all there was to it. The daily grind was going to start all over again. This was the end of all her great hopes. Of Life with a capital L. Of her great plans. She swigged down her green menthe, getting her fingers all sticky.

She'd've started by buying a few dresses, but fabulous ones, and that'd've made her look twenty years younger, and then she'd've gone off to a beauty parlor, where they'd've made her look twenty years younger. Sum total, forty. Which would have left her at fifteen. When you've got the cash, what can't you do! And after that, she'd've gone and seen a guy that sells cars. A super one, she'd have said, with a hood as long as that, and nicely upholstered seats. Something that'd look impressive. She'd have hired a lady's maid and a chauffeur, and en route for Montycarloh. And then she'd've bought a villa at Neuilly as well, with water, gas, electricity, elevator, electric kitchen, fridge, central heating, whyliss, and maybe even a bathroom. She'd start off by filling her cellar with champagne. Every day, at every meal, champagne, except for the morning, when she got up, always the same as usual, cold black pudding and strong red wine.

And this was where it had started. The whole thing. The day when Marcel got himself bumped into by his pal's taxi. It was even the day before, at that, cos it was because of the first guy being reduced to pulp that she'd come back to this caff. What a soppy thing shebeen. Believing a kid, like that! They're liars, kids are, you never ought to believe a thing they say. The little swine. He'd got Ernestine's death on his conscience, after all; not her. Though anyway, what did she care about Ernestine's death. But to have wasted your time, and stuffed your head full of a load of old rubbish, to have imagined a whole lot of tripe. She must've been nuts! Ah, shit. When she thought about it, she could bite her ass with rage. No, really, to've thought for two months that she was going to end up in the skin of a rich old dame and keep gigolos and little fox terrier doggies, to've thought that she could end up, at fifty-five, being able to indulge her every whim, to've thought that because a silly cunt of a brat had told her a lot of tripe that didn't even make sense! Wasn't anything to be proud of in that. No, really, there wasn't an all. And she wouldn't be boasting about it.

She could already see herself arriving at the casino, somewhere where it was sunny, in a place where it was always fine; she could see herself arriving at the casino, with powder thick as that all over her mug, her tits patched up, and dolled up in a three-thousand franc dress, between a couple of well-dressed swells in dinner jackets with their hair oiled down over their noodles; good-looking types, what. And the people'd've said: Who's that, the one with the diamonds big as your fist? Is she Princess Falzar or the Duchess of Frangipani? No, no, they'd have said, the people in the know, that's Mme. Du Belhôtel, the one that goes in for charitable works and antiasthmatic stamps. She was married to an Indian prince, the people's say, and thass the explanation of all her bread. In any case, zwun thing she wouldn't have done, that'd have been play roulette. It's nuts. You lose as much as you like. No, her lovely money, she wouldn't have chucked it on the green baize cloth like that, for it to fly away and her never see it any more. No. She wouldn't have boggled at spending it, that she wouldn't; when it came to fun and games, she'd have been on, all right. But going and chucking her stash into the coffers of the casino—no, she wouldn't have done that.

Just take a look at all these half-wits going by. They still take me for a curé, what's more. Curé! You don't do much work and yet you get respected. And begging for alms, there's something in that. No need of any special knowledge to beg for alms. That could bring me in a little on the side, after all.

And to think that she'd let herself be taken in by that idiotic story, that she'd swallowed it and got Ernestine to swallow it. No, it was too awful to think about.

She pays for her drink and gets up. She goes in the direction of her domicile, which is situated at number ninety-one Paradise Street. She walks; slowly. Her head heavy with thought, she makes her way through the crowd in Lafayette Street. She goes down this street, with bitter regrets restless in her heart. She didn't feel like laughing, she certainly didn't. Occasionally, someone in the crowd would turn around and look at this extraordinary curé who seemed so absorbed in his thoughts. Muss be thinking about the good Lord, they were saying to themselves, the clots. It was when she'd got to the lil square opposite the church of St. Vincent d'Paul that a sports car, but a splendiferous one, stopped. It was—obviously anyone who knows his way around'll already've guessed —it was Pierre's car.

"Hey there," says he.

And Mme. Cloche goes over.

"Good day, M'sieur the curé," says he, very seriously.

"Good day, my son," replied the midwife.

"Got summing to tell you," says he, "summing dead funny, at that."

"And wotizit?" asked Mme. Cloche.

"Well, when he went back home, old Taupe found his door wasn't there."

"Eh?"

"Yes, the door, the famous door, someone's swiped it. That's what I had to say to you. So long."

And the car, with a roar, drove off.

Yes but what do *I* care? Sall the same to me.

Even so, it *is* odd. But apart from that, if instead of stealing his mysterious door, they'd pinched his front door, old Taupe'd've been furious.

Dear Meussieu Marcel and Colleague,

When you receive this letter, you can say farewell to all hope of seizing the riches hidden by M. Gérard Taupe in his hut in Blagny. For, tomorrow morning, at crack of dawn, we are going to steal it, and nothing can stop us accomplishing this exploit. We would be grateful if you would also kindly inform Meussieu Pierre Le Grand of this important occurrence. This will spare you a great deal of unnecessary trouble.

The adventure of the Taupic treasure, then, is coming to an end, and it is ourselves who are going to make it come, this end, and in the manner which we shall consider fitting, in other words, by causing to disappear, for our benefit, the immense fortune of this individual, according to what has been written above.

We dare hope that you will not bear us any ill will for our superiority, for if you were the first to spot this idle money, we shall be the only ones to put it to use; we have no other justification. What is more, we are thus illustrating in a new way the fable of the third robber, and we believe that it was more the desire to participate in this illustration that urged us to this theft than the desire for wealth, ow re sack rough arm s.*

Be that as it may, you look pretty foolish now (long live the foolish! long live the foolish!), and we look pretty rich. So everything's for the best.

With kind regards.

The magic cordon,
The invisible false note.

P.S. As you see, we're writing you an anonymous letter.

Saturnin Belhôtel
Narcense.

"What goings-on!" exclaims Bébé Toutout.

"Um well, um well," goes Théo, not managing to express himself any more lucidly.

"You wouldn't have thought it of your father, would you?"

"Um well, um well," Théo goes on *going*.

"Your father was trying to commit a theft? When he looked so honest. You'd never have guessed that one, would you, my little lad?"

"He hasn't stolen anything, since it was Narcense who. . ."

"Yes, but he was going to. And this Saturnin Belhôtel, do you know him?"

"No."

"There definitely isn't much to be got out of you, my child. Seal the envelope up again now."

Théo, staggered by the curious revelation contained in the letter, reseals it with all the care he's capable of (a lot).

Bébé Toutout supervises him.

"Do your parents come back to lunch?"

"No, I get my own."

"Right. Then you can cook me a steak and French fries."

"French fries? But I don't know how to cook 'em!"

"What a moroon! I'll teach you. You'll see, it's very amusing."

"R'aren't any potatoes."

"You can go and buy some. King Edwards, at forty-five centimes a pound. And for the steak, tell the butcher to choose it carefully—a fillet steak."

"Haven't got any money."

"You surely don't expect me to give you any? Don't you realize that I'm your guest?"

"My guest?"

Théo, with a listless eye, looks at the dwarf, who is stroking his white-haired chin.

"You look like an imbecile this morning, my poor boy. It's the letter that's done that. Cheer up, you'll see others like that in your life. Apart from that, your father's let the other two swindle him, hasn't he?"

"That doesn't surprise me!" Théo bursts out. "Can't even damn well . . ."

"Sh! don't insult your father, even if he isn't, and go and do the shopping. It's already ¼ past 11."

"What about the money?"

"Use your wits. Tell the butcher he'll be paid tomorrow. And stop looking so gormless."

"By the way—are you reckoning on staying here long?"

"All winter."
"Sounds promising."
Then the child and the dwarf contemplate the boiling of the oil in which the French fries are frying.
"Don't you think cooking is amusing?"
"No; sa goddamn bore."
"You'll have to do it every day, though, at lunchtime. I don't want to eat tacks, do I now?"
Théo doen't condescend to reply.
"I wouldn't mind betting you write poetry?"
"I started this summer," Théo replies, blushing. "But I've only written one line, so far."
"Which is?"
"*Mon âme a son mystère, ma vie a son secret.*"
Bébé Toutout counts on his fingers.
"But your one line's defective, my little lad."
"So what? I can't help it. It's a line that'll just have to have thirteen feet, that's all. Why should lines only have twelve feet? It's crazy. My line, I give it an extra foot. Znothing to stop me."
"Let the French fries drain, now."
"There yah."
"Will you remember how to do them, the next time?"
"Course I will, I'm not so stupid I can't fry a few spuds. No!"
"Tell me, Théo, how old are you?"
"Fifteen."
"Have you ever been in love?"
"If anyone asks you, you must tell them you don't know anything about it."
"Théo, you are forgetting the respect you owe me. Look: a white beard, eh! Get it? Well then, give me a serious answer. Have you ever been in love?
Théo sniffs twice and a half to self-possess himself, and:
"I've already run away with a married woman," he boasts.

---

"Clovis, come here."
Thus spake Dominique Belhôtel, and Clovis came here.

"So you're nothing but a rotten little liar, hm?"

And Clovis, who was a good, serious-minded, hard-working child, and who loved his father and mother, burst into tears.

"Daddy, Daddy," he sobbed.

And really, only a heart of stone would have remained untouched.

"Come on, don't cry like that. Tell me all about it."

"I wasn't lying. I heard them . . ."

And Clovis, once again, gave free rein to his tears, as respectable citizens say. Dominique, deeply moved, choked back his sobs; this was his only son, forsooth–his, Dodo's only son, Cloclo.

"Come on, come on, don't cry like that. You know that your aunt's very cross with you. Not at all pleased, old Cloche isn't. You muss understand that. You'd put it into her head that she was going to win in that lottery. And now that she's lost, she's furious. I can understand that. So can you, can't you, me boy?"

"Yes, Dad."

"All right, I forgive you. Come to my arms."

Father and son sob on each other's shoulder; the noblest sentiments wail in the depths of their breasts; well, isn't this touching, each thinks to himself.

"Right; now you're forgiven, tell me all about it, once and for all."

"Znothing to tell. I thought they said what I told Aunt Cloche, they'd said, maybe I didn't hear right. But I was telling the truth, Dad."

"Ah! wharra beautiful thing Truth is! Always tell the truth, Clovis."

"Yes Dad. And Aunt Cloche, will she forgive me?"

"Yes, Clovis."

Another relapse into lachrymation. Belhôtel still has one more question to ask.

"And at X . . . , why did you want to come back?"

"I was frightened, Dad."

"You shouldn't've been."

"But Dad, I thought they were wicked ganggang, wicked gangsters that were trying to kill me. It was Aunt Cloche that'd written to me that they were dangerous. So I was frightened, Dad."

"Snot worthy of a Belhôtel, to be scared! Got it, Clovis?"

"Yes, Dad. Now and under all circumstances, I promise my dear dad, here present, to be of surpassing courage in any ordeal."

"That's right, Clovis. Come into my arms, you are definitely forgiven."

Third and last demonstration of paternal clemency. When Clovis finally escapes from that moist extinguisher that the Dominical waistcoat has become, he too has some questions to ask.

"Is that right, Dad—I'm going to be an engineer?"

"Yes, Clovis, you're going to be an engineer. I promised you you would. I keep my promises."

"Oh, thank you, Dad. Then I'll be going to the lycée this year?

"Yes, Clovis."

"Oh, thank you, Dad."

Clovis, Clovis, the future is yours, as they say. You are serious-minded, hard-working, not too intelligent, but quite intelligent enough, though. Your father has earned enough money to be able to pay for the very highest type of education for you. You will be an engineer, an eminently respectable profession, where your ingenuity will make you outstanding. Perhaps you will even become an inventor, Clovis, and your father and mother will be proud of you. You will regularly describe this splendid trajectory, Clovis, and nothing can prevent you. (Unless he strikes out on the way, but there's no point in telling him that, he's got such a timid nature he'd get in a panic.)

But do not forget one thing, Clovis, which is, when you are being honored on all sides, when you have arrived, when you are privileged to wear a beautiful engineer's uniform, when you are privileged to marry the boss's daughter, then, at that moment, do not despise your relations, your uncle the concierge, your aunt with the midwife, and your father and mother who made so many sacrifices to bring you up. Those are horrible sentiments which reveal contemptible instincts. But Clovis is possesssed only of nobility and honor; we could even make this his crest. Nobility and honor. No, he will not blush for his Uncle Saturnin, even though he is a bit crazy, nor for his father, nor for his mother. Though be become an engineer, an industrialist, a capitalist, a deputy, the president of the Senate, or even the president of the public whatsit (the most glorious uniform to which one may ever aspire), never will he deny his family. Never, never! They will always find some leftovers in the kitchen. One last question.

"So it's true then, Dad. You really have bought a brothel?"

"Yes, Clovis. I signed the contract today, and I've sold this café."

"Which one did you buy, the one in Rouen or the one in Epinal?"

"The one in Epinal."

"I think you were right. The navy, there's nothing much doing there at the moment, whereas the troops, they always keep going."

"Yes, but when there aren't any more soldiers?"

"When'll that be, Dad?"

"Howshd I know?"

"Don't worry, Dad, you'll be rich by then. And when do we leave Blagny?"

"In a month, at the beginning of October."

"And who's going to take Ernestine's place, as assistant madame?"

"Camélia, of course."

"I'd have thought she was very young, Dad, for that job. She won't have enough authority."

"She's the same age as Ernestine."

"I thought Ernestine was very young, too."

"That'll do, Clovis. Don't bother your head about that. Forget about brothels and get on with your maths."

---

*Philosophy, you understand, has made two great mistakes; there are two great omissions in it; in the first place it's omitted to study the different ways of being, primo; and that's no slight omission. But thass still nothing, in comparison; it's also omitted the most important thing—the different ways of not-being. A lump of butter, frinstance—I'm taking the first thing that comes into my noodle—a lump of butter, frixample, it's neither a caravansery, nor a fork nor a cliff, nor a eider down. Because, you see, this way of not-being is precisely its way of being. I'll come back to that. There's still another way of not-being; frixample, the lump of butter that isn't on the table, isn't. That's taking it a step farther. Between the two, there's the isn't-any-longer, and the isn't-yet. In this way each thing is responsible for determining heaps of nonbeings. The lump of butter isn't everything it isn't; it isn't everywhere where it isn't, it stops everything else being where it is, it hasn't always been and won't always be, ekcetera, ekcetera. And similarly, a fairly infinite infinity of nonbeing. So that we can say that this lump of butter is up to its eyes in an infinity of nonbeing, and finally, the thing that seems to be the most important isn't being, but nonbeing. And you can make a distinction: there's what can't be because it's contradictory—the lump of butter is a kettle of fish, And there's what isn't, though it doesn't seem to be contradictory—the lump of butter isn't on this table (whereas in fact it is on it). The strange thing is that what is expressed by a phrase like this: the lump of butter is a kettle of fish—belongs to the category of nonbeing, and yet to a certain extent it is, since you can express it. And so, in one way nonbeing is, and in another way being isn't. And what's more, being is determined by nonbeing; it hasn't got an existence of its own, it emerges from nonbeing and then remerges with it. When the lump of butter wasn't, it wasn't; when it isn't any longer, it won't be any longer. It's as simple as Hello. What is, is what isn't; but it's what is that isn't. The point is that nonbeing isn't on one side and being on the other. There's nonbeing, and that's all, seeing that being isn't. That's where I was trying to get. Things exist, not because they are positively determined—in that case they don't exist—but because they are negatively determined in an infinite multitude of ways. And in this case, they* aren't. *Which* means, and I'll say it once again, that being isn't, but non-being is.

There. Don't worry, we can go a long way with that. Because nothing exists. There is nothing. I myself, I don't exist. You can look at this quantitatively to some extent. Do you understand the word quantitatively? Yes, course you do, you're educated, you are. Well, this is how it is. I can say: I'm this, I'm this, I'm this, ekcetera. But that won't get us very far. On the other hand, I can say to myself: I'm not this, and then this this is the whole universe, present, past and future, it's all I could have done but haven't done, it's all I could have been but haven't been, it's all I won't have been able to do or be, and of course haven't done or been. Faced with all this, what am I? Nothing. I am not. But then, insofar as I'm not, I am. Takes your breath away, donit? Isn't it amazing? Hang on, I haven't finished yet. I'd like you to understand me properly: being, insofar as it is limited, isn't. And on the yuther hand, it's difficult not to agree that what isn't, to some extent, is. Natch, you have to go beyond logic to discover all this. And yet, and yet—what is, is, and what isn't, isn't. But there, I'll tell you the truth: the truth lies in the totality of things, not just in a formula. Even the totality of these formulas, which I'll just go over again so that you can really get them into your noodle:

Being is, nonbeing isn't,
Being isn't, nonbeing is,
Being is, nonbeing is,
Being isn't, nonbeing isn't,

all of which reveal one aspect of the truth; even taken all together, though, all four don't reveal its totaltiy, because if we were to admit that there were only four possible formulas, that would be admitting, primo, a limitation, and secondo, the legitimacy of the principle of contradiction which we have just precisely said isn't legitimate when sa question of totality. Which means that the truth is still somewhere else.

"Oh look here," said Narcense, yawning, "you aren't going to start going on about God, are you?"

"I'm not the sort of man that takes a lace cap for a Homburg hat, am I!" replied Saturnin.

## Seventh Chapter

NARCENCE was trailing along the grands boulevards, not wanting anything, not hoping for anything. He was well and truly fed up. The day before the day before, he had already exhausted the ninety-one possibilities of disposing of the blue door, and the ninety-first had turned out to be just as totally illusory as all the previous ones. For a whole day, with Saturnin, he had tried to find the way out, and had found nothing; this took place at the house of Sophie Isis, at Ça-Hisse-sur-Seine. She looked like a high-class whore, this Sophie. She was always half naked, as you might say; but they didn't pay any attention to her, they were so absorbed in their work. And when they'd finished, when there was no longer any doubt about their defeat, they were so disgusted that they walkéd right by her naked breasts, without touching them. Yet another strange day. They took the door back to the concierge's lodge. Then Saturnin took an ax and made it into firewood, because it was beginning to get cold. On one piece, and by pure chance, he managed to make out, written one on top of the other, the names of Gérard Taupe and a woman; and then a date. They made this into a little parcel which they sent to the junk dealer. That was the end. Narcense was trailing along the grands boulevards. He had fifty francs in his pocket, which he's been lent by Saturnin; they were probably the last, for the concierge was by now pretty hard up. The sort of research he'd been going in for, it came rather expensive. No point in thinking any more about it. Then Narcense perceived very closely, in his memory, a naked breast. It bowled him over.

He looked around him, and saw nothing but women. When they were coming toward him, he caught their eyes; when he was walking behind them, he admired their buttocks, when appropriate. Two or three times, he vaguely thought of following one of these bodies. He walked up and down between the Opéra and the rue du faubourg Montmartre. He stopped outside a movie house and contemplated the photos of a star he admired. On café terraces, women with crossed legs were sitting at tables on which were beers that they were not drinking. The charcoal braziers had been lit; the end of October, it looked as if it was going to be a hard winter, and Narcense saw the legs through a smell of damp charcoal.

Following an attractive walk, he went down a passageway; but, suddenly abandoning the woman he was following, he went into a post card shop and looked at length, not at the New Year's cards, nor at those of politicians, nor at those of boxers, but at the "nudes" and "dishabillés." There was quite a crowd, anyway, in the back of the shop. About ten men of varying ages were flocking around these photos, their throats dry and their hands trembling. Every so often, one would plunge his head into a little movie theater designated by a red lamp as being for the attention of the dilettanti. In an extremely congested little cubbyhole, the proprietress, a dried-up, asexual lady, was keeping her eye on the clientele; some daring ones went so far as to ask to see the special collections, and went out with a naïve smile. All this left Narcense cold, and reciprocal indifference was *de rigueur* among these solitaries. So he carefully examined the various series of "nudes" and "dishabillés," those at eighty-five centimes, those at one franc, and those at two francs. Then he went out into the passageway, turned left at the bottom into a deserted alley and accosted the first woman who appeared. She was a twenty-franc whore, with pretty eyes, a raucous voice and pretensions to vice, pretensions which were in any case unjustified, as the man was shortly afterward able to ascertain, with disappointment. As devoid of intelligence as she was of imagination, she became touching when she asked: What a shittery . . . And when she talked about her kid in the country. Narcense surrendered a packet of cigarettes into the hands of this idiot and went and had a sandwich at the Haussman slot machine.

Then he found himself in the street again and saw, once more, the unique woman whose manifold image appeared to him in the most various guises, which were nevertheless always identical (naturally enough). But this image had lost its power to exalt. One does not make love with impunity; very simply, he was tired. With his last francs, he spent some time in the movies. He didn't understand anything that came yelling in the dark from the screen. Usually, of course, he did understand. But that evening, it wasn't the same. That evening—poverty, and his absurd love. That evening, his scrotum hurt and his head hurt, at one and the same time. And the ghosts shouting themselves hoarse on the taut sheet held not the slightest interest for him.

When he came out, it was around 7. He didn't have a bean left. Just enough to take the metro. At the best time, the time when you keep your elbows tucked in and where you also keep warm. He felt sick when he came out of the tunnel, and shivered in the night.

He passed the lodge without a word, but Saturnin called him back.

"Take a look at this."

He was showing him a parcel, Old Taupe's parcel. Written on it was: Addressee deceased. Return to sender. Narcense shrugged his shoulders. What did he care, no but what *did* he care.

Then Saturnin said:

"Have you seen the paper this evening?"

No. He'd heard the newsmen yelling in the street. What was it?

Talk of war.

What *did* he care, no but *what* did he care?

---

Etienne got up at 6:30; so did Alberte; likewise Théo. Bébé Toutout, though, stayed in bed until about 10. They hurriedly swallowed a cup of coffee, and hurried to the train; the father went to the Audit Bank, the mother to her office, and the son to the lycée. So the dwarf had the run of the house all day. They came home in extended order. Théo arrived first; then Alberte; then Etienne, and it was at the evening meal that the whole family was reunited. And thus the days passed.

And thus the nights passed: they all slept. They usually dreamed very little; Bébé Toutout, on the other hand, had frightful nightmares that tortured him in the middle of the night. He sat up in bed, yelled oo oo oo, and the sweat irrigated his beard. This scared the living daylights out of Théo, thus rudely awakened. Then the dwarf would accuse him of being gutless, pacifier-sucking and lily-livered; Théo, with beating heart, would pull the sheet up over his head. Bébé Toutout would wipe his beard, and calm would reign again until dawn; then that death's-head, the alarm clock, would start chattering at the teeth. With a blow on the occiput, Etienne would stun it; then, his hair standing on end, he'd get out of bed, and so on and so on.

This awakening, the dwarf, as a rule, didn't hear; if he did hear it, he started complaining, and sometimes insisted on their bringing him some coffee and bread and butter in bed; he gulped this down voraciously, and then disappeared under the bedclothes again, while the hard-working family braved the horrible chill of the dawn.

How he occupied his days—that was something of which the hard-working family was totally ignorant, and which they could not even manage to conjecture, in spite of the prodigious efforts of imagination. Sometimes they described his sloth as prodigious, at other times as disgusting, but behind his back, because in front of it they were rather friendly. If he'd been less broke, Etienne would have bought a great big dog who'd have eaten the parasite. He *had* tried to evict him in various ways, but the dwarf always came back again, fortified by his inferiority, adept at every sort of low trick, and endowed with menacing malice. What was more, he was now Théo's friend—his intimate friend and tyrant. He knew everything he did and thought, because he created and controlled these processes. Théo became at will top or bottom of his class (there's a slight exaggeration there—le's say the second or the bottom but one), a chaste adolescent or a little monster of vice; a young man of tolerable inlligence or an incredible cretin. Love your stepfather, Bébé Toutout suggested to him; then Théo thought Etienne was really very nice. Detest him, and Théo felt like breaking rotten eggs over the step-paternal skull.

As for Bébé Toutout, his own tyranny left him entirely cold. It was even completely involuntary. There was only one thing he asked: a nice warm house, where you're fed and where you can sleep; and, whatever happened, not to work. An inexorable marmot, he had found, in the metaphysical bank clerk's half-house, a nest. His dirtiness was on a par with his laziness and his voracity. And that, in any case, had become the great Sunday pastime. They bathed the dwarf. They heated a basinful of water, and threw him into it. He raged, spat like a cat, and clawed like a cat, too. As good an amusement as any other, and hygienic into the bargain. Sometimes Etienne considered heating the water *a bit too much,* and Bébé Toutout would be boiled. But these frightful thoughts did no more than pass through his heart. He didn't dwell on them. It was when he heard a train whistle that he thought of this expedient for the first time. And yet the whistle was very little concerned with the peculiar association of ideas of which its sound had given rise; and the train even less, and the engine driver even less, and they all three went by every day, with the regularity implied by a reasonably worked-out timetable; went by every day, I say, and passed the CHIPS hut which had been boarded-up ever since the departure of the Belhôtels for their boardy-house. Etienne had heard this one Saturday afternoon when he had ventured, alone, onto the territory of this commune that had seen the growth of his being. An individual as amorphous as the reflection of a streetlamp in a patch of mud informed him likewise of the death of the old junk-dealer. He hadn't been to town for two weeks; they discovered him rotting on his mattress; and since various rumors were making the rounds, men of good will searched his miserable abode from top to bottom. The Pics, in particular, dedicated themselves to this end with great zeal. But there was strictly nothing to be found. By order of the mayor, and in the interests of hygiene, this debris was burned.

Etienne never went back to Blagny. He never saw Pierre

Le Grand, who had completely disappeared. When he came out of the Audit Bank, he was always hoping to see him; but Pierre was never there. Slowly, gently, Etienne felt himself diminishing. One day, he found in the back of a drawer a funny sort of gadget that he recognized as the cutter-of-hard-boiled-eggs-in-thin-slices. He took it into the kitchen, so that it could be used. As he turned his head, he thought he caught sight of something like happiness behind him. The sequence of incidents that had led him from a waterproof hat to a fake door seemed to him to be a marvelous adventure, and the time it had taken, a time of bliss. But, as he still doubted appearances, he doubted, and then realized that never, never had he been so unhappy. Then he counted on his fingers the number of days which, with their low-lying brows, separated him from All Saints' Day, holiday and feast day of all corpses.

---

On the beach at R . . . , two bodies were tanning in the sun; one was Pierre and the other was Catherine. She said to him:

"What a marvelous climate! November, already, and the sun's as fierce as it is in August."

"It'll be like this all winter."

"And shall we stay here all winter?"

"We shall stay here all winter?"

"And will you love me all this winter?"

"Yes. This whole winter."

"Tell me about yourself."

"There's nothing to say."

"Tell me some memories. When you were a child."

"My mother was a lion-tamer and my father an acrobat."

"The other day, you said he was a banker."

"That's not the same one. I was saying, then, that my father was an acrobat. In the evenings, after dinner, he used to help my mother clear the table; he'd walk on his hands, and balance the plates on his feet."

"What an idea!"

"When he was in a good mood, he used to hang by his legs from the chandelier and, thus poised above the table, he would eat his dinner. On other occasions, he would hang by his teeth and mix the salad with his toes."

"Disgusting fellow!"

"But he wasn't always so cheerful; when things weren't going very well he took it out on Mother, and he used to stick forks in her behind. But Mother's behind was pretty tough, which meant that all our forks had bent prongs."

"And then what?"

"My father could catch a bus by running backward, and every time he got off he'd do splits."

"And then what?"

"We lived on the second floor for six months. Well, my father neved used the stairs, he always threw himself out of the window and fell on his feet without hurting himself. There was occasional mishaps; one day, he landed on the butcher's dog, a fox terrier that was very highly thought of in the neighborhood. And, as a consequence, we had to move, because people used to shout insults at my father, and some tried to lynch him. After that, we lived on the fifth floor; my father couldn't jump from that height; he used the stairs, but he used to make himself into a ball and roll down to the bottom. There too he had trouble; the concierge didn't care for this way of going downstairs. We moved again. We went to live in a little suburban house, in Noircy-sur-Marne; that was when I started learning white magic, I was thirteen years old.

"How long did you study magic?"

"Seven years."

"You must know a lot of tricks!"

"One or two."

"Why don't you ever display your talents?"

"I think it's vulgar."

They turned over, and exposed their backs to the sun.

"Catherine, you do believe everything I tell you, don't you?"

"Of course, Pierre."

Silently, they absorbed the light. Then they swam over to the hollowed-out rock that the natives called Bunte Bi.

When they got back to the hotel, the proprietor made great gestures at them and spoke to them at length, and with animation; but they didn't understand. So then he showed them a newspaper and Pierre, who could to some extent decipher the language it was written in, was able to read:

THE FRENCH AND THE ETRUSCANS
WILL DECLARE WAR ON EACH OTHER
ON WEDNESDAY NOVEMBER 11TH

And these miscellaneous details:

"Agreement between the two tribes, which had almost been despaired of, has at last been reached; in order to preclude all future discussions relative to the responsibility for the war, they have agreed on common action; the date for the commencement of hostilities has, by common consent, been fixed for November 11th. This day would seem to be especially well chosen, since people will thus be able to celebrate simultaneously an armistice and a declaration of war. On either side, therefore, people are expressing their delight, and both French and Etruscan diplomats may congratulate themselves on having thus achieved a magnificent result."

"*Paris.* The papers today are emphasizing the dangers civilization would incur if the Etruscan barbarians were to be victorious. Among other things, they point out that they do not speak an Indo-European language, that they play the mandolin and that they eat macaroni."

"*Paris.* The King of France, Anatole, and the Queen of the Etruscans, Miss Olini, have decided to break off the game of bezique they were playing by correspondence. 'The interests of the nation,' they have stated, each in his own language, 'take precedence over individual pleasures, even royal ones.' Many Frenchwomen have voluntarily offered their services to replace Miss Olini as Anatole the First's partner."

"*Capua.* The mobilization of the Etruscans is taking place amid the greatest enthusiasm."

"*Paris.* The same thing."

"*New York.* The clash between Gaul and Etruria will probably develop into a world conflagration. The Ligurians and the Iberians will probably join the Gauls; the Umbrians, the

Oscans and the Veneti will probably join the Etruscans. The Polish people have declared they will support their permanent ally and put the Vistula at the disposal of the fringe govermint."

"How awful!" said Catherine. "What a good thing we're a long way, a very long way, anyway from all that."

"Yes," said Pierre, "all that leaves me cold."

---

"Are you sure you've got everything you want?" asked Alberte.

Etienne felt his pockets, his haversack with two days' rations and some thick woolen socks for the future winter trenches; he'd got his tin hat all right, he hadn't forgotten his gas mask. He could go now. He hesitated, turned his head, to see what was on that side, behind him, just once more. They went out. The gate squeaked, Etienne gave Alberte the key. Then they all four, for Bébé Toutout was one of the party, caught the train to town, where Etienne had to change stations in order to get to his mobilization center. The train to town was full. And of all sorts of people. Soldiers joining their regiments, for the most part. Someone had written up on the carriages: *To Capua, To Capua.* Capua was the capital of the Etruscans; they'd just been informed of that by the newspapers, which also explained that these people loaded their guns with macaroni, and that that didn't hurt, and that their mandolins weren't any match for French bombers. In short, the war wouldn't last long and they weren't to worry. Not to mention that it was going to be good for industry. In the train, it was chaos. Women and children were crying. The soldiers joining their regiments were of all sorts and conditions. Some were looking pretty glum, but a lot were boozed. There was a whole contingent of peasants who came from out the Guermantes way and who were as merry as anything. Among them were some who'd been through t'other war. They were singing some of the old songs that dated from those days like *La Madelon, Rosalie,* and it's a long way to Tipperary. There were also, among these joinersup, some who were strenuously discussing what it was all about. It's like this, one was explaining, the Etruscans, it was all their fault, this war, and we French would never have any peace so long as they were around. And it's like this, another one was explaining, it was to defend their bits of land and stop their wives getting violated that they were going to fight the enemy. Now and then someone would yell: Long live France, and others would yell back: Death to the Coches. The Coches, that was what they were beginning to call the Etruscans, and in the paper they'd explained that it was an abbreviation for Etruscoche, which was slang for Etruscan.

And then there were some who weren't saying a word, but that didn't mean that they weren't thinking. They weren't saying a word, on account of there'd been one of them who'd thought out loud, and the peasants from the Guermantes way had slung him out, out of the window, onto the rails.

Bébé Toutout, so as not to be crushed underfoot, had taken refuge in the luggage rack. And from there was going at a rapid pace. "You're joining the Cuirassiers, eh?" someone had started by saying. "Go on, are they going to have *you* in the army?" But the white-bearded dwarf wasn't letting them get away with *that* sort of thing. "Some people may not be big," he told them, "some people may even be small" (you can say that again, interrupted a listener) "but that doesn't stop them having a Frenchman's heart beating in their breasts, does it, comrades?" "Bravo, bravo," they yelled. "Ah! if only I had the great good fortune to be able to be a soldier," sighed Bébé Toutout, folding his hands and looking up at the ceiling where some clever joker had managed to make a cigarette butt stick. "Alas, though! Mother Nature made me too small to go to the front. But I shall serve my country all the same! I shall make bandages, I shall knit mittens for our heroes, and I shall raise the morale of the populace. To Capua! To Capua!"

This homily was greeted by enthusiastic hurrahs. They were passing Blagny. Some hundreds of militiamen surrounded the chemicals factory. That's where they make the gas. We're going to smoke 'em out, the swine. We're going to smoke 'em out of their burrows, the Coches!

And what about Théo? Poor boy. He was still too young to go to war. Like Bébé Toutout, he was out of luck. One on account of his size, the other on account of his age, neither could be a soldier; and the war wasn't going to last long enough for him *even* to be able to join up; twasn't going to be like the last war. Indeed it wasn't. This one was going to be polished off in no time. Three months at the outside. What a thumping they were going to get, the Etruscans. All this was in the papers.

Then they became aware, through a cloud of black dust, of a pall of cops, gendarmes, militiamen, republican guards and curées; it was Paris.

From the Gare du Nord to the Gare de l'Est it was triumphal. Tricolor flags were hanging from every window. Old-gents-with-medals were weeping from the emotion caused by watching the men go by on their way *there*. Lucky guys, who're going to go boom-boom, thought the old-gents-with-medals, and: Long live France, they added, letting a surreptitious tear drop onto their shoulders. And once again French culture was going to be saved, French culture was even going to be nicely fertilized, with something very special—blood and corpses.

At the corner of the rue Saint-Denis, a grocery store that sold macaroni is going up in flames. Farther on, some students are smashing the mandolins in a shop selling musical instruments. And thus everyone is patriotically employed, according to his ability. Of course some women are crying, but they're the ones that aren't very brave. Etienne, followed by his family, finally found his train, which was covered with flowers, vengeful inscriptions and plaintive lags. Charming young ladies are distributing tricolor rosettes and getting their asses felt. Great fun, this war, and of good omen. The Etruscans would be made mincemeat of. Those macaroni-eating barbarians, they'll be beaten by two penn'orth of grated cheese. Any minute now, we'll be entering Capua. Then really, nothing to get excited about; and even the strategists, when they really thought about it, they said they'd never seen a simpler, easier, more amusing war. Then really! And the people who said that you never knew, that the Etruscans knew some filthy dirty tricks, and that there wasn't much to laugh at, well, they got their eyes knocked about a bit with an umbrella, to teach them to speak ill of their native land. After more than two hours, the train started quivering, then whistling, and finally pulled out. Etienne, at the window, was waving his hand (or his handkerchief, doesn't much matter) like everyone else. Théo and Bébé Toutout, very excited, were waving their hats and shouting: To Capua! To Capua! Well, what a lark, this was something different and extraordinary. As for Alberte, she was crying; naturally; because she wasn't a very brave woman.

---

"What's today's communiqué say?" asked the sailor.

"Part of the Etruscan army has got as far as Deuf-Omécourt. They ransacked the customs office and the telegraph office."

"The bastards! They don't respect anything! They're real vandals."

"And they claim to have a civilization!"

"Go on, then."

"An Etruscan regiment, advancing toward a little wood, with the intention of resting and playing the mandolin, has been put to flight by a detachment of cadets."

"Ha! ha! It's quite obvious, victory's around the corner, Hippolyte!"

And they drank their aperitifs with triumphant hearts.

The next day:

"French trooups have occupied the Etruscan town of Malaparte.

"It would be premature to be too precise, today, about the possible consequences of this initial success. What we must keep in mind is that a French brigade has attacked an entrenched Etruscan brigade and put it to flight: the only appropriate word here is 'flight.' Faced with our bowel-net charge, the Etruscans ran for their lives.

"French losses are not excessive, considering their achievement. Our troops packed a prodigious punch."

The next day:

"Our troops still hold Malaparte, and are now facing the edge of the Madera forest, which appears to be seriously organized.

"The Etruscans are said to be getting reinforcements, but were aren't so stupid, we are too.

"The Polish people have declared war on all the enemies of France. King Bougrelas has sent his kind regards to King Anatole, and has borrowed thousands and hundreds from him to feed and wash his troops."

The next day:

"*The latest fashion.* The patriotism of our Frenchwomen is still as ardent as ever. It is well known that we are capturing more of the enemy's guns than we know what to do with; at the suggestion of one of our wittiest matrons, these guns will be sawn up into rings and thus turned into necklaces as simple as they are elegant. They can also be set with pearls and sparklers (as our brave soldiers in the African Battalion would say); but naturally this would be more expensive."

"Cousin Pompon"

The next day:

"During the course of last night, very extensive Etruscan forces, concentrated in the Madera woods, attacked us, yelling at the tops of their voices.

"Faced with this demonstration, the commander of the French troops has withdrawn from Malaparte and mustered his troops slightly to the rear; from his emplacement here he has halted the offensive of the enemy, whose numbers are superior.

"These minor operations were carried out with great brilliance. Really, with great brilliance. In all circumstances, the French infantry, and also the cavalry, artillery, tankery, aviatery and gendarmery have shown themselves far superior to the opposing troops."

The next day:

"Poles five days' march from Capua."

The next day:

"The Malaparte affair: rumors of a most extreme, even a most tendentious, nature have been put about. The events, briefly, were no more than these: an infantry brigade was engaged in a thrust toward Malaparte in order to destroy the information center functioning in that town. Counter-attacked by two Etruscan brigades, it retired, not of its own accord but on the order of the commander of the army corps, who judged the situation to be perilous. Its mission in any case being terminated, there was no reason to keep it there; all the Etruscan forces followed, and hurled themselves against our principal line of defense, which did not give. Our strategic situation remains the same; it is excellent."

The next day:

"The Etruscans are continually putting out false news. They are now even going so far as to talk of their 'victory' at Malaparte.

"French newspapers must daily insist on the systematic falsification of the truth being practiced by the Etruscans. If we allow lies to be spread without denying them, there is some chance of their being believed."

"They're liars, that bunch," said the sailor.

"Don't talk to me about that," agreed the barkeeper, without making his thought any more explicit.

"Well, give me a picon and water, but don't dilute it, eh, I only like it straight."

And they drank their aperitifs, with triumphant hearts.

---

"Huh, there goes Bébé Toutout," said the sailor.

"Call him, then," suggested Hippolyte, and a few seconds later, the dwarf came in.

"Well, friends," he exclaimed heartily, "are you going to stand me a drink?"

"What would you like?"

"A nice rum. Tomorrow, it'll be on me."

"Well, Bébé, what news do you have for us?"

"Pff, pff. Lousy weather, eh, lousy weather."

"That's true enough," conceded the sailor, "talk of lousy weather, it's lousy weather all right, that's true enough."

"And the boss, how's he getting on?" asked Hippolyte.

"He wrote this morning again."

"What's he say?"

The dwarf knocked down his rum and winked.

"Another."

"Good old Bébé! Tell us."

He produced a bloodstained piece of butcher's wrapping paper.

"This is a copy of a card to the brat."

"Read it to us."

"Ahem, ahem, Modane, December the 15th."

"He's in Modane, then?"

"Obviously. I'll go on. My dear Théo. I haven't written to you for a long time, but your mother must have given you my news. I think of you both with much affection and hope to see you again soon, because this war can't last long."

"Ah, you see what he says."

"He duh know anything about it."

"Even so, he muss know more about it than you do behind your counter. He's better placed than you are to know about it, even so."

"That's true enough."

"If he says the war's not going ter last long, that means it's not goingter last long. Dun it?'

"Ah well, all the better."

"What a walloping we're going to give them, the Coches."

"Hang on. Let me read it. Ahem. Can't last long. We haven't seen any action, here. A few planes came and bombed us, but didn't do much damage."

"Ha, ha, ha! their bombs don't go off. They already said that in the paper."

"All they can do is make macaroni."

"Ha ha ha!"

"And even then, French noodles are far better."

"That's true enough."

"I haven't finished," said the dwarf.

"Well, go on, then."

"So I'll see you soon, then, my dear Théo. Love your mother and work hard. Your father: Etienne."

"That's all?"

"Yes, but . . ."

"You want another rum, eh?"

"I believe I do."

"He's a bad one, this Bébé Toutout."

"A nice rum. I've got a letter for the lady in my pocket."

"Oh! you haven't! read it to us."

The rum was poured.

"Ahem, ahem, Modane, December the 15th. My beloved Alberte. I'm in a filthy hole here. We get terribly bored and I don't know what stops me leaving. But where'd I go? I'm caught, and you ought to see what sort of a mousetrap it is, and what a horrible bit of cheese they offered us. It's not possible to run away now. It's extremely cold. It's snowing hard; we are badly billetted, badly heated and badly dressed. The hospital is packed full of patients. About twenty die every day. We bury them in great style. This is our chief occupation. The enemy planes come and bomb us every day, too. Yesterday they blew up the powder magazine. Two hundred and fifty dead. We spent the day picking up the pieces, more or less on all sides. And it was so cold! We don't do anything except bury the dead and get bombed. It can go on like this for a long time. That's another very stupid thing. What am I doing here? It's absurd. If it could last less than four years . . ."

"And then what does he say?"

"If I could only see you again, Alberte, if I could only see you again and once more feel your nipples getting hard . . ."

A very cold, very icy drizzle had started falling. The roofs were shining, the road was gradually turning into a slimy cesspool, and the darkness was dripping down with the rain onto the silent estate. The dwarf went on with his reading, his nose glued to the paper because he was shortsighted and it was pretty dark. Sitting astride his chair, his head in his hands, the sailor was listening without saying a word, and Hippolyte, behind his counter, was still drying the same glass.

"We were bombed again just now," the dwarf went on. "A few more dead. That'll keep us occupied for a bit. It's starting to snow. Ah! if I could see you again, Alberte, if I could see you again."

"Is that all?"

"Isn't that enough for you?"

The rain was carefully cleaning the bistro windows. The mud was encroaching on the pavements. Through the silence, they heard a train coming into the station. The 4:37; it was an hour and a half late. Then Yves le Toltec raised his head.

"You want me to tell you something? Eh? Well, what's got to happen, the civilians have got to hold out, that's my way of thinking."

---

Having put away five rums and six aperitifs, the dwarf was beginning to have had as much as he could carry. He was even forgetting that it was time to go for his shoup. Théo became impatient and went to fetch him. He found the café full of smoke, and stinking, and six or seven men bawling and arguing, perfectly satisfied with both themselves and the world. The dwarf was hiccupping and warbling a patriotic song, in the course of which "truss them" purported to rhyme with Etruscans, and France with lance.

In spite of his protests, Théo extracted him from the midst of the slobbery laughs of the jubilant assembly. He carried him under his arm, because the dwarf would have been quite incapable of avoiding the puddles and mud-patches. The gate squeaked, and then shut again. The steaming shoup was waiting on the table. Alberte was waiting, too.

Théo went in without wiping his feet and deposited Bébé Toutout on a chair. The homunculus was wild-eyed, and stammered some incoherent words. He made a show of picking up a spoon. But five rums and six aperitifs are a lot, even for a dwarf. He dropped his spoon in his plate, nastily splashing the beautiful clean tablecloth, hurriedly tumbled down from his chair, reeled into the kitchen and there, on the floor, puked. After the first few spurts, Théo led him into the bathroom. Very ill, the midget. Once his stomach was empty, he threw himself on to his bed and there fell fast asleep, snoring into his vomit-splashed beard.

When he went back into the dining room, Théo found his mother in tears. He tried to make excuses for the dwarf. That's something that can happen to everyone, to get drunk.

"Oh, I've had enough, enough of that animal, enough of this house, enough of this suburb. Wasting away here, that's fine. But alone. I want to be alone. Take the beast away, step on him, throw him away. I don't ever want to see the hideous little man again. Take him away, take him away."

". . ."

"Waiting here for news, waiting alone in this hole, that's fine. But to have to put up with the presence of that frightful creature. No, I can't go on. I want to be alone, Théo. Take the hideous creature away. No. Don't take him away. Let him stay here. *I'll* go away."

". . ."

"I'm frightened, here."

". . ."

"I'll go and live in Paris. With Mme. Pigeonnier. I saw her yesterday. She offered me a room in her new apartment. Yes, I'll go there. And you can stay here, with the animal."

". . ."

"No, it isn't absurd. It's just like that. I want to. To want something, for once. Just once. To get away from this mud, this swamp. Not to hear that gate squeak any more. That more than anything. For it not to squeak any more. Oh! For it to be over!"

". . ."

"Your father won't say anything. He'll think I'm right. You can be sure of that. He'll think I'm right. And that other thing, you can hear him snoring, snoring, snoring. It's horrible! Why did he come here, that vampire? Oh! to get away! To get away!"

". . ."

"When'll I go? But I don't know. I don't know."

". . ."

"At once. Yes, at once. That snoring, that's too much. I'll go at once."

". . ."

"And you, you'll be able to manage on your own, my little Théo. I'll give you some money every week and you'll get by. Won't you, my little Théo? I'm going. And don't let that dwarf try and find me. He's your friend, isn't he? Let him stay with you! Look after him! Take care of him. Protect him from the rigors of life, of winter. Winter is life; isn't it, Théo? You can hear how he's snoring, your dwarf. And you can hear the rain, the rain that never stops. I'm going somewhere else. Yes, to Mme. Pigeonnier's. She's a charming woman. You don't know her, Théo. You can't possibly judge her. She's genuine, nice, kind. Yes, I will go to her. And you'll stay here with your friend, the dwarf. Promise me you will, Théo! Do you promise?"

". . ."

"What a life, Théo, you can't imagine it. You don't know anything. You don't understand this war. You don't understand your father. Stay here, Théo, in this house. And go to school every day. Work hard. Learn Greek, Latin, maths, history, physics, gym and chemistry. Learn everything properly, Théo. But I—I must go."

". . ."

"Now. Now. Now."

For the last time, the gate squeaked. Théo, at the gate, kissed his mother with all due respect and affection. They felt the very cold, very icy rain falling on their heads. Alberte disappeared, on her way to the station. And Bébé was snoring on his bed, overcome by alcohol. Then Théo was alone, really alone, and there was an imaginary woman in front of him, who was wearing nothing but black stockings (they're terrific, black stockings). Alone, what did he do? He was tired of being alone. Alcohol and masturbation reigned in the half-house, whose inferior plaster was turning to mud.

And as she went down the steps at the Gare du Nord, the steps down to the metro, she met a man who was conspicuous for a scar on his forehead.

---

Saturnin, who had been in the other war, was raised (raise the flag) to the rank of captain; this was the occasion of a glorious orgy. Around 2 in the morning, Saturnin went back to his room; as he didn't have the slightest desire to go to bed, he started to write a few pages which he intended to add to the work he had been preparing for nearly a year:

Could be that some readers, ordinary privates or corporals, have read as far as this, being desirous of educating themselves and eager to understand. Let them tremble, then! For I am t-a-l-k-i-n-g to them: Let them be burned, and then reborn from their ashes! Let them be torn to pieces, and then reborn from their remains! Let them rot, and then be reborn from their putrefaction! Let them be hammered, laminated, stunned, morselated, calcined, fulminated, and then be reborn from their bites! Let them be desperate, and then be reborn from their despair. Let them be shit on, and then reborn from their scatological state! Let them be pissed on, and then reborn from their humiliation! Let them be convulsed, soaked, breeched, plucked, embossed, booted, clogged up, cut up, smashed up, and then let them be reborn from their discomfiture!

But who? How the hell should I know and how the hell should they know themselves!

Gentle, gentle reader, whether you are a private or a corporal, pock-marked or floury-bottomed, I won't pretend any longer—I'm boozed, boozed as a coot, disgustingly boozed. But there's no denying that I preserve my dignity. Yes, I preserve my dignity.

There's sure to be some people who'll tell me: you can't be a real man, because you're not puking. To anybody that says that, I'll say: Who d'you think you are, you scum of the earth? —just take a look at yourself. Looks to me as if you're taking me for someone else. Thanks to these striking, convincing, ineluctable arguments, I shall go on looking like a dignified, powerful, Saturnin sort of guy. Not to mention that, joking apart, it helps my great work on its way. Doesn't it? Look at the number at the bottom of the page in the middle and compare it with the number on the last page, well, there's not much left to read, is there? Some people will be as pleased as anything. I can just imagine them, the idle, lazy wretches, the ones that are rubbing their hands because it'll soon be finished. You needn't be so pleased, my little men. You'll regret it! You can take it from me. But there's other people who're saying: Already! Already finished! no, really, when I think about them I asperge my gullet with the peppermint tea of pride, I massage my skull with the lotion of vanity, I rub my ribs with the Eau de Cologne of self-respect and I polish my toes with the brush of nitwittedness. When I imagine that there's some people who'll go on reading it, who are going on reading it. No, really. Come, my children, let me press you to my heart. You want to go on? Do, then! Go on! Forward! Forward! Forward! Courage!

I certainly am drunk. I might even say that alcohol has made me more obfuscated than the darkest night. But don't think you've got me cornered. Anyone who got that into his head would be orbipercussing his ass with the middle finger of mediocrity. Which would be a great lack of elegance on his part. Tch, tch! However that may be, dear Meussieu corporal or private, kindly accept my heartfelt sympathy and believe me, I remain, yours very truly: Signed: Saturnin on active service, Captain Belhôtel.

---

Over toward Modane, it was snowing so hard and so fast, shells were falling so abundantly, there were so many enemies all around and all about, that the people who were really seriously disguised, I mean the ones with stars on their sleeves and grand crosses on their pectoral muscles, decided to get out of it with their arms and luggage. It was a magnificent retreat. No really, ever since the one from Russia and the one from Charleroi, there had never been a more magnificent one. It was ghastly. The winter was especially terrible, because winter is always decent in periods of gunfire, it does its job well. So some soldiers died because it was cold. There were illnesses, infections, epidemics. Some soldiers died because they were ill. There were also the guns, the machine guns, the shells, the gases. Some soldiers died because they were killed. Ah! it was a magnificent retreat. One of those magnificent retreats that the papers, they say they're strategic, practicly a victry. And every day the guys that had stars on their chests and grand crosses *sulle maniche*, they esspected an unesspected victry on account of the prayers they were sending up to the good Lord and the Virgin Mary and Joan of Arc. But the victry never came, on account of all those myths, they aren't worth two cents. And the Etruscans were occupying towns and villages all over the place. Etienne dragged his kit bag and his miserable boots over roads white with snow, roads ploughed up by shells, roads where the gases that kill people lingered as if they were coming out of fumaroles, you even always had to sleep more than six-foot-three above the ground.

Narcense was a deserter. Bébé Toutout didn't leave it at that. But we won't dwell on this too much. Every day some airplanes made a little trip around the town and sowed a few bombs. Things were collapsing among the civilians, but it must be admitted that they were also enjoying themselves no end. They didn't live in the cellars, because of the gases, because the Etruscans only had heavy gases. So there were great goings-on on the roofs. The night clubs had established themselves up there, under the stars. People danced on the snow. It was so lovely to dance in the cold. And it was dangerous, what was more, as you risked getting pneumonia, bronchitis, tuberculosis and influenza. But what wouldn't people have risked? It was a glorious winter, a glorious winter that killed people off at every turn. And Chrissmas, what a glorious Chrissmas it was. So many couples made love that night that the whole town seemed to be caterwauling. And the snow fell, impassive and cold (even so, we wouldn't want it to be hot), white (even so, we wouldn't want it to be black), impeccable and terrible on the despairing towns where the women eagerly got their bellies filled by the last men still there.

Etienne hadn't got a kit bag any more, nor a rifle, what was the use of it? He hadn't got any boots any more, that was the most annoying thing. He hadn't got a scarf any more. Ah, shit, he'll catch a cold! His regiment (odd sort of possessive pronoun) finally got to Epinal, in little pieces. It wasn't snowing there, but it was freezing. And this war that was supposed to have lasted two or three months. And those idiots of Etruscans who couldn't get around to winning. It was lamentable, it was enough to make you put your eyes out with your thumbs.

At about the same period, that's to say, when it was still

snowing, the G.M.P. heard there was a deserter in town. An anonymous denunciation. Bébé Toutout hadn't wanted to leave it at that. A deserter? That was interesting. They sent some gendarmes to investigate the matter from a little closer. It was true. The man lodging with the Pigeonnier woman was an absentee. They went and picked him up one day when the women were out shopping. They brought him before the officers who'd baptized themselves judges: So you're a deserter? they ask him, and he answered: Yes. And then the brass hats frowned. Seeing that he doesn't want the enemy to kill him, right! we'll be the ones to kill him. In short, they condemned the fellow to death and they stuck him against a wall and they inserted twelve bullets in his skin, in the name of patriotism. That's how Narcense died.

Alberte never knew what had happened to him; the post office is so badly run in wartime.

---

They presented Etienne with a pretty little gold stripe, and stuck him in another regiment; it so happened that his immediate superior was not unknown to him; in fact, his name was Saturnin Belhôtel. They shook each other's mitt in friendly fashion, and Saturnin said to Etienne:

"I'll take you to my brother's place."

My brother's place was 47 rue Thiers, the most expensive, most famous, best-frequented brothel in Epinal. Thirty of the most docile and conscientious girls imaginable worked there. The spondulics were accumulating in Dominique's piggy bank, and when they were visited by generals, Camélia herself, in person, was prepared to do some of the work.

There was quite a bit of pushing and shoving at the door. The two men made their way through the crowd of rutting N.C.O.'s and managed to reach the café. A suffocating smell of tobacco, wine, leather and armpits swamped their nostrils; but, triumphing over this initial revulsion, they crossed the dance floor in the midst of a colossal uproar, and reached the table the boss kept for his brother. The girls swooped down on them. There were cross-eyed ones, skeletal ones, ulcerated ones, slobbering ones, dilapidated ones, bald ones, snotty-nosed ones, elephantiac ones, bandy-legged ones; they were all smiling and wiggling their asses.

"Lay off, lay off!" Saturnin yelled at them crudely, and then he shouted:

"Camélia! Where are Tata and Rara?"

Seeing that Saturnin was the boss's brother, they were sent to him; two rather pretty girls, tuberculous to the seventh degree, came and sat down beside him, squealing a little, as they were anxious to seem gay. This tore their chests out of them, and when they'd finished scraping out their lungs, they laughed like anything. By some astonishing mystery, their eyes still seemed to expect something out of this immense fuckery. They were given some glasses and the wherewithal to fill them, after which no one took any more notice of them. The player piano gave painful birth to a waltz, and stripes and naked breasts revolved to its rhythm.

Then Saturnin said:

"Well?"

Etienne replied:

"Well?"

These were serious questions. How could they answer them? Where could they start? With the door? When he thought about the door, Etienne couldn't get over it. Could they talk about that now? What a bad joke. What the hell could they have done with it? But who on earth cared about it now?

"Do you remember Les Mygales? That's where we met. In an odd sort of way, I must say. I haven't often had the opportunity of meeting you since. What about the guy who was strung up in the tree, do you know what happened to him?"

"He deserted."

Etienne swallowed the potion that had been placed in front of him, a potion very probably made from bidet water, the nectar of brothels and the hydromel of whorehouses. To desert. He leaned over to Saturnin:

"Braver that I am," he murmured.

"Don't talk like that in front of the girls," muttered Saturnin. "They repeat everything you say."

And he moved his gold braid up and down over Tata's stomach.

"Shall we go up?" she suggested, but the ex-concierge didn't condescend to answer.

"Your door, that was all hokum," he said to Etienne.

"I knew it was."

"We really went to some trouble, Narcense and I did, to find a worthy place to put it. We carted it from apartment to apartment, from castle to manor house, from hotel to barracks, always hoping to discover the lost room that corresponded to it."

"And you didn't find it?"

"No. Naturally we didn't. And yet we were operating methodically, we were following a genuine clue. Nothing to be done, though, it was all imagination. In the end, we burned it. As we were breaking it up, I noticed the name Taupe carved on one of the bits, next to the name of a woman."

"Yes, his name, Gérard Taupe. I knew that, too. A souvenir of a love affair, that door"

"Then you must also know?"

"That he's dead. Yes. Prewar stuff, all that. Don't you think? Tell me, what's happened to your sister, Mme. Cloche?"

"Already decorated three times for heroism."

"It's not true!"

"It is. Blood excites her. And what about your pal, Pierre Le Grand?

"Well now, I haven't the slightest idea what's become of him. He's another strange one."

"And your missus?"

"All right. Thanks."

"And your big son?"

"He's at the lycée, working for his exams."

The women were getting impatient.

"Shall we go up?" they kept asking every five minutes.

But the two men went on talking without a break, and were swapping reminiscences of their childhood. Finally, Camélia came to call them to order; the girls were wanted elsewhere. So they went up, fucked, and came down again and went on drinking.

The heavy atmosphere muffled the shouts and songs; the player piano barely scratched them and words were dissipated in slow and ineffective oscillations. Idle words. Outside there was a foot of snow and minus fifteen times as many degrees centigrade.

Etienne and Saturnin couldn't make up their minds to leave.

"Don't you find that nothingness absorbs being," said the latter to the former, who retorted:

"Wouldn't you rather say that being conjugates nothingness?"

When they'd reached their seventeenth glass of liquor, they fell asleep.

A colleague, Lieutenant Themistocles Troc, recognized them dozing on their table and went up and shook them, bellowing in their ears:

"What, no more love!"

They woke up, blinking, with matted mouths.

Outside, it was a cold as chastity.

---

Toward March, the fine weather returned in the form of incessant rain. The civilian and military populations splattered through the mud, seasoned with gas and shells. The French achieved a few victories as a consequence of magic operations, such as ministerial changes, the placarding of speeches, the unveiling of monuments and the execution of female spies of great beauty.

During the whole of April, no one cast a single clout, but May was superb. The vegetation vegetated admirably; the boidies perched on the telegraph wires and sang gaily, and the sky became bluer every day. In Obonne, life went by in mild and senile fashion, to all appearances extremely placidly. In fact, a lot of things were happening. Examples: Théo deflowered the cobbler's daughter and the piano teacher's daughter; Bébé Toutout distributed candies to young children in exchange for trifling services; Hippolyte, inflamed by the new wine, made advances to Cléopastor, the gendarme, but was rejected with scorn, for Sergeant Pourlèche alone occupied his heart. Every evening, Meussieu Exossé and Meussieu Fruit became inebriated with studying the supposed plans of the general staff and moving fickle lags over a map of Europe. When they got home, with sticky mustaches and dripping noses, each got belabored by his respective missus as she thought of all those elegant officer-druggists wielding huge retorts.

One Saturday evening, the bell of the half-house rang; Théo ran to answer it. A kid with a suitcase in his hand was waiting behind the gate.

"Are you Clovis Belhôtel?" asked Théo, who'd been told by his stepfather that Clovis was coming, fleeing from Epinal where a beriberi epidemic was raging.

The gate squeaked. Clovis went in. It was 10 o'clock. It was dark. They had eaten. Bébé Toutout was looking closely at the naked women in the *Gaulois,* a rag so named in order to give its intending readers a good idea of what it was all about. Clovis put down his suitcase and did not conceal his stupefaction at the sight of this extraordinary creature; who raised his nose.

"Hello, my little man," he said calmly.

"This is Bébé Toutout," Théo explained. "He lives here."

Clovis sat down. They offered him something to eat; he had. What he wanted was a drink. Some wine, preferably.

"How old are you?" Théo asked him.

"Fifteen," replied Clovis.

"I'm sixteen. What class are you in?"

"The second."

"I'm in the first. I'm taking my exams this year. I'll let you have my lecture notes."

"Thanks."

"By the way, do you smoke?"

"Of course."

"Well, here's a pack of cigarettes. They don't cost me much, you know. Sa little sort of business I do."

"Ah."

"By the way, what does your old man do?"

"He keeps a brothel."

"A what?" said Théo, staggered.

"Ha ha!" cackled Bébé Toutout, "Théo that doesn't know what a brothel is! What a boob!

Théo, disdaining the midget's jests, showed that he did know:

"So your old man, he keeps a bawdyhouse, then?"

"Yes. It was the most terrific cathouse in the whole of Epinal. But what with this beriberi epidemic, he had to go somewhere else. To Verdun, that's where he is now."

"Did you take advantage of it?"

"That's just it."

"That's just what?"

Clovis laughed, without deigning to explain. Then he inquired:

"What time are you going to Mass tomorrow?"

They didn't answer. He's going to the bad, this one!

---

In June, a second floor was built on to the Marcel house, and it soon got around that you could meet some pretty girls there. A bearded dwarf, armed with a revolver to see there weren't any breaches of the peace, received the customers and sent them away with their genitories and wallets empty.

"Well now, fifty francs to sleep with a kid of fifteen with fresh, hard breasts (you've never touched anything like 'em), you think that's too much, do you, you old cuckold?" said Bébé Toutout to the curé of Obonne, who'd come to consume.

The venerable priest (he'd been treating himself to the Eucharist every day for the previous forty years), rejoined:

"After all, Meussieu Bébé Toutout, for you, a sincere practicing Catholic, one of the most faithful of the faithful, a regular attendant at vespers as well as at matins, a pillar of the Church, a champion of the faith, to try and make me pay fifty francs, me! God's representative on earth!"

"It's not a question of God, but of cunt," retorted Bébé Toutout. "Hand over your fifty francs. It's a terrible thing to be such a skinflint. And when I think that you raked in at least fifty Masses after the last battle."

Upstairs, Ivoine and Colberte, the daughter of the piano

teacher were knitting socks for their brothers who were fighting the barbarians; in another corner of the room, Théo and Clovis were reading:

"Seen the paper?" said Théo to Clovis. "They explain that the so-called victory of the Etruscans doesn't mean a thing. The Poles are going to take them from the rear—it's a strategic maneuver, you see."

"Ah," said Clovis, "none of this would have happened if there hadn't been an atheist government. This war is God's punishment."

"You think so?" Théo asked him anxiously.

"Of course. The padre at Epinal proved that to me. France is expiating its impiety in blood."

Ivoine and Colberte stopped work for a moment and fervently kissed the little medals they wore hanging between their tits.

"My papa was always blaspheming. It's a lot of balls, he used to say, meaning religion. He was killed. He must be in hell. It was God's will," said one of them.

"And what about mine," said the other. "The dirty old pig. He used to deceive my mother, and how he did, and he laughed at her because she went to Mass. He seduced all the kids who came to the house. His impurity has been punished all right. He caught syphilis at Peyra-Cave and died of it."

"Since when do people die of syphilis?" asked Théo skeptically.

"Oh, Ida know," said Colberte, "Any rate, he died of an illness."

"You're slightly talking crap," Théo went on. "My stepfather, he never went to church and he isn't dead yet."

"Yes, but that may be to come," retorted Clovis intelligently.

The two girls giggled, and Théo followed suit. But this laughter was shattered by Bébé Toutout's voice yelling:

"Ivoine! Colberte! Come on down! Za customer!"

"Coming, coming," replied the two kids in their clear voices, putting their work down on the table.

They went down. Théo said:

"Who is it, d'you think, downstairs?"

"No idea."

"By the way, Clovis. Have you seen in the paper that . . ."
They both started mocking the incredible absurdities of the enemy. Ivoine came back up.
"Who was it?"
"The curé."
"Well, he's not bothered."
"He preached a lovely sermon the other day," murmured Ivoine, smiling blissfully.
She took up her work again.
"He's always asking for money," Théo grumbled.
"What's that matter," retorted Clovis, "if we don't give him any and if he comes and spends it here?"
Then he suggested enlarging the house, adding on a café, because the café trade, that rakes it in. And increasing the number of girls.
"Have to talk to Bébé Toutout about that," replied Théo, suddenly absorbed in a passage in the fourth volume of *Les Misérables.*
"Bébé Toutout, Bébé Toutout!" exclaimed Clovis, exasperated.
Then, after a silence, he asked incoherently:
"By the way, your mother then, she live all by herself in Paris?"
"Yes."
"Whereabouts?"
"She lives with a woman friend."
Bébé Toutout, who'd just come upstairs, added:
"You might just as well tell your pal that she went off with a guy."
Théo didn't flinch.
"Yes. And he was even a deserter, which is worse. She was living with him."
"I see it all," said Clovis, scornfully, "your mother's just a whore."
Théo hung his head, and Bébé Toutout, a few seconds later, bellowed with rage because he'd just caught his beard in the door of the safe where he'd been tucking away the curé's fifty francs.

# XCI

SOME decades later, the war was still not over. Naturally, there weren't an awful lot of people left upright, so that Etienne had finally become a field marshal, and so had Saturnin. They were both holding out outside Carentan with an army of eight men against the Etruscan army of some thirty people, including the queen, who, with age, had become Mrs. Olini. One evening when the Gallic army (because, with time, France had become Gaul again) had fallen asleep in the middle of a clearing around a nice wood fire, a crafty Etruscan came and pinched all the dreaming soldiers' weapons. The next morning, there was nothing to do but to surrender. The war was over. Toward evening, an Etruscan general came to fetch the two captive field marshals, who had been shut up in a hut; the queen was inviting them to dinner: A tribute to the conquered, she said. They buckled on their breastplates, polished their calves, cleaned out the interior of their noses and followed the guide.

In the forest, in the middle of the same clearing where the whole Gallic army had got itself all balled up in the manner narrated above, a vigorous banquet had been prepared, composed for a roast boar and boiled chestnuts, the whole washed down with hydromel. They took their seats. Then a herald tomtommed and the queen appeared. Not without astonishment, Etienne and Saturnin recognized Mme. Cloche.

"How are you?" asked the first, with presence of mind.

"Ah, Cloche of Cloches!" exclaimed the second.

"Well, my lambs," said she, "you must be amazed eh? to meet me again here. Talk about surprises, this must be a surprise. Apart from that, it's quite some time since we saw each other. Years and years. A mere nothing. And you, you've come up in the world. Field marshals of Gaul. That's nothing to sneeze at."

The two men bowed politely. Then they asked for news of their friends and relations. Most of them had been slung, kerplunk! into the clayey earth. Théo, though, was a prolific, second-class, in the Argentine.

"That's a fine situation," said Mme. Cloche. "And what about the guy that tried to hang him?"

"Who was that?" asked Etienne.

"Yiy-yi-yi," said Saturnin. "Let's not talk about all that. It's ancient history."

"Ah, of course," agreed his sister. "Well, aren't you drinking?" she exclaimed indignantly.

And torrents of hydromel flowed down their gullets.

"Howja spend your time?" she asked, a few bottles later.

"In the old days, we used to go in for metaphysics," replied Etienne.

"We still do, from time to time," added Saturnin, "but less and less."

"How come?"

"Because of the rain."

"Well," yelled the queen, rising up into the night, which was illuminated by a bit of round tallow which someone's demented thumbs had pummeled into the likeness of a human face, "well, the rain, that's me . . ."

"Snot true," said Saturnin.

"Hey, you-ou, so you take me for a liar, now, do you?"

"Oh no-o, oh no no no!"

"Well, I am, I'm the rain! The rain that dissolves the constellations and upsets kingdoms, the rain that inundates empires and macerates republics, the rains that makes your shoes stick in the mud and runs down your neck, the rain that trickles down dirty windowpanes and rolls down to the gutter, the rain that shits everybody up and makes no sense. And I am also, pay attention now, the sun that defecates onto the heads of harvesters, that skins naked women, that scorches trees, that pulverizes roads. And I am also the icy patches on the roads, that cause accidents, and the ice on the ponds, that cracks under the feet of the obese, and the snow that sends a chill down your spine, and the hail that splits your skull, and the fog that macerates your lungs. Yo soy also the summer months, the spring months that breed venereal diseases, bring faces out in pimples and cause stomachs to swell. Zhur swee the spring, that sells a sprig of lily of the valley for a franc, and the summer that kills people off because they live too intensely: I'm the autumn, that causes all the fruit to rot, and the winter that sells its boxwood on Parmesan Day. Ich bin the storm that howls with the wolves, the tempestuous tempest, the blizzard that blitzes the lizards, the hurricane that hurries you into your coffin, the gale with its hail, the cyclone on its bicycle, the thunder with its icicles, and the lightning that lights life. Eyeamme . . ."

"I insist on see-ying," interrupted Saturnin, who was getting a little rimy.

Etienne nudged him, thus inviting him to silence.

"For the last ten years, I've been studying up on meteorology," the queen explains.

"It's very interesting," said Etienne, conciliatorily.

"In the old days, when I was old," Mme. Cloche went on, "I had a very different routine. In those days, I was the queen of the mustard pot, the empress of pants' seats, the goddess of the truss. I used to inspire nocturnal dastardy and diurnal poltroonery. Always in a bad temper, I used to distribute cancer boxes. I was a bog attendant in the Tuileries gardens. I was an aborting ragpicker, a pox-promoting procuress, a lynch-promoting janitress. My lovers' feet stank, and when we'd finished copulating, I used to beat them up with a poker."

"Ch-charming," mumbled Saturnin. "Cidronie, my sister, you're ch-charming."

She shrugged her shoulders.

"You make yourself sound very clever, the way you stammer, but I bet you can't even count up to ten any more."

"Zat a riddle?" her brother asked. "Saul beyond me, I'll just let you go on chatting."

"Right; let's go. Close your fists, open your fingers at the same time as me, and count: won, tool, tree, fore! fife, sick, zen, ate, nein! in tent. With your toes, you can go on from lemon to empty, but you're too boozed for that."

"O my sweatster Cloche, what a lelaugh hic," hiccupped the ex-concierge.

"Yes, that's really very amusing," Etienne acknowledged.

"*I* didn't think that one up," said the queen. "Sin the book."

"What book?" asked the two field marshals errant.

"Well, this one. The one we're in now, which repeats everything we say as we say it and which follows us and tells about us, a sure piece of blotting paper that's been stuck onto our lives."

"That's another odd business," said Saturnin. "You create yourself as time goes on, and then the book immejately comes and snaps you up with its fie's fleet scrawl. Yep, that's the way we are, and that's how all the people around us are, o queen my sister, your shit-squittery generals, your soldier-ants, and the fish in the nearby pond that can't get to sleep. Double life, double knots. Oo ya ya."

"And what ja think of what's written down?" his sister asked him.

"The philosophical passages, my dears, they aren't so hot. I say that because of the progress. The progress of my thought, natch. Better and better, you understand, that's what I'm getting. So things that go back years and years, back to my quadragenarian youth, well, you can imagine, I find them a bit transparent."

"Personally, after all, I'm not dissatisfied," said Etienne. "I seem innocent, and I appear in an attractive light. And then, I have an interesting life, my story is instructive—exemplary, even."

"You needn't try to be so clever," said Mme. Cloche. "If you go on kicking each other like that, you'll break your tibias. I'll be frank with you. Well, I shall never forgive myself for being taken in the way I was taken in. About the door. And the infuriating thing is that it's written down, all the way along, and right here. Ah, shit!"

"Well," said Etienne benevolently, "you'll have to suppress that episode—you can just literally cross it all out."

"Literaturely," added Saturnin.

"Snot possible," said Mme. Cloche. "It's done, it's done. No way of going back on it. Ah, what a shame!"

"Personally," said Saturnin, "I can't see there's anything to get in such a stew about. It happens to everybody, to get made a silly bastard of. But if it really upsets you so much, you've only got to start all over again."

"You're screwy, my brother. Yever known people to be able to take back things they did?"

"No, but we will know it."

"Then you think I can rub time out and start again?"

"Try. In the circumstances you're in now. Remake your life, eh, you old bitch."

"That'll do, that'll do. But it's absurd, what you're saying. After all, time's time. The past's the past."

"Swot *you* say."

"And what if I fall into the trap all over again?"

"Squite likely you'll be just as credulous. Anyway, you'll see. Rub it all out, I tell you. I'll come with you."

"So'll I," said Etienne.

"Then you mean to say, time, it's just nothing? No more history?" asked the queen.

"What does that matter?" she was answered.

She shrugged her shoulders.

So they left the clearing outside Carentan and, passing through the temporal miscarriages of eternity, came one June evening to the gates of the town. They separated without a word, because they didn't know each other any more, never having known each other. A concierge took to his lodge, a midwife set up shop. A man flattened himself against the gate of a suburban half-house in which, patiently awaiting the vespertine shoup, a child was squinting at an obscene photo. The gate squeaked. The man became flat.

A mask traversed the air, causing people of multiple and complex lives to disappear, and took human form at a café terrace. The silhouette of a man appeared in profile; so, simultaneously, did thousands. There really were thousands.

# NOTES

63 If you call for *des cartes* in a café, the waiter will bring you some playing cards.

131 Théo has lifted his first line from Arvers (Alexis-Félix) (1806-50). This poet is now only remembered for just one sonnet—but this is known all over France simply as "*le sonnet d'Arvers.*" It begins:

*Mon âme a son secret, ma vie a son mystère,*

Théo's version has one foot too many because, by reversing the two halves of this line, he makes it necessary to pronounce the e in *mystère,* which, at the end of the line, would be mute.

140 There is a pleasant French mnemonic for the square on the hypotenuse:

*Le carré de l'hypoténuse*
*est égal, si je ne m'abuse,*
*à la somme des deux carrés*
*construits sur les autres côtés.*

140 Inaudi. An illiterate shepherd who was a mathematical genius and appeared later in circuses and music halls.

238 *Auri sacra fames.*